CW00449139

FOUR BORDERS TO FREEDOM

One boy's arduous journey to freedom

Bahram Fakouri

RUMI PRESS

First published in the United Kingdom in December 2020.

Copyright © 2020 Dr Bahram Fakouri

All rights reserved.
No part of this publication may be reproduced, distributed, or transmitted in any form or by any means, including photocopying, recording, or electronic or mechanical methods, without the prior written permission of the publisher, except in the case of brief quotations embodied in critical reviews and certain non-commercial uses permitted by copyright law.

For permission requests, write to the publisher at the address below

Rumi Press Ltd
82 Adagio Point
London, SE83FJ
United Kingdom

A NOTE FOR THE READER

I initially wrote this story in Farsi, my native language, in the form of a diary while experiencing the events described in this book. Regrettably, the diary no longer exists, as I had to destroy it in order to protect my genuine identity.

In 2005 and 2006, I wrote the main part of the manuscript in German on my laptop. Unfortunately, the laptop was stolen from my temporary hospital accommodation in 2007, and I subsequently lost the manuscript as I didn't have any backup saved elsewhere. After this traumatic event, I didn't feel like having enough motivation to write the story again.

In 2014 and 2015, while practicing in London I wrote the same story for the third time, but this time in English. I added two to three pages to my writings on a daily basis and emailed it to myself every night before retiring to bed. By doing so, I wanted to make sure that it was safe from any natural and manmade disaster. Once the manuscript was completed in 2015, Ms Michelle Elvy, author and manuscript assessor from New Zeeland, kindly helped me edit it and shared invaluable tips.

Despite the fact that the editing was completed in 2016, I decided to defer the publication and wait for a more suitable time as I didn't wish to displease some of the individuals in the story who are still alive and live in various parts of the world.

The names of the majority of people involved in this story have been changed in order to protect their privacy. I am convinced that they can easily identify themselves while reading the book.

I hope you enjoy reading the story.

Bahram Fakouri

December 2020

This book is dedicated to my parents and my uncles Taghi and Jamshid.

CONTENTS

CHAPTER ONE

THE MIDDLE OF THE STORY

He shouted hysterically. "This is my last question to you, stubborn child. Are you going to pay my money within twenty-four hours or not?"

I shifted uncomfortably in my seat, puzzled how to answer this question: I found myself in unfamiliar territory, surrounded by strange people, feeling as if I'd never find a way out. And I had no way to pay the amount this thug was looking for.

He leaned in close, so close I could smell his foul breath that dropped the oxygen level in the air dramatically.

"I don't know how I could do that," I said carefully. "I have no money. But you know that already."

"Then, I am going to sell you as a slave."

This took me by complete surprise.

"I thought slavery was abandoned decades ago." I tried to remain calm, tried to reason with the man.

"That is what you think," he came back quickly with a sly smile. "But there are many slaves in this country — and soon you will be one of them."

"What would I do as a slave? Do I have to put rings on my ears and nose? Learn how to fly a carpet, perhaps?" I was quickly losing my rational grip. I really thought he was putting me on.

"You are young and healthy and will be in demand for physical labour in this country. You will come with us now."

He led me to a truck in the dark of night and insisted I get in. We drove for about two hours — I could see nothing of the landscape, and we passed no other cars. At an hour that must have been near 9 pm, we arrived at a gated farm far out in the country.

Maher — that was his name, the man who insisted he would trade me as a commodity — got out of the pickup truck and spoke in low tones with a man sitting next to the gate. I could not make out anything, but I had studied Maher enough by now to imagine him: his thin frame, his proud yet pointy shoulders, his short spiky hair, the way he cocked his head so self-assuredly, his suspicious eyes. I watched the shadows as the man opened the gate and we passed through, continuing along a lengthy driveway. There were men scattered beside the driveway. I peered through my window into the dark; some of the shapes appeared to be just boys — as young as thirteen or fourteen.

The driver stopped the vehicle some fifty yards beyond the main gate. In the moonlight, I could see a large house on one side of the driveway and an array of several sheds, a cottage, and barns a bit further away. Men were walking in and out of the buildings.

Maher told the driver and me to wait for him in the truck. He walked toward a tall man standing in the driveway and shook his hand. They talked for a few minutes, after which he signaled for the driver and me to exit the vehicle and join him. We entered a sizeable cottage — perhaps 150 square yards. The floor was covered by cheap, faded carpets, and an old man was sitting in one corner of the room, with many tea glasses around him. I could only assume he was responsible for hot beverages. I was longing for something to drink, but given my situation decided to remain silent.

Maher motioned for the driver and me to sit down on the floor. He then left the cottage, saying nothing at all. I asked the driver what we were doing there, but the driver only shrugged his shoulders.

It is difficult to determine a genuine from a non-genuine shrug.

Ben shifts in his seat. The woman in front of him is holding the paper with her left hand, and her right hand is resting gently in her lap. She peers down through reading glasses at the paper she's reading. She sits very still. Her stillness makes Ben nervous, but he does not dare interrupt.

Finally, she looks up over the rim of her glasses straight at Ben. "A slave?" You were being sold as a slave?"

"It is the truth." There was nothing else to say. "We concluded on the phone last week that I should write it down, and I have."

The psychologist is a woman in her mid-forties. Blond hair short, a blue suit with a white blouse. She looks formal.

"So, Benjamin," she says, putting his paper down on her without a sound. "How do you feel, now that you've written down this part of your story?"

"Please call me Ben as everyone does. You know I don't think I need to be here."

"I didn't ask you to come. You made the appointment on your own."

"You are correct, but I was forced to come here. I really have no say in it."

"You have freedoms here, you know. You make your own choices."

"Of course. But I'm not sure I like my choices."

"Why don't you tell me why you finally decided to come to see me? Even before I read your story further."

"I need a statement from you at the end of these sessions stating I have participated successfully. Your writing is required if the college director wants to help me do my final exams."

The counselor smiles.

"You are here only for the certificate? You don't really want to tell me your story? Nothing bothers you?"

"It seems everybody I talk to on the college staff wants me to tell my story. I'm tired of having to do it. Every time I explain my history and my journey here, I remember too much."

"You were sold as a slave – or at least threatened. I think that may be something you need to talk about."

"Yes… but I can't talk about it. It's too hard…." Ben hesitates, then whispers. "The humiliation, the degradation. The terror…"

"I'm sorry about that, Ben – I do not want you to relive things that are too terrible. That's why we've agreed that you write it down."

"But I find it hard to sit here and watch you read it. You know I have some difficulties behind me. Isn't that enough? Couldn't I just drop in a few times for backgammon or chess, and then you could confirm to my teachers that I have been here and things are fine?"

"That would mean I would have to lie. That's not in line with the code of professional conduct and practice. It's out of the question. Either you come or you don't — but if you come to these sessions, you'll have to share your story."

Ben sighs. "As far as I can see, having me retell my life story does me no good. The only advantage seems yours, in that, I pay you for the sessions."

"Few things are free in this world. Have you had counselling before and found it useless?"

"Well, no."

"Then how do you know it might not be helpful?"

"I just don't believe in these things."

"You don't believe in something you've never tried — is that what you're saying? Look, I talk to my clients the way we are talking right now. I am not going to prescribe medication and I am not going to perform surgery on your brain. It is going to be a conversation. You write down what you like, and we can talk through the rest. How can it hurt to chat?"

"I mean you no disrespect, but please understand that I don't think I have any emotional issues that need to be addressed by a professional. I went through tough times in my life, some of them exceedingly tough — life and death tough. But I managed without anybody meddling with my emotional or psychological health. I am emotionally resilient and can get through life's crises and challenges on my own."

"I appreciate your resilience, Ben. But it's obvious that this time you have not managed the challenges very well, since your teachers seem to generally agree you need to come here. We all have imperfections. We all have our little day-to-day issues, our small battlefields. As you have indicated, most of us deal with them pretty well, most of the time. It's called life. One needs professional guidance if his problems are objectively or subjectively too big to deal with — if they affect the person's adjustment or effectiveness in negative ways. There is nothing wrong with asking for help with those sorts of challenges."

Ben wants to object but the psychologist seems to talk without taking a breath.

"People generally consult a medical doctor if they have a physical illness, but some ignore emotional or psychological conditions. It's easier to ignore emotional problems, even though they can cause more damage to the person than somatic or physical conditions. Our thoughts, emotions and psyche function in direct correlation with our physical body; that means your physical condition can impact your emotions and vice versa. You should go to the library and look up the word psychosomatic."

Ben hesitates before responding.

"It is embarrassing telling my friends that I am seeing a counsellor at my age. They would think I have gone nuts and that something is seriously wrong with me. They'll begin avoiding me."

"It sounds like you know that none of your associates have ever had counselling or may have needed it. But are you so certain, Ben? I have a large practice and it has always been full; my colleagues' experiences are similar to mine. Having adjustment difficulties, or going through tough emotional times at some stage in life, is part of our normal development; these issues do not make one less of a human being or depreciate his human value."

Ben feels a trickle of sweat drip down the back of his neck. He wishes the psychologist would go back to talking about what he's written down. Somehow that's easier than this. Words like 'adjustment difficulties' make him feel inadequate. What will his friends say when he's labelled as someone with 'adjustment difficulties'?

As if she can read his mind, the psychologist continues. "Why do you have to tell them at all? Your friends, I mean. You come here for yourself, not your friends."

Well, that much makes sense to him.

"Look, Ben," she continues as she uncrosses her legs and sits forward. "There is a bottom line here that really defines your situation. If you don't come for sessions, or if you come but don't cooperate, I cannot give the confirmation your college requires. I am sorry, but I have to adhere to both the rules and my own principles. Perhaps we will merely verify your contention that you have no problems. That wouldn't be all bad, would it?"

Ben sighs and crosses his feet.

"I guess I should write down the rest of my life story – all of it – as I've done for today's session so when I am asked to tell it, I can just hand out copies."

The psychologist smiles.

"Actually, I think it is a good idea to continue with this exercise. I think you should write down what you think you want to tell me. It seems the best way for us to proceed. What you have given me here shows tremendous insight – and your ability to tell a story. So I propose you keep writing excerpts from your life – whatever you think you need to share. I will read the excerpts during our scheduled sessions. Do you think it is easier for you to express your feelings and your stories in writing than orally?"

Ben manages another smile and then becomes serious.

"I know your counselling is confidential, but have you had someone like me before?"

"Do you mean a client who did not want to talk with me and share his concerns?"

"No, I mean someone who writes down his stories and hands them over to you?"

"I have seen many clients who were more comfortable using unconventional methods to express their feelings and concerns. I often find I need to customise the approach. Some people find the act of writing therapeutic."

"You might be right. Back home, when I was much younger, I used to write down things that happened to me. I did feel better when I noted my concerns and feelings. It forced me to give them form and substance."

Ben sees no way out of his current situation. His dean has insisted that he see a psychologist. His advisors are concerned, and his main goal in life is to graduate from university.

"OK. May I book just one session a week with you since I will need time to do the writing? During my journey here I wrote a lot about my experiences, but had to destroy it at one point to keep from being found out and extradited back to my country. If I'm going to do it, I want to do it right – not give you any wrong impressions. Maybe I should also give a copy to Miss Finn, my professor who suggested I come here. She's the one who will be checking in with you to make sure I am coming to the sessions and cooperating."

"How you go about it, of course, is up to you. Each session is one hour long. I will read your material and in the time we have left we will discuss it. I may have questions and you may have questions, too. Everything you say remains confidential. It won't be fodder for tale-telling in teacher meetings."

"Shall I continue with this part of my story? When I was sold as a slave?"

"You write about whatever you think you want to tell me about yourself. You may continue with this part of the story and then go backward or forward. If you think your upbringing played a crucial role for your current concerns, tell me about that. You can go both directions. Our stories are not always as linear as we may think."

Ben nods thoughtfully.

"That makes sense, I guess. Should I narrate it in the third person like I'm standing back and looking things over, or tell it like a first-person story?"

"Write however feels comfortable. How you choose to do it may actually give you some important insight into yourself. Stories, feelings, even random thoughts will all be fine. You spoke of writing about things when you were younger. Did you keep a diary or journal as a boy?"

"Yes, in fact, just about ever since I was a teenager, but not a word since I came here to Germany. I suppose you think that means something. Most of the entries in my diary are from my mid- and late-teens."

"It is good you have that. For me, write your current story as it comes to you. The earlier stories will surface in time – I am sure of it."

Ben is not so sure of how much of his story will 'surface' but he's willing to give this a try. Really, he has no choice. He stands and offers his hand for a shake.

He leaves the room feeling no different than he did yesterday. But something has already begun to shift. It will take some time before he can recognise it – and even longer before he can touch it.

CHAPTER TWO

HOW MUCH IS
A BOY WORTH?

I looked at the driver, hoping for something more than a shrug.
"I know very little about Maher's business deals," he managed.

During the next two hours, several men, including Maher, entered the cottage and sat on the floor. Maher placed himself next to a man who appeared to be the owner of the house and farm. He looked to be 60 years old with an odd appearance: a full moustache on his lip and closely cropped chin whiskers, but no hair on his head. He was called Sahib by the other men.

Maher did most of the talking. They glanced in my direction from time to time. Clearly, I was of great interest – or at least a key subject of their conversation.

When it came time for a late supper, two men put bread and big plates of rice in front of us where the driver and I sat on the floor. One man, carrying a watering can in one hand and a metal bowl in the other, walked in front of us and asked us to wash our hands. Clearly not for hygiene.

The men across the room ate with their hands from the shared rice plate. Another new custom for me. I just ate the bread that was laid in front of me.

After the meal most of the men left the cottage, but Sahib remained sitting next to Maher. Maher beckoned me to sit next to him.

"How long have you been in Pakistan?" Sahib, which literally means 'owner' in the Urdu language, spoke to me in English.

"A few weeks."

"Do you like it here?"

"That is a difficult question because I have not seen a lot here, not yet. I think I need more time to be able to give you an honest answer. I must confess I do not like how I have been brought here."

"You seem to be a bright young man. How did you end up here?"

"By *here* do you mean Pakistan or in your house?"

He offered a brief smile.

"Here in my house."

"Maher brought me."

"Do you know why you are here?"

"Not having been told outright, this is the best I can figure: Maher keeps insisting that I owe him money and wants to find a way to get his money from me." I rubbed my bruised eye – it had swelled in the last several hours and felt quite sore by now. "He beat me earlier today, thinking that would get his money. But I do not have the money. So his last threat was to sell me as a slave."

I thought I saw a flicker of sympathy pass across Sahib's face, but I knew this was a dangerous game. I did the best I could to remain composed. "I assume," I said heavily, "he wants you to purchase me as if I were an item."

Sahib looked me in the eye. "Your assumption is correct. He asked me to buy you from him so that he can make up his losses. But tell me, why don't you pay him his money back?"

How many times would I have to say the same thing? Surely these men knew exactly how I came to be in this situation? I exhaled and said slowly, "I don't have any money."

I decided to keep going, as I had Sahib's attention. "The man who asked Maher to help me get from Iran to Pakistan has reason to believe that Maher has been dishonest and corrupt. He does not think Maher used the money he provided to him for the purposes for which it was intended. Assuming that is true, I owe him nothing and he has no claim on me, correct?"

Maher remained silent. I counted on the fact that Maher's English was not good enough to understand. I specifically tried to couch it in words I understood would be unfamiliar to him. If I had to return with Maher I didn't want him to know I had offended him.

Sahib listened intently. I was certain he understood.

"How much do you think you are worth?" he asked.

"You are a man of difficult questions. I am not sure I can give you an answer because I believe that all human life is both precious and priceless. Human beings should not be for purchase. They are not for purchase in my country."

"People are for sale in many countries. Undoubtedly in your country as well. Perhaps you've not heard of it. You are very young."

"I don't know how else to respond."

"Accept what I just said because it is the reality in this world. Did you see the young boys on my farm when you drove through the main gate?

"Yes, I saw a few of them carrying things in and out of the sheds."

"I have bought those boys; they are mine and I own them. I can do with them whatever I want."

"You are saying you bought them as slaves?"

"You can call it what you want, but I paid for them and they work for me. I can also sell them if I want to."

"I am perplexed and don't know what to say. My history books said that slavery was abandoned in most countries ages ago."

"What you read in books differs from the reality of our world. You should not believe all the things you read or hear on the radio or see on TV."

"If those young boys work for you, then their work needs to be remunerated. What I mean is that after a while they should be able to buy themselves free from you — pay you what you paid for them."

"It is not as simple as you think. The money they earn is less than the cost of their accommodation and food. In fact they owe me more money the longer they stay and work for me."

"That is unfair. You are saying that these people can never be freed up from their slavery because you refuse to pay them what they are clearly worth to you. I cannot believe that we have slaves in the mid-eighties. May I ask your religion?"

"I am a Muslim. I think you are, too?"

"I was born a Muslim as my parents are Muslim, but I am not practicing. I have never been to a mosque to attend a prayer. Are these young men, your slaves, Muslims too?"

"Some of them, yes."

"How do you justify that as a Muslim you can own and trade in slaves? I thought slavery is *haram* or forbidden in Islam."

"No, your information is not accurate. Slavery has been a part of all religions, including Christianity and Islam."

"I have learned that slaves were people captured during wars, mainly women and children. Since there hasn't been such a war in the current generation, we should not have any slaves."

"Again, it is not as simple as you think. These children have very poor parents who cannot feed them. They would end up on the streets and probably become beggars or criminals if they survived beyond their tenth birthdays. I give them the opportunity to work and learn and survive. I have taken them from the streets and given them shelter and sustenance."

"But you don't actually pay them any salary."

"Why should I? I have bought them from their parents. This means I have already paid their salary in advance. They work for me and they live and eat here for free. What is the whole purpose of getting a job? To earn money for food and shelter. These kids get their meals and shelter for free – something their parents could not offer them. I think it is a fair trade. I am a humanitarian, you see."

I felt my ears grow hot. "No man who usurps another man's freedom is a humanitarian. I am sorry, Sir, but you are making these kids pay for their parents' failure and misery. That should have nothing to do with them. Is this legal here, in this country, to buy and sell people?"

"Well, not officially, but the lawmakers know that we take these kids from the streets and protect them. I am providing a service for the government, you see. And I charge them nothing for it."

"It is still unfathomable to me. Don't these children escape from you?"

"Where should they go? Do you think they have a better life in the outside world? Certainly not. They would starve in a month and they all know that. Most of them don't leave the farm at all and if any of them do escape we can easily retrieve them."

"If someone reports you to the police, wouldn't you be in trouble?"

Sahib poured more tea. "You are a very nosey young man," he finally said, pushing a cup toward me. "But most people don't ask questions like this, so I will answer. The local policemen know about what we do, sure, and they occasionally come to my place and have meals with my men. And, I should also add," – and here Sahib raised his cup – "the police even help me find my boys if they run away. I make their jobs easier."

I cringed at the idea of *his* boys. "Your words make it confusing. A bad solution to a bad problem solves nothing."

"You don't need to think about it if it causes you confusion. Just accept things the way they are. There is always a reason why God wants things to be run in certain ways."

"There you go twisting things with words again." Someone here had to say the truth. "The whole situation is manmade so I cannot understand why you relate things to God."

"You are too young to understand it now, but accept the facts as they are. One day you will comprehend." He seemed so sure of himself.

"You sound like my math teacher. He always said, 'Learn things by heart; if you don't understand them now, one day you will figure them out!'"

"He must have been a wise man."

"Math, Sir, is *not* life."

Sahib smiled and shrugged. We apparently agreed to disagree.

"Anyway," I continued, "I think I should be concerned on this particular night about my destiny. May I ask you for an honest answer concerning why I am here now and what the plan is?"

"The fact remains the fact. You owe Maher money. He asked me to get his money back from you. If you don't repay your debt, he can do with you whatever he wishes. I am sort of a debt collector, too. I can give him the money you owe him and you will be mine. You can work for me."

"Except for the fact I do not owe him any money."

He ignored my comeback.

I continued. "And what do you mean by that? You want me to work on your farm for the rest of my life? An entire life is worth only a few thousand dollars to you?"

Again, he overlooked my argument, but at least he offered a response.

"I have other businesses, too, which might interest you more than the physical jobs on the farm."

"What are the other businesses?"

As soon as I said it, I recoiled at myself. I couldn't believe I had asked that question. It suggested that I accepted his premise.

"I will go into that with you later. They require intelligence and common sense – both of which you seem to have in abundance. We can offer anyone a tailored profession according to his aptitude and skills. You don't have to stay in this house. You can work freely outside, sure." He leaned in close and delivered his punch line. "But you need to remain loyal to me and my business associates; otherwise your health or life expectancy may be compromised."

"I understand your threat, but I still don't understand the nature of your proposals. Can I choose what I want to do?"

"I will explain things to you later."

Sahib turned to face Maher and asked directly, "How much does the young man have to pay you?"

"2,000 US dollars."

"I will give you 1,200 US dollars. He will stay here with me and you will leave my farm."

Maher asked for time to talk with the driver outside and stood. Sahib and I sat in awkward silence during his absence. I shifted in my uncomfortable seat, looked around for want of anything else to do. The room was massive and made me feel small and insignificant. The walls were whitish without any posters or paintings, and the floor was covered by several cheap carpets in total disharmony. It was a place that was the opposite of homey; indeed, I felt very far from home by now. The sweat dripped down my back a little more. I could not believe that they were buying and selling me like a young bull. I wondered if it were all just a ploy to frighten me – but to what end?

Clearly, I was an object of interest to them. An *object*.

It was some time before Maher came back and sat again next to Sahib. When he finally spoke, it was succinct: he would accept the offer and would leave me there for 1,200 US dollars.

I looked at Maher and spoke to him in Farsi.

"I cannot believe what you are doing. You are a disgrace for all men. Even as a human trafficker you could still have some dignity and honour – helping people to freedom. You promised you would transfer me to Europe within days and now you are trading my freedom against 1,200 US dollars?"

My anger emboldened me. Perhaps too much. I said in a voice stronger than a seventeen-year-old boy should have, speaking to a human trafficker of Maher's nature, "My family is large. When you return to Iran always keep one eye out behind you."

Maher was not moved in the slightest. "You have had your time to pay my debt," he replied calmly. "But you didn't, and now I cannot wait anymore. This is the end of our chapter and we will probably never see each other again."

Sahib stood and turned to Maher.

"I think you have talked enough and should leave here, now. I will come out with you and give you the money at the gate."

Sahib then looked at me and told me to remain seated until he came back.

I was distraught. I felt betrayed by Maher, by life, by God if there was one outside my being. This whole situation had all been built on a lie – it was as if Maher had convinced himself his lie was true. He had *stolen* my money. And now, I was now in no better position than when we'd met, when he'd agreed to help me get across the border to freedom.

I owed him nothing.

And here I was stuck with Sahib. Better or worse than Maher – I could not be sure. I compared what little I knew of Sahib with the brute Maher to see if either possessed any true human decency. Sahib was brighter and more knowledgeable compared with Maher who was obtuse and intellectually dull. But would Sahib be any fairer in his dealings with me? Either way, my destiny was yet again in someone else's hands. My road to freedom was not any surer.

Sahib returned to the cottage later and suggested that I could sleep there and we would talk about my duties the following day. Several of the farm workers also stayed the night in the cottage.

Frau Bosch, it turns out, is the psychologist's name.

Ben arrived on time for his second session – it's a Tuesday – and now sits opposite her while she gently turns the pages. For a brief moment he closes his eyes and listens. He can hear the birds outside the window – swallows, he thinks – but not even her breath. She is quieter than a mouse, there on the other side of her large mahogany desk.

His pages are hand-written. In German, of course. He has learned to speak fluently and his written skills are also coming along very well – enough to earn him entry at the university. A lot of good that has done him: his road to freedom has landed him in a psychologist's office, bound and constrained yet again.

Ben fidgets. Finally, Frau Bosch looks up. But she does not speak. This makes Ben nervous.

"I hope what I have prepared will provide you with useful information."

"I'm eager to learn about you," she says. "I wonder, as I read these pages, how you came to be in this extraordinary scenario you describe here."

She seems sincere.

"I tried to indicate some of my feelings and perceptions where they seemed important. I found myself recalling, so I tried to recreate them. They aren't word for word, I'm sure."

Frau Bosch sits back, adjusts her glasses, and glances back down at the pages. "Shall I continue then? Or would you like to talk first?"

Ben is not really in the mood to talk. Not yet. "Go on," he says.

Next time he will bring a book or homework. He feels slightly uncomfortable sitting across the large desk, watching someone read his life story. He is grateful for the small smile and nod she offers before dropping her gaze to his pages once more.

At least she does not shrug.

My introduction to the human trafficking business did not begin with Maher. It began much earlier — though it was bound to get worse before my path led to anywhere close to what I had imagined, as a young boy, as the free world. It began with a lawyer and a man named Sinam.

The lawyer and I arrived at the small airport of Zahedan early in the morning. This was early summer and the heat was already up. Zahedan was about 720 miles away from the capital city, Teheran. The capital of Iran's Baluchistan Province, Zahedan was close to both Pakistan and Afghanistan. Most inhabitants there were of Baluch ethnicity and spoke the Baluchi language. I knew very little about the city and province. I learned in school about the Taftan Volcano, which is quite close to Zahedan. It had been idle since the early twentieth century. Rostam, the primary hero in Ferdowsi's Shahnahmeh, descended from that area. Besides that, I knew nothing of this city or this part of my home country.

Zahedan was dusty. Located next to Kavir-e-loot Desert, it was hot in the summer and cool in the winter. The city held no attraction for Iranian tourists and had always been associated with tensions between various religious groups and smugglers of drugs like opium from Afghanistan.

Most men in Zahedan wore long beards, white robes, and the round religious cap that was most likely part of their religious dress code. Women wore burqa that covered the whole body.

The majority of the population in Zahedan were Sunnis, a minority in the country since most Muslims in Iran belong to Shia. Sunni and Shia are two branches of Islam, and they split over the rightful successor of the prophet Mohammed. Sunnis chose Abu-Bakr, Mohammad's companion, and Shias chose Ali, Mohammad's son-in-law. Shias believe in Ali, his two sons, Hassan and Hussain, and nine successive Imams as the holy leaders of Islam. Nearly ninety per cent of the Muslims in the world are Sunnis. The majority of Shias live in Iran, Iraq, Syria, Pakistan and Turkey.

I asked the lawyer whether there were interesting attractions in Zahedan that could entice tourists. The lawyer said that the city had very few redeeming characteristics. It housed drug dealers, human traffickers and accommodated a huge number of refugees from Afghanistan who escaped from the Afghan-Russia war. He didn't think the city was in any way an attraction for foreign tourists at that time.

The streets in Zahedan were crowded with people, and I was surprised to see young boys selling drinking water from buckets on the streets. I learned that there was a shortage of pure drinking water in the city. The tap water in Zahedan was contaminated.

We eventually arrived at a hotel that looked very old, but was acceptable for short stays. The receptionist, a young man, asked me to hand over my ID to him and said it would be returned upon checkout. He further explained that every hotel guest was required to leave his ID at the hotel reception desk so police could check their identities later in the evening.

The lawyer asked me to go to the room and said that he would join me later; he needed to make several phone calls.

The room was on the first floor. It was small with two single beds, a wash sink and a ceiling fan. I watched the bustling street scene through the window and waited for the lawyer. He returned half an hour later. I asked him what the news was and he said that the middleman who would help get me out of the country would come to our hotel that evening to pick me up.

The lawyer planned to stay in Zahedan for just the one night and fly back home the following day. After that, I'd be in the care of someone completely unknown to me. At least with the lawyer, my first contact on my journey to freedom, I had someone who knew my father.

I started to realise this was the point of no return. It was very warm in the room and I was soon covered in sweat. I turned on the fan and threw myself on the bed, hoping for a nap. Sleep only came in fits and starts.

Several hours later we went for a walk and to get some food. We came upon a fast-food restaurant, which served typical Iranian sandwiches. I asked one of the other customers if there were any interesting places to visit around the area. The man indicated there was a large mosque and the university building, but I could tell by his demeanour that he did not think they were impressive. The lawyer preferred not to raise any suspicions by walking around the city, so we returned to the hotel and waited for the middleman, Sinam.

He arrived at our hotel room at nine o'clock that evening. Sinam was in his early thirties and had been born and bred in that city.

He sat on the bed next to the lawyer and started in on details of my trip. He said that he was not involved in human trafficking, but he knew people who were. He said he would take me to his friend's house, and that friend would take over from there. I had the impression that Sinam was doing the lawyer a favour by transferring me abroad. Perhaps it involved repaying some debt.

Sinam asked the lawyer to stay in the hotel in order to avoid contact with the other men. He stood, signalling it was time for me to go with him.

I thanked the lawyer for his company and support and we parted with a handshake. I lifted my bag and followed Sinam out of the room and into the street.

We walked towards Sinam's pickup truck, which was parked some fifty yards down the street. Once in the truck, Sinam explained that the place we were heading was not the sort of house I was probably used to. He warned that I would see illegal items there and that I should behave as if none of it seemed out of the ordinary to me. We arrived at the house some forty-five minutes later.

Excitement welled up inside me. Finally, it seemed I was on my way. I would be leaving Iran, the only country I'd ever known, for a free life.

Sinam knocked on the door, explaining it was a secret knock known to him and people inside. After a short wait a man opened the door, greeted us, looked me over for a moment and then asked us to follow him. We entered a sparsely furnished house looking to contain four or five rooms. I saw four men sitting in the living room – on the floor, no chairs – smoking an opium pipe. They ranged from 25 to 40 years old and were wearing

Baluchi clothes. They were gathered around a small metal container filled with hot coals used to heat up the opium in the bowl of the pipe.

The men shook our hands and asked us to join them on the floor. We sat while Sinam talked to the one who seemed to be the head of the group. They spoke in the Baluchi language.

I was unable to understand their conversation so my focus wandered to the other men. Some lay on their backs after inhaling the opium. There were four machine guns standing against the wall in one corner of the room and assorted related items in an open wooden crate next to them. I remembered Sinam's remark that I would see unusual things in the house, so I tried to remain cool as if it were all a part of my normal routine.

Sinam introduced the head of the group to me. His name was Sardar. I smiled and nodded at the man and he smiled back.

"Do you know anyone who went to Europe through Zahedan and Pakistan?"

"No, Sir. None at all."

"Listen to me, Ben. I am not personally in the human transferring business. It is too much of a hassle and is not lucrative. Sinam is a dear friend of mine and he asked me to find a person who can take you to Pakistan and then to your destination, wherever it is. I found an Afghan man named Maher who claims to be good at this job. He has never done anything for me, and in fact I am going to see him for the first time tonight or tomorrow morning. I have asked one of my best drivers to take you and Maher to the border and drop you off at the place that Maher has stipulated. The crossing into Pakistan will be done by Maher and his connections. Do you have any questions?"

"I have questions, yes, but since you are not handling my transfer yourself you will not be able to answer them. They concern my stay in Pakistan. I think I will wait and ask Maher."

"I am sure Maher can explain the itinerary."

"Perhaps one question, Sir. Do you know when we will start the journey?"

"When Maher and the driver arrive here. That may still be sometime during the night."

Sinam asked me if he could leave me with the men. I saw no real alternative and nodded. I thanked him for his help.

Before Sinam left the house, he handed Sardar a sports bag filled with money. It was the payment for my transfer. I was exhausted, physically and emotionally, so I asked Sardar if there was a place I could rest. He showed me into an adjoining room with mats on the floor and said he would wake me when the men arrived.

Three handlers down – one to go the rest of the way. Or so it appeared.

Frau Bosch pulls her glasses from her head and looks at Ben. "You write so calmly about this. As if it's almost not you going through this. Going to a new city, dealing with all these new people. Preparing to leave your own country forever. How old were you?"

"Seventeen."

Ben sees Frau Bosch wince, just slightly. He thinks she's about to say something else but then she puts her glasses back on her nose and lowers her eyes once more.

I used my handbag of clothes as a pillow and fell asleep immediately. I slept through to six o'clock the next morning; I woke confused and apprehensive when I realised that no one had awakened me during the night. I got up and found several new men sleeping in the hallway and living room, and Sardar sitting in the living room. He beckoned. He reported that the men had not arrived during the night, then assured me things were fine and they should be along shortly.

"Don't worry, Ben," he said with a pat. "Your travel ticket will not expire."

I appreciated the attempt at humour, but my anxiety sat like lead in my gut.

Sardar suggested that I rest a bit more until everyone in the house was awake. I lay down again, but could not sleep. My mind was awhirl with questions.

Sometime later, there was a knock at the front door. One of the men opened it and a tall young man entered the house.

It turned out that he was the driver, Pooya, a local man in his late twenties. He had an athletic build and a pleasant smile. Sardar introduced us, explaining that I was the passenger who wanted to go to Pakistan. We shook hands. Pooya asked if I had ever been to Pakistan. I said no and asked whether he had been there. He said he occasionally went to some of the small Pakistani border villages, but had not been to the large cities – Islamabad or Karachi. He explained that he spoke Baluchi and had spent time in the Baluch province of Pakistan several years before.

I wasn't sure what I expected to hear or whether what I had heard really made any difference.

Pooya turned back to Sardar and asked when the main man – Maher – would arrive.

"Hopefully, very soon. We have waited for him all night."

A few minutes later the front door opened and one of Sardar's men escorted the man who would arrange my transfer across the border inside. Maher was tall, slim and a bit browner than the other men in the room. He wore the traditional Pashtun clothes – a pair of bulky trousers, a long dress called a perahan, which ended at the knees, and a coat without sleeves.

The men sat in front of Pooya and me. Sardar offered Maher tea and they chatted briefly about their mutual friend who had recommended Maher. He explained that Pooya was a dependable driver who knew the outlying country very well. He would take them to the spot near the border where Maher wished to be dropped off. He also explained that I was a relative of one of his friends and that he expected Maher would take good care of me and not subject me to any unpleasant experiences or undue risks.

"Have you been in the business long?" Sardar asked.

"A number of years. Just last week I sent a couple to Sweden. That I am still in business attests to the fact I have been quite successful."

He then addressed both of us.

"I know many capable people in Karachi who will be able to solve the passport and visa problem. Once inside Pakistan, our first stop will be Quetta. It is an 8-hour drive beyond the border. From there, we will go to Karachi. From the time we arrive there, Ben will be at his destination in Europe within three to four days."

I listened carefully and was filled with confidence that the man knew what he was doing. I was happy and excited that my dream would soon be my reality. Europe, which had seemed so far away and out of reach for so long, was about to happen for me. I would not allow my head to consider the possibility that Maher might be stretching the truth about his successes or skill.

Sardar reassured me that what Maher had said was in fact true. He asked me if I had any questions for Maher.

I shook my head. "You have already answered them well."

Maher finished the meeting by stating that he was a man of honour and skill and would deliver what he promised. I wondered why he would feel the need to point this out. Surely a man of honour simply acted as a man of honour.

Pooya, who had been listening to the conversation, asked Maher whether he had only me as a passenger or if there would be more people on this trip.

Maher replied that he had a tailored transfer plan for each passenger, and this trip was just for me. He continued that it was also a matter of confidentiality and he had always respected his clients' wishes to remain anonymous despite the fact that he had a long waiting list for passengers wishing to be taken to Europe and Canada.

This seemed like an excellent and convincing answer. Everyone nodded congenially.

Sardar thanked Maher for his preferential treatment, making provisions for me on such short notice. He handed over the money bag – an Adidas sports bag. Sardar told him that it was exactly 3,000 US dollars and that he would get him the rest once we arrived in Karachi. Maher seemed to be satisfied with the arrangement and thanked Sardar. I pointed to my bag and asked Maher what I could take with me.

"You can take your small sports bag with clothes. You will need to be able to carry it. That won't present a problem."

Maher, Pooya and I left Sardar's house around noon in Pooya's Toyota pickup truck, with me squeezed between the two other men. The pickup was several years old and its exterior looked unremarkable.

Except for the bullet holes in the doors.

I hoped the bullet holes were from only one shooting. But there were many – visible from the inside, which meant they went clear through – and I could not be sure. And even one shooting was more than I cared to witness first-hand.

And so we set out. I was unnerved but kept quiet. Neither Maher nor Pooya seemed likely to answer questions about outrunning shooters.

We drove through the streets of the city and made our way toward the motorway. It was a very hot day and the truck was without air conditioning. We were soon sweating. Maher leaned his head against the door frame and minutes later was asleep.

Pooya smiled at me. "Where are you from, Ben?"

"Next to the Caspian Sea. Have you been to any cities in northern Iran?"

"I wanted to go there once, but something happened and I had to cancel my trip. I heard it is beautiful over there, certainly not hot like here."

"It gets warm in the summer, but not as hot as it is here. We also use fans at home in the summer. They help make the heat manageable. Where are you from?

"From a village not far from Zahedan."

"You were born and bred here, then?"

"Yes, but I did my military service in Yazd, about 430 miles away. That was several years ago. I lived there for the better part of a year. Have you ever been to Yazd?"

"No, but I understand it is an old city."

"That's right. In fact, it is one of the oldest cities in the world. It is a beautiful place and was a magnet for tourists before the Islamic Revolution. Nowadays, you hardly see tourists anywhere because the war has disrupted so much in the country."

"I don't remember much from the time before the revolution, but people say that we had lots of tourists in the country and the borders were open for everyone."

"That's right. The country was open to tourists and our people could travel to many countries without a visa, but things changed dramatically after the revolution; we can hardly go anywhere now. I think we can still travel to Turkey without a visa. Why didn't you want to go to Turkey instead of Pakistan?"

"I heard the borders to Turkey were tight and that it was almost impossible to slip in illegally."

"I guess I have no idea about that since we are so far away from Turkey."

"Didn't you want to go abroad yourself, Pooya? I mean, you are so close to the borders?"

"I have been to several Pakistan border towns, but I did not want to live there. I prefer to be in my city."

"I didn't mean living in Pakistan, but going to Europe through Pakistan."

"Do you think I would have a better life in Europe? My friends and family live here. Besides, people go to Europe to study. I am not into studying, so I wouldn't know what to do in Europe. I think Europe is for people who are very ambitious and want to obtain academic degrees. Me?" – Pooya shrugged his shoulders – "I finished high school with a good deal of difficulty and was just happy that I eventually made it. I am not put together to be a good student. If my parents had not forced me, I would not have finished high school. My father was working on other people's farms and wanted me to find a better job. He was so happy that I finished. I'm not really sure it has helped me."

"You seem to be a smart man. Is this driver job your side line or your career?"

Pooya began laughing.

"This is a temporary job for me. Whenever I need extra cash I drive people to the border, but it is not my main job. After my time in the military I started buying and selling cars, but I ended up in prison. When I was released after two years things were not the same. I could not find any interesting job that I could qualify for. I borrowed some money from relatives and bought this pickup truck and have been in the hauling business since."

I asked Pooya why he was in prison.

"I killed someone who asked too many questions. I was then sentenced to two years."

"Really? Two years for killing a human being is nothing. You must have had very good connections to get such a mild sentence!"

He shot a broad smile in my direction.

"I am pulling your leg, Ben. I had a friend, a member of the Iranian Mojahedin party, who was arrested by the revolutionary guards. He mentioned my name during his trial – and that led to my arrest." Pooya sighed. "It is a long story, Ben, but I was imprisoned for providing assistance to a regime opponent. I was released after two years, when they finally realised that I was not bright enough to bring down the government."

"What happened to the friend who involved you?"

"He was fortunate that he was not executed. He was sentenced to five years when it was determined that he was a very small fish in the movement. I don't know where he went after his release. He probably left the country like many others. Do you belong to any of these anti-government parties? Given your location, you could be a member of the communist party, Tudeh. Am I right?"

"Could be, yes, but no, I am not affiliated with any party. From what I've seen, politics only seems to bring sorrow and danger."

"I am glad that you don't belong to the communist party or I would have to kill you."

I was taken aback for just a moment before his smile blossomed again.

"Ah. More leg pulling, I assume."

He nodded and explained his dislike of the communists.

"I don't like them at all. In my opinion, they are just doing a disservice to this country. I regard them as spies for the Soviet Union."

"I know some people in my city who sympathise with the communist party, but they do not take any action against the government."

Several moments of silence followed.

"Tell me Pooya, how long since you have taken someone like me to the border?"

"Last year."

"Really? That was a long time ago. Do you remember the roads?"

"Two weeks ago, I was transporting something and had to drive through these mountains. No worries; I know my way."

"Where are we going now?"

"We are still safe using public roads. That will have to change shortly. There will be an increased presence of border patrol as we near Pakistan. We will be travelling through the desert and have to watch that we are not located by authorities. We will take a break somewhere in the mountains and wait for darkness. Our destination is a village where Maher's guide should be waiting for you. I think it takes four or five hours to walk from that village to Pakistan. We still have hours before we reach our destination."

Sometime later Pooya turned right, off the asphalt road, onto an uneven path strewn with stones. We were constantly jostled front and back and side to side. At times we bounced off the seat and our heads hit the ceiling. As a four-year-old I would have loved it – but not so much that day.

"We need helmets for protection in here," I said. An attempt at a joke.

Pooya laughed and looked at me.

"What doesn't kill you makes you stronger, Ben."

We both laughed. At that point Pooya stopped talking and concentrated on his driving. He also seemed to be watching the rises on both sides of the road.

"What are you looking for?" I asked.

"Bandits who hide behind these small hills and ambush people like us. Some of my friends have fallen prey to them. I would not want to share the same experience."

"So, this is where it begins to get dangerous? It sounds scary. Are the bandits armed?"

"Most people in this area are armed despite the fact that being caught with a weapon might get a person years in prison. Didn't you see the machine guns in Sardar's house?"

"Yes, I saw them, but pretended as if they were nothing out of the ordinary in my life. I was instructed to be cool."

"Good advice. Living here is like living in the Wild West days in America. You need to defend yourself, your family and belongings."

"I have not been to the Wild West. I don't know how they live there."

"Me neither. I was referring to the saying. Don't take it seriously. I don't think anyone needs to carry a gun in Europe. Maybe in America, from what I hear."

"Are these bandits seriously dangerous? I mean, do they kill people as well as rob them?"

"Oh, yes, they are looking for young men from the Caspian Sea. And when they catch them, they show no mercy."

That time he didn't get me.

"You are hilarious. You should try your hand as a stand-up comedian."

"Honest answer. No. I have heard no reports that the robbers here ever liquidate their victims. They are just after valuable items — mainly money, watches and rings."

"Are you armed, too, Pooya? Do you have any weapon hidden anywhere in your pickup truck?"

"That will be a question I won't answer. You will have to be satisfied with that."

I figured the nature of his response suggested he probably was armed. Which made me feel, strangely, a bit better.

With one large lurch to the right – a deep pothole that Pooya deftly avoided – Maher woke up and asked Pooya about our location. The path through the mountains was dangerous, but Pooya was a skilled driver and managed to keep his truck under control, although at greatly reduced speed from the motorway. As we neared the far end of the mountain path, Pooya slowed and pulled over to the side hiding the truck between small, brush-covered hills.

"I must not drive further during the light of day. Just ahead lies a wide expanse of flat desert, and the border police patrol that area very closely."

And so we stopped.

We got out to stretch our legs.

Maher said that his whole body ached and that he needed a smoke to relieve his pain. He lit a cigarette. I walked a few yards away and found a suitable spot to urinate. After walking around the truck several times to work out the kinks, Pooya said that he was going to take a nap in the pickup. We would have an hour and a half or so until it would be dark enough to continue. Maher joined him in the truck.

I was left out. I didn't mind, as I was glad to escape the heat of the truck. I sat on a large rock next to the truck and thought about my parents. I knew they would be worried about me. Too much time had passed since I left home. Too much had happened already, but there was no way of getting a message to them to tell them of my adventure so far. There was nothing I could do about that. My intention was not to cause them distress in any way. But there was no way to contact them until I was safely on the other side.

Soon. Once I arrived in Pakistan, I would call them and let them know of my safe departure from our country.

For now, I was in the middle of nowhere. And when night fell, it got totally dark. I had never seen such a blanket of black – for as far as I could see in any direction.

Pooya awoke and got out of the truck, looking out into the darkness as if to get his bearings.

"It seems a bit scary with no light around us," I said, pointing out the obvious.

"Now we begin the challenging part of our trip," he said. "I have to drive with the truck's headlights off most of the time so we can't be seen by the border police. Soon, lights will come into view in the distance and I will drive toward them across the desert. I know which lights to aim for."

I sighed a fairly loud sigh. Pooya put his hand on my shoulder.

"It might seem frightening, Ben, but believe me, we will be fine. I have done it before. I know what I'm doing."

"Oh, I trust you fully, Pooya. It's just this nervous breakdown I'm having that I'm not so sure about."

We chuckled. I was glad for the little squeeze that Pooya administered to my shoulder before turning back to the truck. I understood it was a form of reassurance, and it helped. I nodded my appreciation into the darkness even if he couldn't see it.

We began moving forward at a very slow pace. Pooya would turn the headlights on for just a few seconds every minute or so to view the terrain immediately ahead. He kept to the path for some time. It was unnerving to be moving along and unable to see. I came to appreciate the value of my eyesight all over again. We all focused on the road and did what we could to keep us on the right path.

The lights he had mentioned came into view as tiny specks on the far horizon. It was impossible to judge distance in the darkness, but they were clearly many miles away. At one point I gagged as the uneven ride had made me queasy. Pooya asked if I wanted to stop for a few minutes. I was so eager to get to our destination that I declined and mounted a mental defence against my physical problem. Had there been time, I am sure I would have been fascinated by how well my defence worked.

I had come to like Pooya in the few hours I had known him. Even so, I was somewhat surprised by his thoughtfulness; compassion just didn't fit my picture of people in his line of work. I had heard terrible stories about human traffickers and their associates allowing horrible things to happen to the people in their care.

Pooya and Maher exchanged very few words the entire trip and I wondered why. I didn't feel comfortable asking in Maher's presence, but decided I would ask Pooya more about their relationship later, if the opportunity arose.

Pooya offered that we were still a long hour from our destination and suggested a short break. I really needed to relieve myself. The ride had been nerve-racking. We all seemed ready for a short stop. It had been a mentally exhausting journey, surrounded by all that dark.

The men opened their doors and got out.

Pooya screamed. "Oh, my God. Be careful."

By that time my feet were also on the ground. Maher put out his hand to keep me from proceeding. Pooya reached inside the cab and flashed the lights ever so briefly. What it revealed was unbelievable. My legs became weak and I let myself down to sit on the ground next to the vehicle.

"We are lucky to be still alive," Maher said.

Pooya had stopped the pickup truck at the very edge of a deep sinkhole. The vehicle's front bumper extended out over it. The front tyres were just inches from the edge. The others joined me on the ground. We sat and stared at each other.

Eventually, Pooya broke the silence.

"One of us must have an amazing guardian angel watching over us tonight, and I doubt it's you or me, Maher."

He smiled — I could make out his teeth in the black of night.

"I think we should be grateful for Ben's bladder condition that forced us to stop at that point."

I urinated for the second time in an hour. It must have been my anxiety, as I usually had supreme bladder capacity. But I too was glad I needed that pitstop.

Fifteen minutes later we were on our way again — relieved in more than one way. After backing up and moving around the hole, Pooya again set his eyes on the distant lights. They grew larger as we neared them. After a short time, he stopped again with directions for Maher and me.

"You two need to stand up behind the cab in the bed and keep watch. You will be better able to take in the full 360-degree view from back there. Let me know if you suspect anything."

Maher and I climbed into the bed of the truck.

"Watch with your ears as well as your eyes. You will hear vehicles long before you will see them. That gives us a slight advantage I believe."

I asked Pooya if he had a flashlight in his vehicle to use intermittently instead of the headlights. From our vantage point standing in the bed of the truck, I thought it would help, and the beam was less likely to be seen from a distance.

Both men agreed it was a good plan. Pooya removed a flashlight from under his seat and handed it back around through his window.

Maher took it and stood next to me while Pooya began inching along into the darkness. We reached a wider expanse of flat desert so sticking to the path was less important, which was a good thing because Pooya said that by then we were far too close to use the lights at all.

There was a low rail across the back of the roof of the cab that we could hold onto to maintain our balance. Pooya had been right; this made a far better vantage point from which to assess our situation. At one point we came upon four camels with sacks on their back. No one seemed to be accompanying them. Maher asked Pooya to stop and see what they were carrying, but Pooya said that they should leave the camels alone as they certainly belonged to someone and they were most likely carrying opium to their owner. It was a common practice in that area and opium traffickers were not people with whom we wanted to get involved.

Maher smiled at me and commented that Pooya was a man of principles and he liked people who adhered to their principles — especially when that worked to save his neck.

Although the remainder of the trip was not without its dangers and harrowing moments, we eventually arrived safely in the small village where we had been headed. We stopped beside a one-room clay house that was lit by oil lamps.

"I hope this is the right place." Pooya let out an uncertain sigh.

"The guide does not seem to be here," Maher said looking around. "I may have to find another way forward."

I was already growing concerned, feeling my gut tighten when Maher added, "No need to worry, Ben. I am going to find another solution and get you across the border into Pakistan."

"But how," I asked, "if your man has failed to show up? Without any guide we might walk in the desert for days and probably starve to death. Maybe you have heard that some people needed 40 years for a trip that should have taken just 11 days."

"I will find the way myself without a guide. I know the area. This really isn't rocket science. We are here and the border is out there." He made a large sweeping motion with his hand.

Pooya appeared to doubt Maher's contention that it would be an easy task. He asked a few questions about the route Maher would take, understanding the security risks. He seemed to indicate the area was very hard to get to know, especially if one were to take a different route across the border each time. I liked Pooya's questions; they revealed a man who considered the many dangerous angles to such a crossing. I was not so sure I liked Maher's answers.

Pooya asked Maher whether he knew anyone in the village.

"No. Each time I just randomly choose one of the smallest villages close to the border. Just give me a few moments and I will have things figured out."

The idea of choosing a place randomly was both reassuring and unsettling.

I was suddenly hungry and asked Pooya if there was a shop in the area where we could purchase food.

"Unfortunately, not. We should have thought to bring some."

I asked Maher how long a walk it would be before we arrived in Pakistan.

"Only four to five hours."

"In that case I can wait to eat," I said.

Pooya, who had been the voice of reason throughout the trip, expressed his concern.

"Based on my experience, everything will have to fall into place perfectly for you to make that schedule. Things seldom go on schedule around here. I think you need to eat before you begin – just in case. Give me a few minutes to see if I can get some food from one of these houses. I will be back soon. The people in this area are generous and compassionate."

Pooya walked to the house next door and knocked at the wooden door. It was larger and in a better state of repair than the hut by which we were parked. A sleepy young man opened the narrow door. It seemed that Pooya apologised for waking him. They conversed in the Baluchi language. The man turned, and closed the door. Pooya continued to stand there. I took that as a good sign.

After a few minutes the man returned with loaves of bread and a large jar of water. Pooya offered him money, but he waved it off. I could see from where I sat how Pooya tucked money into the man's trouser pocket. Apparently, he then asked the man if he knew a guide who could take his companions to the Pakistan border – he pointed at Maher and me.

The man leaned out his door and looked us over as he contemplated the request. Presently he looked back at Pooya and nodded. Then he turned and motioned for Pooya to follow. Maher and I were to remain at the truck.

After fifteen minutes – which stretched into an eternity for me – they returned. Pooya wore a broad grin. He said he had arranged for an old man who had walked the area for seventy years to guide us. He asked for very little money.

Maher considered the possibility for just a few seconds before nodding in agreement. Apparently, the money would not be a problem. I felt much better knowing we would have a genuinely knowledgeable, home-grown guide. I sensed that Maher was relieved as well.

When Maher moved a few yards away to pass water, Pooya spoke to me in lowered tones. He said he had some reservations about Maher's competence. He hoped he was wrong, but suggested that I keep alert at all times. He said and hoped that his feeling was wrong, and asked me to take good care of myself.

It posed a new quandary: should I continue or go back, considering the new insight from Pooya?

After a few minutes Maher returned and announced he was ready for the final leg of our trip to the border. I finished eating and took a long drink and made the decision to continue, with added watchfulness.

A few minutes later an ancient looking man approached out of the darkness. Pooya shook his hand, but offered no real introduction. Maher asked the old man if he knew how to get us to the border without being seen. The old man, whose first language was clearly Baluchi, spoke to Maher in broken Farsi saying that he knew where the Mirjaveh border – the Iranian border – was, and that he would get us there unobserved.

Maher paid the old man the amount Pooya had negotiated. The old man didn't bother to count it. The guide asked for permission to go home to leave the money there and come back. Maher told him that he should return soon since he wanted to set off immediately.

Pooya shook my hand one final time and wished me good luck. I thanked him for providing my transportation and wished him success in life.

The old man joined us once more and motioned for us to follow him. He turned and set a steady pace to the east.

I walked a few steps behind the guide and Maher a few steps behind me. I carried my small bag of clothes and Maher his sports bag with the money and perhaps other things. I found it more difficult to keep pace with the guide than I had anticipated, but was determined to be up to it. The old man was short and thin, but fit and able. His face was leathery and wrinkled. He reminded me of Nabi, my great grandmother's servant.

From time to time he used his flashlight to survey the ground ahead to make sure it offered safe passage. The ground was uneven and cluttered with small rocks. In the first hour of our travel, we continued across the rocky area. The trees and other plants were unfamiliar to me; they were unique to that desert area and like the old man, I supposed, were designed to survive long periods of harsh, dry conditions.

Maher and I stumbled each from time to time. I soon came to understand and appreciate the reason behind the old man's high stepping gait. Before long I was walking with little difficulty.

The rocky surface gave way, and after several hours we found ourselves on the flat desert surface. The old man stopped and pointed into the distance. We could see the lights of what appeared to be a village not far away. I wondered if this meant we had already crossed the border. I was hopeful but didn't ask.

When the sky displayed the first streaks of light for the new day, Maher called us to a stop.

"That is a border police station up there. What are you trying to pull, old man? I said we needed a place to cross without being detected."

The station was a large building with a high, sturdy fence stretching in both directions from its sides. It was well lit inside and out. There were gates on each side of the border. That was everything we did not need.

The old man pointed as if he had completed his end of the bargain. Maher grew agitated.

"We didn't want to come to the police station crossing. We need to cross into Pakistan *undetected*. I told you that. It is the reason we are using your service. Otherwise we could have travelled the road in the truck."

With the two of them speaking in Baluchi, I had to use my imagination and read their facial expression and tone. Maher's demeanour became angrier and louder and his body language suggested complete frustration.

It crossed my mind that considering the language barrier, it might well have been that the old man had misunderstood Maher's purpose, having interpreted the message as getting us undetected to the border station.

As the discussion continued, I realised how tired I had become from walking in shoes that had clearly not been designed for such a cross-country hike. I sat on the ground and took off my shoes and massaged my feet. I figured the guide and Maher would eventually find a common ground and stop arguing. Unfortunately, it only worsened. Maher had a very short fuse. He began throwing easy punches at the old man's shoulder and chest. I jumped to my feet and moved in between them, asking them to calm down. But Maher took his jackknife from his front pocket and I realised I was not succeeding in calming the situation.

The old man fell to the ground and appeared to be in pain from Maher's punches. I felt bad for the old guide, but shared Maher's frustration.

But when Maher threatened to slaughter him, I did my best to push Maher away.

"Come on, Maher, please stop and put the knife back in your pocket. He is old enough to be your grandfather. It isn't right for you to start a physical fight with him."

"He is a useless and greedy man. He has brought us here so we will be caught."

"I think it is more likely that there was some confusion in understanding what you wanted."

I asked Maher to quiet down and sit on the ground before the border patrol heard the commotion and were upon us. That accomplished, I went back to see the old man.

"Do you know this area yourself?" I asked Maher over my shoulder, while checking over the old man's body for serious damage. "You must remember where you crossed with those that came before me."

"No, I've not been at this place before, and I don't know how we can get to the other side."

"But you said you have done this before."

"Not at this location. I am really annoyed and angry now. You should not talk to me for a while. I am warning you. I am not in the mood for this discussion."

I felt panic rising in my chest. Things had suddenly deteriorated — perhaps to a point they couldn't be repaired. It seemed obvious that sticking around there could only make things worse. I spoke to the old man in simple Farsi.

"Can you take us back to the village?"

The old man struggled to his feet, shaking off my attempts at helping him. He started walking back the way we had come. I hurried into my shoes and picked up my bag. I had been following him for several minutes before Maher caught up with us. He again began cursing at the old man.

Now it was my turn to become angry — an unfamiliar and unpleasant state for me. I addressed Maher.

"Can you please stop swearing? Cursing does not change a thing. What we need is a new plan that has some promise of getting me into Pakistan. It will soon be light and we need to have a plan before we are seen. Swearing accomplishes none of that for us."

"I warned you before and I am warning you one more time," he came back. "You should watch your words with me."

"Otherwise what? Otherwise you will take out your jack knife again? Is that your way of dealing with all problems?"

Through the exchange our guide had not varied one bit in his stride. I continued, directing my next set of concerns to the old man.

"We need to find cover – trees or brush where we can get out of sight."

I remembered we had walked through a wooded area along a very small river.

"How about the stream?" I asked, hoping this was a good suggestion.

The old man appeared to agree and veered slightly to our left – toward what I assumed was the narrow river.

An hour later, relief swept over me at the mere sight of the green trees and plants with the small river running through the valley. We came upon a secluded spot: momentary peace. The old man and I sat on the ground, our backs up against two tree trunks. Maher eventually joined us after a period of pacing and snorting.

We settled in to think and devise a new plan. Perhaps the old man knew something that would be helpful to me. Before, he had clearly not been thinking along the necessary path.

"Any ideas?" I asked, just throwing it out, hoping it would ignite a useful brainstorming session. Maher offered a plan – of sorts.

"We will go back to the area of the border police station tonight and try to find a gap in the fence. I don't see any other alternative, considering where we are."

I was relieved that Maher had managed to calm down to the point of being rational again, but slightly alarmed that he still saw himself in charge of the undertaking. I remembered Pooya's caution.

"Do you know where to look for such an opening?" I asked.

"No. I don't."

I rolled my eyes, mostly intentionally. He tried to explain what he meant, and I sensed he was scrambling to regain his authority, or to at least appear not completely incompetent.

"The border fence is about eight feet high and made of wire mesh. Razor wire runs along the top. Any gaps or openings are only temporary – wind, fallen trees, perhaps cut by someone trying to cross. It is constantly patrolled and when a problem is discovered it is repaired immediately. It is a matter of each new pass making the repairs."

It made sense. I felt myself relaxing again, even though, as plans go, that really didn't amount to much.

And I was starving again.

"We don't have any food for today," I said. "Should we stay here or go back to the village and return tonight?"

"No, we are staying here," Maher said. "That would be just too much walking – to go to the village and to come back."

The old man had been listening and had understood enough to get the gist of the conversation. He stood and looked down at me.

"I go back village. Return, bread and water this evening. Old legs can walk forever."

He pointed at them.

I believed him on both levels – that he would return *and* have food for us. I hoped I hadn't read too much of my great grandmother's old servant Nabi into him and that he really was trustworthy in his own right.

Maher and I went just a bit further into the wooded area for cover from any eyes that might pass by. It was a bit closer to the stream, and the sound of the running water was soothing and somehow reassuring. We lay down in the grass and slept. A few hours later, I awoke and spent some time exploring. From the trash left behind I could tell others had used the place as their stopover as well. It turned out to be a fully unremarkable area, possessing nothing that even really sparked my imagination. As noon approached it grew quite hot so I unbuttoned my shirt. I smiled to myself when I realised that was the most excitement I had experienced since arriving there at the river bank.

Maher woke and asked me for the time. He sat up and stretched and began to talk as if the unpleasant exchanges of the near past had not occurred.

His remarks were driven by hunger.

"I wish we had some of those cold drinks and biscuits that are just a few miles away to the east of the border."

It didn't represent our reality so I didn't reply.

"Aren't you hungry, Ben?"

"Yes, and thirsty, too."

"You can drink the river water."

"I don't think it looks clean and I don't want to contract some awful disease. The old man said he would bring bread and water later on. I understand he was telling us this water is not drinkable."

"Do you really think he will come back? Don't be naive. We are on our own here."

"You seem to have trust issues. I think he seemed to be an honest man and I think he will come back just like he said. We have to wait until it grows dark anyway. I believe by then he will have returned."

I wasn't about to escalate the discussion into an argument – something that seemed to come far too easily for the man, so I stopped at that. I was quite uncomfortable leaving my safety and perhaps my future in the hands of such a superficial pessimist. I figured my best course of action was to avoid future conversations so I lay down and pretended to be asleep. I would try to remain polite, but keep words between us to a minimum.

Finally, the sun hit the horizon and the steady blue of the daytime sky began to melt into darker shades of orange and yellow. Although I appreciated a beautiful sunset, I was impatient for darkness to overtake us. I was hungry. I was thirsty – my goodness, how I was thirsty! For my physical needs and for other, more philosophical reasons, I needed that old man to reappear.

Hours passed. It grew dark. Remaining quiet, as we were, added a mysterious, worrisome element to the area that I had not noticed the night before. I felt an ominous chill. Very few words passed between us.

Then, a noise.

I sat up straight. "You hear that?" I whispered.

"What?"

"Somebody's footsteps swishing through the grass."

Maher stood and became immediately attentive.

"I don't hear anything. I think thirst and hunger are causing you to hallucinate. I told you the old man won't be back. We need to make ready to return to the fence."

I no longer heard anything either. I felt my shoulders slump and my stomach growl.

"I guess I share your view now. It is time to start, like you say. Perhaps we will be luckier tonight."

I wasn't sure I believed that, but allowing the possibility couldn't hurt.

As we bent down to pick up our bags, I heard the noise again — and so did Maher. Footsteps! Maher signalled for me to remain quiet. They became louder as who or whatever it was moved closer. Before long the beam from a flashlight came into view. It stopped at our clearing and rose to shine on us. I held my breath — what else could I do? It moved to illuminate the face of the person carrying it.

It was the old man.

At once I felt both relieved and smug. Though I opted not to share either emotion with Maher.

It was a reunion punctuated with my nervous laughter. The guide lowered his load to the ground and sat at my feet. I was so overjoyed that I knelt down and administered a fully awkward hug. He returned it. I was more moved by the old man's gesture than I expected I would be. It was hard to know how to express my appreciation. That immediately became a secondary consideration to the food and drink — especially the drink. I had never in my entire life been that thirsty. It overrode my hunger a hundredfold. We drank and ate and then drank some more. The old man took none of it for himself.

"Eat. Drink if you need to," I said to him.

He smiled and shook his head.

I whispered to Maher, "Please give the old man 20 US dollars as a token of our appreciation. What he has done is really extraordinary. Like you said, he could have just disappeared from our lives forever. Think of the money as payment for a lost bet — to me."

Unexpectedly, Maher smiled.

"I will give him twenty-five just so you don't think I am stingy."

Maher opened his bag and counted 25 US dollars into his hand. The old man looked puzzled.

Maher also offered his hand for a shake and mumbled something resembling an apology for what happened on the previous night. The old man thanked him for the money and said he would accompany us to the border if we wished.

I didn't wait for Maher to respond. I said that we would be happy to have him go with us to the border again. Maher stated no argument and offered the man a hand up.

Once again, the old man walked ahead of me and Maher brought up the rear. We walked for about an hour when we came upon the Mirjaveh border just ahead.

When we were several hundred yards from the fence, the old man asked us to lie down and crawl toward the border station. I didn't understand, but had come to trust him. Apparently, so had Maher because he followed his suggestion as well. The building was a beacon of light out of the black of the night and bustled with activity. There were people inside and armed, uniformed soldiers outside. The roads to and from were well lit by tall lampposts that spread an eerie blue tinted light across the area. There were many vehicles parked there.

Maher whispered to us. "The fence extends away from the building on the other side of the road. We need to make our way over there and follow it out perhaps several hundred yards. If there is a gap, it will be out there. The fence here is too well lit. Out there, it trails into the darkness."

What he said made sense. The old man nodded.

We remained right there on the ground for some time, observing and learning the routine. We determined that a police SUV drove away from the border control building at regular intervals and returned after about fifteen minutes. The old man said that the SUV drove along the border fence for two or three miles and returned. He suggested that we should move back along the road several hundred yards away from the border control station where we could cross the main road in the darkness.

Maher accepted the guide's suggestion. We crawled along well to the right of the road on the rocky desert ground. It soon fell into darkness away from the lampposts.

And then we were at a road. And just like that, Maher suggested that the old man had fulfilled his obligation and that he should return home. We would manage the rest on our own.

I had mixed feelings about that. It was probably true and yet the old man seemed to have spent the day figuring details that had been invaluable up to that point. I did not want to lose him. But Maher seemed in charge again.

With only a little hesitation, the old guide nodded, shook our hands and wished us luck on our way.

Maher asked me to strap his small bag onto his back because he needed his hands free for crawling; we needed to be far speedier than what we had managed up to then. With no difficulty, I dragged my small bag along tied to my right wrist.

When we began crawling, Maher pointed out that I would be able to crawl faster and with less effort if I let my knees touch my elbows with each movement. He was right.

"You seem to know a good deal about manoeuvring like this," I said.

"A survival skill I acquired when I fought in the war in Afghanistan."

A new piece of information. One I was glad to have — I figured such experience gave us at least a slight edge I hadn't counted on.

By then we both had skinned elbows, lower arms and palms. I had no doubt the pain was going to be worth it once I had achieved freedom in Pakistan.

We crawled on for about fifteen minutes, taking several very short breaks to unfold our bodies. At one point, after the SUV had passed us on the road, Maher finally suggested that we could start walking, with our bodies bent forward. We moved to the other side of the road and kept going for many minutes. We veered to our left and continued through the darkness toward the fence at a gentle angle.

It was at that time we learned there was another SUV patrolling that section of fence. As it approached, with its spotlight scanning the ground on both sides, we hurried back out of the light's effective range. The soldiers moved on and we again approached the fence. We felt our way along it, moving away from the building. We not only found no opening, but determined that the mesh wire was buried a foot into the ground to prevent escape from below. A disheartening discovery, to say the least.

We heard the vehicle returning and ran back into the darkness where we lay flat until it had passed. Then, we tried again, covering perhaps 250 yards before the patrol returned. We hid. It was a game of cat and mouse. Knowing I was the mouse made it quite unnerving. The mouse never won. I began to believe the security net was just too well maintained for us to penetrate it. Maher said the fence extended perhaps twenty miles. My spirits hit bottom.

Maher insisted that we continue our search. After close to an hour we came upon a small gap in the mesh wire. It was at the location of a temporary patch where it seemed the wire had actually been cut. It signalled that some other person hopeful of escape had been there before us. A ten-foot-wide section of wire had been unrolled across the broken section and wired in place to cover it. I managed to untwist several of the wires that held the patch in place and slip in between the two sections. I was through. Maher was a slightly larger person. I stayed and untwisted several more wires until he was there beside me. We saw the lights from the patrol vehicle coming back toward us in the distance. At Maher's suggestion we replaced the twists so the patrolmen would be none the wiser. The SUV drew dangerously close. We bent low and ran out into the darkness – out into what I was sure was Pakistan. We didn't stop for five minutes until, finally, needing to catch our breath, we collapsed onto the ground.

At the same moment, as we lay there on our backs, we each extended our hands for a shake. We had made it work. Despite my growing doubts about the man on the other end, I was certain it was the most meaningful shake of my life.

"We made it," I said, not quite believing it. My freedom had been hard won, but here we were, soaking up the promise of the world on the other side of the fence.

Maher smiled. "I told you."

The psychologist finishes reading the pages and sits back, removing her reading glasses and shaking her head.

"Goosebumps, Ben. I was terrified just reading your account. And so many disappointments in such a short amount of time. I admire the emotional strength you exhibited."

"It was terrifying," Ben admits. "Had I been spotted within fifty yards of the fence I could have been shot where I stood, no questions asked. Fortunately, the full significance of that did not hit me during those final crucial hours."

"Adrenaline," suggests Frau Bosch.

"Yes, perhaps. But also, looking back, I attribute it to that feeling of invincibility that adolescent males carry with them. Thinking about it, I think it's amazing any teen boy ever reaches manhood."

"A good insight. Fortunately for you, it seems to have worked in your favour. Do you have dreams about that time?"

Ben smiles and shrugs.

"Which ones?"

She winces and sighs.

"Same time next week?"

"Sure."

CHAPTER THREE

A FAIRY-TALE BEGINNING

O nce upon a time – no, seriously.

Frau Bosch smiles at Ben. A genuine smile. Ben feels almost comfortable.

"We're going back to the beginning today, I see," she says.

Ben notes the interest in her tone. "Yes, I thought it was time."

"It is always good to consider our roots, to see where we came from. In your case, I think it may be a complicated story."

Ben does not respond. Frau Bosch has only read a small portion of his story so far. She has no idea.

"Will I find Nabi in this section?"

"Yes." Ben is secretly pleased she remembers his mention of his old servant. "Nabi, Banu, Maryam and all the rest. They were important to me as a boy. They –" He hesitates, feeling his throat constrict. "Well, they are important."

Once upon a time – no, seriously.

As I recall, it was a sunny spring day. I was in the orchard that belonged to my maternal great uncle and great grandmother. It was quiet there and conducive to thinking and wondering about the great questions in life. It had become my place of contemplation. The branches in the orchard moved as if dancing in concert with the breeze. I was fifteen and, like most teens, if I didn't need to be moving, I was reclining. That morning found me lying on the grass on my back with my arms lying gently across my chest. I had positioned my chemistry and biology books under my head as a headrest.

I was looking at the clouds and tried to remember from geography what they were called. They had to be stratus or cumulus since I was pretty sure the third one was nimbus and that was the darker one that brought rain. Gradually I sorted it out and concluded they had to be stratus since they were not the fluffy ones resembling cauliflower. I think it is often useful to establish an answer by the rule of exclusion, although even at that age I knew it had limited use in life. With the school year soon ending, the purpose of my time in the orchard that day was to prepare for my final biology and chemistry exams. For some reason, or reasons, I was unable to control my thoughts and found it impossible to focus on my studies.

At one point, the sound of approaching footsteps returned my attention from the nebulous images in the sky to my real world. Turning my head toward the sounds, I saw they belonged to my grandmother, Maryam. I sat up cross-legged to greet her, offering my usual smile.

"Is your back pain better today?" I asked. She was short and underweight, and she looked frail.

"It would have been manageable if I had not had so many household chores. It fell on me to take care of Banu, tending to her daily hygiene requirements and changing her position in bed."

Banu was her mother-in-law. She admitted to being eighty years old so who knew her actual age. A strong, attractive woman, she was well respected in every way. Her husband – businessman and land owner – had been assassinated as a young man, leaving her and her four sons on their own. She never remarried. Her husband had been a successful farmer and landowner, and she ran his business on her own. She rented out her farmland to several local farmers. That generated enough income for her to raise her sons, one of whom was my late maternal grandfather.

Banu had fallen on the stairs several weeks before and broken her hip. Her doctor insisted on bed rest for three months in order to heal her ancient bones. This was how she came to need regular care. Banu's grandchildren were at home on the weekends and took care of her then. During the weekdays, Maryam was her primary caregiver. Sometimes Banu's youngest daughter-in-law helped, but really it was mostly up to Maryam.

Unlike Maryam, Banu was tall and big-boned, making Maryam's tasks a real physical challenge. But Maryam was a patient woman, known as a person with amazing endurance and willpower. Everyone felt badly that life had not treated her fairly.

Maryam had been living with Banu ever since her split with my grandfather. The story is that he fell in love with and married another woman – took a second wife, permitted under Muslim law. Together they built a second family, something that was not uncommon for affluent people in Iran at that time. But what was permissible by law was not permissible by Banu. As soon as she learned that her son had fallen in love with another woman, she asked him to leave her house where he, Maryam, and their five children had been living. My grandfather bought a new house for him and his second wife. Maryam stopped talking to him, but maintained a working relationship with his second wife and later with his stepchildren, too. Maryam never remarried. She would have had difficulty finding a man at that time who would marry her and contribute to the support of her and five children. Banu stayed with her daughter-in-law and raised her children, one of whom became my mother.

Maryam was a proud woman who never openly complained about things, despite her difficult lot in life.

"You must stop lifting heavy things," I said to Maryam. "Your back pain will never get better."

"Listen, Ben, you are still a child and cannot understand these things, but there are things in life which are more painful than physical maladies and more challenging to bear than physical torment."

Emotional conditions were harder to manage than physical ailments, she said. She was right: I didn't completely understand what she had been through in her life. She was probably referring to multiple ordeals in her life. I didn't push her for more. I watched as she walked across the courtyard, stooped low from her intense back pain.

What I did understand was that she didn't like consulting physicians, that she did not believe they could change the natural course of a disease. I figured that her trust in medical doctors had been broken when she lost her eldest son at twenty-eight from a brain haemorrhage following a car accident. That had been some years before – way before my time. Competent and well-known neurosurgeons from across the country were brought to him by helicopter, but his life could not be saved. He had just graduated from university with a degree in engineering. Family and friends alike were proud of him and his achievements, and his loss left a huge, unfilled void in the family. His death had broken Maryam. I think each year since she stooped a little more.

At the time of my uncle's death, I was ten years old and his funeral was only the second I had attended, the first having been my paternal grandmother's one year before. Any funeral is sad, but a funeral for a man so young is almost unbearable. I will never forget the relatives crying, screaming and weeping at the wake. Some collapsed into unconsciousness; a few needed to be taken to hospital. I was too young to understand death, let alone such unfathomable grieving.

But even if I could not understand them fully, the funerals had their impact. Like many of my cousins, I had horrible nightmares about death and about the ceremonies around it. I dreamed of wakes and creepy processions. Hearses entered my dreams as much as anything else. And I soon realised that my trauma was as real as that of anyone else: these events were just as terrible for a small boy who could not fully understand their nature.

My paternal grandmother's death had made an impression, too. She had been bedridden, mentally confused and with far too many of those end of life physical embarrassments of the elderly. In the end, her passing was a relief. It was her life at the end that was hardest for those who loved her. I recall hearing my grandfather – her husband – pray to God for her death; he was sure his wife would not have wished to live with Alzheimer's and its many hideous effects.

After her death, I asked my grandfather why he had wished for her to die.

He tried to explain.

"She was the love of my life as long as she was alive. When she became terminally ill and persistently confused, her life became meaningless to her – frightening, also, I have to imagine. Lying in her bed those last weeks she became like the undead. I could not take care of her anymore, as I am old. I thought she became a burden for all family members, and I could not stand seeing her losing her dignity any longer. So I prayed to God to release her and the family by her death."

I fidgeted, not knowing what to say.

"You know, Benjamin, letting people go is also part of the loving process in life and everyone needs to learn that. It is my wish that my God has mercy with me and won't keep me alive if I am going to be a burden for my family."

I figured that message was directed equally to God and me.

That afternoon, Maryam asked me to come to their house. She was baking bread – the special kind for which she was famous in the family. She did her baking in a special clay oven, which occupied a tailored shed in the

46

backyard. I couldn't turn her down. Upon arriving at her place, I went to Banu's room; I know about old women and guilt, and I felt ashamed that I hadn't visited her more frequently. But Banu was happy to see me. She reached out and took my hand, offering a smile. She patted the edge of the mattress and I sat. We spoke briefly about my parents.

I remember looking at her and imagining her as a young and energetic woman moving through her world with aplomb. There were stories about her younger years that painted Banu as a resolute and visionary woman with strong willpower. People said that Banu was focussed, determined and passionate about her orchards and farm plots. She was a businesswoman through and through; she could mobilise people to achieve her objectives. She did things on her own terms, never kowtowing to the wealthy and dominant landowners of the time. She amassed her own wealth, even while raising four boys on her own after the death of her husband – quite unprecedented in Iran at the time. Yet she remained humble and helped people in need whenever she could. Her long list of accomplishments included building roads and bridges, for which the local people revered her for years and years.

I can only marvel at what she might have accomplished had she not been illiterate. She believed that education was the key to success for most people and knew it would have eased her life, opened up more paths. She was, however, living proof that there was a route other than a school education that could also lead to a fulfilled and successful life.

"Bring me my purse," Banu said suddenly to Maryam, calling from her bed. Maryam went to fetch the purse from its hiding place, only known to the two of them. Soon Maryam arrived with a small leather bag. Banu opened it and gave me a few coins to buy cookies. Banu was a generous lady. But she was slightly out of touch by then – for a teenage boy the amount she offered was too small to purchase anything of significance. Still, I thanked her as if it were. My parents and teachers taught me that it was the intention or thought behind that gift that counted most.

Later, my change clanking in my pocket, I took a seat in the garden. Under the tall bitter orange trees chickens, geese and turkeys clucked and pecked busily, while cats lounged languidly nearby under the grapefruit trees. They seemed to enjoy a peaceful co-existence, these animals – something that appeared to be difficult for human beings, the crown of evolution. I contemplated the congenial yard activity and waited for a taste of Maryam's bread. Nabi was also there, sitting next to the oven, waiting patiently for the fresh bread. One of Banu's servants, Nabi had worked for Banu most of his life. He must have been in his seventies by then – he was married with no children and had spent all of his life as part of my family. He proudly owned a small house a few hundred yards down the road, but most of the time he stayed in Banu's house.

"Where's Max?" I asked. Max was the German shepherd who barked incessantly at the front gate whenever anyone passed. Nabi said Max was unwell, possibly poisoned by some hostile individuals – a real possibility as the neighbours didn't like the noisy beast. We then laughed about the running family joke as to whether Max's Farsi was better than Nabi's German. Nabi was good-natured about his learning difficulty, verbal tasks and pronunciation being very difficult for him, his vocabulary no more than a hundred words. He could not recall the names of commonplace items so called everything a 'thing'. Nonfamily members could not have a meaningful conversation with him, but family members understood him very well. We knew he felt most comfortable at Banu's house, avoiding having to mingle with the outside world. Nabi was diligent and loyal to the family members and in his own way liked everyone in the family. Growing up, I spent a good deal of time around Nabi and liked him. Nabi played with me and became my reliable means of transportation back and forth between my place and Banu's.

And he often sat in the garden with me and waited for Maryam's bread.

The only person Nabi was not on good terms with was Gorgin, Banu's other servant, who was a deaf mute and had worked for Banu for more than fifty years.

I often wondered why Banu had chosen servants who were unable to talk well or to express themselves in a conventional way. I told myself it was because Banu had a kind heart and wanted to provide them with a sheltered place where they could feel comfortable and useful. Back when Nabi and Gorgin were children, there were no employment possibilities for deaf-mutes and people with learning difficulties. Later on, however, I came to believe that both parties – Banu and the servants – had benefited from their symbiotic relationship. Perhaps it suited Banu to have servants and housekeepers she knew depended so much on her; perhaps this loyalty created a kind of coherence in the household.

At any rate, Nabi and Gorgin never sat next to each other and went out of their way to avoid each other. A funny fact, since communication between them was nearly impossible, even if they tried.

"Why is the German Shepherd important to you, Ben?" Frau Bosch looks up from reading and poses a simple question – but Ben answers with a blank face.

"I mean, it's an odd detail in there, don't you think? I am reading about your family – and even your close connection with your grandmother's servant – and then, in the middle of this, is Max, the German dog. It strikes me as an odd detail."

Ben is stumped. Which is not usually the case. He wonders now, too, why Max appears in his memory. And whether Max was in fact poisoned that day.

"I've not really thought of it," Ben says, "but I supposed Max's possible poisoning was a bit of a warning to me – perhaps it told me, even then, even when I was so young and naive, that life takes sudden and violent turns. Even if you are a dog."

Frau Bosch raises an eyebrow, says simply, "Indeed. Point taken, Ben."

And continues reading.

It was dusk by the time I left the orchard. Just outside the gate I ran into a village boy, Sam. He was perhaps twenty years old and recently released from prison.

We shook hands. I asked about his plans. He said he was going to finish high school and then study architecture, because he was good at drawing. I avoided inquiring about prison life but Sam brought up his three years in prison anyway. His face looked drawn and heavy with regret. I knew all about his crime, of course – everyone did. I did not want to talk about it, though. His prison sentence was the result of an affair with his neighbour's wife; he was caught with her in bed by the husband – he was sentenced to three years in prison, and the woman got five.

Had Sam not been a teenager or had he been married, he and the woman would have both received death by stoning, or, at a minimum, a life sentence. Such is the way of life in my country since the Islamic Revolution. These were heavy topics for a boy on his way home after a happy afternoon with Banu and Maryam's special bread. My mood was light and I was not sure I wanted to talk about prison or sex.

But Sam wanted to talk. I tried to listen only partly as Sam went on about his time in prison, but I was intrigued when he arrived at the end of his story, when he concluded that, looking back on it, he may have been fortunate that he ended up there for those years. That he regarded it as a kind of blessing.

I was perplexed by his contention. I could not imagine spending so much as one day in prison. I was taught that prison was for people who had lost the control over their lives and were incapable of making sound decisions. I asked Sam how he could view prison at all in good light.

"Listen," he said, leaning in close. "While I was in prison, some of my friends were executed by the government because they belonged to the opposition party. Some were killed in the Iran-Iraq war. You are too young to think about politics, Ben, but you will one day understand. On the balance of probabilities, I could have been dead by now if I had not been in prison. Either executed for my political beliefs or killed in war. Either way, I see the prison sentence as a kind of divine intervention to preserve my life."

Sam was right, of course. I had little interest in politics – and up to that point my concerns centred wholly around school and family life. I am the eldest son and have three younger brothers – three, four and thirteen years my junior. My relationship with the two younger brothers was not good at that time since they had recently broken my piggy bank and spent all my savings – nearly thirty US dollars. Seems they urgently needed money and my piggy bank was the only source at hand. They never told me how they spent it, but promised to pay the money back with interest when they were older. But I didn't believe them and decided to keep my new piggy bank hidden from them. My father scolded them for what they had done and actually compensated me for my loss. He asked me not to tell my brothers about that.

Such was a typical worry for me at age fifteen. I was fortunate because my parents understood I was a sensible boy with an independent mind. They had no doubts I would have a bright future. They were proud of my school achievements. Perhaps, partly because of that, I, too, grew to be proud of my accomplishments and came to believe in myself.

I shuddered late that night as I thought of Sam and his three years in prison, and his friends whose lives had been cut short. I vowed to make my father proud.

My father failed to complete high school but had grown to be a well-respected man in his community. He trained as a mechanic and worked on special textile machines for a large, well-known manufacturer. He also owned some land and a welding workshop manufacturing iron doors and windows for commercial and residential buildings and aluminium water tanks for orchards. Financially, he did well.

I respected my father, even though as I grew older, I didn't share his views on a wide variety of subjects. I often challenged his ideas, in the typical way of a teenager. My mother – Roya – was a hardworking housewife, busy raising four children and running the farmland. Like my father, she'd left high school before she graduated, and went to work helping her mother, Maryam, and grandmother, Banu, tend to their farmlands. She was a very smart woman and grasped things quickly.

Mother was from a wealthy family and her parents wanted her to marry an educated man with money. But Mother was smart and strong-willed, and when her parents arranged for her to be introduced to a high school teacher ten years her senior, she rejected the man and told her parents that she would prefer to stay single for the rest of her life than marry a man she did not fancy. That was around the time my parents met – my father was working on Mother's parents' farmland and fell in love with her.

But what was a poor boy to do? Father knew her parents would not approve of him, since he was penniless, with neither formal education nor a good job. He was a handsome young man, but Roya's parents thought he could not make a living with his looks.

So he started seeing Roya secretly. On one occasion the two of them were caught together by the house servant, Nabi. Nabi asked Father to stop seeing Roya because she was above his class and not suited to him; otherwise, Nabi threatened, he would inform Roya's family members, who could cause my father serious trouble.

My father was resourceful. He devised a new plan that involved getting approval from Nabi first. He avoided a confrontation with the man, understanding that any further discussion with the important house servant would have lost the game before it began. He believed that if Nabi approved of him, he would have an excellent chance of obtaining Roya's parents' approval, too.

Father's Trojan horse strategy was two-tiered. First, he stopped contacting Roya for a short time after the confrontation with Nabi. Instead, he began cultivating a friendship with him. He occasionally took him to a restaurant or bar and also invited him to the cinema. He worked months on building that relationship. Then, when Nabi eventually became his ally, he started praising my father to Roya's mother and grandmother. The friendship paid off, and my father received approval to marry the girl he loved.

These were my parents, even before they became parents: a woman independent and strong enough to say no to an arranged marriage at the time when the arranged marriage was customary in most families, and a man persistent and clever enough to bend the situation to his advantage.

And my father remained friends with Nabi into adulthood. Even well after I was born, the old servant regularly came to our house for dinner, beer or wine before the alcohol became forbidden.

I finished dinner and went to my room with my crossword puzzle, a much-loved pastime that had even won me some prizes in competitions. That evening, however, I could not focus my attention on the puzzles and finally threw the book to the floor. My thoughts were not on the puzzle – they kept drifting to my conversation with Sam. The idea of prison worried me; I was pretty sure I would be mortified and broken if I had to spend time in prison. I understood Sam's story, but I would never regard a prison term as a blessing.

So I decided that night that I would never go to prison. How would I achieve this? Well, I would begin by not sleeping with a man's wife. But besides that, I would focus on the things within my immediate control: my schooling, my sport and my general attitude. The first was easy: I knew how to apply myself to my studies. The second item was more of a challenge, as there were few opportunities for me to participate in my favourites – boxing and martial arts. The fact was, at that time, if someone wanted to learn a martial art, he was required to have a letter of character reference from the local Islamic Committee stating that he was a good Muslim who would pose no potential harm to the Islamic Revolution. Since I did not participate in any religious activities, such a recommendation was out of the question.

That left my attitude – and a final option for improving myself. In those days, every young man had to consider whether to join the military and go to war. But I was not sure I was ready to become a hero. I understood the experience of war might increase my independence and emotional strength – maybe it would even make me fearless. And I saw how all those characteristics would be useful in life.

It was 1980 when Saddam Hussein invaded my country. At a time, Iran found itself in a place of great national weakness: the Islamic Revolution had occurred the year before, and with it the vast majority of capable leaders – governmental and military – had fled, been imprisoned or executed.

Unlike Iraq, Iran suddenly did not have any allies and was left on its own, having to fight with out-dated weapons and inexperienced leaders. The government tried to compensate for those disadvantages with overwhelming manpower. Because of that, it even recruited teenagers. Many young men joined up. But joining the military would not be palatable for my parents. I could have joined one of the many paramilitary groups involved in the war if I wanted — because they did not require parental permission. I was worried about going against my parents' wishes, but there was a lot more at stake: the clerics promised immediate admittance to Paradise for any soldier killed in the war.

My chemistry teacher was against any war. He made the point that there could be no winner in the end. He spoke vehemently about the many losers, how war burdens those young people who happen to survive with a life that is crippled or emotionally damaged, how veterans usually end up as a burden for their family members and quite often commit suicide. He despised those people who brainwashed teenagers and mobilised them for war by promising a superior afterlife, who assured them their deaths would gain them the key to open the gate to Paradise. Never mind that he was trying in his own way to cast his influence over us; I couldn't help but agree with him. At fifteen, I had serious doubts about gaining entry to Paradise by killing other human beings in a war that I knew little about.

My town had plenty of martyrs — too many boys from my high school whose lives had been taken by the war, buried now as a reminder of my country's quest for greatness. I did not like the idea of dying for any cause at my age. I preferred the mortal life on earth that I understood. I had plans that could only be put into practice on earth and I was not sure if they were suitable for the afterlife. For one thing, I very much looked forward to having an intimate relationship with at least one or two girls on earth before I departed this world. Indeed, at that point in my young life, I had yet to see a young woman naked — except for my mother. The only naked girls I'd viewed were in the glossy pages of a *Playboy* magazine illegally imported by my friend Emin's brother following his heart surgery in Germany. Emin and I figured his doctor prescribed him the magazine as a way to keep his heart pumping. He usually locked the magazine up in his Samsonite attaché case in his parents' farmhouse but Emin found out the codes for the case. Every few months we looked forward to going to Emin's house to have a look at the luscious women in the magazine pages. At times our efforts were in vain; some days, we found Emin's brother at home, with the precious attaché case next to him, impenetrable. I suggested we should steal the magazine from his brother, but Emin regarded the magazine as a CPR machine with special life-saving value for his brother, and so did not approve my suggestion. I still wanted to take the magazine so we could look more than every few months, but Emin was adamant: he was sure that if we took it away his brother's heart might stop beating. Of course, we didn't want to compromise his heath, since he had done a great service to us by importing the magazine in the first place. So we contented ourselves with our secret sneak peeks, glad also that Emin's brother hadn't been caught with the contraband at the airport – which would have resulted in a long jail sentence, and in his case most certainly death, without the CPR unit.

In the end I dismissed the idea of going to the war as preposterous and not in line with my life plan, so I also deleted that option from my list. Put simply, I would have to hold out for the benefits that would accrue from being a hero in the here and now. I doubted if I – a pimply teen full of impure and lustful thoughts – qualified for Paradise anyway.

With 'war hero' checked off my list, I turned my attention to my circle of friends, wondering if I could change my friends or find additional friends who could influence me more positively. It would not be an easy task. I only had three or four friends and most of them were relatives. In that time and place it was not easy to find peers who were compatible with my take on life, or who had similar interests. And really, since much of my spare time was spent earning extra money or attending language classes, or trying to please Father with my welding, I had little time for friends.

Yes: *welding*. From the time I turned thirteen, my father wanted me to learn something practical, apart from what I was learning in school. It was my father's suggestion that I learn welding – his early trade, after all. I began spending most of my spare time at the welding workshop and learned how to build doors and windows. I worked hard, ever mindful of my father, ever wanting to be a good son. But I really did not like it. It was repetitive and boring, and it left a burning sensation in my eyes, which disrupted my sleep. How could a boy of my ambition make something of himself if he was stuck wearing a welder's helmet? This was a dead-end job that used none of my imaginary gifts! I wanted to spend my nights dreaming of poetry, or at least girls from Emin's brother's magazine – not rubbing my eyes and wincing at the pain. No, the welding profession did not seem to fit with my image of myself. I could not see it in my future.

But I did not want to disappoint Father, so I needed a back-up plan.

I needed a role model, someone whose fine example I could follow. The only problem was, I was living in a place with very few role models for an outward-thinking teenager. This was Iran at the beginning of the eighties.

Like most of my contemporaries, my life had become sheltered with the revolution. I knew about very few foreign athletes, singers or actors. Most of the national newspapers stopped writing about western celebrities and role models, and foreign magazines and newspapers had been banned by the state. I watched very little TV because it, too, had become so very uninteresting. There were only two channels and they were controlled by the state. They offered nothing of interest to a person my age, with the typical programmes that included endless religious discussions, East European World War Two movies focusing on resistance and defence tactics, and a few select – and repeated – Samurai movies from Japan.

The Islamic Revolution had changed everything and narrowed society. Many people who had once been available as role models had been accused of embezzlement, racketeering and treason. Or worse: they were accused of being against God and Islamic values. Some were fortunate and managed to leave the country before their arrest warrants were served. As a result of this mass emigration, there were hardly any singers, actors or writers left in the country. There was virtually a cultural void, with no strong public figures for a boy of my age to look to. While kids in other parts of the world may have been celebrating the rise of Bono or Bjork, we didn't even have pop stars setting an example. Never mind second-wave feminism or cross-cultural discussions like the rise of the Neo-Expressionism or graffiti art with widespread political and cultural meaning – those were as far out of reach as the moon.

Iran of the early 1980s offered very few role models. My situation was similar to many teens. What we needed were freethinking and independent-minded heroes. Nothing about my country at that time engendered such traits.

I decided to study other people in my situation and looked first to find a role model among my relatives. If I were not to be a welder, this would be a sure way to ease myself away from the burden of following in my father's footsteps. I would give him something to be proud of by looking to my uncles.

But none of my five uncles qualified. Most of them were good men and fun to be with, but they could not be regarded as role models. As a matter of fact, my third eldest maternal uncle was so irregular in school attendance that he didn't graduate until he was twenty-two. He spent most of his school time with like-minded friends, playing cards, smoking cigarettes, drinking illegally brewed alcohol, engaging in reckless behaviour and committing minor criminal acts. He was stigmatised and written off by the other family members at an early age. And he wasn't offered any kind of professional support that might have altered – meaning, *improved* – his life. He blamed his father for his problems; his father, my maternal grandfather, started smoking opium at the age of fifteen and became so addicted that he couldn't manage two or three hours without it. Opium was inexpensive at that time and its consumption was widely spread throughout the country. My grandfather consumed it for almost sixty-five years until he passed away at the age of eighty. His physical dependence on opium prevented him from engaging in work and any serious social activities. He had managed to earn a living renting out the land he inherited from his father.

Sadly, there weren't any uncles who I looked up to. I needed to look beyond my horizons – and I soon fixated on my maternal great uncle, Banu's youngest son: at least thirty-five years older than I and living in Germany. A physician, he was highly respected by all our family members. He was the first college graduate in the family. I had only seen him once and when it came right down to it, I knew very little about him. What of his accomplishments? What ambitions had set him on his course? I needed to know those things, if I was to follow in his path. But he was very far away – an impossible distance, really, for a boy in a small town.

No, I needed someone who was easily accessible and whose achievements were apparent – someone I could readily study up close, first-hand.

"I'm beginning to get the picture, Ben." Frau Bosch pours a glass of water from a glass jar and offers one to Ben. He has not been talking but his mouth is dry.

"My life as a boy was good – I could not really complain."

"Right – and so you don't. I see that, Ben. But I also see that Iran in 1980 could not contain you. I see a lot of pain and confusion there. Already."

"You have no idea. My troubles had not even begun yet..."

"Yes, I can tell," says Frau Bosch, and Ben thinks he sees a small smile forming. "Tell me, Ben, what music did you listen to as a boy?"

"How does that relate?"

"Just curious."

"Well there were of course illegal copies of Michael Jackson back then. I knew him, of course – and other international pop stars. But my musical heroes, if I had any at all, were the Iranian musicians who were banned after the Islamic Revolution."

"Do you listen to them today? These Iranian musicians?"

"No. Strangely — no. At the moment I listen more to the German musicians such as Groenemeyer, Lindenberg and Westernhagen."

So, I picked up my crossword from the floor and tucked it in my drawer. Then I took out pencil and paper eliminated most of the options I had listed for changing my life. I soon found myself downhearted and went to bed. It crossed my mind that I could also ask my uncle, Omid, for some guidance next time when I meet him.

I woke late, around noon. The sun was shining and I had ideas — lots of ideas. I would eat breakfast and start on my list of things immediately.

It was Friday: the weekend in Iran. My parents and brothers were not in the house; I thought they might have gone to my grandmother's. While I was making breakfast, my paternal grandfather, who lived with my family, entered the kitchen. He looked pale and sad. He said that one of his old friends was seriously ill and might die soon. He asked me to come to his room after I finished eating. I felt great empathy for him. I had not seen Grandfather so shattered and sorrowful since the death of my grandmother.

He was a healthy and fit man and had seldom ever been ill. He married my grandmother while in his early twenties. She was a widow ten years his senior with three children. Eventually he became the biological father of two sons, my father and another son who died from pneumonia at the age of seven. He'd been living with my family since the death of his wife a few years earlier. My brothers and I felt very close to him.

When I finished eating, I went to Grandfather's room and sat next to him. I asked him if there was anything I could do to make the situation less painful and to comfort him. He patted my hand.

"Benjamin, listen to me, son. What I said earlier was not true — about my friend." He hesitated, then said, "I need you to be strong. The truth is this is about your uncle, Omid. He was involved in a serious car accident this morning and passed away at the scene. Your parents went to your grandfather's house. Most of the relatives are with them by now."

I became limp. My shoulders slumped. I was speechless and had difficulty breathing. Grandfather brought me a glass of water and put his arm around my shoulders, trying to comfort me. I remember just sitting there staring at the wall for some time absorbing the situation. It seemed like a dream... my mind was racing... could this be true? It was as if I were waiting to wake up and find the news had been the stuff of a nightmare.

Soon I went to my room and dropped face down onto my bed. I began weeping. Grandfather allowed me my privacy. I remember asking God to undo the tragic accident. Perhaps it had been a mistake – perhaps the information had been inaccurate.

I even spun other possibilities in my frantic mind: perhaps someone stole Omid's wallet or bag and this was a case of mistaken identity. Anything to erase the possibility of this being Omid, dead. Omid, my closest uncle: fun, diligent, good looking and focussed on his goals. Omid, who had high school with a good grade average; Omid, one of the few soldiers who survived, unscathed, his eighteen months of military service in the Iran-Iraq war. Omid, dead at only twenty-three years old.

His goal was to study at a university in Germany. The accident occurred as he was on his way to the German embassy in the capital city. He was one of three passengers in a taxi which collided with a truck. All four in the vehicle had been killed.

Following Omid's death, I remained in a state of grief and depression for weeks. Of all my relatives, it had been Omid who would motivate and encourage me to focus on the important things in life. One of my earliest memories of him was from when I was just six years old. At that time, my close friends, Reza and Emin, started their first year of primary school and I wanted to attend, too. But I could not attend because I was a few months younger and the rules dictated that I wait one more year. I was more than a little upset and demanded that my father do something about it. He tried, but found the rules were hard and fast.

I felt upset and could not accept the fact that I would always be one year behind my friends: they would graduate from high school one year earlier and would start earning money earlier, and with that head start they would surely be more successful than I. So I asked Uncle Omid to teach me the first year's school subjects so I could keep up with my friends. I was persistent and Omid, seeing how important it was to me, would not disappoint me. He understood all about being hopeful and determined. We spent a good deal of his free time together that year. In the end I had learned all the material that a student had to learn in the first year. Omid asked his father, my grandfather, who was very influential despite his addiction to opium, if he would talk to the local congressman to get me placed in second year with my friends. As a result, the congressman asked the principal of the local primary school to look into the matter. The principal set up an interview, and Omid accompanied me to the office.

I was primed and confident. The principal, who was a very caring and kind man, asked me a substantial number of questions, which sampled all the subjects. In the end he was satisfied with my knowledge and agreed that I could skip the first year if I passed all the exams at the end of the school year. I was out of my mind with gratitude for the opportunity. I had no doubt about my ability to pass the exams and promised the principal and my uncle that I would not disappoint them.

It all worked out according to my expectations. I skipped the first year and started primary school at the second year level with my friends.

During the weeks after Omid's death, I spent a good deal of time remembering my years with him. Initially, I felt intense sadness about my loss. Gradually, after weeks of mourning and grief, I began to realise that the really good things about our relationship would always remain with me. Perhaps I had my role model after all. My spirits improved. I started finding ways to make my life more interesting – and to gain more independence.

And soon life resumed, even with a semblance of normalcy. I got back to considering the options for improving my life. A windfall came one day when I overheard my parents discussing Aunt Pardis, my mother's sister.

Pardis was married to Shervin and lived some ten miles away. They owned a big house in the city and a farmhouse in a village. They seldom used their city house and soon I began wondering about life in the city – what it could do to change my course. I thought the city would offer plenty of opportunities for a boy of my potential – I just had to get there. So I screwed up the courage to ask if I could move there. I was excited at the prospect, but needed my parents' and aunt's approval. How would I convince them of my crazy plan? How would I gain their support – to let a teenage boy live in the city?

I had seldom given my parents any reason not to trust me. I realised that in light of my uncle's death my parents might be a bit overprotective and less easily convinced to allow me to leave them and go live with my aunt. Regardless, I was impatient and did not want to wait so much as one more day. I approached the discussion with as much optimism – and maturity – as I could muster.

I decided I should probably talk to my mother first and convince her that the move would be in my best interest. If my mother agreed to the move, she could help obtain approval from my father. My teenager intuition was keen – I knew a few things about how homes operated. In most families the wife was the person who was really in charge and made the most important decisions. Getting Mother on board was critical to the plan's success.

In my mind I listed the points I felt I needed to make so I would be well prepared for the conversation. I explained to Mother that if I could go live with Auntie Pardis I would be closer to my high school — no more than a ten-minute walk — and I would have access to the city library, where the students usually went to prepare for their exams. I also argued that I could learn to become more independent since I would be on my own on many days when Pardis was back at the farm; I would also need to learn how to cook for myself and in all other ways tend to the important tasks of my life.

My presentation was apparently a good one. Mother did not object to my plan and promised to talk to my father when the time was suitable. She was good to her word and approached him within the next few days. My father's response was predictable, coming from his view as a practical man; his main concerns centred on my ability to resist peer pressure and to maintain a good group of friends. He specifically asked me to promise I would stay away from illegally brewed alcohol, cigarettes and opium. He said nothing of magazines with naked women, and I did not bring them up. I heartily agreed to his terms: I pointed out that I had known enough people among our own relatives who ruined their lives with opium and other kinds of addictions and assured him I would most certainly avoid them.

My parents agreed to let me have a trial period of three months with my aunt. If, during that time, my school performance remained high and I kept out of trouble, I could stay there as long as my aunt was okay with the arrangement. I was delighted with my parents' requirements and knew that my Aunt Pardis and her husband, Shervin, would be glad to have me at their place.

I understood, too, that the success or failure of the move was strictly on my shoulders. I liked that most of all. I believed in myself.

CHAPTER FOUR

DREAMS AND REALITIES

My parents were quite close to Aunt Pardis and Uncle Shervin and they regularly spent time together, meeting at least once a week to eat together. So at their next dinner engagement, Mother brought up the topic and, as I expected, Pardis and Shervin met the idea with great enthusiasm. They asked that I come as soon as possible.

Several weeks later – at the age of sixteen – I gathered my things and made the move. Their two-storey house was located near the centre of the city. I was given a room on the first floor, with a big window that faced a small road. I fit in almost immediately; I felt comfortable with Pardis and Shervin and homesickness never befell me, not once. At first it was difficult to believe I had really shifted my life into the city. But it took me no time at all to feel my new freedom: I was essentially on my own most of the time. I spent much of my free time with my two friends Emin and Reza. We had our own space and time either at my aunt's house or at Emin's brother's house, which was also adult-free during the week. Most of my relatives owned two houses, typically one on their farmland and one in the city. All of them owned large farms so they spent most of their time at their country homes leaving the city houses vacant. So Emin, Reza and I had plenty of room to be left alone.

But we didn't get into too much trouble. Schooling kept me busy; I attended the same school as my long-time friends, Emin and Reza, even though I was not in the same classroom. The three of us were diligent students and spent most of our spare time together outside school. We were very different people – Emin was the youngest child in his family, with siblings two to twenty years older than he, so he was very much independent and strong-willed, while Reza was the only son in his family and therefore slightly spoiled – but we had similar drive and interests, and we'd been inseparable from a young age. I suggested that we all attend a private English language class once a week to improve our vocabulary and fluency – English was the language of the world, after all. The class was taught by one of the better-known teachers in the city, a teacher in a different high school. He graduated from a university in Canada and approached teaching the language hands-on, insisting that students learn the subject while in the classroom without any obligatory homework. No homework? Unheard of! But his methods really worked, and soon we were satisfied with our progress, chattering more with each week of learning.

This new kind of intellectual stimulation only further supported my already jaundiced view of the school system. For me, high school operated like a prison: once we entered in the morning we could not leave until 2:30 without written permission from the principal or one of his four deputies. Mine was the largest boys' high school in the city and accommodated nearly 1,000 students. The building was a new, huge complex constructed of concrete – impressively prison-like, to be sure. Rumour was the old, wooden building had been burned down by some of the former students, and I'd even heard that one of my uncles and his friends had been responsible – something about it being an act of revenge for failing the final year in high school. The police had not found the perpetrators. But it was a story that had great appeal to me.

Each new classroom accommodated twenty-five to thirty students. The students varied greatly in age; this was the time of the Iran-Iraq war, so some students intentionally failed their final exams in order to remain students. So many boys back then wanted to avoid becoming soldiers, and going to war. The majority of students opposed the war and did not share the establishment's view. Occasionally, some students who were openly involved in anti-government activities were taken away from the classrooms by members of the revolutionary guard. The underage ones were, fortunately, only cautioned or punished by expulsion. Older students had to face harsher punishments, however, such as imprisonment – and imprisonment for anti-government activity usually lasted a significant number of years.

In contrast, there were students who joined the war at the early ages of thirteen or fourteen. Those were students I did not understand; most came from religious families with extreme views, families who regarded the war as holy – therefore requiring each Muslim to be a part of it.

Which meant that freedom of speech, especially with regard to the Iran-Iraq war, hardly existed in either the schools or society. One dared not express his dissatisfaction with the government or governmental decisions. Discussions about the establishment, war or any tangential social concerns were therefore off limits – especially so in schools, between teachers and students. The religion teachers were the only instructors who openly sympathised with the government and tried to mobilise the students to join the war, as the country needed soldiers. But for the most parts my teachers, like my Canadian-educated English teacher, kept mum about their views on government, war and politics.

We wondered, of course, about the qualifications of some of our teachers. Looking back on it, it's a wonder that someone like Mr Canada was even allowed to partake in the system. There were rumours that some of the religion or philosophy teachers had not graduated from universities and had been given positions as high school teachers because they were staunch government supporters or were actively involved in establishing the current government. Those were the teachers I liked to avoid – though there was really no doing so. I could choose my outside classes, like English, but my days were regulated and strict, moving with the other prisoners from Islamic philosophy to religion to Arabic. Despite the conventional wisdom and against all universal laws known to mankind, in my country we could alter and rewrite the past after the Islamic revolution – one of the few abilities and skills acquired after the Shah was overthrown. We successfully managed to attribute all previous achievements and advancements to the religion and all defeat, failure and misery to the non-religious rulers of the country. As one famous writer said, "who controls the past controls the future and who controls the present controls the past."

Morality and religion were discussed and taught regularly in classrooms and on TV by some religious preachers and teachers. Some of them dared introduce us new role models who were omnipotent historic religious figures such as Imams and their innumerable children; they were allegedly the most intelligent and knowledgeable beings with supernatural power – stronger than our childhood heroes such as Superman, Spider-man and Batman all together.

Listening to some of those preachers revealed how imperfect, small, superficial, impure and fallible we mortals were. These individuals also blamed the western countries for our poor choices and our lack of success. Interestingly, some people in my country believed them.

During the first few years after the Islamic Revolution Iran saw many opposition parties form, some of which favoured a more moderate government, some urging more radical change, and yet others actively desiring an anti-Islamic government. Most of those opposition parties were banned by the end of 1981. The more militant members of those parties started fighting the ruling party, their outrage moving them even as far as acts of violence. Indeed, key government members, including the country's president and prime minister – Rajai and Bahonar – were allegedly assassinated by resistors in August 1981. In return, the government's special guard arrested and executed many of the opposition members. I remember all this clearly – it was an important moment in establishing my resolve.

The biggest opposition party was Mojahedin – a party which gained many teenage members who believed if they eventually came to power they would bring democracy to the country and fight the injustices and inequalities in society. I knew plenty of people who held such dreams.

Many teenagers my age blamed the older generation for the political upheaval. They toppled the Shah Pahlavi and terminated his dynasty without making any provisions for filling the subsequent power vacuum. This resulted in a period of chaos.

My first contact with the Mojahedin came one night at a friend's house, when he introduced me to a beautiful girl. Funny enough, that's how stories often begin. A boy, a beautiful girl. In this case...

One warm spring evening, one of my school friends invited me to his house for dinner, asking me to arrive early enough so we could study chemistry together. Shayan was three years older than the other students in our class, having repeated each of the three years in high school. He joked about wanting to learn all school subjects meticulously, taking two years for each regular high school year – but we knew better. We knew Shayan was one of those students intentionally delaying his graduation to avoid the military. His performance in physics, biology and chemistry was appalling – and held him back. But his high grades in essays and literature revealed his real intellect and abilities.

I arrived at Shayan's place early as arranged, and I helped him with chemistry in his room for about an hour. When we moved to the living room after our session, Shayan's cousin, Susan, was there talking to Shayan's mother. Susan was nearly the same age as Shayan. When Susan saw me, she quickly covered her hair with the headscarf; she had not known there was a guest. I admired her without and with a headscarf.

Shayan greeted Susan and introduced her to me. He said that Susan was a member of the opposition party in Iran – the Mojahedin.

I could tell Shayan wanted us to talk politics, but Susan would have no part of it – at first.

Susan responded to Shayan's initial queries with a simple shrug: "I think you are trying to wind me up again, but you won't succeed tonight."

I liked her immensely – anyone who could resist Shayan's prodding was a worthy opponent.

"Will you at least tell me and my friend, do you think that your party would form a better government for this country than the current one?"

"Certainly. That much I will tell you. It's simple: Because we will make sure that each individual has the freedom of speech and can practise the religion they want too. I believe we could have everything that people in Europe and America have. In my party, we think our people deserve to take their destiny into their own hands."

That's all Shayan needed; he lit into her with a barrage of questions.

"Do you really think you can implement freedom of speech in this country? I don't think it would work well here because we have religious people who do not accept any criticism whatsoever. The establishment already promised freedom of speech as well as a lot of other things, but as we know they were empty promises. Why should we believe *your* party's promises? You know, Susan, your party is a religious party just like the current government. I cannot believe that you would make things better. Your party coming to power would just mean one religious viewpoint replacing another."

Susan raised her head to respond, but Shayan was not finished yet.

"Religion should be separate from politics, like it is in western countries. We need a secular government like the European governments. You know my view about religions, my dear cousin. Let me quote Karl Marx again: *'Religion is opium to the people.'* We need politicians whose religion does not interfere with their decision-making process. Religion is a personal matter and should not be used as a means to prosecute other people. You religious guys become extremists when you obtain power and one should not believe you."

I was sure I saw Susan roll her eyes at the mention of Karl Marx. Now it was her turn.

"You really think your communist party can offer a better solution to this country, Shayan? Your party has betrayed this country throughout our history the same as all our rulers have. You guys come up with quotes from Karl Marx, Lenin and like-minded comrades and think you can save these people from their misery with platitudes. Look at the Soviet Union and all the Eastern European countries and see if any of them have *really* been successful. You should also look at comrade Pol Pot and his atrocities in Cambodia. If you have time, read George Orwell's *Animal Farm* or *1984* and find out what is going on in your comrades' countries. And now it's my turn to quote from the past – let's look at Voltaire, shall we? *'God gave us the gift of life; it depends on us to give ourselves the gift of living well.'* We deserve to live under better conditions. That is our birth right and it is what I am fighting for."

"I am not an active member of the Tudeh Party," Shayan shot back. "I am just a sympathiser. We do not have extreme views like you guys and don't try to demonise and insult other people because of their beliefs. We did not betray anyone. This country had great leaders too; people like Mosaddegh, Cyrus the Great and a few other kings. Do not throw out the baby with bathwater, Susan."

"You are wrong again, Shayan. I agree that Mosaddegh was a great man who did a lot for this country but don't think there was a single king or ruler who served this country well. We say Cyrus the Great was excellent and oh yes people love to say great things about him, but he lived twenty-five hundred years ago so how do we know much about him, really? He was a 'great' ruler – he most certainly had blood on his hands. How can you be so sure that all accounts about Cyrus the Great are accurate? At any rate, what I am saying is that monarchy is not an acceptable form of government in any civilised country."

"That's a poor generalisation, Susan. It is not correct to think all individuals with socialist views think similarly and act like Pol Pot. He was a mentally deranged individual who became a socialist leader; I don't think being a socialist made him a killing machine. You said earlier, you are going to fight with this government, but you must know you can't succeed. Just look at how many of you are being executed on a daily basis. You don't mind losing your life even when you know you won't achieve anything? I would call it suicide. You should rethink your strategies. You may win one or the other street battle, but you will lose the war against the government in the end. You don't need to be a brain surgeon to foresee that."

"We are fighting for a cause and if we are killed, we become martyrs. I am okay with that and it does not frighten me. I think I would be honoured if I lost my life fighting for the freedom of my beloved country."

I stiffened at that – this was sounding awfully close to fanaticism, the kind of fanaticism that made me squirm in my seat. And Shayan said what I was thinking, too.

"Unlike you, I guess, I love myself and I don't want to be killed and become a martyr. I appreciate it if people are killed while defending their country against foreign invaders, but I find it disturbing to fight against my next door neighbour because we think our subjective views about our country are incompatible."

"You are entitled to your view, Shayan, and don't worry about me."

"But I am concerned about you, because I really like you despite the fact that your mind has been corrupted by a lot of religious mumbo-jumbo. I don't want you to be harmed, cousin. Even the mere thought of it makes me sick to my stomach. You know the likelihood that your kind will eventually be imprisoned or more likely, executed. In prison, virgin or unmarried women are raped by prison guards before they are executed so they cannot go to Paradise. Why am I pointing all that out to you today? Because I don't want you to end up that way. My caution to you is that you should choose your battles wisely and make certain you are not starting a skirmish that is doomed to failure. A dead soldier can be of no help to his army."

Susan smiled and left the living room.

Shayan looked at me and said, "I hope that Susan and I did not confuse you. My advice to you is to stay out of these parties and concentrate on your school work."

I offered a weak smile and said that I was apolitical and did not wish to be involved in any such activity at my age. The long exchange had been both informative and extremely unnerving for me. Privately, I was impressed at how determined and passionate Susan was. I was also impressed by her knowledge of history. I had a nodding acquaintance with Karl Marx and had only recently heard about George Orwell's *Animal Farm* – a topic in my private English lessons.

I just wanted to live a calm and quiet life, and that evening demonstrated to me that I did not want to get mixed up in any of those parties or the violence that seemed to inevitably follow from such adamant beliefs.

But what choice did I have? In Iran of the early 1980s, one had to choose – there was no staying out of politics. You either followed one party or the other. There was no room for middle-ground thinking. This was becoming clear to me already – and it made me afraid for my future. I was a middle-ground person.

Perhaps I needed to reconsider my future there in my country.

"So we come to a turning point," Frau Bosch concludes from the section of Ben's story.

"Yes, you could say that," Ben agrees. But he does not elaborate. He knows what's coming next. This week's writing has not been unpleasant. This week marks the first time in many months he has allowed some of the old fears and disappointments to surface long enough to be relieved with any degree of honesty.

His counsellor sits back in her chair and resumes. Ben senses she is eager to read what he has written; this gives him a good feeling. He can't define it further – he feels nervous but also relieved.

Finally, someone will hear what happened to the young boy.

I enjoyed my stay at my aunt's and uncle's house and especially the time I had with Uncle Shervin. He was a tall, strong man with an imposing beard; he resembled the Islamic Revolutionary guards. When he entered an establishment, most people were intimidated by his appearance. The reality was just the opposite – he and his family were victims of the Islamic Revolution and were displeased with the ruling party in the country. He was one of nine children. His father was one of the wealthiest landowners in the city.

In 1977 Shervin was imprisoned for involuntary manslaughter as the result of a vehicle accident; he was released shortly after the revolution. The accident was a terrible occurrence that happened on an otherwise joyous occasion. Shervin had been the driver of a pickup truck carrying fifteen people to a friend's wedding ceremony; the truck skidded off the road and overturned. As a result of the accident, ten people died and several more were seriously injured. He received a lesser sentence because his lawyer proved that Shervin warned the passengers ahead of time not to get on the truck and even refused to start it initially. But he drove the truck after being persuaded by the enthusiastic wedding guests that nothing would happen to them during the short journey between the bride's and groom's houses. In the end he was the one who had made the decision to drive, so he had to assume some fault for it.

Shervin himself was badly injured in the accident, but his psychological traumas were far more significant. For weeks afterwards he suffered from mutism and posttraumatic stress disorder lasted a good deal longer. His condition required a long period of professional treatment. Shervin had been engaged to my Aunt Pardis before the accident and married her following his release from prison. I always thought their bond was somehow rooted in the time they spent apart, how Pardis had stuck with him through that impossibly hard time, that their love for each other endured even when he was in prison.

I learned even more about Shervin's history living with him and my Aunt Pardis. I knew a little of his background, but living under his roof, I was exposed to more of his own history – and his own experience with post- Islamic Revolution Iran. Shervin was a well-read, business-minded son who ran many of his father's enterprises. After the Islamic Revolution a portion of their farmland was occupied by some of the local farmers who contended they had leased the land for a number of years so they were entitled to keep it for themselves. A similar thing had happened to both my grandfather and great uncle. It was a common misunderstanding, or convenient contention, and many of the big landowners lost sizeable portions of their holdings to the local farmers. Even when the misdeeds had been proved in court, the local authorities did not have the manpower to enforce their judgments. The government's focus was on the war effort and local law enforcement often went wanting. The illegal redistribution of land continued.

The state asked the big landowners to appeal to the occupier's common sense, to leave their land, or wait until the war was over and the country was in a better situation so that the state could deal with the problem appropriately. The illegal occupants chose to wait for the latter to occur, in the meantime earning tidy sums from the land they held and used.

Meanwhile, Reza's father – my great uncle – was also one of the local big land owners whose land was taken over by thirty local farmers one Friday afternoon. A kind of irrational rage accompanied such take-overs. Reza's father and his four housekeepers had to escape in order not to be slaughtered, while the occupiers entered his orange orchard and cut down nearly five hundred orange trees, already in their third and fourth years of growth.

Such waste. Such is the way of revolution. I recall kind of involuntary weeping once the news about trees broke to me, as I would spend some time in that orchard on school holidays.

Most of my relatives were stigmatised as anti-revolutionary, which in many eyes made us proponents of ex-king, Shah. We were told that we would be watched very closely and that one day, when the revolutionary guard had collected sufficient evidence against us, we would be removed from Islamic society. It was an amorphous threat, which made it all the more frightening.

We were more protected in the city, where we could blend in, and it was much harder to single out previously wealthy land-owners. Even so, I occasionally experienced hostility from local people who had become irrationally religious after the revolution. They became members of the armed, post-revolutionary guard, and the unbridled authority that came with the position made them even more dangerous. City life was, however, better there than in the outlying areas of the country.

Prior to my move into the city, I felt the threats more acutely. My family's dysfunctional relationship with the local revolutionary guards was at its lowest point in the early 1980s, and we were socially disadvantaged and became easy targets for some of the local revolutionaries and radicals. Several of my close relatives were accused of being against the ruling party at that time and were taken away unexpectedly in the middle of night to unknown places by the local revolutionary guards. Some of my younger cousins and I were blatantly threatened to face justice when the time was right – a threat that usually meant corporal punishment, imprisonment and psychological torment – if we were fortunate.

My move to my aunt's house significantly reduced those sorts of encounters and I was far less worried about unexpected physical attacks. Nevertheless, I occasionally received intimidating messages from the same fanatics.

And those threats, even in the city, soon became too much to bear. The radicals seemed to find me, even though I tried my best to stay out of political discussions. Over time, I found it difficult to cope with the intimidation and changed my high school to the neighbouring city, about twenty miles away from my aunt's house. Despite some commuting difficulties, I enjoyed the new high school with its good teachers and competitive students.

Until I met Hassan.

Hassan was a member of the Islamic committee in my new school. I was familiar with these groups – religious committees in each high school, consisting of five to ten bearded hard-line government party activists. They were fierce in their commitment, and below-average in their academic performance. Most important, they were linked with the paramilitary army and feared by most students.

Their job was spying other students.

Hassan seemed to be around nineteen years old. His dress code and appearance revealed his extreme religiosity, and I knew from my first glance that he would be a staunch government supporter. He asked me to take a seat in front of his desk. I sat down on the chair and looked at him directly. I could not hide my disapproval: everything about his way of dress – long beard and untucked shirt with top button done – revealed someone who was trouble, and ruin for my country. I could not hide how I despised him; I could not hide my contempt.

I could think of no reason for my being there – my brain raced, wondering what they could have seen me doing – and felt anxious. Regardless of my actions – or lack thereof – it was not a good sign to be sitting in front of this fellow.

"Brother, we know that you are new in our high school. Could you tell me why you have come here?"

The first question was easy enough to answer. I exhaled.

"I had difficulty with a few students in my previous high school and decided to change my school. Is it a crime?"

"It is not, but it is very suspicious."

"In what way?" I held onto my confidence.

"Brother, we have heard on the grapevine that you and your family don't cooperate with our Islamic government and also insult our faithful and religious brothers in your area."

"Your information is inaccurate. I have never made any disparaging remark about anyone from our government in public. I admit that I have criticised one or two of your so-called religious brothers, but I think they deserved it. By the way, they are not representing our government, but themselves."

"We also know that you listen to our enemies' radios that try to ruin our young people's character. Not only do you listen to these radios but you also disseminate their views among your classmates. Just look at your clothing – jeans trousers, colourful belt. And your shoes. All that shows you are sucking up to Europeans and Americans and are against our Islamic norms."

"I admit that I sometimes listen to the foreign radios the way I listen to the local radio but it is just for keeping up-to-date with the current affairs so I am not ignorant. My views about a variety of subjects in life are based on my *personal* experience – I am not advertising anyone else's views."

I felt my answers were good so far, so I added: "It is true that at times I happen to have the same take on one subject like our enemies if I may say so."

Hassan didn't seem to like that, as I saw his expression grow sterner.

"Brother, we have been watching you for a few weeks and have gathered intelligence that leads us to believe that you are not suitable for this school. You're lucky we cannot expel you from this high school, but you should know you won't receive any reference of good character from us – which is essential if you want to go to a college or get a job after your graduation."

Suddenly, the conversation had taken a turn – and I was caught off-guard. I could not help the heat rising. "This is outrageous!" I responded. "I can't believe your tactics – that you indirectly ask me to leave the school because you heard something negative about me from your companions, who have unresolved issues with my family – *not me.*"

"We have never seen you taking part in a prayer at school, and you have not attended any rally organised by us since you have been here. If we put things together, we come to obvious conclusions."

"You make things so easy for yourself."

"Brother, I am sorry."

"Stop calling me brother, as one would not treat his brother this way." Now my ire was really up. "By the way," I added, "if I had a brother like you, I would kill myself – or probably him."

I stood up, slammed the door and walked away from his office.

I was in a befuddled state and didn't know where to go next. I knew that my parents did not have any workable solution so I asked Shervin for advice. He suggested that I should find a smaller high school in the same city, with no reputation, to complete my high school education. Upon his recommendation, I found a small high school that was reputed to be a place for underachieving students, plus students who were slightly older and tougher. The only problem was that the school needed permission from the Department of Education in order to enrol me in the middle of the school year. Which of course resulted in a problem larger than I had imagined.

The government official in the Department of Education refused to issue permission for change of my high school as he thought it was against the law. I felt quite desperate and showed up repeatedly in his office, begging him for assistance. He didn't want to change his view whatsoever and demanded that I leave his office. I asked my relatives for advice – whether any of them knew anyone who could intervene on my behalf. It was Shervin who said I should talk to the head of the Department of Education. So the following day I went back there and asked to see the head of the department. After a one-hour wait I was ushered into his office. He stood up, shook my hand and asked me to sit down. His behaviour was confusing for me as these kinds of folks hardly respect the public and hardly shake a hand.

"Benjamin, what brings you here to my office?" he began. "My secretary said you were waiting to see me today. I am sorry that you had to wait so long. As soon as I heard it was you, I asked my secretary to send you in.

"I am sorry, Sir, do we know each other?" The man's face seemed familiar to me but I was sure that I didn't hear his name before.

"I have changed my last name and this is the reason why you don't know me," he confided. "I was your principal when you started your primary school. Does it ring a bell?"

Of course! Now I could see! I knew him by his previous name.

He was a kind man – principal of the school, the same one who allowed me to skip the first year in primary school. We had a brief exchange, and he then phoned the man in charge of my case and asked him to call my new high school and facilitate the transfer without any delay. He then insisted I should be able to attend my new high school on the same day.

I was delighted that I could enrol in high school again, at last.

To my surprise, the atmosphere in the classrooms and high school was to my liking, and I made a few friends over time and was able to settle down and focus. There were of course a few ultra-religious teachers who would ask students to join the war; even in a smaller school, I could not escape the fanatics. But the principal and his deputies were slightly liberal and did not ask students to pray at noon. To my surprise, there were several diligent students in my classroom and I had to study hard in order to keep up with them. I still lived with aunt's family and soon felt settled again, enjoying the challenges and even new friends in my new high school.

I still met regularly with Emin and Reza, even though I was in a different school. Together, we joined a gymnasium where we met two to three times a week in order to do more exercises. Our gym was in a poor state, very cold in the winter and hot in the summer. It stank badly most of the time but it was the only place we could go for physical activities that did not require any reference of good character. We were young men now and interested in gentle weightlifting – how else could we become more physically presentable for the beautiful teenage girls we encountered in our city streets, walking to school or sitting in small groups in the parks on weekends?

Meeting girls was more than challenging. To begin with, boys and girls had to attend separate schools, so it was very hard to find a reason to chat up girls on the streets or accompany them to a local café. Further, walking next to girls or teens mingling together in public was strictly forbidden. We needed to improvise new ways, therefore, away from the eyes of the morality guards, to be able to talk to girls. If we met girls we wanted to talk to, we usually walked one or two steps behind, as they strolled languidly down the streets, and tried to speak to them from a safe distance. It was not an ideal way to begin a relationship. Our success rate was hit or miss. Sometimes the girls looked back — and if they didn't like us they bombarded us with swear words. If, on the other hand, they fancied us they revealed their liking with a smile. We would then ask them to go to a place, usually a bookshop, which was relatively safe.

If the bookshop meeting was successful, we tried even harder. Getting the phone number from a girl was practically impossible — a boy had to be very good, had to have the winning combination of the excellent art of conversation and good looks in order to get a girl's number at the first encounter. We occasionally succeeded. But only occasionally — at best, one out of ten attempts. Ferdowsi, the famous Iranian Poet, stated in his Shahnameh that the hero, Rostam, had to go through seven ordeals in order to achieve his ultimate goal. If you received the girl's number, your problems only increased; you needed to be resourceful and develop a strategy in order to accomplish your objective. The next challenge was when to call her house so that she picks up the phone and not her parents.

Back then, it was our experience that virtually all parents did not want their daughters to communicate with a boy. We had plenty of crafty strategies. We sometimes employed the help of our female relatives our age, asking them to call the girl and make out to be the girl's friend. Once she was on the phone we took the receiver and talked to the girl. Of course, making contact was only one step — having anything to say was quite another. Most of the time we did not offer much beyond talking about the school subjects and hobbies. We kept it light. We tried our best. And for a teen boy in 1983 Iran, that little chat would have an immense positive emotional effect. My friends and I felt boosted for days, even weeks, if we managed to make that kind of contact. And even if these phone calls rarely ended up in a real date, we were over the moon for days after a brief phone chat with a girl. Our morale was lifted quite high.

Probably because our expectations were so low.

"Ah, Ben — I am glad to see that some of your childhood was filled with the events of typical adolescence. Girls and secret phone calls. You write with such humour about those times in your life, and I am struck by the contrast between that and the kind of terror that these extreme religious groups caused, even in schools."

Ben feels pleased at the praise – he thinks back fondly on his early memories of girls, though those seem so far in the distance now.

"Yes, thank you. The next part will tell more from the last of my high school years – the darker side of my reality."

Frau Bosch shifts slightly. "I will be sorry to hear of further troubles – but of course that is why we are here, Ben."

"Of course."

Ben looks out the window. A small blue bird lands on the sill, pecks briefly at the wood, then flies to the trees.

It was early evening and dark when I arrived at my auntie's house following a small workout at the gym. I was on my own as my aunt and her husband were on their farmland. A knock at the door interrupted my reading. I got up from the sofa and went to open it. In front of me was a young bearded man, dressed like the revolutionary guards. He greeted me and showed me a picture of a man, asking whether the man lived on my street. I looked at the photo and replied that I had not seen him around. The bearded man then asked if there were other people in the house, if he could ask them the same question. I replied that I was the only one in the house at that time. He then apologised for the disturbance and walked away. I closed the door.

Several minutes later, I again heard someone banging on the door. When I pulled the door handle down several men pushed the door in, forcefully, and I lost my footing and fell on the floor. Before I could respond further, someone pulled a fabric sack over my head and I was told to keep quiet.

They introduced themselves as a paramilitary force and said to follow them without any resistance if I want to remain alive. I was placed in the rear seat of a vehicle – between two men. By the way I had to climb up into it, I thought it was perhaps an SUV. The car started moving and no one said a word.

I could hardly breathe with my head still inside the cotton sack; my heartbeat went to the roof and my breathing became faster, shallower. I started shivering.

The man to my right spoke. "We were told that you have been very vocal and despise people like us."

"Can you take the sack off my head?" I asked, trying to remain calm. "I am having difficulty breathing."

"Stop talking and shut up, then you can breathe."

The car drove on for about forty minutes before it stopped. The car door opened and I was instructed to walk with the men who guided me on either side. We entered a building and I was forced to sit on a wooden chair. My hands were still tied and my head covered with a sack. To say I was scared would be an understatement. I was terrified.

Someone approached. The sack was taken from my head and my eyes adjusted in the dim light. It seemed to me that we were in a disused factory workshop. In front of me were three armed men – young men, slightly older than me. Their uniform revealed that they were members of the revolutionary guards. I knew one of them – the short one. He lived in the area where my parents and grandparents lived. I had once engaged in a short but bitter – and public – quarrel with him. I called him a useless Gargoyle, a bigot, a hypocrite.

That was more than one year ago before I moved to my aunt's house.

The short man looked at me with his blunt face and smiled. "You thought you could say nasty things about us and get away easily? Did you really think you could hide from us?"

"Why should I hide from you?" I said, ever the rationalist. "I didn't do anything illegal, and, as you know, I have lived with my aunt since last year. I am not hiding at all. Besides, it is impossible to keep it secret from you guys. I think the only place you can't gain access to is a few cubic inches within my skull."

"We know you hate us and I have to say, the feeling is mutual. We find infidels like you disgusting. It would be a pleasure to send you to hell." Gargoyle sought confirmation from the husky guy and the one with Dumbo ears standing next to him as he spoke. Confirmation came in the form of eager nods.

I was frightened, immediately regretted my inappropriate response and kept asking God to save me, to not end my life here. But it is difficult to find the right words when your hands are tied and three maniacs with machine guns stand in front of you – in a shabby factory – looking for a reason to make use of their weapons. I put my head down like a boy who was ashamed of doing something inappropriate. Then I looked at Gargoyle who I knew was a primary school dropout and said.

"I have never intended to insult you or anyone we both know. We had a heated argument last year and used unfavourable adjectives for each other. In hindsight, it was an error of judgement and I profusely apologise for it."

"Why apologise now? Have you forgotten the offensive messages you have sent to us by other people? Why aren't you now as tough as you were before? Are you frightened now, you bastard?"

Was I frightened? No doubt. I was about to crawl out of my own skin with fright. I was a boy with a good deal of education and smarts, but no one had yet taught me how to talk reasonably with a handful of unhinged armed lunatics, or how to appease them, sitting as I was with hands tied in a derelict factory. I must have missed that lesson in school. And I was now paying dearly for it.

My heartbeat rose steadily and my whole body kept shaking. My brain seemed to have switched off completely. I was out of ideas. I wished there had been a way to stop my body from trembling; I knew this was revealing my fear far too much, and I didn't want these thugs to see how frightened I was. The short man, the one I thought of as Gargoyle, kept talking, insulting my family and me with whatever vulgar adjectives he could sling. I wasn't sure if I was listening to him all the time even when I heard him talking. At one point he stopped opening and closing his mouth so I knew he was expecting a response from me.

I saw that as my chance. "Listen my friend," I said, trying to sound not nearly as scared as I was. "We know each other, and our families do, too. You father worked on my grandfather's farm for many decades. I don't think your father would approve of your action now. I am sure we could resolve the issues in an acceptable way without using a gun. Again, you have my apologies. Don't you see any other option at all?"

He snarled. "Don't mention my father at all. Your grandfather and all his family members belong to the feudal society and will be punished soon. People like you always regret what they have done to others when they are in trouble. Don't you think we know why you are being polite and reasonable now and not using your big words, you son of a bitch?"

I was desperate to know how the maniac would react if we could turn our situation around, but I could not express what I had on my mind. Once again, I tried to ask them to use their common sense.

"Obviously I cannot change things that happened in the past by my family members, but I always try to improve myself and become a better person, maybe in line with your norms."

"I don't think people like you can change at all," he spat. "And they should not deserve a second chance."

"But I am still a teenager and probably ten years younger than you, so I am confident I have the potential to change to a better person. Please give me a chance."

Before I finished my sentence, the living Gargoyle gave a signal to the husky man with his head, and the other lunatic walked towards me, stood in front me and looked into my eyes with an indescribable hatred. He then picked the sack off the floor next to me and pulled it over my head.

Crack-crackle-rat-tat-tat! Suddenly, I heard shooting from a machine gun directly beside me. I thought I was shot. I thought I was going to die. Then there was silence. My head was still covered by the sack. I didn't feel any pain – and I could still breathe. I had a kind of burning feeling in my skin and buzzing in my ears. My seat felt wet and I initially thought I might have been shot and was losing blood. I didn't have any real experience with death and I wondered how it felt when a person dies. I wondered if this was death, this slow realisation that I was still alive but soon to fade. I expected to go through a kind of tunnel soon and then, maybe, see a light somewhere. Immersed as I was in those thoughts, I was startled when someone removed the sack from my head and greeted me with a hideous smile.

I was still in the same factory. With the same cretins. I was not dead.

Which was a relief in more ways than one. I would have been utterly disappointed if these people had been the first beings to see in the afterlife.

The sadistic man, Gargoyle, walked to me and squatted next to my chair. He looked at me while heating up the end of his machine gun barrel, a Kalashnikov, with a cigarette lighter.

I felt uncomfortable and became even more agitated, but I tried to be brave so I didn't say a word. I looked at him and what he was doing: this action was meant to scare me, same as the shooting before. And then I remembered Michael Strogof – the character in Jule Verne's novel who was blinded by a hot blade. I panicked more. Gargoyle nodded and the man with Dumbo ears picked up the sack and pulled it over my head once more, despite my resistance. I begged them to stop torturing me and let me go.

Gargoyle seemed to take special pleasure in his actions and began quoting a verse from the Quran, loudly. I didn't understand but I knew enough to sense it was about punishments of traitors or enemies. When I felt hot metal against my left midfoot, I instinctively tried to jump from my chair. I was stopped by someone pushing my shoulder down with his hands.

Soon Gargoyle pulled the sack from my head and put his greasy face down so close to mine I could feel his hot, rancid breath.

"I just branded you like cattle to remind you that you cannot escape from God's forces. By the way, don't forget your diaper when you go out, big mouth."

I didn't feel much pain from the skin burn but I felt mortified, ashamed of myself, speechless. I had difficulty breathing, as if a huge metal belt was placed around my chest so that my lungs were unable to expand.

Two men grabbed my arms and forced me up, pulled the sack again over my head and made me walk with them. I was placed in the same car between two men, and the car started moving. I asked where they were taking me; one responded that I would soon see myself. This wasn't the sick man I already knew; his accent was different. I wondered how many of them were in this merry band.

The vehicle eventually stopped, the car door opened and I was forced to leave the car by one man holding my arm and pulling me out the door. I was taken to a place and pushed down to the ground. The men asked me not to move. I felt them untie the rope around my wrists. I was then instructed to take off my slippers and trousers. I still had the sack over my head and I was beyond mortified. I asked them if it was necessary to take off my trousers and one responded, cruelly, that my trousers were wet anyway and should be removed as they stunk.

I reluctantly did as I was instructed. I was told to sit on the ground and to keep my eyes closed while they removed the sack from my head. One of them took off the sack from my head while the other immediately pulled my trousers over my head. They were both laughing loudly. This obviously brought them great pleasure.

I was asked to first count down from fifty to zero and then, and only then, could I remove the trousers from my head.

I didn't know where I was so I waited for about thirty seconds before I took the trousers off my head. I found myself sitting in my aunt's yard. I felt paralysed; my heart palpitated and my breath was coming short and fast. My teeth were chattering, and I did not have energy left to stand up and go in the house. I remained seated, naked on the ground, for minutes before I stood and found my way to the door.

I walked in the bathroom directly, turned on the shower. My legs were wobbly and I felt utterly powerless as I sank to the bottom of the shower, the hot water spilling over my shaking body. Warm water ran over my head and back. I thought I would never leave that place. And then a wailing started

— as if from another body, so loud was it, so foreign to me. It was coming from my throat, from my chest, from my belly. I started crying so loudly I had difficulty controlling myself. It was as if my body did not belong to me anymore. It was some time — minutes? hours? — before I stopped weeping and regained my composure, although I was unable to stop shivering.

By the time I went to bed, early morning light was shining through the window shades. I knew that my aunt and uncle would not come home that day, and I was glad to be alone. I did not want them to see me so devastated, so defenceless. So broken.

In bed, the uncontrolled weeping and shaking went on for a long time. I don't know what time it was when I finally passed out. I woke up hours later, feeling numb all over my body. I did not feel like walking to school. I remained in bed and got up around noon.

And then I was angry. I moved through the afternoon thinking about revenge. Had I possessed a gun I would have killed those psychopaths with no remorse and pissed on their skulls.

The sober truth that frustrated me was that I knew it was impossible for me to get to these madmen and their clan. I was fully aware that I could not launch an offensive against these people. The only way to face what happened to me was by cultivating my mental toughness to help me to better deal with fanatics like this — extremists who take justice into their own hands and violate other people's rights. The more I thought about ways to comfort myself, the more depressed and frustrated I became. Only after hours of contemplating my horrible state did I come up with an idea that helped erase the previous day from my memory. I acted on it that very day. But I won't disclose it to anyone — one humiliation is enough. This is something I take to my grave.

I explained my absence from school with a tale of food poisoning and bad diarrhoea.

The psychologist puts the pages down and looks at Ben for several seconds before saying anything.

"I am sorry that you went through pain and humiliation at a young age. It was clearly an experience with many layers, wasn't it? The mock execution, the branding..."

She is trained to be empathetic and non-judgemental, but her eyes wander involuntarily to Ben's foot. He moves his feet – the scar is something he carries but he does not wish to speak of it. He does not wish to ever speak of these matters. This is why he's written it down, after all.

Some things are better left unsaid.

After the events of that night, I lost something in me, but I was unable to explain what it was. I spent a lot of time at home and hardly went out. I stopped attending the gymnasium. Over time I kept asking myself how I could flourish and achieve my full potential in an environment, in which I could hardly function normally as a teenager. I did not belong to any opposition party but that was irrelevant; what I learned that night was that my fate was in the hands of a few extremist revolutionaries – if they wanted to, they could simply decide to eliminate me. They could claim anything: there was Ben, taking part in one anti-government demonstration or activity; there was Ben, slinging slogans against Islam. Such accusations could imprison an innocent individual for a very long time or even result in a death penalty. I knew many young people who were imprisoned with fabricated charges and without any proper court proceedings. There were judges in each city who were known for their harsh punishment – and execution was not out of the question. Some of the county courts enforced the death penalty swiftly and hardly ever waited for the Supreme Court ruling. One of my uncle's friends was executed by firing squad a few days after the judge's ruling – never mind that a couple months later the High Court overruled the district judge's decision and acquitted the poor guy. His parents received an apology from the district court for the miscarriage of justice that resulted in their son's killing. The apology also included the reassurance that their innocent son would end up in Paradise.

I was not alone in my frustrations with the violation of human rights and freedom of speech and of the press. My friends and I did not like living in a country where we were regularly threatened because of our family's status or because we lacked the required interest in participating in religious activities. A large percent of teens was looking for a way to escape from the country and live in Europe, the USA or Canada. The government did not want young people to leave the country and even prohibited male teenagers older than fifteen from applying for passports.

This ban opened up a new line of business for human smugglers. These were individuals, usually of questionable character themselves, who facilitated the illegal transportation of people to other countries. Although it became a popular and lucrative business for the smugglers, it was very risky because those who were arrested for engaging in it were typically executed.

But despite the risks, I needed to get out. By the way, I felt an urge to leave this place and all its injustices behind. The city was a good move for me – but it wasn't enough. I really wanted to live in a place where I could exercise my reasonable human rights. I spent a good deal of time trying to figure a way of getting to the United States of America, but I knew the time had passed when I would be allowed to apply for a passport. I was now seventeen. No way was I going to get a visa to the US.

Besides that, relations between Iran and the United States had grown quite hostile in the late 1970s and became worse during the first few years after the Islamic Revolution, inflamed by the taking of American diplomats as hostage, the closing of the US embassy and the ensuing crisis.

I got to the point where I could not imagine remaining in my country once I finished high school. All of my future dreams took place outside my country. I visualised a university degree and a peaceful life in Europe. I knew my goals did not align with my present reality.

I talked to Emin and Reza about their lives and what they would like to do in the future. They shared the view that we should leave the country and build a life somewhere else. Reza's father had many influential friends and Reza thought, therefore, that he would be the first one of us to emigrate. Emin and I knew that, because of our ages, it was impossible for us to leave the country legally.

So we began investigating alternatives.

My view was that we should find someone who could smuggle us out of the country as soon as possible since the longer we remained there, the more difficult the situation would become. We promised each other to use all our available connections to find a relatively safe way out of the country.

Little did we know, such a thing did not exist.

CHAPTER FIVE

GOING ABROAD

"Good to see you, Ben. Looks like a lot of pages in your folder this week."

"There are. I really got into writing the past few days."

"Any reactions?"

"Many — a potpourri, you might say. Maybe there will be time at the end to talk about some of them."

Frau Bosch adjusts her glasses and begins reading. It appears to Ben that reading what he has written is more important to her than talking with him. Which is just as well, since he's been made to come to these sessions but prefers not to talk about his life.

Not one bit.

I was in my final year of high school and I understood that if I really intended to escape from the country, it was now or never. The year following graduation I would be obliged to serve in the country's mandatory military service, which meant fighting in the war. I began collecting information about the various means available for leaving the country, but all options were illegal and more or less risky.

One day I was introduced to a retired Iranian military officer by a distant relative and was told that the officer had useful connections with smugglers who could prepare illegal passports and visas and transfer young people abroad. I approached the officer and asked if he could help me get to Canada or Europe. He said that transferring people to Canada was very challenging, but that it was somewhat easier to send passengers to Sweden, the Netherlands and Germany. I could imagine living in Germany since I had relatives there. Besides, I had managed to take German lessons privately, alongside my English lessons, and by now could effectively speak and understand the language.

The officer introduced me to the main man – nicknamed The Colonel – who was in charge of transferring passengers abroad. The Colonel did not explain how he planned to take me to Europe, but said it would cost 5,000 US dollars and that I needed to pay half of the money in advance and the other half when I arrived in the neighbouring country of Turkey. The Colonel said that he was going to send two passengers abroad the following week and, once they arrived in Europe, I would be in line to leave next. He added that those two passengers were from my previous high school.

Things were going to move fast. It was hard to believe I would be leaving the country so soon. I talked with my friends Emin and Reza and we compared notes: Reza had found a way for himself, a plan designed for only one person so he could not take me along; and Emin was still undecided and wanted to have a discussion with his brothers to see if they would agree to fund his transfer.

My father was the stumbling block. He was not keen about sending me abroad illegally and asked me to wait while he searched for a safer means for me. He thought it was prudent not to rush.

I was terribly disappointed. But I waited as my father suggested, all the while hoping to be contacted by The Colonel. When I did not hear from him, I contacted the middleman who had introduced me to The Colonel. I learned from him that The Colonel's man who was making the transfers had been arrested in a small town on the border with Turkey – and that The Colonel had disappeared.

So much for that possibility.

I was devastated. But at least I had not given him any money. And with time I came to see that I should forget The Colonel and his smugglers, since it was clearly not as safe as I had been led to believe. Being imprisoned for attempting to leave the country would certainly be worse than remaining there in my current state, which was, one could argue, a more or less free man.

For the time being, I dropped my search.

Weeks later, I accompanied my friend, Reza, to the local telecom office for an international phone call. While sitting in the waiting area we chatted about the lifestyle in Europe and North America. After a few minutes, the operator called Reza to the booth to take his phone call. I remained in the waiting area. A Mullah, a Muslim preacher with turban, who had been sitting close to me turned to greet me. He said he couldn't help overhear my conversation about life in Europe and asked if my friend or I wished to go abroad. If so, he said, he might be able to help.

"Are you serious?" I asked. "Are you pulling my leg, or are you an agent of the government?"

The Mullah responded that he had been an influential Mullah prior to the current government and had been defrocked after the Islamic Revolution. He still knew a few individuals who transferred young people abroad.

He gave me his phone number and asked me to call him to set up a more private meeting. I was surprised by the chance encounter and more than a bit suspicious. I told Reza about the conversation with the Mullah. Reza urged me to meet with him and find out more.

Later, I spoke with Shervin about the encounter and asked if he knew the Mullah. He didn't know him, but also urged me to phone him and ask for a meeting. Several days later, I made the call and arranged to meet him at his place the following evening. I told Emin and Reza about it. They joked that I should watch out because the Mullah just might be into teenage boys.

"Maybe he liked the look of your jeans," said Reza.

"Maybe he wants to invite you to more than tea," said Emin.

I could appreciate their humour, but I wished they were taking this more seriously. It just might turn out to be the biggest event of my life so far.

I arrived on time and rang the doorbell. He lived in a mansion that sat one block from my high school. I had seen it before, but paid little attention to it. The Mullah opened the door and motioned me inside. He seemed to be alone there. I was suddenly a bit uneasy, but put on a smile and tried not to telegraph my nerves. The Mullah shook my hand and showed me into the living room. He turned on the television and asked me to watch TV until he finished his prayers next door. He was gone some ten minutes. When he returned, he sat next to me on the sofa and, oddly I thought, turned up the volume on the TV. He whispered into my ear that the house might be bugged. He continued to speak in low tones.

He skipped small talk and got right to the point. He said he enjoyed helping young people fulfil their dreams and made it clear that he would not take money for his services. As it turned out, 'his services' involved putting me in contact with those who went about making such transfers. He explained that he would take me to his house in Tehran where he would introduce me to friends who undertook that kind of illegal transfer and they would tell me how much it would cost. If the smugglers and I agreed to work together, I could pay him any amount of money that I thought was appropriate for the service. He had me repeat the details to him to make certain I understood. I was asked to meet him at his house in the capital city a few weeks later where he would introduce me to the Facilitators – his word for smugglers.

Later, I informed both my father and Shervin about the prospective meeting in Tehran. They each advised me to go ahead and have the conversation with the smugglers, but to ask for time to consider their offer and the details of the method they proposed.

When I met with the Mullah and his friend in his house, which sat in an affluent area of Tehran, I learned that I would fly from Tehran's international airport with a fake passport, visa and identification card, and it would cost about six thousand US dollars. If I decided to use their service, I needed to pay three thousand US dollars in advance and the rest on the day of departure. I asked the man how he could guarantee the safe departure from the country's airport and he responded – honestly, I supposed – that there could be no guarantee in that kind of undertaking, but they would do their best to make it succeed for me. I asked him if he could introduce me to someone he had successfully sent abroad. He said those individuals did not wish to be contacted by potential passengers for fear of being found out themselves.

The Mullah asked me to trust his man to do his very best; after all, if I were arrested at the airport, they would all be in serious trouble. I supposed that made good sense.

I returned to my city and talked with Shervin about the Mullah's Facilitator and the money he required for the transfer. Shervin promised he would enquire about the plan and find out what the chances were that anyone my age could actually leave the country with a fake passport. Shervin thought it would be improbable, at least through the main airport, since the security was very tight and the revolutionary guards were ever vigilant for young deserters.

Nonetheless, Shervin did ask his friends, and they advised him to avoid trying an escape through the international airport. They were convinced that the likelihood of being arrested and ending up in prison was astronomically high. I had let my hopes rise unrealistically, I guessed, and was immensely disappointed that my second attempt at escape was also flawed.

Following repeated dashed hopes, my disappointment turned into anger. I wanted to be able to blame somebody, but there was nobody to blame. I tried to console myself with a quote from Martin Luther King – one I had read in a magazine earlier: '*We must accept finite disappointment, but never lose infinite hope.*' In those days of waiting and trying and failing, those words became far more meaningful to me.

So I resumed my focus on my studies and resolved to be patient. Soon, knowledge of another route opened up. I learned that, in essence, there were two often successful options to escape from the country; one was through Turkey and the other through Pakistan. Most people preferred Turkey, since it was a more liberal country and was closer to Europe. But Pakistan was a viable option, I was told.

My friend, Shayan, introduced me to a lawyer who knew smugglers who were apparently regularly transferring passengers abroad. The lawyer acted as a contact and promised to update me after communicating with the other party. He would only reveal that the person lived in a settlement on the border with Pakistan and the transfer would be through Pakistan. With this new information, I managed to keep my expectations under control and assumed a 'wait and see' perspective.

I informed my father and Shervin about the lawyer, hoping they may have heard something of him. Shervin had heard about him from a mutual friend. He was a young lawyer who had recently graduated from university and now worked in a different city. My father asked Shervin to meet the lawyer first and find out how safe this new route was and how much it would cost. A few days later, Shervin and I went to the lawyer's house, which was there in the same city.

The lawyer was a secretive and careful man. He said that I would wait in Tehran for a phone call from his man and then I could fly to the border city. I would be picked up by the man there and would leave the country whenever the circumstances were suitable. He also asked to receive half the fee in advance and the rest once I arrived in Pakistan. In total, he asked for five thousand US dollars.

The lawyer did not disclose the actual details of the plan, but he seemed genuinely optimistic about the skill of his people and the track record they had established. In the end, Shervin and I were satisfied with the lawyer's explanation of the dangers that might delay the transfer or even block it.

When Shervin and I explained the plan to my father, he agreed that the lawyer appeared to be the man for the job and decided to meet with him the next time.

Days later, the lawyer phoned Shervin and asked him to bring my father and me to his place to finalise the arrangements. He also asked for some money in advance so that he could set things in motion. It appeared everybody up and down the line required something in advance.

The three of us went to the lawyer's house a week later. He explained that he had contacted his man and things were ready to proceed. My father asked the lawyer if he had completed this kind of transfer before and his answer was no – which was honest, I supposed, but not reassuring. The lawyer went on to explain that he, personally, had no interest in the smuggling business, but he had known the man who was going to transfer me for a long time, and said he had been involved in successfully smuggling people for years. At last, he gave us the man's name – Sinam. He had been born and raised in the border city of Zahedan, and he had long known how to arrive in Pakistan undetected.

I asked the lawyer if I would be the only passenger. I would be the only one he knew of, but Sinam might have others that would join the trip. Such details were not shared for obvious reasons. I wouldn't know until I arrived at the border town.

The lawyer was clearly optimistic that the mission would be successful. I asked him what I could take with me. He said I had to travel light and was not to take more than five kilograms of things, since I would have to carry all my items myself on the hike across the border. At the end of the meeting, my father handed the required money to the lawyer, again asking for reassurance that his men at the border were professionals and would take good care of me. He looked the man in his eyes and said that the money was of no value compared to my safety and well-being. I knew that was his feeling, of course, but it was somehow very special to hear the words. The lawyer promised to take care of me and to make sure that I would be safe throughout the transfer. He asked me not to say farewell to any of my relatives and friends for fear that information might fall into the wrong hands and jeopardise the trip, leading to enormous complications not only for me, but for those who might follow. He asked me to wait to phone my friends and relatives once I reached my final destination. At that time, I could explain why I had not been able to say goodbye to them earlier.

During the days leading up to my journey, I spent some time with many of my favourite relatives and friends. Those were emotional times for me, but I did not say anything that might telegraph my upcoming trip.

I also spent a few days with Emin and Reza and indicated I might be transferred out of the country soon. They understood not to ask for details or a time schedule or to speak of it with anybody else. They were good and loyal friends. Reza said that his father was still looking for a legal way to send him abroad so he would be able to travel back home after leaving the country.

Emin was torn between the legal and the illegal, but came to share Reza's view that he should leave his country lawfully so that he could return to his parents whenever he wished. He decided to do his military service first and then leave the country legally.

I was not concerned about my return to the country whatsoever. I believed that over time the laws of the country would change and people who left the country illegally would be welcomed back without any sanctions. My country needed bright, young, talented people and to restrict them from coming back would only work against its future.

Two weeks later, I received a phone call from the lawyer asking me to prepare for the journey. I was to go to the lawyer's house when called – very likely during the following two days. I was both excited and frightened. I could not describe my underlying joy in words. I walked on air for two days.

On the eve of my trip, my Aunt Pardis and Shervin, Maryam and Banu joined my family and me at our house. My parents were quite emotional as I expected them to be. Of course, we would miss each other greatly. They were clearly worried about my safety. Although the lawyer had been very reassuring, it was clear that things could go wrong, that I could be arrested somewhere along the border or have to put my life at risk if anything got off track. Such worries weighed more on my parents than on me; such grave concerns were less of a problem from my adolescent perspective. I was a jumble of nerves – most of them fuelled by excitement, not worry.

After dinner we sat in the living room with tea, delicious Persian cookies, cake, watermelon and various nuts on the coffee table. It was Shervin who started the conversation that needed to be held. He spoke about logistics, money and my need for a shoemaker. We talked in hushed tones, even in the privacy of our home.

"So, Ben, how do you feel about your upcoming journey?"

"I'm doing alright. A little frightened, but it's certainly not overwhelming. I am very happy that I have finally found a way out of here."

"I suppose you have considered that you will miss your family and your friends?"

"Of course, but this is moving into *my* life. Everybody has to do it one way or another. Missing friends and relatives is part of that process. I have faith that the laws will soon change and I can come home legally to visit."

"Are you taking money with you for your use or just the money you need to give to the lawyer?"

"I am taking a few hundred US dollars and an old twenty-dollar gold coin that my mother gave to me. It's worth at least one thousand US dollars. I need to hide it somewhere so that nobody knows about it during my trip."

"Why not just take money instead?"

"Money takes a lot of space and would be hard to conceal. The coin does not. I think I should hide it in the heel of my shoe so it will be with me all the time."

"I agree you need to be careful; after all, the people you're dealing with are willing to work outside the law so they may not be fully trustworthy. My advice is to trust them no more than you must."

I remember nodding, thinking it was good advice. There had been times when I was too trusting and that naivety always came back to bite me.

Shervin continued. "And you need a good shoemaker."

Up until then, I had agreed with everything Shervin had said. But I could not see why I needed new shoes. My runners seemed perfectly suitable for the journey.

"You find a shoemaker you can trust and get him to insert the coin for you. I would stay with him while he works, otherwise you might experience an unpleasant surprise later."

"I think you mean a shock, Uncle Shervin! I won't let the coin out of my sight while he is working on it." I liked Shervin's plan.

But none of us knew a good shoemaker, so that topic was dropped for the time being.

It was my aunt who spoke next. "Ben, are you really feeling good that you are leaving here?"

"I am not happy to leave you, but happy about the prospect of a better future for myself. I wish there were no need for this kind of move. I suppose no one likes to leave relatives and friends and everything that is familiar to live in a strange, foreign country."

"So, you think you will be happier somewhere else?"

I wondered if Aunt Pardis pressed the issue more for her sake than mine. It was really the most difficult of the several questions I had been pondering.

"Honestly, I don't know the answer to that," I replied, slowly, "but in my mind I think I would be happier in a place where I have more freedom than I do here. I know you all say that happiness is a state of mind and a person won't be happier by a mere change of location, but I think that might not apply to all human beings."

Pardis tried one more time.

"You are giving up your life and everything here. Don't you think you might regret it one day?"

Shervin attempted to come to my aid.

"Remember what Rumi said. '*Don't grieve. Anything you lose comes back to you in another form.*'

"I didn't know that one from Rumi, but he was a very wise man and he is probably saying the truth."

My mother seemed to take up my aunt's point of view.

"Ben, why are you not content to live here like most other teenagers?"

"Mother, why do you think all people should think the same way? We are unique beings and choose different ways of life. Why did you marry my father and not the man preferred by your parents? You were slightly different too. I think I have your genes! I cannot allow myself to be average with small dreams and goals."

"I really do appreciate your view, you know," she said. "If it were a conventional and safe trip, I would encourage it."

She reached out and patted my hand.

"Not everything in life comes with guarantees or can be achieved easily without risks," I tried to sound strong, for my mother and for myself. "I wish I would have found a better solution, but as you know this is the only available option at the moment and I don't want to wait here years for something better."

At the base of their concerns was of course their worry over my safety and also their own. Life could become very difficult for them if it was discovered that I left the country illegally.

"It could make trouble for us with the revolutionary guard," said my mother, and I knew she was right. "You know they are looking for excuses to harass us."

"I know," I conceded. "But if something happens to me, you could say that I made my decision privately, without your knowledge. And Mother, you should not pay attention to our neighbours. Many of them don't like me in the first place. Some of them regard me as an anti-revolutionary despite the fact that they have never talked to me and don't know my views." I felt myself slipping into a bit of a rage, recalling the wrongs against me. "Most of these radical guys in the neighbourhood operate from a point of uninformed opinion and seem unable to evaluate the obvious facts. They hardly make use of their brains; all they can do is regurgitate other people's opinions."

My mother winced – she was worried, I could tell, that I would say too much. But I was not finished.

"Did you also forget what these people did to my classmate's cows on their farm? Do you remember, Mother, how they slaughtered them overnight simply because the owner's family belonged to the Baha'i faith? You know, the only things we have in common with these armed extremists are the air we breathe and the streets we use."

Shervin came to my defence. And it's probably a good thing someone stopped me there. It seemed I had plenty of reasons to leave, and I was not afraid to say them.

"Ben is right. Most of these men with exaggerated and distorted religious views have forfeited the full use of their mental faculties. As one wise Irishman said, 'Two per cent of people think, three per cent think that they think, and ninety-five per cent would rather die than think.' I could also quote Einstein who said, '*Two things are infinite, the universe and human stupidity.*'"

I appreciated my uncle's support. "I couldn't agree more with your comments," I said.

Mother made another effort.

"We have a lot of religious people here who are kind, moderate, very supportive – and don't like or accept the religious radicals. Remember, the radicals form just a small percentage of Muslims."

I felt the need to express my view further.

"Unfortunately, it is the minority that ruins the majority's reputation. A few unruly teenagers make all teens suspect. Somebody said it only takes one rotten orange to spoil the basket. In our country we are experiencing that everywhere."

"Roya is right," Shervin said. "We must distinguish between peace-loving moderate Muslims, living in comfort with other religions for centuries here, from the fanatics who have gained ground since the Islamic Revolution. In this country about two and a half centuries ago under Cyrus the Great, each individual could practise his religion without any fear of repression. We learned in school that Cyrus defeated King Nebonidas from Babylon and freed up thousands of Jews and helped them go to Jerusalem to rebuild their temple."

"I read about Cyrus the Great, too," I said, "and what he did. If it was true what he achieved, he must have been a great leader but, unfortunately, different from his successors."

"You are right," Shervin continued. "Cyrus was the one who devised the oldest charter of human rights, which was written on a Cyrus Cylinder. Most of the references to the days of the kings have been removed from the textbooks since the Islamic Revolution. I am surprised you know as much about him as you seem to. Cyrus was regarded as a messiah, a person who saved people from misery."

"Things were satisfactory – great, even – in Iran centuries ago, but during the past decades – in my lifetime – they have taken a turn for worse."

"Not everything, Ben, but certainly fanaticism and radicalism have grown as you have indicated. When I was a child, I was told that human dignity is inviolable, but things are not the same now. For some people religion has become the only important aspect of life. Perhaps you heard about the judge who ordered the execution of three of his own sons because the religious views they espoused deviated from their parents' view. As far as I know, the sons were living good lives, never having stolen or taken another human life. They simply opposed their father's religious view."

"What would you do if your son did not believe as you do?" I asked. "Would you ban him from your family and stop talking to him?"

"You know I was born a Muslim, Ben, but really don't practise the religion. When I was a child I had to pray and fast because I was asked by my parents to do so. When I turned twenty years old, I stopped praying and I also stopped fasting regularly. These days, I do not fast and do not pray at all. My views about religion have clearly changed as I've grown older."

I saw my father nod in agreement, but my mother remained silent. Meanwhile, Pardis got up and rattled dishes in the kitchen.

Shervin continued. "I regard a religion as a hobby that makes the person happier, calmer and comforts him or her in a number of ways. I like playing volleyball and you like playing football and we both enjoy those things because we feel better about ourselves and our teams afterwards. I have no intention of trying to convince you to convert to volleyball or to tell you volleyball is superior to football. It should be the same with religion; each individual should practise what works for him and no one should try to impose his beliefs on other human beings. Of course, there need to be some limit on hurtful extremist views. I am still working on that."

"I agree with you," I said. "And that is one of the reasons that I don't want to live here since it is obvious one can hardly practise or express his positions when they differ from those who are in power."

"As far as I know, most European countries have a secular state, and religion or God does not play any role in their constitution" said Shervin. "I don't mean that the Europeans are not religious; I think most of them profess a religion. But they have separated their religion from the state. I believe it should be the ultimate goal in our country, too."

"You are probably right about the long term for our country, but facts are facts: at this time, we cannot express differing views freely without serious consequences. I must live in the here and now. I can't wait around for changes that may or may not take place."

And thus, we arrived at the very basis of my motivation to leave.

"I think we have never talked about these things seriously before," Shervin said, "and tonight I felt the need to tell you my personal views about our society, country and religion. You need to hear these things before you leave us."

"I appreciate that – and one day I will find a way to tell you about my future country's society, religion and constitution when the right time comes."

By then my aunt had wandered back into the room. She seemed to have accepted that I was leaving and that she could have no influence on my decision.

"Ben, do you think you will come back here to live someday?"

I felt the need to be honest in my answer and had to form my response carefully from what I knew at that moment. I sighed and rubbed my palms together.

"I doubt if I will. Remember, none of our relatives who have left here have returned home from Europe. They come here to visit, but do not want to live here. I imagine that wherever I study and begin my career I will stay. I know you understand that, wherever I am, I will still love all of you and will think about you every day. I carry parts of each of you buried within me as important elements of my beliefs and my goals, and character."

Pardis began weeping: "Of course we know those things."

I was glad that Shervin could sum things up – for I felt a lump in my own throat.

"Ben, you are a teenager with your life ahead of you. You will be living in a free society, which will provide you an abundance of opportunities. You can become an engineer, physician, teacher or whatever eventually catches your fancy. Clearly, you would be insane to return here as long as things remain as they are today."

"Things might change over time. One can never know the future. If this country again becomes an attractive place for living with liberal laws and freedom of expression, I would not rule out my possible return."

The conversation continued when my grandfather entered the room. I asked him if he had a piece of advice for me or anything he would like to tell me before my journey. He thought for a moment and nodded as he took a seat.

"Every human being is looking for expansion in life; it can be knowledge, money, power, beauty, strength or whatever. I think you are not different from the rest of your species except your way is slightly unorthodox. You will be fine as long as you believe in yourself and maintain that belief with unshakeable faith. My advice is that you should go, discover and revel in the talent which is in you, as that is your God-given right. Do know that I believe in you."

Tears formed in my eyes, but for some reason I was determined not to release them. I nodded. He understood my appreciation.

Unnecessarily, Shervin tried to further explain what grandfather had said.

"What your grandfather means is what our great Sufi, Rumi, said, *what you seek is seeking you.*"

"I forgot that you are such a staunch fan of Rumi, Shervin."

"You should also remember the following quote from Rumi when you feel low or depressed during your journey: '*You are not only a drop in the ocean, but a powerful and mighty ocean in a drop.*'"

"Thank you for that. I will remember it on my rainy days."

My father had been listening attentively and was finally ready to say what was on his mind.

"You know that I think you can become a successful person right here in this country, too, and don't need to leave us to achieve that goal."

He became tearful, but continued.

"I respect your decision and support you as much as I can. We love you unconditionally regardless of your education, income and social status. When we had arguments and disagreements in the past, it was because we wanted to be certain you understood our way and why we thought it was the best way for you. We understand that we are not infallible. It is our hope that you will come to understand that same thing about yourself, as well."

"You are a good father and I am grateful for all the things you have done for me. I know you never did a thing without having my best interest at heart. Don't worry about me and don't be tearful. It is not as if I am going to die now."

"Understand that even when you are fifty years old, you will still be my son and my feeling for you will be the same. You outgrew my lap, but never my heart."

"I will continue to do my best to remain a good son. I hope you understand that has always been my intention."

"Certainly, I do. You have been a good son; I would say most of the time. Of course, there was that incident when you were sixteen and you drove my car on the highway and were chased by the police!"

Finally, a humorous moment to make us all laugh.

"I did not have a driving licence, but I had nearly twenty hours of driving lessons. You knew I could drive better than many people with a licence."

Shervin jumped in.

"You might be correct, but no driving without a driving licence in your new land! You must avoid potential problems."

I responded – perhaps I shouldn't have.

"Uncle. You bend the rules whenever you want to. How often did you ask me to drive your car and take you to various places despite the fact that I did not have a driving licence?"

"It was different when I was sitting next to you in the car, Ben."

"I don't think the law would have seen it differently if the police had caught me, but I am glad things went well. Do you have any other embarrassing issues you wish to reveal about me tonight?"

We both smiled.

"A few, but the night is still young."

It brought smiles across the room. Shervin was on a roll.

"Tell us the ice cream parlour story, or I will tell it my way."

I'm sure I blushed and perhaps became a bit uneasy.

"I thought you could keep secrets, Uncle! I trusted you with that story."

"If you were not leaving the country, I would have kept it as a secret, but this may be my last chance to embarrass you about it."

"It seems, then, that I don't have any choice. When I was about thirteen, Emin, Reza and I used to go to a well-known ice cream parlour at least once a month. Customers would order ice cream, eat it inside, and would pay the bill on the way out. The three of us would order ice cream and cake, and sit there and eat. Then two of us would leave the café and one would remain; we took turns. If the two of us who left were asked whether we had paid for the ice cream, we would say our friend sitting there would pay for all of us. After ten minutes, the third person would leave the café – paying only for himself. We justified it as being our unique way to demonstrate our frustration with society. We stopped doing it after a while."

My father clearly didn't understand.

"Showing frustration by not paying the café owner the money?"

"In retrospect, I understand it was wrong, but I don't think we bankrupted him with our action. At that age we lumped all people with power as part of society's *establishment*. It seemed to us a shop owner shared in the power."

"Any other unpaid invoices we need to divvy up for you before it is too late?" Father asked, now more comfortable with the lighter turn the conversation had taken.

"Nothing else as far as my memory serves," I said.

But Shervin wouldn't give up.

"What about the book in the university bookshop?"

"Shervin, I'm beginning to see it was a mistake to trust you with my secrets."

"Come on, Ben, tell us."

"Okay. When I was fourteen, I wanted to buy a book about cell biology from the bookshop. I went there often and looked at the book. It sold for one hundred rials. I didn't have enough money to buy it immediately so had to wait. The price of the book had been written inside the back cover page with a pencil. Eventually, I managed to save the money to purchase it. When I went to the bookshop, however, I saw that the price had doubled within those two weeks. Having only one hundred rials, I became upset. I was not of a mind to wait several more weeks to earn the additional money, so I took the book and hid it under my jumper. Then, I went to the shopkeeper and handed over my 100-rial-note to him saying I found the money on the floor between the bookshelves. He looked at me and thanked me for my honesty. So, I indirectly paid the original price for the book."

"You could have asked him if he would sell the book for the original price of 100 rials," Pardis said.

"But, my way was easier. At least that's what I thought at the time."

Shervin came to my defence, again.

"Come on; most people have stolen things and don't have a guilty conscience over it. If I was the owner and he would have come to my shop and told me what he had done, I would forgive him and let him keep it. He didn't go there with the intention of stealing the book. In reality it was the shopkeeper's greed that created the situation, which led Ben to do what he did."

Pardis disagreed.

"One cannot blame the shopkeeper for somebody stealing items from his shop. We are not talking about a hungry man who steals food to survive. It was about a book, which probably wasn't that essential."

I told her I understood her point.

"Maybe I should go back and give him the rest of the money."

"No, forget that," Shervin said. "I don't think you should do anything because you have already paid him the original price. It's not like you will end up in hell for it."

"Don't mention hell, Shervin. It reminds me of a book I once had to read. I was looking for a challenge and entered a book reading competition for students. It was about a book called *Ma'ad* or *Resurrection* written by a grand ayatollah named Dastgheib, who was assassinated some time ago. In his book he presents numerous examples of people who did unpleasant things in their lives and ended up in hell for eternal punishment. After I read the book, I had nightmares for days. Emin warned me not to read it, but I didn't listen to him. I read it for the competition because they promised to take the winners on a weeklong trip."

"Was that after you stole the biology book?" Pardis asked.

"Yes. Two years later. Let's drop it because I am a reformed citizen now."

"How did the competition go?" Shervin asked.

"You would not believe what happened. Five of us tried to win the competition. I think some of the students stopped reading the book before they finished it because it was not for everyone."

"You mean, it was not for faint-hearted individuals?" Shervin said, seeking clarification.

"That's right."

Pardis wanted to know what happened.

"The organisers did something different from what they had promised. They told us that they didn't have any money to take the five of us on a trip, but each winner received a box full of similar books."

"Maybe you should have taken those books to the bookshop where you took your biology book from," Shervin suggested. "You could have left them on a shelf without anyone noticing it."

"That didn't cross my mind, but I suppose it could have been an option."

Pardis pressed the issue raised in the book.

"Do you now believe in resurrection and afterlife after reading that book?"

"Honestly, I don't know whether I do or not. I don't know anyone who returned from hell and reported accurately about the temperature, torture strategies and entertainment options."

"Now, Ben, don't make fun of it," she said. "I believe in an afterlife. Otherwise our life on earth does not make sense."

The illogical nature of that made absolutely no sense to me, but I let it pass – almost.

"I think Omar Khayyam, the famous philosopher and poet, held a different view when he said, 'Men talk of heaven – there is no heaven but here. Men talk of hell – there is no hell but here. Men of hereafters talk about future lives – O love, there is no other life – but here.'"

"He is not the only poet who thinks that way," Shervin went on. "He has many poems about life. One of them, which I like, goes, 'Realise this: one day your soul will depart from your body and you will be drawn behind the curtain that floats between us and the unknown. While you wait for that moment, be happy, because you don't know where you came from and you don't know where you will be going.'"

I agreed with Shervin's take on it with a series of nods.

"I like his poems. Some of them are great. My favourite is, '*My coming brought no profit to the sky, nor does my going swell its glory. My two ears have never heard anyone that could say, why I came here and why I will go away.*'"

"He was also an astronomer and a great mathematician, you know," Shervin added. "Ben, you should know about his fields of expertise."

"I think he modified the Iranian calendar and was into geometry, but I don't know about it in detail. Most of those subjects are taught at universities and not in high schools."

Pardis sighed.

"We should leave Khayyam to rest in peace and change the topic. How did we end up quoting Khayyam?"

"Ben was talking about hell and afterlife, which took us to Khayyam who was not sure whether there is existence after our mortal life."

"Oh, yes. Of course, there is an afterlife. Read the Quran and the Bible. Do you think that those books lie or promise something which does not exist?"

Shervin responded first.

"I personally believe in an afterlife, but I know many people who believe in the big bang theory and think that some chemical reactions created life about four billion years ago. They don't believe in God, supernatural power or infinite intelligence and they are pretty smart people."

Mother was moved to speak.

"Of course, there is an afterlife. People who think differently should read the holy books like Pardis said. If there is no heaven or hell, what happens to all the monsters and despots like Hitler or Saddam who killed so many innocent people?"

Shervin attempted a response.

"You accept what is written in *those* holy books, but other people believe what they read in *other* books. Not everyone shares your views about creation, for example. To be honest, I don't know where or if the malicious people receive their punishments. They probably get away with it if they have not been punished in this world. What do you think, Ben?"

It felt special to be asked as if my opinion was valued.

"It is a very sensitive issue and I believe that every individual should find a solution for himself. I am still fighting with indecision, but my favourite poet Khayyam says, '*Beyond the earth, beyond the farthest skies, I try to find Heaven and Hell. Then I hear a solemn voice that says: Heaven and hell are inside.*'"

Pardis looked puzzled, disturbed even.

"I didn't know that Khayyam was a nonbeliever."

"He questioned many things, but did not clearly state what he believed," Shervin explained. "He also questioned the purpose of his life in the verse Ben quoted. I think he says that heaven and hell are inside our head."

"Ben, what did you learn about heaven and hell from the book competition you mentioned before?" Pardis asked.

"I also needed to read several chapters from other books in order to comprehend the author's texts and be optimally prepared for the competition. I learned that heaven has five hundred levels and the top level, for instance, is allocated to prophets, martyrs, religious celebrities and grand ayatollahs. The lowest level is for people who just made it into Paradise. Hell is located below Paradise, has seven levels and also seven gates. It offers different torture options based on the severity of the individual's sins and is not a nice place to be."

My father had been silent for some time but now spoke up again.

"Does anyone know whether a person can get out of the hell or is the consignment to hell for the rest of time?"

"I think God will eventually close down hell," Shervin said, "and everyone will end up in paradise. Ben, what have you read?"

"I could not find a definitive answer about it, but I tend to agree that it is the way you just described. I hope you are not going to ask me about the different kinds of punishment in hell, now."

"Tell me this, then. Do you think the punishment in hell is worse than what we experience in this life?"

Pardis answered before I could mount a response.

"Shervin, you are a joker. Of course, the punishment in hell is harsher than here. It is said that the fire in hell is seventy times hotter than the fire on earth."

"In that case, Ben, listen carefully and don't do anything which can place you there."

I couldn't help myself – I had to respond.

"I am baffled by the exact description of punishments in hell and rewards in Paradise despite the fact that no individual has returned from the afterlife to explain the conditions in hell and heaven. You ask two religious experts and you receive two different descriptions. Besides, not all religions are in agreement about hell and heaven. Some religions posit no hell. This matter does not concern me at the moment. Perhaps, I will think about it later in my life."

We talked into the early morning hours. We covered many topics. It was a kind of discussion in which I had not been included before. As the night hours wore on, I felt privileged and secure in my family. This was like my rite of passage into the wide-ranging family philosophic base. My knowledge and beliefs seemed important and, even when they differed from the others, I was still accepted and loved.

We did not turn in until nearly two that next morning.

The following day, the lawyer phoned Shervin and said the time had come to send me to

his house in Tehran for transfer.

"You have a dynamic family, Ben." Frau Bosch speaks softly this time. "You must miss them very much."

"Of course, I do. My family is everything to me."

"But your freedom is more?"

"Yes," said Ben, glad that Frau Bosch got it. "A man's freedom is infinitely more."

My father, Shervin and I drove to the lawyer's house in the capital city. Once they had said their good-byes to me, I suddenly realised the cord had been cut – I was about to face the unknown on my own. It was what I wanted. That did not mitigate the anxiety that crept through my being or quell the several tearless sobs that convulsed my chest.

The lawyer had intentionally not explained my travel plan to my father and Shervin. He said it had to remain confidential and it still might change at the last minute. Later, he explained to me that he and I needed to fly to the border city, Zahedan, and once we arrived there, the other man would take charge. At that point the lawyer – my only tie to my old life at that point – would also become a part of my past.

I spent the night at the lawyer's house. The following morning, we went by taxi to the national airport, which was about an hour's drive away. It was the largest airport in the country with many different terminals. The lawyer and I were dropped off at the domestic terminal. It was going on six o'clock on a bright and breezy morning. Police and special revolutionary guards were visible in every corner of the airport. I enquired why there were so many of them. He said the guards were there to protect the planes from being tampered with and to keep opponents of the government from leaving the country with fake credentials. I hoped they would not suspect me of such things.

We entered the domestic area of the airport and after receiving our boarding cards and passing the security check, we entered the airside of the huge building.

I felt relieved that I had not been stopped by inquisitive guards asking difficult questions. Zahedan was not a holiday resort and when young people travelled there it was often a step on their way to escape from the country. Part of me felt guilty just being there. The rest of me was terrified.

We sat in a café next to the departure gate and ordered black tea.

"Ben, in just two hours, you will be significantly closer to your destination. This could be your last tea in Tehran for decades – perhaps for the rest of your life. You do understand that once you have left illegally it is not possible for you to re-enter."

"I know. I don't mind if I must stay away for a decade or so, but not for the rest of my life. I would miss a lot of things here. It is where my family is. The laws in this country change often and I'm counting on that."

"Why don't you want to stay here? Do you have a reason other than the common one?"

"You mean that we feel our freedom is compromised and our basic rights are violated?"

He nodded.

I continued.

"I think I will be able to unfold my intellectual potential easier in a country where I won't be monitored so strictly by the state."

"Are you saying that other governments do not watch their own people?"

"I understand they do. I was talking about the developed countries where such surveillance is for the protection of the citizens, not just for those in power to maintain their power. As you know, the dose makes the poison."

Again, he nodded.

"I have not been to Europe yet, but I know that all of the countries there have their own intelligence agencies. There is MI5 in the United Kingdom, FBI in the USA, BND in Germany. I don't think there is any country without an intelligence agency."

"Again, I refer to the dose. Are you implying that people in Europe are monitored to the same degree as here and for the same purposes? I know it varies from country to country. I don't think Russia can be regarded as a free country. I would say people have a very different – much less restrictive – kind of freedom under Helmut Schmidt in Germany than under Gorbachev in Russia at this moment in history, but either is better than here. I have not been to Europe, either, but my common sense cannot accept what you are suggesting. You are what, only about thirty years old? Don't you want to go abroad and study or live there – get a first-hand impression of what life can be like there?"

"I wish I could, but I have two families to feed. I have two wives and they need me, and I cannot take them abroad. They aren't what you would call compatible – with each other, I mean."

"Two wives? I thought that was more common in my grandfather's generation."

"Yes, that's true. Do you not have any relatives with two wives?"

"My maternal grandfather has two wives, but the first one stopped communicating with him after his second marriage."

"As it happens, I married my first wife and then started studying in a distant town while she and my children remained in my hometown. Human nature being what it is, I started an affair with a girl in my university town."

"But how did you manage? I mean, there are strict laws..."

"Yes – a problem! We were caught by the morality police. I was given two options: marry her or go to prison. Most people my age with two wives have a similar story. Once you and your girlfriend are caught by the morality police you really have only one option – namely, marrying her."

"Men are the same all over the world," the lawyer continued. "Sexual desire is the same here and in Europe. Nationality does not restrict affairs of the heart – or loins. But an affair here, in this country, can devastate the rest of your life."

"I understand a man can have four wives in Islam. Do you know of such men?"

"I don't know if anyone would practise that in its extreme, here. I think a man's physical and emotional well-being would be affected, since he would have to work all the time to feed them. He would also have to be very rich because he would have to purchase houses and jewels for them and take them on holiday. There is no study about the life expectancy of men with two wives in this country. I think they don't live long or probably end up in a psychiatric institution."

I couldn't tell if he was joking. "Why not buy one big house and all live together?"

"In my experience wives don't even want to live in the same city, let alone the same house. Things have changed since the old days."

"You are right, I suppose. Even my grandfather's wives did not want to live in the same house. Do you treat them equally?"

"Treating them equally? Impossible! Their needs and wants are very different. I do my best to keep each of them happy. They have different tastes and I cannot buy the same gift twice. They also desire different holiday destinations and as I said before, it is hard work, satisfying two women." He wagged his finger then and concluded, "I do not recommend having two wives."

For me, this was a whole new world. I had never given much thought to the topic of wife management.

He smiled and looked at his watch.

"I think we need to board the plane now."

Frau Bosch wears a curious expression.

"Do you have strong views on marriage, Ben?"

"I think a man and a woman should marry if they love each other."

"Was the idea of multiple spouses offensive to you?"

"Not at all. It is the way of my culture. But as the lawyer pointed out to me, a man must be very rich to support multiple wives."

"Not for a poor academic student, then."

Ben chuckles. "No. Not for me. Not at all. I personally don't even believe in marriage."

"I imagine you have feelings about leaving the country and facing the unknown."

We were now thirty-thousand feet above the ground and flying at a speed of several hundred kilometres per hour away from everything I had heretofore known.

It was as if the lawyer had read my mind. I was excited, but also deeply sad now. I worried about my family – I hoped they didn't think it was my intention to abandon them. I suddenly felt awkward.

"It is a fully foreign and rather indescribable feeling," I said. "I'm questioning whether I have let my relatives down, leaving them there in their situation. Somehow I feel guilty for my decision."

"Why guilty? And why do you think they are in an unpleasant predicament at the moment?"

"They have to live in this country and face the rationing and all the sanctions and restrictions imposed on them while I am going to a place of abundance, with no lines for bread, cooking oil, sugar and petrol."

"Those are the stresses of wartime and people understand that. Once the war is over, things could return to normal, even in our country, Ben. The war has been on us for years, but it will eventually end and we will face a better time."

I knew he was trying to comfort me but I still felt quite low.

The lawyer continued. "In the city where you have lived, up north, you have not really experienced the full impact of war, so your lifestyle has not been seriously affected. You know that closer to the fighting, millions of people have been bombed and had to evacuate their home cities. So many places are now in ruins. Those people have lost everything, including family members and friends. Some have had to move to camps in other cities. Your family is among the fortunate."

"I understand what you're saying – and I know it's true. I am grateful to God or the supreme power for keeping my family and me safe throughout these years. I tend to take all that for granted. My literature teacher kept quoting the poet Saadi Shirazi: '*I cried because I lost my shoes until I saw a man who lost his feet.*' If I feel depressed and low, I try to comfort myself with that adage. Sometimes I forget. But you are right; I should not feel sad or guilty. I have made the best decision on my own that I knew how to make."

"You have made the decision to go abroad – let's say in a less conventional way – and need to overcome every obstacle that appears. Keep your spirits high and lower your expectations during your trip. A lawyer friend of mine says it is better to be a pessimist than an optimist because pessimism is likely to decrease anxiety and improve the performance."

That gave me a lot to think about. I decided to look at my expectations more closely. What was I really expecting here? Could I even imagine life after landing in a new land? So far, I had only focused on leaving – the arrival would be something else entirely.

"My view is that one should be a *realist*, Ben, and tend to be more optimistic than pessimistic. *Hope for the best, be prepared for the worst.*"

I looked out the window as he spoke, but his words lingered.

"Will we be landing soon?"

He nodded and looked across in front of me to see out the window.

"Are we going to be picked up by your man at the airport?"

"No, we will get a room in a hotel and I will call the middleman from there. Our first problem will be to get out of the airport without any difficulty."

"Do you have any tips for me if I am questioned about why I came to this city?"

"Just look very surprised at the question and say you are my friend and are accompanying me – make it sound like it is an everyday occurrence. Be yourself and don't look frightened."

I wondered just how I was to not look frightened when my knees were knocking together and my breathing rate was far from normal.

CHAPTER SIX

MANAGING EXPECTATIONS

I expected to be happy – overjoyed, even – at managing my escape to Pakistan, but when I finally realised what I had accomplished the feeling extended well beyond that. All those ups and downs of disappointment and all that uncertainty and worrisome undercurrent had faded.

I was lying in a ditch with a man I barely knew and trusted even less, and I was overcome by an extended state of elation.

"We made it," I said again.

Maher patted me on the shoulder and said, "Best be moving on."

"A brief comment, Ben," Frau Bosch said, "now that your story has brought us safely inside the border."

"Of course." Ben feels today will be easier than the last session. His story is tumbling forth every time he sits down with his pen and paper. He is surprised his counsellor can read his handwriting, but she has yet to complain.

"It's about this word 'expectations'. I am thinking of that expression, *Hope for the best, be prepared for the worst*. May I ask how well your general expectations are being met since you arrived in Germany?"

"Very well, actually. I believe the identity problems are only a tiny glitch on my path to a positive future. Hoping for the best, yes. But cautious even so."

"You seem to feel more in control of your destiny."

"Exactly. *Destinies,* I suppose. Plural, that is." Frau Bosch smiles at that.

"I am finding," Ben explains, "that life is composed of many paths, not just one – not the way I used to think."

"So far, has the writing – the remembering – been helpful for you?"

"Yes. I am really just beginning to understand that."

And so we hurried on, Maher and I. Once safely inside Pakistan – well away from the border – we found a shallow sinkhole in which we could rest and relax out of sight temporarily until we could locate a place that would be safe to stay for the remainder of the night.

But soon we were not alone. Three young Baluchi men approached us. Maher told me not to say anything. He greeted the men and they joined us on the ground.

They looked me over closely. One pointed to the jeans I was wearing.

"The boy looks Iranian. Is he an illegal?"

"Goodness, no," Maher said, offering a laid-back believable smile.

"His pants. He doesn't look to be from here."

"I can see how you could be confused. He is one of my mother's cousins. He slipped across the border into Iran with me last week. I had business there. Now we are returning. He has been wearing jeans in order to fit in with the young men there. No time for him to change yet. He is a deaf mute and does not understand what we are talking about now. It would be good if you could smile at him."

"We are sorry about his condition. He must be very brave to accompany you on such a journey."

They all forced smiles and nods – more than seemed reasonable.

"What is the situation in Zahedan?" one asked.

"You know Zahedan," Maher replied, sounding casual. "It struggles on."

I followed Maher's lead and remained silent. When he finally stood, so did I, moving to his side away from the others. With what seemed to be a series of very odd gestures – Maher's attempt at faking sign language, which would have been comical were it not for the serious nature of our situation – Maher indicated we should be going. I nodded. He turned and began walking. I stepped in behind him and followed.

After a few yards, Maher whispered, "Those men are looking for illegal passengers in order to receive hush money to keep quiet about them. It is a widespread racket in this area. I believe they are harmless, but still," – he shot me a scornful look – "you should have worn Afghan or Baluchi clothes."

"How could I have known to do that? You should have told me when we first met."

"Everything will be fine, now. All sorts of clothing are worn in the cities of Pakistan."

I had grown really thirsty again and the bread was not filling.

"Could we find some water and maybe something sweet – cookies?"

"Look at the lights there. We will arrive in a few minutes. There is a small shop. It's always open. We can buy some fizzy drinks and biscuits."

"It sounds like you have already been here."

"Yes, I know most of the villages around the borders. Over the years I have passed through all these villages and towns. It was just that we came at it from a different direction this time – for security reasons, as I explained."

His explanation made sense, but Pooya's caution remained in the back of my mind.

Five minutes later we arrived at the shop – part of a very small settlement. My eyes were drawn immediately to the big fridge out front. It was filled with fizzy drinks. I removed a bottle of Schweppes and drank it down within seconds, then took a second bottle and sat sipping it for some time, sitting on the ground next to the door. Maher joined me and also quickly downed two bottles of soda. I went into the shop and got two packs of biscuits for us.

A few minutes later our thirst and our hunger had been satisfied. Maher steered me in the direction of a small open building just beyond the little shop. Several men were sleeping on the floor. We lay down using our handbags for pillows.

Exhausted, we fell asleep within minutes. Maher woke me up at nine o'clock the following morning. We found a place for tea and bread and then set our sights on finding a driver to take us to Quetta, which was the next big city and the capital of Baluch province.

Maher stood and spoke in a loud voice.

"Who will take us to Quetta?"

A young boy approached us and said he knew of somebody. Maher handed him a one-dollar-note and the boy, promising to back soon, bowed and ran off.

"How long a drive is it?" I asked.

"Quite some way. A six- or seven-hour drive from here, depending on how the traffic is moving."

"It will just be good to be riding. My leather shoes make walking very uncomfortable. You need to make sure your future passengers wear shoes better suited to hiking. I'll be dealing with blisters for a week."

"A point well taken. Make me a list of your suggestions. I have the feeling you will have several."

"I wish your previous passenger would have left some valuable tips for me."

He smiled and I returned it. We had a strange relationship.

The boy returned, saying he had found a driver. Maher agreed to the price and offered the boy another dollar. I thought the kid's cheeks were going to bust.

We had several hours to wait until the driver's arrival at noon, so we found a place in the shade and lay on the ground. By 12:30 I was impatient.

Maher tried to calm my worries. "Here, noon is an unspecified period that spans mid-day. Be patient. Time is different here than you are used to – more a useful generalization than a precise measurement."

And Maher was correct. My fretting had been for nothing. The driver was a young Afghan man with a Toyota pickup truck with four doors and four seats – a step up in terms of transportation. I sat in the rear seat and Maher up next to the driver. The young man explained that it would be a long drive to Quetta and we could take a nap if we wanted. I said I was so excited that I wanted to feel and see every minute of the trip. Maher, on the other hand, closed his eyes and fell into a deep sleep.

"Do you know where you are staying in Quetta?" the driver asked.

"I have no idea. Captain Maher takes care of things like that."

He nodded and grew silent. I had questions, of course – my grandfather always said I had too many questions.

"Why do so many Afghan people live in Pakistan?"

"To escape the Afghanistan and Soviet Union war. It has gone on for a long time. Many people who lived in the border towns crossed over and now make their lives here. The business environment in Pakistan has been very kind to most of us. I have several partners who are also Afghan."

I didn't pursue just what his business was — transportation, perhaps. Perhaps something else. I was learning which questions not to ask.

"I had several passengers from your country last week. They had arrived in Pakistan illegally, too. I took them to Karachi — a very long drive, almost fifteen hours."

"I take it you have known Maher before."

"What makes you think that?"

"You seem to have assumed I am an illegal."

He smiled and nodded. I took that to mean I was not going to get the whole story.

"I have heard about him from mutual acquaintances, but I met him in person for the first time this afternoon. I only knew his name because the boy heard you call him by name, and told me. Did you know Maher is known as Maher Disco among his friends? Around here if you say Maher Disco, somebody close by is bound to know who you are talking about."

"Where does the Disco come from?"

"Maher spent so much time in discotheques that if a friend was looking for him he knew right where to find him."

"Did you fight with Mujahedin against the Soviet army?"

"Yes, I fought with Mujahedin for a short while. It was a terrible time. I don't think Maher was ever with Mujahedin. I suspect it was inconsistent with his lifestyle. He was more into partying, girls — you know."

"What did you do before the war in your country?"

"I finished high school and wanted to go to Moscow to study, but once the war began that was no longer possible."

"What did you want to study?"

"I wanted to be an engineer."

"I am sorry things didn't work out for you."

"I am happy that I am still alive since many people have been killed in that war. I am glad *you* are alive, also, considering your own war with Saddam."

"Thank you. Me, too, of course."

"I have been told that your fellow countrymen in Iran do not treat Afghan refugees fairly."

"Really? I don't know about that. Where I lived, we did not see many Afghan asylums. I remember seeing a few who worked in the construction industry, but I don't know about unfair treatment."

It was true. In our area we had many Iranian war refugees who had to leave their cities in the war zones. I knew that even some of them were not treated nicely by their own countrymen. "People don't seem to like outsiders moving in close to them," I reflected. "From what I've seen it does not matter if they come from another country or another city within the same country."

"I wonder why people are that way," he asked.

"I suspect they are afraid of losing their jobs to the newcomers. Maybe they are also afraid the others will somehow dilute their traditions or something, or influence them or their children away from their beliefs. I wish I did know."

He seemed to want to explore the topic more.

"I have been told that in your country all Afghans are regarded as drug dealers or people who increased the unemployment rate of Iranians in the labour market."

But I wasn't sure how to respond so I tried to keep it general. "Like I said, I am not aware of such feelings towards Afghans. I imagine one can find xenophobes in every country who find reasons to blame the foreigners for their misery and failure. My family taught me to be receptive, tolerant and not to judge a book by its cover. Are Afghans treated well in Pakistan?"

"I am not sure how to answer that. Some are and some aren't. You hear different reports. I suppose we expect to be treated better in your country than elsewhere because we speak your language."

"I am embarrassed to hear that we mistreat you in my country. I have to believe that the people with good common sense agree with me that the refugees should not be disparaged or put down."

"I was told that in some areas in your country businesses put up signs stating that entrance by Afghans is prohibited."

I had an uneasy feeling in my stomach. How did this driver know so much more about my country than I did? "I don't know about such things. I think this subject is just embarrassing for me and my lack of relevant information on the topics you bring up puts me at an unfair disadvantage."

I realised how defensive I sounded, but I didn't know how else to respond. So I added, simply, "I think we should change the topic."

And to my relief, the driver said, "I agree with you. Understand I didn't mean to attack you personally."

I nodded and shrugged. But I *had* felt attacked.

About that time Maher woke up from his nap and looked around to get his bearings.

"I will need to stop up ahead. I'll tell you where."

In about ten minutes we arrived in an area where there were a number of small shops lining both sides of the road. It wasn't really a village. Maher signalled for the driver to stop.

"Just wait here. I'll be back in a few minutes."

After about fifteen minutes, Maher returned with a massive piece of hashish in his hand. It resembled a thin layer of brownie. I didn't know what it was, but it seemed from the driver's reaction that I should have. The driver started laughing and said to Maher, "You cheeky boy!"

Maher laughed along with him.

"We need to celebrate the boy's entrance to Pakistan! What could be better than this?"

I was baffled and did not know how to respond. So again, I smiled and shrugged.

And said, innocently, "What is that?"

They burst out laughing.

"What kind of school did you go to anyway?" said Maher. "This is Afghan hashish, one of the best forms in the world. It is pure and made here, a few miles away from us. Are you telling us you have never smoked hashish?"

"Honestly, no. I have never even smoked a cigarette. Well, there was that time when I was ten and my friends and I wanted to know how it was to smoke, but that just made me sick. I have seen weed at school, but it looked different."

"I can see that I need to teach you some important lessons," Maher said. "Weed is from the dry part of the same plant and unlike hashish it does not contain the sap or resin. Hashish is much stronger than what you are calling weed."

I tried to remain calm. "My grandfather was an opium addict and I think one addict in the family is more than enough."

"I guess you answered my next question," said Maher, not unkindly. "If you have not smoked hashish before, you should not start with it today. Please enjoy the scenery while the two of us 'men' enjoy our special cigarette."

Maher mixed a bit of hashish with tobacco and rolled two cigarettes. He handed one to the driver. The driver and Maher smoked and sang separate songs, neither of which I understood. They puffed a lot of smoke inside the cab of the truck. I coughed. I asked them to roll the side windows down, as I was quite uncomfortable about the whole scene.

Perhaps they were right: perhaps I *was* less of a man than they were.

They said it would be a pity to waste all that valuable smoke, opening the windows, but did as I asked, half-grumbling, half-joking. Opening the windows wasn't enough, however; I soon came to feel light headed and nauseated. I really needed more fresh air. And I think the 'men' took perverted pleasure in my obvious discomfort.

It was Friday – the weekend – and there were not many cars on the road. We drove on for two-and-half hours. With every new mile away from the border I could feel myself relaxing. *That* was about to come to an abrupt halt.

Just ahead were multiple police cars blocking the motorway. Standing beside them were no fewer than ten armed policemen. It was too late to make any sort of turn that would seem legitimate and we were signalled to stop. Several of the armed policemen surrounded the pickup and asked us to get out. We did as we were told, of course. Several policemen searched the vehicle. They found the remaining hashish on the floor of the vehicle. One of the policemen motioned to the officer in charge to come to our truck.

My first thought was that they were looking for drugs and that was what they had found. I'm sure my blood pressure rose. The officer approached us and asked the driver in English how many passengers he had brought from Iran.

"Just one."

"Are you sure you have not dropped off any passengers back between the border and here?"

"I have not. This young man, Ben, is the only passenger in my vehicle and I am not the smuggler. My job is to take these two people to Quetta and that is all I know."

It sounded like he had just sold me out. I listened further.

The officer moved away from the driver and approached me.

"You must be the passenger. Show me your passport."

"I do not have any passport, but I have an ID. Here."

I handed it over.

"This is an Iranian ID, which is in Farsi. It is not part of a travel document. In order to come into this country you need to have a valid passport and a visa. You think we are so stupid that anyone can enter this country without an appropriate travel document?"

"No, Sir. That is not at all what I think. I respect this country very much. My life was endangered in my country and I escaped from it to what I thought would be a safe haven here in your country."

He walked around me looking me over.

"To me you don't look like someone who would be in such danger. Who brought you to Pakistan?"

"A man from a village in Iran took me through the border and he left me once I was on Pakistan's soil."

The officer approached Maher.

"Are you the boss here?"

"No, Sir, I have nothing to be the boss of. The young man asked me how to get to Quetta this morning. I said that I was going there today and he could join me if he could pay part of the driver's fee."

One of the policemen had opened Maher's bag and positioned it for the officer to take a look inside.

"Where does the money in your bag come from?"

"This is my money from the vehicle I sold recently. I plan to use it to buy another one in Quetta. I hear prices are better in the city than out here."

"Do you really think that we are idiots here and don't know how you dirty dogs operate? You think you can do whatever you want to in this country. You will pay dearly for this one."

"Sir, I am not a smuggler. I told you the truth. This young boy was already on Pakistan's soil when I met him, therefore I cannot be accused of smuggling him into Pakistan."

Okay, so they were both selling me out.

"You all tell the same lie. Human traffickers like you should be hanged on the spot."

He turned and walked away, telling the young policemen to handcuff all three of us. He approached me again shaking his finger in my face.

"Because of you my weekend has been ruined. You are going to prison for a long time so that you will not get these ideas in your head again."

My heart sank. I had never been so frightened before – not even when I was captured by those paramilitary hoodlums. I started to shake and began saying all the wrong things: I begged for mercy; I offered him money if he would release me.

He became openly angry and hit me in my face with his fist.

With that punch I fell to the ground and found I was bleeding from my mouth. One of the policemen helped me stand up and walked me to the prisoner transport van to join Maher and the driver. My right canine tooth had been loosened and my mouth continued to bleed. The van drove off with us in the back. Three of them sat in the van and a police car and the pickup followed.

The policeman who had helped me up changed the handcuffs so my arms were in front. He said that way I could put pressure on my mouth to control the bleeding. I thanked him. That surprised both of us, I think.

Maher sat in front of me and told me he was sorry about the punch I had received from the police officer. He said I should not be too worried and thanked me for not incriminating him. He explained that keeping us in jail would not benefit anyone in the country and we would be released soon.

Those words should have made me feel better, but they didn't. I was upset, disappointed, humiliated and in pain. I had no idea what lay ahead, having never been in trouble with the law before. I had heard terrible stories about prison. I took several deep breaths hoping that would help me regain my composure. To some extent, it did. The pit of my stomach felt like it weighed thirty pounds. I managed to whisper forward to Maher that I didn't think we should be talking. He stopped.

We arrived at the police station in Dalbandin. It had been a thirty-minute ride. We were taken to a small room – a temporary holding area. Its metal door was locked from the outside. We were told there would be a preliminary hearing in a little while. We sat on the dirty floor, waiting.

It seemed clear that the driver and Maher really were not concerned. They were soon asleep. My adrenalin level was so high that a nap was out of the question. The pain in my mouth and jaw grew worse. My head ached and throbbed. I asked the policeman who was just outside the door if I could use the washroom to clean up my face. I must say I was surprised when he opened the door and led me to a sink outside. A few minutes later I returned to the small room and sat there waiting for the officer responsible for the hearing.

He eventually arrived and approached the three of us. He asked the driver to follow him to his office in the adjacent building. After thirty minutes the driver returned and said that he was free to go, but his pickup truck would remain impounded until everything had been sorted out. I wondered if that was a good omen for me.

Maher was taken next. He also returned after half an hour saying he was free to go, as well. He would wait to hear the outcome of my session. The interrogating officer asked me to take a seat in front of his desk. It was then I first noticed the blood down the front of my shirt.

The officer was a middle-aged man and asked me to provide personal details such as name, address and date of birth. He then asked me where I first met the other men. I continued to follow Maher's lead from before.

"As I said before, I met Maher in Pakistan soon after I crossed the border and asked him if he knew someone who could take me to Quetta. He said he was going there and I joined him."

"How much did you have to pay him for the transfer from your country to here? Where is your final destination?"

I put on a puzzled face and repeated my position.

"Like I said earlier, I met him in Pakistan. I was brought to Pakistan by an old man from an Iranian village close to the border."

"Listen to me, young man, you will stay here in this prison until you confess the name of the people who brought you to Pakistan. There is no other option. It is the only chance for you. We are very patient and have plenty of space in our jail to hold people like you. I am telling you that we can break anyone. I am asking you one more time about the name of the smuggler. Who brought you to Pakistan?"

"I don't have any name other than Old Man. That is what he asked me to call him. You must know traffickers don't use their real names."

I felt good about that final touch. It didn't seem to change anything, however.

"You have had your chance and you did not use it wisely."

The officer accompanied me out of his office and asked the policeman to take me to their main jail, which, I found, was located in the same building. In the meantime, Maher and the driver had left the police station. The jail resembled a horse stable more than a jail. The cell was about fifty square yards, had one metal door and two, sizeable, metal-barred windows without glass; the floor was hard packed soil. The walls of the prison cell were made of sun-dried mud. There were no furnishings. Five prisoners were sitting on the floor.

I tried to conceal my fear as I entered the cell. I sat in one corner away from the others. The other inmates looked me over. One asked my name. I said it, but offered nothing more.

It soon became obvious that the floor was to be my chair, my bed, my table and from the smell, my emergency washroom. The only light came in from the yard outside the windows.

I sat there, leaning back against the wall with my eyes closed. Perhaps I could nap. Perhaps I could close my eyes and open them again to discover this had all been a bad dream. But my thoughts were a whirlwind of negative images and questions that unsettled my mind. How would this affect my life? How did Pakistan deal with illegals? Would I ever see my family again?

In a short time, a policeman entered the cell and brought six metal bowls, a bucket of soup and bread. Supper. I refused to eat anything and remained seated. Partly because I felt sick in every cell of my body, partly as an act of rebellion against my situation.

Sleep arrived in fits and starts, sitting against the wall. Sometime during the night, I woke up shivering and cold. There were no provisions for cold so I wrapped my arms around my knees and waited for the warmth of day to return.

The sun rose, announcing Saturday, a half day in Pakistan. The policeman opened the cell door and, one by one, let us use the only toilet. I'm not sure what I expected, but it was filthy beyond anything I would have imagined. The contents of my stomach threatened to leave me, and violently. There was no sink, only a water tap next to the wall outside. We were given time to wash our hands and face the best we could without soap or towel. I slipped out of my shirt and ran water over the blood, hoping it had not yet set. Most of it had not. I wrung out my shirt and put it back on.

Back in the cell I became aware for the first time how badly the other prisoners smelled. Which was probably true of me as well; it had been some time since I had showered.

For breakfast we were served tea and bread there in the cell. By then I was quite hungry and didn't turn down what was offered. As I ate I looked around the room hoping it would not have to be my home for very long. A cave in the hills would have been better. I thought about Maher. I hoped he was taking steps toward my release.

By noon I moved back and forth between feeling frightened and bored. I had nothing to do — no books or newspapers. And the other men spoke a language I didn't understand. They made no attempt to talk with me.

Before lunch, a policeman opened the door and beckoned to me, asking that I follow him. I was taken to an office. I had not seen this officer before. He looked to be thirty-five years old. I nodded — the only greeting I would offer.

"Have a seat, Benjamin."

He motioned with his arm. I sat in the chair, which sat beside his desk. There was also a bench across one wall.

"How has your stay been, so far?"

"I assume you would not expect me to say excellent?"

He smiled and chuckled.

"Prison is not meant to be the Taj Mahal Hotel, young man. Are you saying our jail is worse than those in your country?"

"No, Sir. This is my first time inside any jail, anywhere. For a jail it may offer excellent accommodations. I have nothing to compare it with."

"I read in your file that you did not name the smugglers who helped you enter Pakistan."

"But I did. Old Man. That was the only name he gave me. That is the truth and ten years in this place cannot change the truth. I could make up a name, but it would just send you chasing after shadows. I don't know what more to say. I am trying to cooperate."

"You could not convince my colleague of that yesterday. It is why he detained you."

"Can you tell me what happens to me now? I'm just a teenager and believe it is wrong for me to be imprisoned with older men."

"You seem to be well informed and know your rights. This is not a prison and you are only in custody here until a decision is made about how to handle your case. The prison is in a different place. Inmates are not sent to the main prison until after they go before a judge and have been sentenced. You still have some time here."

"Can you tell me what happened to the men who were with me – I mean the driver and the man named Maher who offered me the ride?"

"The driver owes a fine. Once that is paid his pickup truck, which has been impounded, will be returned to him and he will be free to leave. The other man – Maher, you call him – was set free after paying a fine."

"I suppose you have had illegal people like me here before. What happened to them?"

"It depends on the court's decision. Most of the time they are fined by the court and released or they are sent back to the border and have to leave our country."

"Do you know how long I have to wait for the court to make a decision?"

"Two to three weeks maximum. You won't stay here for long. I might be able to help speed up the proceedings."

"That would certainly be very nice of you, Sir. I would be forever grateful."

"Now, you need to go back to your cell."

I thanked him again and was escorted back to what appeared would be my home for some time. The break from the horrific odour had been welcome, but made it seem even worse upon my return.

Nothing else happened that day – minutes morphed into hours and hours into complete boredom. The other prisoners talked to each other and laughed a lot. I got the idea they were trying to best each other with dirty jokes. I sat. I paced. I did squats and push-ups. Then I did it all over again. The meals were identical one to the other: tea, soup, bread and gravy. I drank the tea, never wanting to be thirsty again like I had been in the desert. The soup smelled disgusting and contained things I did not recognise. The gravy turned my stomach on sight. I ate the bread.

The friendliest any of the others became was when the youngest of the lot would give me some of his bread when he noticed it was all I ate. I nodded and offered a quick smile. We shared no words. The others seemed to anticipate the meals and devoured them with great joy. Evidently our backgrounds had been quite different. I thought it would have been an advantage had I been less over-particular about the food.

I did not hear anything from the jail officer for several days, and with each passing day my worry grew. Two inmates were taken from the cell, which left just four of us. Out of desperation I asked to speak to the officer whose office I had visited several days before. I was surprised when the request was granted. I stood in front of his desk.

"Good day, Sir. Excuse my forwardness, but I am wondering if you have any news for me."

"I understand your impatience. I was your age once. The courts are very busy these days and your case is just not considered urgent. Your turn will come when your turn comes."

None of that had been helpful. If anything, it deepened my growing depression.

"You said last time that you might be able to shorten my stay here, but did not explain more. Can you tell me more about that?"

The officer smiled and motioned for me to take a seat in the chair beside his desk. I couldn't dislike him. Beyond that I had no opinion.

"Tell me about yourself?"

"Like what, Sir?"

"Did you leave a girlfriend behind?"

"No, not that I don't desire one, but it was not easy – dangerous even – to have a girlfriend in my country."

"Tell me more about that."

I felt myself relaxing a bit. The mere act of talking to somebody who could converse in English was unbelievably satisfying.

"Well, if a boy and girl go out and are seen together in public, they could be arrested by the Morals Police and forced to get married. That is the reason most boys don't have girlfriends. There have been girls I liked very much – but in my country it has to be from afar."

"Did you have any relationship with a man in the past?"

The question confused me. I didn't want to seem naive so offered something.

"No, Sir, I have never had anything with a man."

"Why not? It is not a bad thing. Actually, it is quite normal that men attend to each other's needs."

"I have a few best friends – guy friends. Nothing intimate ever went on between us if that's what you are referring to. We were just best friends and we all liked girls. Most of us used to chat up girls on the streets and walk behind them in the local shopping centre and ask for their phone numbers. My evening fantasies are about girls, not men."

"So, that was *then*. What would you say now if a man would like to have something with you?"

"The idea is distasteful to me, Sir."

I became fearful about where the conversation was heading. The officer scooted his chair closer to mine and put his hand on my lap.

"If I were you, young man, I would not reject it. You might like it. It might even earn privileges or speed things up."

I stood up, eager to put distance between myself and this conversation. Beyond that I had no plan. "I am sorry," I said quite suddenly. "I think I don't feel well. I... I need to throw up. My system is not used to this food." I waited too many seconds, then added, "I need to leave the room, please."

He allowed me to go back to my cell. The inclination to vomit had only been partly an excuse to leave. It was less driven by the food, however, than the disgust I was feeling. I fought to keep things down.

I was so confused – not about my sexuality, but about my new dilemma. The officer was basically in charge of me. I assumed he had the power to punish me. He had brought the idea of a relationship up once. He could bring it up again.

A new sense of desperation settled in under my skin, down to my bones. I had heard stories about the fate of young boys in prison, but it had not entered my thoughts since arriving there. None of the men in my cell had made any moves on me. The idea of guards participating in such things had never entered my mind.

During those days, the site of the pickup in the yard had been reassuring. Each morning when I was taken outside to wash up, I looked for it. I knew it meant the driver was still around – a connection to the outside world, for me. And then it was gone. Just like that. I felt good for the driver, but sorry about the lost connection.

Days passed. And more days.

I received no notice of a court date and wasn't about to ask to see that officer again. So I waited.

Three new prisoners were added to my cell. They appeared to know each other well — perhaps arrested for the same offence. They were loud, rowdy and disrespectful. They spat on the ground and threw air kisses to the other inmates and each other. I did my best to avoid eye contact. But that wasn't always possible.

On one occasion two of the new arrivals approached me and sat next to me on the ground – one on each side. The leader of the group asked my name and where I was from. He spoke in English. His skills were clearly minimal. The other one put his hand on my calf. I stood up and asked them to go away and threatened to call the guard. The men laughed as if it had been great fun to scare the teenager. They moved away continuing to throw me kisses.

I became panic stricken and began hyperventilating. I did not know how to respond without aggravating the situation. I most certainly could not fend them off.

I did not want to call the guard and provoke the men more, so I sat in my corner, knees up, arms folded across them, head down.

The men kept their distance the rest of the day. I sat there terrified. Darkness overtook the room as night approached. I hated the night to come. I didn't eat supper. I lay down against the wall with my face positioned to keep watch on the others. I dozed, off and on. At one point when my eyes fluttered open there was a man's face just inches from mine.

I made a move to get up, but the man – a strong man – held my shoulder down and clapped a hand across my mouth. I squirmed trying to stand, but he rolled me onto my back and positioned himself on top of me. He reached for my crotch and squeezed what he found there. I managed to bring my knee up between his legs in a powerful thrust, which apparently did just what I had intended. He rolled off groaning, holding himself. I watched as he crawled toward his friends who apparently found the whole scene hilarious. The other inmates were watching us in the moonlight.

I sat up hugging myself, horrified and breathing rapidly. Clearly, I was not safe there. Tears came unchecked, wetting my cheeks. I fell over onto my side and remained there, as still as possible.

I blamed Maher for my predicament. I needed to get out of there. The only thing to do was to risk another meeting with the officer; hoping he could move me from that cell.

Apparently, I slept some because I woke up at first light.

When the guard brought tea and bread, I spoke to him at the door in low tones, asking if I could see the officer as soon as possible. The guard wanted a reason. I replied that I did not feel safe there with the new inmates who had made threatening gestures toward me. I wished to change cells.

The guard laughed and said that nobody had ever died in that cell, and besides, there was no other place for me. He went through the stock routine about this being prison and not a hotel. He left it at that and walked away.

I grabbed a hunk of bread and went back to my spot, my head and gut suddenly screaming with desperation. The scariest of the new arrivals continued to taunt me from across the room with air kisses and pulling at his crotch. His cronies enjoyed the show. I forced myself to watch sober-faced, thinking it represented some show of strength on my part. I would not let him get the better of me. I had to at least appear strong, even if I was quaking inside.

Very soon, the guard called my name and I moved quickly to the open door. With no explanation I was taken to the officer's room. I hesitated just inside the door and chose to sit on the bench across the front of the room rather than take the chair that I had previously occupied.

The officer watched my manoeuvre with apparent interest.

"So, what does my young prisoner have on his mind today?"

I had already forgotten the words I had arranged the night before so I just began speaking.

"Sir, I don't feel safe in the jail here. One of the new men woke me up last night and tried to touch my genitalia and when I wanted to scream, he put his hand on my mouth. I kneed his groin and he left me alone, but I feel sure it will happen again. I think that proves that being in that cell is not a safe place for me."

"You seem to keep forgetting that you are a criminal just like the others in your cell. Entering this country, the way you did is unlawful and is why you are here. You have to wait until the court rules on your case. There is nothing I can do for you. We don't have another cell for prisoners who are awaiting their hearing. You will just have to put up with the situation. You should have thought about the possibilities earlier."

"You are saying you are not powerful enough to do anything to protect me? I am sure a man in your position could do something to protect me if you wanted to."

I would wait and see if flattery had any effect on him.

"Why should I protect you more than the others? You ignored and humiliated me right here in this office the other day. I showed you my admiration and passion and you dismissed it – and me. I regarded that as an insult."

"This is all quite confusing for me. I am a normal young man with normal urges to do things with girls. To this point in my life I have lived with that and the frustrations that go along with it. I don't believe a man should be forced to do things against his beliefs. That would be *you* not respecting my needs. Why do you present it as a one way street where only your needs are worth considering?"

He ignored the logic of my argument, which I thought had been well presented.

"You are in a jail away from girls. Men have needs as you indicated. In jail men learn how to take care of each other. You did not hear me out the other day. I wanted you to let me touch you and wanted you to treat me like your girlfriend."

"How can I treat you like a girlfriend when you are a man, and I don't fancy a man?"

"If you want, you could imagine I am a girl. You will see that many men sleep with each other here and it is not regarded as a bad thing."

"You mean here in the prison?"

"No, I mean in this area and this country. It goes on in all countries. Men get intimate with each other when there is no woman around. Surely you should understand that by your age." He looked at me with a hard stare.

"What you describe has not been a part of my life or that of my friends. Perhaps such things are just different in my town. The fact is that I don't want to be touched by a man and I think one should respect that."

"I have received your message and I hope the other inmates don't harass you anymore. I can't be by your side all the time. Now go back to your cell and try to be less tense."

I left the room having failed in my mission. I was clearly on my own. Back in the cell I saw that the three gang members were occupying my corner. I moved to the one opposite them and sat. It was darker there well away from the window. I kept my eyes averted from the others, looking at my hands, the floor, up toward the window. Eventually I sat back, closed my eyes and pretended to take a nap. Sleep didn't come. My mind was filled with visions about what had happened the night before. I was sure it was not over. I was sure next time the man would have help. I sensed unpleasant things were yet to come.

Again, I drank tea and ate bread for supper. The friendly inmate who had shared with me was no longer there. Several hours into darkness most of the prisoners lay down to sleep. I did also – there in my new corner. The three gang members continued to sit, chat and laugh across the room. They had stopped glancing in my direction. I hoped that was a good sign. Perhaps what had transpired before had just been some sort of hazing for the new guy. I could only hope.

Later that night after the gang members finally quieted down, I felt a sense of relief and positioned myself on my side, my head turned into the cell and cushioned against my arm. I allowed myself to enter that twilight zone between remaining alert and slipping toward sleep. I was suddenly roused when I felt someone putting a piece of cloth over my head and face. My head was forced to one side and pressed against the floor. I felt the full weight of someone on top of me. I struggled against it, but found I was unable to move. The intense pressure on my face, neck and shoulders made it difficult for me to breathe.

The pain and tension in my neck and shoulders grew worse. A second person pushed me from behind so that I was positioned on my chest and belly; he then straddled my legs across my calves and worked to pull my trousers down. I tried to move – anything – but with the weight of at least two of the other inmates on me, it was impossible. At one point I managed to roll onto one side by throwing my elbows, landing them wherever I found somebody else's bulk. They retaliated with punches to my buttocks, lower back and upper arms. It went on for what seemed an eternity – in reality probably no more than three minutes. Long enough to inflict terrible bruises I suspected.

Eventually, they stood and moved away. I turned onto my stomach and pulled myself a few feet closer to the door. Exhausted, I gave up and just lay there. It was then I first realised I was crying – my face lay in a muddy pool of my tears. I took inventory. I could turn my head, but only with great pain. The same for moving my arms and legs. My chest had been compressed by a very heavy man's weight and I felt sure I had bruised ribs. Every breath caused excruciating pain throughout my chest. I had to breathe so I had to put up with that.

Equally as bad as the pain was the degradation and humiliation I felt. Nothing of a sexual nature had occurred, but the process disgusted me. It also sent the message that anytime they wanted to they could take me. I had never felt so helpless. My frightening inclination was to grab any one of them by the throat and choke the life out of his body not caring at that point what happened to me as a result of it. I was sure my upper arms and behind were badly bruised as the punching had gone on relentlessly for some time. I hoped my kidneys hadn't been damaged.

For the next several hours it seemed a strain just to lay there motionless. At some point the tears stopped. My collar was wet with mud from where I had lain on the tear-soaked floor.

The following morning when it was my turn to use the toilet and clean up outside I could not respond to the guard's call. He came over to me and nudged me in my ribs as if to awaken me. I groaned at the intense pain. Tears started again. The guard knelt down beside me. He saw my cheeks raw from crying and from having been roughly forced against the floor. He tried to sit me up. I was no help at all in that process. Again, terrible pain found its way to every corner of my body. He could see the bruises to my face and neck. He opened my shirt and examined the deep bruises on my arms and shoulders. He looked at my lower back.

He motioned to one of the non-gang related men to help him stand me up and move me outside. He told me to wash up. I made what motions in that direction I could. Outside in the light my condition became at once obvious to him. He asked me what had happened. I was astonished at the question — surely it was obvious. It was then I realised I had also sustained damage to my windpipe in addition to the injury to my neck. Speaking was beyond painful — almost impossible. So, I remained quiet, managing to take a long drink from the tap then letting the water wash across my face.

The man who was helping me stood there winced when he got a peek at my shoulder and arm. I managed to speak directly into the guard's face.

"I need to see the head of this prison, now!"

The guard looked as if he felt sorry for me.

"He will be here in an hour. I will try to get him to see you."

I removed my shirt and scooped up water from the tap to clean the cuts on my arms and torso. It was more time than I should have been allowed, but the guard made no attempt to stop or even hurry me.

He asked in a somewhat confidential tone: "Who did this to you?"

I looked at him for a long moment.

"I suppose the list of suspects is pretty small, don't you? Besides, I could not see in the dark."

The guard shrugged and looked ashamed.

"I am sorry for what happened, but one cannot choose his own group of inmates in prison."

With the continued help of the man from my cell, they took me to the original holding cell, where I had been held initially along with the driver and Maher. He told me I would wait there while he contacted the superintendent. I was left alone for many hours. I lay on the floor on my side, my knees bent. That was the least excruciating position I could find. I had no idea how I would get up.

It must have been nearing noon when the guard returned.

"You will come with me, now."

I opened my eyes and stared up at him.

"A little help, if you will."

He managed it in a mostly gentle and even caring manner. I shuffled along behind him down a long hall to a new office. The sign on the door read 'SUPERINTENDENT' in three languages. As it turned out he was the same officer to whom I had previously talked in the smaller office. I doubted if that could be good.

He stood and winced as I entered. I struggled to pull myself back into my shirt. They were required there. He rounded the desk.

"What happened to you?"

He turned me around and then back to the front.

"The things I predicted when we last spoke came to pass last night. I was no match for the three of them."

"Tell me exactly what happened."

The sequence of events was jumbled in my head so I assembled them into what I figured was a logical order.

"I was lying there on the floor dozing when the gang members draped some sort of cloth around my head — like a blindfold, perhaps. At first I expected it to be doused with something that would put me to sleep. It wasn't. They held me down on the ground and tried to sexually harass me, pulling down my pants and pummelling my buttocks and back with their fists. They pushed my neck and face down hard against the ground and beat me while I was in a position that didn't allow me to defend myself. They spent a good deal of time pounding their fists into my upper arms. I think you saw the bruising."

The superintendent nodded, wincing again. The beating had happened on his watch and he was plainly uncomfortable about that. He tried to make the case that his hands were tied by the system as if to alleviate himself of any culpability.

"I am sorry for what has happened, but how could we have prevented it? I don't have sufficient staff to stand watch over every cell, every hour, of every day. We only have that one cell in which to hold prisoners who are awaiting their first hearing. You are not our typical prisoner. I understood that from the outset. You are cultured and well-bred, not the likes of the dogs we have here — drug dealers, rapists, thieves and on down the list of the dregs of humanity. It is unfortunate that your kind must mingle with them, but that is our system."

He opened the office door and called one of the guards to him. He spoke in a language I did not understand. He closed the door and faced me.

"I will try to gain your release within the next few days. I will call the court and recommend an expeditious hearing. That much I can do. The court typically calls youngsters last because the adults have more pressing responsibilities to attend to on the outside – family, business, and so on."

Within five minutes he had apologised for the system, for himself and just then for the court system. I figured I really must be a mess to look at. I would have smiled at that had it not been so painful.

Presently, the guard he had dispatched minutes before returned with a small pack of biscuits and a pot of tea. The officer presented it to me and said he would return soon. He left. I drank and eventually managed to eat. It hurt to swallow, but I knew I needed to eat. I took tiny bites and let the tea just flow down my throat. I figured I needed food to rebuild my body and my strength. It was so painful – moving my jaws and neck.

As he was leaving the room I asked if I could see a doctor. He said they had no doctor for the prisoners. He did, however, move to his desk and hand me an aspirin. It was better than nothing, I supposed. In fact, I had the presence of mind to understand it was the best he had to offer me.

I remained in the office alone. It was a real treat to be alone if only for a few minutes. I drank some tea and forced myself to eat a few biscuits. I lay back along a bench, my feet dragging the floor. The pain was not subsiding. If anything, I had become one large mass of throbbing hurt. I fell asleep in that position.

Sometime later – I had no good estimate of how long I had been asleep – the superintendent re-entered the office. I awoke and struggled to sit up. I apologised for having stretched out on the bench. I wasn't sure why. He let it go.

"How are you feeling, now?" he asked.

I took a moment to assess my situation.

"My neck is killing me. I think something is not right with my neck."

"Such things work themselves out. I'm sure you will be fine again. I think you can go back to your cell now."

That was not what I needed – nor expected – to hear.

"Can you assure me the men will not attack me again? I am here at your doing, not mine. It should be your responsibility to afford me a safe place.

The court has not even found me guilty of anything. If I have to go back at least give me something to protect myself with."

"What do you mean, *something*? You know you cannot have a knife or a club in the jail. They would soon have it and be turning it on you. You don't need a murder charge in addition to your current problem. Now you must return to your jail cell."

I saw his logic about possessing a weapon. He apparently did not see mine about deserving to be protected when in his custody. There was no reason to pursue that. I thanked him for the tea, biscuit and for the aspirin. He opened the door and a guard escorted me back to the cell.

There had been some changes made there. The gang members who assaulted me were handcuffed and chained to the pillar in the middle of the cell, which limited their movements to sitting and standing. When they saw me, they started laughing again and throwing me kisses. I went to my corner and avoided looking in their direction. I felt fear and anxiety drain away. I felt lighter. I sat, not giving them the satisfaction of seeing how painful it was to move.

The gangsters did not receive meals that day. It was apparently considered full and appropriate punishment for what they had done to me.

My harassers remained in chains for the remainder of my stay there. Two days later the guard informed me while giving me bread for breakfast that I would be leaving jail that day. The court had made a decision in my case. I figured it was good news, but not sufficient news.

"Where will I be going?"

"I haven't been told."

My life was about to take a new twist.

But even that required a good deal of waiting. I spent the next several hours with pain-filled pacing and biting at my fingernails. I had never bitten my nails before in my life.

Early in the afternoon the guard called my name. I thought I was going to throw up. He walked me to the office where I had first encountered the man who I later discovered was the superintendent. Another officer was sitting behind the desk. He asked me to take a seat and pointed to the chair beside him. He folded his hands on the desk and offered a smile. I took that as a good sign. He spoke.

"This is the day we all have been waiting for."

That seemed an odd way to begin – the day *everybody* had been waiting for. I didn't understand. He soon clarified it.

"The decision has been made by the judge and it is pleasant news. You are not going to prison. You are being sent to the United Nations High Commissioner for Refugees in Quetta. There you will be helped with your asylum application. Now you must be happy. After all these difficulties, you are going forward."

He seemed to know a lot about my case even though I had never seen him before. I felt the need to thank somebody and he was who I had available.

"I am really grateful for your support, Sir – or whoever moved this along for me. If I am to make my way there on my own, I will need directions."

"Two of our local policemen will be taking you. They are waiting for you now."

"I really appreciate your kindness."

He walked me to the door from where the two policemen escorted me to a police SUV. It seemed too good to be true.

One policeman sat in the rear seat with me. The other sat in the passenger seat beside the driver. The vehicle headed toward the motorway. I wondered how I could go about contacting Maher. He had the money and the contacts for my transfer to Europe. Despite the man's bouts of incompetence, he was all I had so I figured I needed to see what he had to offer. Although in my mind I had been blaming him for my time in jail, I understood it had just been unfortunate timing – our truck on the road at the time of the roadblock.

My mind whirled, jumping from one topic to others in no particular order or logical sequence. I was not paying attention to the journey whatsoever. After a time I began studying the terrain outside. I recognised the area and said as much to the policemen.

"What's going on? We are heading back the way I came."

"That's right," he said puzzled at my reaction. "We are taking you to Taftan, Pakistan's border town with Iran."

"You must be mistaken. I was told you were taking me to Quetta."

"Who told you that?"

"The officer in the police station; the one who handed me over to you."

The three men in the car began chuckling.

133

CHAPTER SEVEN

TWO STEPS FORWARD, ONE STEP BACK

"But I need to get to Quetta!" I made my voice as adamant as possible. But once again, I was feeling a creeping fear.

The truck trundled on, and the man beside me offered the explanation.

"He just didn't want to make you upset – make you hard for us to handle. That's why he told you the story about going to Quetta. Why should we take you to Quetta? We are not a transport service for illegal immigrants. Our orders are to hand you over to the border police at the Pakistan/Iran border."

"Why are you sending me back? I don't want to go back."

"We didn't make the decision, kid, but we have to execute it. We cannot change anything for you."

I slumped back in the seat. Tears came and I felt no embarrassment about allowing them. Up and down. How many more times could I take the ups and downs? The officer had seemed so sincere I just couldn't believe it had been a lie. Perhaps it was time for me to stop trusting anybody.

I began focusing on a new fear: what terrible things would be done to me back in Iran. I had heard horror stories about the way captured escapees were treated. One of my friends said his older brother had seen a returned escapee who was tortured badly by the border guards so he became completely paralysed. Whatever part of me that held my sanity was rapidly crumbling. At that point I figured anything, no matter how outlandish, would be worth a try.

"I am sure you don't want to see me executed – and that is likely what will happen. You don't understand my situation with the Iranian government. Please, just drop me off. There is no way your superiors will find out. Please don't let this be the day I die."

The policemen became more serious but did not seem moved to let me go.

I tried again. "I do not have any money, but my wrist watch is worth three hundred US dollars."

"You stop talking, now. There is nothing we can do for you. We are under orders. We have transfer papers to be signed and returned to our headquarters. You will need to try again once back in Iran."

"It will be impossible for me to try again once I have been imprisoned. Or executed."

The officer sitting beside me swallowed hard and studied my face, then turned away.

They began ignoring my very presence in the vehicle and began talking amongst themselves in their own language. I crossed my arms and sat back contemplating my likely fate — prison. Several hours later we arrived in Taftan, the town where Maher and I had met the driver of the pickup.

Darkness was falling when we stopped in front of the local police station. I shook with fear as I was led inside and taken by one of the local policemen. I was sure I would faint, or at the very least throw up.

As they turned to leave, the policemen who had ridden with me in the back seat came to me and wished me luck. He looked sad for me.

"I really do wish things could have worked out differently for you, young man."

The Taftan policeman who had taken custody of me turned me around so I was facing him.

"Are you ill, boy? You don't look well."

"Maybe if I can just sit down for a few minutes, my dizziness will pass," I said.

He allowed it, but continued to talk with me.

"You are here to be extradited, as you know. The sooner we do it, the better."

I felt sick and thought I would pass out. "Honestly, I don't care anymore if you want to extradite me now or later," I said. "Or if you want to shoot me here and now. Once I am in the hands of the Iranian authorities I am as good as dead anyway."

Just then, a distinguished looking man entered the station. It grew quiet and everybody turned toward him — reverently. It appeared he was important. He had two men with him — clearly his bodyguards.

The officer who seemed to be in charge of the station approached him, offering a modest bow. They talked quietly for several minutes. There were quick glances in my direction. I didn't understand, but I had stopped trying to understand. I had given up — fully and completely. Whatever happened would happen: I had no life out in front of me.

Hope was gone. It was all over.

Unlike the rest of the people in the room, who had snapped to attention at the man's arrival, I remained sitting on a bench hunched over with my arms resting on my legs

I didn't see the man approaching me.

Suddenly a pair of shiny, leather shoes and the legs of expensive-looking trousers came into view. I followed them upward with my eyes, but couldn't stand.

The man maintained a serious expression as he looked down and spoke to me.

"May I ask which city you are from?" He sounded pleasant, not demanding like I expected.

"A city on the Caspian Sea. I am not sure you would know the name. Have you been to northern Iran?"

Even as I answered I remained puzzled at the exchange. The police officer in charge offered a brief explanation.

"This is Haji, the tribal leader in Taftan. Most revere him as the most powerful man in the area."

At that point I managed to stand up as a sign of respect to Haji. Haji extended his hand as a clear offer to shake.

"I have been to Mashad and Zahedan several times, but not to northern Iran."

Haji and the officer talked in their language again for several minutes. I didn't understand a word. Haji turned back to me speaking flawless English.

"I have asked the officer to allow you to join me in my house tonight so you can experience our more favourable hospitality — different from that extended to you during your recent ordeal. You could still go back to your country tomorrow."

"I certainly don't understand what's going on," I replied, and I realised I should sound more grateful. But I continued on, "It appears I have no choice but to go back to my country. I would consider it a privilege to be able to put that off one more day, however."

The man offered a fine smile. I think I managed one in return.

"It is settled, then. My man will take you to my car. I will join you shortly."

There was no coercion involved. His man walked beside me and pointed the way. He opened the rear door for me and, seeing I had difficulty moving, assisted me. He closed the door and stood beside the car.

Ups and downs: if nothing else, the yo-yoing of my experiences and emotions would surely drive me insane.

I tried to relax while sitting in Haji's car, waiting. I took several deep breaths. I realised that giving up had been easy – that I had resigned to an early death over the horrors of an Iranian prison, and that this resignation was a relief. Now, I found myself needing the transition back to a state of momentary hope. I didn't know if I had that kind of strength left.

I moved my mind in another direction and reflected on Haji. I estimated he was near fifty years of age, give or take. He was wearing the local Baluchi clothes. He chose his words carefully – I had no way of knowing why. He appeared to be in excellent physical shape, despite an expanded waistline.

For some reason I wondered how many wives he had.

He returned to the car – expensive, spacious and a Japanese make I didn't know. He sat beside me in the rear. His men sat up front. The one I had come to know was the driver. It was a twenty-minute drive from the police station to Haji's house. Our attempts at small talk were awkward and soon ceased. Instead, I listened to a monologue about the scenery that would have been there had it been light.

When we arrived, I followed Haji through tall, expensive double doors and turned right into the spacious living room. He indicated with his arm for me to take a seat on the many floor cushions. I was surprised that there was no sofa in his living room but did as my host asked. One of his men accompanied us and offered water. I gladly accepted it, downed it without ceremony, and was given a refill. Haji puttered at something across the room as if buying time. A few minutes later five men entered the living room and took seats nearby.

Haji also sat and began what seemed to be a serious conversation. I continued to feel baffled by this hospitality – by what I was doing here at all. He asked me about my family and my ambitions, and how I came to end up in prison. Believing I had nothing to lose, I provided honest answers, offering details to the extent that seemed reasonable.

After a short time, food was served. I soon saw the custom was for everyone to wash his hands in a small container, which was passed among us, before beginning to eat.

I had no appetite so settled for tea.

"My young friend," Haji smiled. "You are so slim and pale because you do not eat. You should take better care of yourself. Look at me and the others here; we never say no to good food. You should eat with us now and I will promise to help you."

A hint of better times ahead: Haji would help me. I had no idea what it meant but I returned the men's smiles and offered my plate for food.

After the meal, Haji got down to business.

"The officer informed me you are going to be extradited back to your country – that you entered ours illegally. I could help you by setting you free here in Taftan. It is up to you. Know, however, if the police here in Pakistan arrest you again, my name is not to come up. You must live with great caution. Being caught a second time would put you in danger of a long sentence. Our story would be that you escaped. Are we understood?"

"Yes, Sir. I am so grateful to you for your generosity. I would never mention your name. I don't understand why you are doing this for me."

"Some things in life we must just accept."

I had difficulty believing any of what had already happened – so I just smiled and thanked him.

"I pay a visit to our local police station once a month. I wanted to do it this morning but something came up and I could not go there. I believe either my or your God wanted us to meet up this afternoon."

I must have looked perplexed but managed to thank him once again for his kindness.

"Do you need money?" Haji asked.

"I will be fine."

I had no money, of course, but I didn't feel comfortable to receive any more from the man. My freedom was the ultimate gift.

"Could I, though, ask for local clothing and head cover? Dressed as I am, I have little chance of remaining free, you understand."

Haji nodded at his man who was soon back with everything I needed.

When we retired for the night I stayed in a room just off the living room where Haji's men slept. There were thick rugs to sleep on and the air smelled fresh and clean. At least for those next few hours, life seemed very good.

I was exhausted, both physically and mentally. I fell asleep immediately and slept through to seven the next morning when I was awakened by the sound of the outside door closing. The others were gone. I walked to the toilet where I removed and discarded my old clothes – filthy and blood-soaked – and changed into my new ones. They felt so good – clean and fresh. My old shoes were dirty and scuffed, but still had good soles and would be serviceable. I did my best to clean them up.

The turban proved to be a challenge. I struggled for a while and gave up.

In the hall, one of Haji's men beckoned for me to enter the living room, where I was given tea and bread. For the first time in weeks I was genuinely hungry. There were several men sitting there. Haji was not among them. One of the men asked me if I needed help with the turban. I was happy to have his assistance. The man rolled the turban and placed it on my head. It had been less a lesson and more a helpful service. I tried to note the various turns so I could figure it out later for myself.

After breakfast I asked the man who helped me – who also spoke some English – if he could direct me to the town centre.

"I want to take the bus to Quetta and wonder if someone could get me to the station."

One of Haji's men offered to see that I got there. Since I did not have any money left I decided to sell my wristwatch. I would do that with great reluctance since it had been a gift from my paternal grandfather. I knew he would approve, considering my current circumstances.

Passing a store window, I looked myself over: I looked good and was sure I would not stand out as different from any other local young man my age. It felt like I was wearing a body mask that offered a complete disguise.

At the town centre I entered a shop next to the bus station and asked if they would buy my wristwatch. The man offered me a very low price. I moved on. Eventually, I sold it for what seemed a fairer price, and I purchased my ticket at the bus station. It cost a good deal less than I thought it would. The extra money felt good in my pocket.

The bus for Quetta left at noon, which meant I had to wait a few more hours. I walked around the town centre and had my shoes polished, remaining close to the bus station and always amongst people. It was surprising to see that most of the people there were men. The few women I did see were covered from head to toe in burqas.

When I finally boarded the bus I took a seat near the rear by a window. There were lots of travellers. A young man took the seat next to me. The trip started twenty minutes late. The bus moved slowly. I overheard others talking and learned the trip to Quetta might take up to twenty-four hours. I had been so involved in finally getting a ticket I had failed to ask about the duration.

I kept a very low profile while sitting on the old bus and covered the exposed part of my face with the hanging portion of the turban. I wanted to be left along, but the young man beside me spoke to me in the Baluchi language, and I held up my hands in the universal gesture indicating that I hadn't understood. In Farsi I asked if he were Afghan, thinking we might find a common language. He repeated my gesture with a smile.

I settled in for what looked would be a quiet journey. I turned my attention out the window and began planning what I should do when I arrived in Quetta. The passenger sitting behind me tapped me on my shoulder and asked where I came from. I had been thinking about a response to that question so turned slightly in my seat and offered it.

"Originally from Kabul Afghanistan, but spent many years in Iran and am now on my way to Quetta."

The passenger smiled and said, "I have lived in Kabul, too. Which part did you live in?"

"I was a child when my parents moved to Iran – I don't remember where we lived but our house was next to a mosque."

"Your accent is Iranian. It means you went to school in Iran?"

"Yes, I went to school for a number of years there, as my accent betrays, I believe."

In the local language, he asked the person sitting next to me if he would exchange seats. The passenger from the rear moved closer and introduced himself as Amir, shaking my hand.

Amir looked to be about thirty-five years old. He had black hair, wore a small hat and sported a two-week growth of beard. The man was inquisitive – not something I had counted on, or desired.

"Where did you get your turban? Iranian men do not wear turbans."

"I got my clothes in Taftan. I like all the room they afford – more comfortable than a pair of jeans. The storekeeper insisted on the turban."

I moved my arms as if to demonstrate what I meant.

"What is your job?" Amir asked.

"I was a student when I was in Iran… I don't know what I am going to do in the future."

"You should come to Afghanistan and join the Mujahedin and fight against the Russians. You can also meet Ahmad Shah Massood, the world-famous commander. "

That option had not made the top one thousand on my list of possibilities, but I smiled and nodded.; had I wanted to fight, I could have stayed in my own country and fought there. I wouldn't go to a war even if Heracles, the Greek hero, or Rostam, the hero from the Shahnameh, or both at the same time asked me to join them.

"I will think about it," I said agreeably. "Maybe sometime in the future."

"You are a young man and you could be very helpful for us."

Suddenly I thought I understood. He was on a recruiting mission. I tried to turn the conversation back on him.

"Are you a member of Afghan Mujahedin?"

"Yes. I am on leave and going to visit some relatives in Dalbandin, but will go back to Afghanistan soon."

"What is your job?"

"I fight too, but I am now recruiting fighters and am also into other administrative things."

I felt smug for having figured him out.

He continued. "If you mean what I did before, I was a student in Kabul University. I studied engineering, but could not finish it once the war started."

I asked if he would teach me some Afghan slang – words unique to Afghans. I indicated that I wanted to be able to fit in. Amir grinned and nodded. By evening I had quite a stock of useful words and phrases – a number of them not fit for mixed company. I practised them inside my head.

The bus stopped every few hours for fifteen to twenty minutes. The passengers used the time to pray, use the toilets or eat something. It was late in the evening when the bus arrived in Dalbandin, the very place I had been arrested and was detained. A wave of anxiety accompanied this stop, and I felt an increased need to remain out of sight.

I hoped that the police would not come on the bus and check passengers' IDs. It was the first time that possible problem had entered my thoughts. I slid down in the seat and pretended to be asleep.

Amir stood to leave and shook my hand. Many other passengers also left. I did my best to remain inconspicuous there in my seat. I hoped my rapidly thumping heartbeat could not be seen through my clothes. I was grateful for the ample material of the garments.

The psychologist puts down Ben's story.

"My goodness. The danger and agony just didn't stop for you, did it?"

Ben shrugs. He knows this has been a tough chapter to read.

"I must admit that my hope was that today's instalment would be filled with good things for you — safe havens, supportive new acquaintances. How did you feel while you were writing, Ben?"

"The way you would imagine, I suppose — I relived the events, and the feelings — especially the terror. It was a difficult phase to write about. I have heard that it can be therapeutic to revisit one's fears. I should certainly be well 'therapeu-ed' by now."

They share a smile over Ben's newly coined term.

"Do you find it so?"

"For the most part, yes, I suppose so. I find it hard to re-live the pain, but also perhaps necessary."

"You've written a lot of your story, Ben — and you do it well. Have you written anything else?"

"Just my university papers."

"Do you read a lot outside of your classes?"

"Yes. Like most students, I read if I have time. The international classics. Hemingway, Dickens. And of course, now that I'm here, Goethe and Kafka. Grass, too."

"They are some of our most important storytellers. We are a country rich in the tradition of literature, as you know."

"Yes — one of the many reasons I am glad to be here."

"What is your favourite book? Do you have any?"

"Maybe the old man and the sea from Hemingway?"

"How so?"

"Because the old man, Santiago, demonstrated an unwavering faith in himself despite multiple failures. He didn't let his external circumstances distract him from his goal."

"Interesting observation. Maybe you will share your favourite passages?"

"Yes, but first, I must continue with my own story, no?"

"Yes, Ben — of course. That is your goal with me. *Your* story."

By the time the bus moved on, nearly a quarter of the passengers were new. I pretended to be sleeping and did not look at the new passenger next to me. Over the next few hours, I slept intermittently.

It was early in the morning when we arrived in a town called Nushki. Again, a large number of the passengers left the bus for prayer and to use the washrooms. That time I also left the bus in order to go to the toilet.

It was not the day I had anticipated. As I walked back toward the bus, there he was — Maher, weaving his way through the crowd toward me, offering his hand and a big smile. Seeing him made me feel both happy and disturbed. I accepted his hand with a smile, of course.

"I knew I would find you here, boy."

I could tell his enthusiasm was genuine. My first words surprised me a bit, but they were the ones that had been hanging at the forefront of my mind for weeks.

"Tell me where you were all those days I was in that medieval jail in Dalbandin! Where were you when they forced me back to the border, when I thought I was going to be met by a firing squad? I came within a hair's breadth of being returned to Iran! I probably owe my life to Haji from Pakistan's border town."

There had been a good deal more anger in my tone than I had either intended or anticipated.

"I was waiting for you the entire time," Maher responded coolly. "But I was unable to do anything for you while you were in jail. Between the staff at the jail and the several layers of the court system, it was difficult to offer an appropriate bribe. Finally, I managed it and got you released from jail. You should be happy about that."

"Excuse me; *you* managed to release me from jail? How did you do that?"

"I found an influential and willing middle man – between the prison system and the courts. He took my money and gave no promises. It took a while. I waited outside for several days until I saw the police taking you from the building. You looked so happy, I figured things had worked out."

"I'm afraid somebody took your money and then sent me back to the border at Taftan for extradition. It was a good solution for them; I see now that it filled their pockets as well as solving the problem that my presence was causing."

His explanation had only partly quieted my rage. I still felt indignant.

"How did you find me?"

"I followed you back to Taftan and learned Haji had taken you under his wing and invited you to his house. His bodyguards were intimidating and have the reputation of shooting at the slightest provocation. I thought Haji might have assigned you a travelling companion – a bodyguard for the bus trip. We have been following you. This is the first time I have been convinced you are really on your own. I assume the man who left you at Dalbandin was your protector."

"No. I had no man. He was just another passenger although he was a seasoned veteran of the Afghan war."

Maher nodded.

"Who are you with now?" I wondered. "You keep saying 'we'."

"Me and a driver."

"The same guy again? And with a chunk of hashish in the vehicle?"

"No, this time I have a good friend of mine as a driver."

"You know that you messed up last time. If you hadn't purchased the hashish and hadn't told your buddies at the shop that you had a passenger from Iran, I would not have gone to that jail – where I had to endure hunger, thirst, filth and sexual harassment, as well as beatings. This is all your fault, Maher. You failed to keep your mouth shut. You and your hashish!"

I realised that I had raised my voice. People were beginning to re-board the bus.

"Please don't shout at me, Ben. I am sorry. I don't know what more to say. I am here with you now."

"What do you want from me?"

"Now we can finish your journey. In Quetta you will need my help – help you set you on your way. Without it you would probably just be walking into another period of confinement."

He stepped off toward where cars were parked. I looked at the bus and then back at him. What he said made sense. Even though I wanted to prove that I could handle things myself, he made it clear that I couldn't.

So I followed him. We stopped at a tan pickup, smaller than the first one. The seat was only really wide enough for two. I managed to squeeze between the driver and Maher.

The driver was a man Maher's age. I could tell from their conversation that they had known each other a long time.

"So, what is your plan?" I asked.

"Like I said, we are going to Quetta and once we are there, I will sort out the rest – make contacts and so on. We do have a problem."

That was the last thing I wanted to hear. I sighed. "What is the problem?"

"I had to use all the money to get you released."

"What do you mean, *all* of the money? As I remember you had nearly 3,000 US dollars in your bag – sixty per cent of the money for my transfer."

"It cost 4,000 US dollars to buy your freedom from jail. I had to add 1,000 US dollars from my own money. Let me calculate how much I have spent for you to this date; I would say about 5000 US dollars. Your man in Iran needs to pay me 2000 US dollars in order for us just to be even. I need some more money to find you a passport and ticket to Europe. I would say at least 2,500 US dollars more. You ask your middleman in Iran to send 4,500 US dollars at once and there will be no need to have him send any more money."

"I will call the man in Iran, but my father only agreed to pay him 5,000 US dollars for the entire trip."

"How could I have known that we would be arrested?" Maher asked.

"You presented yourself as a professional. You said you knew your business very well. You said you have sent many people to Europe and other parts of the world. I would say you should have computed the risks in your calculations. At the very least you should have known to be cautious that day we were arrested."

"Look, my friend. Just explain that the situation got out of hand and that you will remain here in limbo, dodging the authorities, until the money is available."

"Do you have a receipt for the money you allegedly paid for my release?" I asked.

"Of course I don't have any receipt. People who take bribes don't offer receipts. But I have been honest with you."

"I have not contacted my parents or the lawyer since we left Zahedan almost three weeks ago. I'm sure they are worried by now. I need to call them soon and tell them that I am alive. I think you need to contact Sardar and tell him why you need more money. He is the one who introduced you to Sinam, who can get in touch with the lawyer."

"No, I don't know Sardar very well and won't call anyone. *You* are the one who owes me money. *You* have to call up your people in your country and get it."

"You do understand that, for all I know, you had nothing to do with my release from prison! For all I know, you are just making the assertion to swindle me out of my parents' money."

Maher bristled. "Here is your situation, Ben. It will take 4,500 US dollars to complete your journey. Take it or leave it."

I could have taken it as a threat, but his tone made it sound like my reality.

I folded my arms across my chest and began thinking about my options. Maher apparently took this as an act of defiance.

"Listen to me. I don't care who you are going to call today, but one way or another you need to pay me 2,000 US dollars to be able to walk free from me. You give me my money back and you are free to do whatever you want to."

"What do you do if I don't pay? Will I remain your prisoner?" A horrible prospect, but one I had to reckon with.

"I don't think you want to hear what we Mujahedin do to Russian soldiers and captives."

"Do you even know what the word Mujahedin means? It is about as far from threatening helpless teenagers as it can be." Now I was just disgusted.

"I am so disappointed in you. I will call my father tomorrow and we will see what happens."

Maher remained defiant. Guilt clearly didn't work with members of his brand of the Mujahedin. "As I said before, you will pay me 2,000 US dollars soon. How you get the money is your problem."

I was disillusioned and upset. It was clear that Maher had not paid bribe money to the jail or the court in Dalbandin. Had he, the court's verdict would not have been the worst one possible. I would have been set free or at least turned over to him. Still, I didn't have many options.

I chose to remain quiet for the next two hours. The driver asked Maher what the current plan was. Maher no longer even pretended to have any redeeming qualities.

"We are going to Quetta. From there Ben will make a phone call to get the money. When it arrives we will be finished. I think Ben does not wish to be transferred to Europe anymore, so we'll go our own ways in Quetta."

I had had it with him and let go with a two-minute tirade, outlining his incompetence and my desire to never see him again. I called him a number of disparaging names that would have been best left unsaid. Maher responded in kind, shouting at me and proving many of the points I had just made.

He ended with a harsh final note. "Listen, brat. Say one more nasty thing about me and I will send your corpse to your middleman in Zahedan. This is my last warning."

Whether that threat had been serious or not, I understood he could inflict unbearable pain on me. I shut up.

An awkward silence followed as we drove on. The driver pulled off the road near a stand of trees to relieve himself. I walked around to the rear of the truck and stretched my arms and legs, unfolding myself after an uncomfortable ride squeezed between Maher and the driver on the narrow seat. They talked together out of my earshot.

"Where will we stay the next few days?" the driver asked when we got back in the car.

"I don't know yet," said Maher. "We don't have any money for lodging. Things could change after the phone call."

Clearly, he really needed the money from me.

If I was already concerned over my current prospects, the arrival in Quetta did not lighten my mood. I don't know what I was expecting, but what I saw was not it. Quetta was surrounded by beautiful hills and was well known for the fine fruit orchards those hills held. It was the largest city in Baluchistan province and was only a one-hour drive from the Afghanistan border. But it was not what I'd call beautiful. It was a city of contrasts. The streets, especially in the poorer sections, overflowed with migrants and refugees from Afghanistan who had come to escape the war. The locals stood out. They were mostly men wearing Baluchi clothes. There were only a few women to be seen and most wore the traditional Islamic burqa. A few, however, wore no head cover.

That had not been the case in Iran since the Islamic Revolution in 1979. I must say I was intrigued, seeing women with no covering.

We pulled into a small convenience store. Maher purchased drinks and a roll of biscuits for each of us. I supposed he needed to keep me alive and functioning until he received his money. Somehow even that thought was not really reassuring. We stood next to the vehicle and drank and ate.

Maher continued to look around.

"We need to find a place for Ben to make a phone call."

I was happy with the suggestion. We found the telecom shop and I asked the shop assistant to dial my home number. I became excited when I heard it ringing on the other end.

"Hello," came my mother's familiar voice.

"Mother. It's me Benjamin."

Predictably she began crying, but didn't let that interfere.

"It has been so long. We thought something had happened to you, but we could not go to the police for help. Are you in Europe? I have not left the house since you left the country… I've been waiting for your phone call. Are you feeling well?"

"Yes, Mother, things are great here. We arrived in Pakistan easily. The man in charge took a private car and we went to a small town, and we holed up for some time. That was the reason we did not have access to a phone. As you can understand, things are a bit different here. I am fine so you can stop worrying. I will try to do better with the phone calls. Can I talk to Father?"

"Sure. He is standing here right next to me, listening."

"Goodbye, Mother. I love you."

"Son," my father began.

Explaining my situation to my father was not easy. I told him of the unexpected additional charges, without mentioning jail. I lumped the extra fees into 'unexpected developments'. I felt bad lying to my father – but I knew I would feel even worse if I told him the truth. I did not want my mother to worry any more. I suggested my father should talk to the lawyer in Tehran to try to send the additional money.

"I don't understand why the man is asking you for the money." My father sounded understandably frustrated. "He should call the middleman in Zahedan. I will talk to the lawyer and will see what he suggests." I was glad he did not press me too much. Then he asked, "Are you really okay, Ben? Not disappointed with the decision to leave the country in this way?"

"I am fine," I lied. Then added, "And very happy with the decision. The man here is taking care of me with three meals a day and places to sleep at night. I could not have a better guide. He keeps me entertained and I have never been bored. He was an excellent choice. I'm told I need to put the phone down now. I am going to call you tomorrow and hear what you find out and get the lawyer's phone number. Give my regards to the family. Goodbye for now."

"You were making fun of me on the phone. I don't think it was funny."

"What I was doing," I said, angrily, "was lying my butt off to save yours. If I had told my father the truth, you'd have never seen another dime. Anyway, I didn't want to worry my parents with stories about your incompetence. I said what I thought I had to say and that's that."

"What did they say about money?"

"My father does not know much about the money or my transfer —he has given the lawyer carte blanche. We need to talk to the lawyer. We have to call him tomorrow."

I could tell he was not happy or satisfied, but he said no more about it. I ignored him.

"I am really exhausted," I said. "We need to find a place to sleep now."

I sensed I was assuming more of a take-charge attitude. Time would tell how that would work out.

"I told you I don't have any money now to stay in a guesthouse, but we will find a place to sleep."

Maher and the driver conferred for a moment then reported they knew of a place.

"I want to walk around a bit before sleep. It seems like I have been sitting forever," I said.

Maher agreed.

"Twenty minutes," he said gruffly.

It felt good to move. I noticed that I could move with less pain than before and took that as a tiny victory for my side. We strolled along the busy streets in the commercial district. They were filled with other walkers, street vendors and the ever-present beggars. I figured many of them were Afghans since they spoke Farsi and Pashto.

I was surprised with the number of shops that sold music tapes and videocassettes. Many of them played very loud music out into the street through loudspeakers. I lagged a bit to listen. That was very unlike things in my country.

After the walk, Maher directed us to the small cottage of one of his friends. It was a single room. There was a water tap and a toilet about twenty yards from the main door. They were shared by many people. Soap was not a commodity. I washed up as best I could and returned to the cottage.

Maher's friend spoke Pashto with Maher so I understood very little of it. I found a place on the floor in the shadows and fell asleep while the others were still talking and laughing.

The first words out of Maher's mouth the following morning were about making the phone call immediately.

"Whenever you wish, we can call the lawyer and I will ask him for money," I said.

"We will go back to the phone shop where we were yesterday and you will sort things out," Maher suggested.

"And we can have a cup of tea and bread somewhere," I said. I was not asking.

We left the cottage and drove back to the phone shop. I asked to eat immediately, before making the phone call. There was a traditional café nearby, which served tea and food. It was run by two Afghan men who spoke Farsi. The food was acceptable and inexpensive since the café mostly served the refugees.

Maher then accompanied me to the phone shop and I called my parents. My father asked me for the number of the phone I was calling from. He would have the lawyer call us right back. It was the only arrangement that was acceptable to the lawyer.

We waited in the phone shop for the return phone call. It came a little less than an hour later.

The lawyer was all business.

"Are you with Maher now?"

"Yes, we are together now and he sends his regards."

"Why does he need the additional money?"

"It is a long story, but he had to pay money to release me from jail on our way to Quetta. He used 2,000 US dollars of his own money to arrange it. If I am to be able to continue using his service, we need to pay him more money."

"Is he listening now to what I am saying to you?"

I tried to disguise my answer, not understanding the intention of his question.

"That would not be so."

"Just say yes or no now. Did you see him paying money?"

"No."

"Do you believe that he paid money?"

"No."

"Are you his hostage now?"

"Yes."

"If you can escape from him, do it and find somewhere safe and call me."

"Yes. Just a moment I will need paper and pencil."

I asked Maher to go find what I needed. As soon as he left, I spoke in a low tone, and rapidly.

"Listen, he is disingenuous, ill-tempered and not very bright. He lied about transferring passengers abroad before. He is a dilettante as far as illegal transfer is concerned. I think I am his first. He has no moral compass and has become very scary."

Maher returned with the pencil and a pad. The lawyer continued.

"Tell him I will find some money over the next few days. I will call you in three days at this same time."

"Sounds good, Sir. Thank you. I will talk with you again soon."

More gibberish to set up my answer to what I expected to be Maher's next question.

"Why did you want a pen and paper? You didn't use it."

"The lawyer said he was going to give me his office phone number, but he later changed his mind and said it would be safer if he would give us a call in this shop in three days. Sorry if you had to pay for it."

"Why does he need three days?" Maher asked.

"To send the money out of Iran, I imagine – a lot of red tape, I gather."

Maher became agitated.

"This is taking far too long. You and your people are not taking me seriously. Next time you will insist on immediate delivery. I will settle for nothing less, or you will face a lot of hurt."

I believed him, but tried to continue to assert myself. I had to believe I really was in the driver's seat – and in a way I was.

"Maher, threatening me does not help our relationship. The lawyer said he would phone us in three days and there is nothing I can do to change that. Remember, I mean nothing to him but a few bucks. Make this more difficult and we'll never hear from him again."

Clearly, I was getting pretty good at this.

"I will agree to just three more days."

"Three more days before what? How will hurting or killing me help your situation? You know I have played no part in causing your problem."

"You will see what I am capable of, Ben. I will contact your parents directly. They will pay in order to save your life."

"Such an attempt would make you an international criminal. You are far too smart to risk that."

"You just wait and see."

The implication was almost humorous, but I ignored it.

"I guess we'll have to wait and see for at least three days. But all this makes me wonder about something: Why is the driver still with you? What is his role, really?"

"He brought me here and he also lent me some money to pay for your release. He is waiting around for his money. Once we have received it we will set you off on your own."

That conversation had run its course.

"We can go to the same place where we stayed last night, but we have to buy some bread and fizzy drinks first."

We made the purchase and returned to the cottage. Clearly, he still had some money.

I knew if I were going to escape I needed additional information about the layout of the city and its public transportation system. I had seen buses.

Later that day, I told Maher I wanted to go to the city – that I thought we all needed to get away from those same four walls for a while. Maher said that he was not in a mood to go out and did not want me to go anywhere without him.

"Why don't you want me to go out on my own?" I needed to know if I was really his hostage.

"It is not a safe place for someone without a passport; you don't dare risk that. If the police ask you for your passport, what would you do?"

"I'm quite sure most of the people around here don't have a passport and probably don't even know what one is. I don't see the police harassing them."

"As long as you have not paid me my money, I don't want you to go out and put yourself at risk. Once you have paid your dues, you are free and can do whatever you want to."

I remained there the rest of the day without complaining. The following day, Maher left the cottage for the city, leaving the driver and the tenant of the cottage with me to make sure I didn't leave. My position was clear: I was a hostage.

Three days later, at the appointed time, we drove to the phone shop to wait for the lawyer's phone call – which was late. Lawyers!

As with the first time, I took the phone and mostly just listened.

"Do you have any new information for me," he asked. "Say yes or no."

"Not sure. Perhaps. Maher sends his regards and says he needs his money urgently and cannot wait any longer."

I paused a few seconds as if listening, then continued.

"Yes, for now I am healthy, thank you."

I had extended the yes/no approach hoping to provide more information. I hoped the lawyer got the message that I was in trouble.

"Are you his hostage?"

"Oh, yes indeed. I've heard clouds may roll in, also."

"I talked to Sinam; you are right. He found out that Maher lied to them about transferring passengers abroad. I am sorry for that, but you need to make the best of the situation. Get away from him and call me. Immediately."

He repeated his phone number, and I memorized it without giving anything away.

"Yes, Sir. The humidity is very *sticky* here, however."

I hoped he understood it was my situation that was sticky – escape would be difficult.

"So we can expect the money in two days? You will send it to this phone store in Maher's name... Yes, I'm sure he has appropriate ID... That will make Maher very happy."

That probably just confused the lawyer, but I again needed to set things up for me back here.

I hung up.

"So, the money will be transferred to me here in two days – all of it? You did well, Ben. I really would have disliked having to harm you. You and your big words have grown on me."

Maher tried to sling an arm around my shoulder, but I ducked away from it.

"Well, I am glad you feel that way about me because it isn't exactly like it sounded. The lawyer is still working on the transfer. Apparently, he doesn't believe you so they have not approved the transfer. He wants to investigate and in two days will have a final answer."

I hoped I had bought two more days. I figured using the same old three-day delay would no longer be acceptable. Assuming my statements about Maher had been close to accurate, I hoped he would go along with it. The reaction was not what I had hoped for.

Maher grabbed my forearm firmly and dragged me out of the telecom shop. There he suddenly slapped me and punched me in the chest and shoulder, hard, several times.

"Now you are acting crazy," I said.

He landed a hard knuckle into my flank. It momentarily disabled my leg and I fell to the pavement. He kicked me in my still tender ribs. I had difficulty taking a breath and lay there gasping. Wanting to avoid another boot to my ribs I struggled to my feet. None of the passers-by looked twice.

"You have lost your mind," I said, backing away several yards.

He came after me and pushed me in my chest with both of his hands. I lost my balance and for a second time fell onto my back. Maher walked toward me as if prepared to kick me again. By then the driver and two men from the phone shop moved in and restrained him. Several men gathered, wanting to know what was taking place. The driver offered a lie he hoped would satisfy them.

"They are cousins. Just a disagreement. It will be fine."

I lay there shocked and frightened by the unexpected degree of the man's rage.

Maher told the men who were gathering that I was a traitor, that I had deserted the Mujahidin. Clearly, he hoped to let the Afghans do his dirty work for him. I trembled with terror and was unable to move.

"I am not even from your country. How can I be a traitor?" I managed to say, weakly.

Maher took advantage of my attempt.

"If you are from a different country, show your passport and prove it."

"Listen to my accent – Iranian. I can't even make myself sound Afghan."

At some point Maher added the phrase 'Russian traitor' for good measure. The murmur *traitor* spread across the crowd. I looked up at Maher. He looked deranged.

He and the driver picked me up under my arms and dragged me toward the truck. I had nothing left with which to struggle against them.

"We will find an Islamic Judge and get things settled once and for all," Maher called back to the gathering.

Many of them cheered.

They placed me on the seat between them. They closed the doors.

Maher took a knife from his pocket. He held it to my throat.

"Listen, you dog. I can kill you here and no one will do anything to me. Did you see how the crowd looked at you before? If I hadn't taken you to the truck, they would have killed you with their bare hands. This was your first lesson. You will learn the rest soon."

"I hate you, Maher," I said. "You are the dregs of humanity."

He turned to the driver. "More of his big words." And he turned back to me offering a malevolent smile. "I don't care at all about how you feel toward me. I will get my money out of you, one way or the other. I've heard that Iranian families have been known to pay huge sums just to get the bodies of their executed sons back from their government. Now, sit quietly here until we are home; otherwise I will cut your ear off with my knife. Then there can be the other ear, then your tongue – you get the idea."

I believed his threats. He was clearly a sadistic monster. I recalled a teacher once saying that it did no good to try logic on a crazy person. I remained quiet.

Before getting out of the truck at the cottage, Maher spoke to me.

"From now on, you are not going anywhere without one of us accompanying you."

"You mean I am to stay here in your cottage?"

"Yes, you stay here until I decide which way will get me the most money for you."

Shortly after arriving at the cottage Maher left again, and I was left in the driver's care. Maher muttered something about slaughtering me like a sheep if I attempted to escape. That, of course made no sense. I was his meal ticket. But I also realised I could not assume logic with a man like Maher.

In Maher's absence I lay down and hoped to regain my strength – again!

Two hours later – it was evening – Maher returned to the cottage accompanied by the man who was the official tenant of the cottage. They sat across the room from me and began an earnest conversation in whispers. I made out words here and there, but much of it was in Pashto.

After their hushed brainstorming, Maher turned to me.

"This is my last question to you. Are you going to pay my money within twenty-four hours or not?"

And that is how I came to be a part of the dangerous world of slave trading.

CHAPTER EIGHT

VERILY, AFTER EVERY DIFFICULTY, THERE IS RELIEF

The following morning, I was awakened by the voices of men already at work outside. I went to the door and saw many people, teenagers and men, carrying sacks. I could not tell what they were doing but I assumed this was their job — their life. I approached one of the boys who looked about fifteen years old and asked if he was happy working there. He did not understand my language, but he smiled just the same.

I felt heartbroken and distressed for the youngsters. They were there due to the misfortune of their birth, and for no other reason. I had many unanswered questions. I viewed Sahib's practice of child labour as morally reprehensible and ethically wrong. I knew it would be condemned in most countries. I wondered, however, if the poverty here has made it acceptable.

I counted more than a dozen workers on the farm. What would I answer if I were asked what I could do? What work could I possibly contribute — work that may well keep me alive? I could drive tractors and other small agricultural machines on the farm; I had learned how to drive those machines on my grandfather's farm during summer holidays.

Frau Bosch puts the pages she's been reading neatly on her desk.

"It seems I am the one who is benefiting from what you are writing. Ben, this is a real education for me. I had no idea human slavery was so widespread. I can only imagine how terrible it must have been."

"You will see more as you read on."

"Did you come to some conclusion about Sahib and Maher — the worthiness of their values and approaches to life?"

"I think I am still appraising that. Neither deserves a place in civilised society. Both believed the rationalisations they constructed to defend themselves — neither exhibited much guilt. Or, maybe neither had a conscience and therefore no guilt. Perhaps we can talk about whether that is possible — to be completely devoid of a conscience. Sometimes I wonder about myself in that way. Experiences have hardened me — closed off emotions. I believe I may be getting a handle on it, but still..."

"I look forward to those discussions. We will have them."

"Good. But first — maybe you need to read further."

"Yes. I certainly do."

A man approached me and motioned for me to follow him. We headed into the house and he showed me into the living room. He was one of the men in Sahib's personal service — working more on a professional or personal level, I believed. He dressed well and moved with a degree of grace or distinction the others didn't. He motioned for me to take a chair, and left.

The furniture was nice — comfortable. There were posters and pictures on the wall. On one of the posters was a verse from the Quran: '*Verily, after every difficulty, there is relief.*' It caught my attention and made me wonder why that would be important to a slave owner and trader. Perhaps it was intended for those in his employ or those he owned.

Sahib entered the living room and took a chair facing me. He was all smiles.

"Did you sleep well?"

"I haven't really slept well since I left my family. I am fine — not happy about being here, understand, but fine. An interesting verse there on the poster."

"You mean the one stating relief will come after every difficulty?"

"Yes. I must say that relief has eluded me so far on this entire journey."

"You must not give up on that. We are intelligent creatures of God Almighty, and we are here to make something out of our lives, something positive and something better than our fathers had. My parents were poverty-stricken and I was very poor when I was a child and young teenager, but I was ambitious and had big dreams. I have always been looking for ways to advance myself."

I could not wince at the idea of Sahib advancing himself while all these young men and boys were working as slaves. Something felt severely out of balance.

"We are on earth for increase and advancement," he continued. "And we are not here to be happy with less. The issue is that many people are satisfied with less – little – and they cannot even contemplate having more than what they need for survival. They cannot imagine, even in their dreams, what it is to own more than they can eat or wear at the moment."

"But does that justify men being held back? Is ignorance a justification?" I needed to ask this question, for it's one that had plagued me since arrival.

"Look at the men who work for me. Most of them hardly use their God-given brain and cannot imagine being independent and living on their own in a better future. They cannot imagine being free or living a life of their own. They are not even free in their imagination because if they were they would not be here today."

"So you condemn them just because they lack imagination?"

"No, Ben. I don't condemn them. I merely think more about what God has given me. That is a difference between the others and me on this farm. I was almost one of them when I was young, but decided to change my way of thinking – the goals I set. I started thinking like a big landowner even when I had nothing. I *imagined* I had a huge acreage and people were working for me and driving me around and running my business even back while I was still a poor worker. I occasionally wondered what the richest landowner in my country would do in some situation or how he would deal with a problem I faced. I did not have the confidence to share my dreams with my peers because I knew they would ridicule me. Still, I kept dreaming big with no fears, formulating and reformulating images of the life I would have."

"I didn't allow anything to make me give up. I found that it was not enough to think big; you had to devise a plan and adhere to it. Everything starts with an idea, imagination or a very strong desire for change. Once you feel the strong desire for change, believe in it and keep focusing on it day and night, you will be surprised how it takes over and comes true for you."

"Belief will set you free, then?"

"This is not my original idea. Other men have known it in earlier centuries. It is also written in the Quran, '*God will not change the condition of people, until they change what is in themselves.'* I am not a Quran interpreter, but for me it means flushing your mind of all the barriers and limitations and giving free rein to your imagination."

I had to admit this man was growing on me. He was quite different from any others my journey had offered me thus far. I sensed he liked the dialogue, even craved it. He was a creative man, after all.

"It is an interesting view on life and I quite like it," I admitted, "because I put my faith in the power of imagination and belief, too. I also believe that I was not the property of my country, so I left it a few weeks ago. Similarly, I don't think I belong here. Most of my maternal relatives are big landowners like you, but I cannot imagine being a landowner and living on a farm. I have envisaged my future completely different to the situation I am in now, but despite opposition and countless setbacks, I am hopeful I will soon achieve my goals." I realised I was perhaps pushing too far, but I kept on, as I felt there was a connection, however distant it may be, between Sahib's philosophical position and my path to freedom. "That may seem humorous to you, considering my situation and my precarious relationship with you. I knew before I started my journey that I didn't want to live an ordinary life. And I knew that this meant that I need to face and conquer extraordinary challenges. You merely present for me one more set of challenges to conquer."

I saw his eyebrows raise ever so slightly, and quickly added, "I didn't mean to offend you by that."

"No, I am not offended, and as much as I really do enjoy conversations such as this, the fact is that I have invested in you – so you need to generate some income for me. That was my reason for having you brought to me this morning."

"How can I earn the money you have paid for me by working for you? You said the men here work to pay for their accommodation and food. How can I earn 1,200 US dollars above and beyond that? We need to reconfigure things – *re-imagine* them – or not even a hundred years in your employ will see me free."

"I need to explain something before I answer the last part of your question. It is true that I have paid 1,200 US dollars for you. That does not mean I will sell you for 1,200 US dollars. I am in the business to make a profit. You can understand that. To begin with, you are worth much more than that just like you are – clever, creative and focussed. Your value changes based on your expertise and your willingness to use your acquired knowledge."

"What you are saying is that you took the petty-minded, greedy, short-sighted Maher to the proverbial cleaners."

Sahib smiled the broadest smile I have seen.

"I like that description of Maher, and your conclusion is correct. I am quite sure we will find a suitable profession for you. Working on land is not for a young man like you. You deserve something more fitted to your intelligence and drive."

"You must have something in mind for me or I wouldn't be here this morning."

Throughout the conversations I had come to feel free to speak my mind with no fear of rebuke or retaliation. This was different from any relationship I had ever experienced.

"We are going to visit a friend and a business partner of mine today. Be patient. I have already talked to him on the phone, and his ideas fit your unique characteristics."

He asked me to follow him. We left his house, got in a four-wheel drive SUV and drove off. It was just the two of us. While on the way, I learned a few more things about my slave-trade superior. He had not learned to read and write, for example, until his late teenage years – my age. He also asked questions about my parents' occupation and wanted to hear more about my ambitions in life. The conversation flowed easily.

After driving for nearly an hour we arrived at a gated house. The gatekeeper waved and swung it open and we entered. Clearly, Sahib was known there.

He parked his vehicle at the end of the long driveway and indicated for me to follow him to the house. It was a big house with many rooms, lavishly decorated from what I could see. There were virtually no people to be seen – unlike at Sahib's place.

One man – the housekeeper I, assumed – greeted us and instructed us to take seats in the living room. This room was huge with many chairs, a dining table, several sofas and coffee tables. In many ways it was western in design, unlike Sahib's more traditional, Middle Eastern décor. It impressed me as having been built recently. There were paintings and pictures on the walls and handmade, expensive-looking rugs covered the floor.

In a few minutes, a tall man wearing a Pakistani suit entered the living room. He was in his mid-fifties and clean-shaven, and he wore an expensive Rado watch on his left wrist. Sahib stood so I did as well. The man embraced Sahib and shook my hand. He sat opposite us on a sofa.

The housekeeper served tea. I hoped for biscuits or bread as well. I hadn't eaten that morning.

Soon Sahib and the host, called Arif, began talking in Urdu. I assumed it related to our visit, which was simultaneously none of my business and yet all about me. Their conversation continued for ten minutes while I sipped my tea. Everything seemed quite cordial. I could not understand more than a word here and there, but tried not to look bored.

Arif adjusted his position and looked directly at me. Apparently it was now my turn.

He spoke in English.

"So, what do you think of Pakistan?"

I was surprised by this first question — and flummoxed as to how to answer. "Honestly," I began, "I have seen both good and bad here — more bad, I'm sorry to report, but I keep an open mind."

Both men laughed and offered smiles. It occurred to me that Sahib was relating to me more like a proud father than my owner. There was something oddly paternalistic in his interest in me. Something that kept me safe, I felt, but also made me a bit uncomfortable. Too much familiarity, perhaps — while at the same time clearly my advocate and protector.

I would need to think later about how those positions are compared. For now, I needed to stay focused on the topic at hand — whatever that was.

Arif spoke.

"We don't have Ayatollahs in our country as you do in Iran, but we have a president Zia, who is no better than the men in charge in your country. I think we Muslims in the Middle East are cursed by God, and the governments are the divine retribution he has visited upon us. I would say we are better off here than your fellow countrymen are in Iran. We are not involved in any official international war. We have President Ali Bhutto to thank for promoting the development of a nuclear weapon so that we can defend ourselves against Indian threats — otherwise, they would have wiped us out by now. You understand how much we hate each other."

I wondered what any of that had to do with me, but I was grateful Arif was addressing me with such broad geo-political concerns. Still, I was not sure how to respond, and I was glad when Sahib looked at Arif and jumped in.

"Do you think we have an atom bomb now?" he asked.

The conversation took an unexpected left turn at that point.

"I heard that professor Abdul Qadeer Khan has completed the development of the nuclear bomb," Arif offered.

Sahib responded. "Insha'Allah (if Allah wills it), it is not just a rumour, but I do believe the reality is that we have the atom bomb now. Do you think Khan designed and created the atom bomb on his own from scratch or he had help from other countries?"

The topic seemed quite important to them both, and I could merely listen. I could follow most of what they were saying.

"Do you really think we can build a nuclear weapon on our own without any foreign support?" Arif said, more than asked. "We don't have the necessary infrastructure in our country. Kahn had to have had support from European countries, but who cares. The important thing is that we own an atom bomb; how we obtained it is irrelevant."

That statement contained an uncomfortable parallel to the way Sahib thought about me.

I listened to their conversation out of politeness, but was dying to know what these men had planned for *me* and how they wanted to exploit my 'characteristics', as it had been put. At that point I felt certain neither one had truly benevolent intentions with regard to me, no matter how intellectual the tone of the conversation.

Presently, Arif addressed me again.

"I hear you want to do business with us?"

I offered a weak smile. "It doesn't seem I have a choice in the matter."

Arif shrugged and continued.

"Sahib and I are business associates and have always been honest with each other like we will be with you. We keep our promises, reward loyalty, and punish betrayal severely. We know influential people in every department of the government. We know how things are run and get done in this country. Like everywhere else in this world, it is all about the right connections and relationships. What I am saying is that we are the best at what we do and how we do it. We are giving you an opportunity to work with us."

"Go on," I said.

"Ben, I am going to make you a business proposal, which can thrust you to the next level in achieving your goals in life. If you want to succeed, you will, and as I mentioned, it will provide you with a brighter future. There are risks involved, but the risks are minimal and the benefits are great. We can see in you an ambitious and motivated young man who is unafraid of tackling extraordinary tasks. It was not an easy undertaking to enter our country illegally and yet you succeeded; my proposal is far less hazardous than what you have already accomplished. As I said, you will be a changed young man and one with invaluable experience."

I was beginning to worry – for he was setting up the potential for success a little too hard. I could tell that with these men there would be a catch. There was always a catch.

"This is what you will do. You will fly to Athens in Greece and carry two small but very expensive rugs with you. These handmade rugs are valuable beyond your imagination. In Athens, you will hand them over to a good friend of mine. He will pick you up from the airport and will be with you for one or two days before sending you back to Pakistan. The entire trip will take no more than three to four days and when you have returned, you will have paid most of your dues to Sahib."

"What are you saying, that I merely –"

"I am saying that you will be nearly free again."

I couldn't help but wonder why my role was necessary in the scenario just laid out before me. "Why don't you ship the rugs by post or some other delivery service?"

"These are very expensive and we don't want them to get lost or damaged or stolen by customs."

"Then why not use signed or recorded delivery that makes sure the item was delivered by signature?"

"Of course we know all the delivery options, but they are still not safe enough either here or in Greece. It is hard to say which country is more corrupt. So, we prefer to send them by a person we can trust completely."

"Aren't you afraid that I will steal your rugs and disappear?"

"First, you value your life too much. Second, you are too intelligent to pass up such a once-in-a-lifetime opportunity such as this – to earn your freedom."

He was making a very good case, but one problem remained.

"There is a fly in the ointment," I said, "because I do not have a passport; otherwise I would have left my country legally."

"We know about that, so we will provide you with a passport. We have a friend who is in, shall we call it, foreign affairs, and he knows his job very well."

"Is it illegal to transport rugs to the other countries from here?"

"Not at all."

"Why don't you do it yourself or use someone you have trusted for some time?"

"I cannot do that because I am not allowed to leave my country due to my stand on our government, and Sahib is too busy with his business. It is less a matter of trust than it is certainty. Certainty comes with the need to avoid dire repercussions for failure – like in your case – the first point I made a moment ago."

"What happens to me if I am questioned or arrested at the airport here? Wouldn't they ask me where I purchased the carpets?"

"We have that handled, too. We have our man at the airport and he will see that your departure goes flawlessly. We will also give you a legitimate receipt for the rugs so you can say you have bought the rugs here. Believe me, you can depart from here safely and won't encounter any difficulties. It would be against our interests to have it any other way, don't you see."

"What about the airport in Athens? I seem to remember that it is forbidden to import expensive goods there. One of the Greek men I met in my home country mentioned it once."

"You were misinformed. *We* know that the carpets are very expensive, but the layman at the airport will not know about it and when you show him a receipt stating the price of the carpets they cannot object. You will not be subjected to any sort of hassle for two little rugs."

"If they want customs fees for the rugs in Athens, what should I do?"

"We will see that you have a few hundred US dollars in case you have to pay customs and if they need more you can get it from our man in Athens. You should not worry about Athens, as there is corruption at all levels in Greece, too. We have thought about everything and you are travelling well-prepared."

I looked directly at Sahib.

"Am I free after my return?"

"If you succeed, probably yes."

"*If* and *probably* don't fill me with confidence, you understand."

"You must trust us."

He was right, and I had no option.

Arif continued. "Now we need to contact a friend of mine to arrange the passport for you. It will be a four- or five-hour drive. I will arrange food for the trip."

And thus ended our meeting. Soon thereafter, we were all in Sahib's vehicle driving back from the province, Sindh, toward Quetta. I rode in the back seat and the men talked up front. Some of the road signs were familiar to me since Maher had taken me through the same roads to Sahib's.

It was early afternoon when we arrived at our destination. We were to see a man named Rashid who — I assumed — was an expert in counterfeit passports and IDs. Rashid was in his mid-thirties and originally from Afghanistan. He spoke both Urdu and English quite well.

Secure inside Rashid's small house, we were presented with a large piece of luggage containing hundreds of fake and original passports from a variety of countries. Rashid took one look at me and declared me a perfect match for one of his fake Portuguese passports. He guaranteed it could not be distinguished from an original.

"What about the language?" I asked. "I don't speak Portuguese so it won't work. And what about a visa? You need to find something better."

I wondered if this had been some kind of test. I felt the two men who had brought me here watching closely.

"If you are from a European country, you receive the visa when you enter Greece. They are not very strict," replied Rashid. "I also have Spanish, German, British and Greek — actually all European countries. If your destination was not Greece, I could offer you this Greek passport," — he held it up with a proud air — "which is a masterpiece."

"I need to be able to speak the language of the country of the passport," I said insistently. "Otherwise, the risk of being arrested is astronomically high. I don't want an Iranian passport because if I get arrested, I will be sent back to Iran — and that's the last thing I want." This seemed an evident statement of fact, but I wasn't taking any chances. "What about an Afghan passport?" I added.

Rashid smiled.

"No one fakes Afghan passports because you can easily obtain one from the consulate in Karachi if you are from Afghanistan."

"I can speak Farsi in an Afghan accent. I could say that I am an Afghan who lived in Iran so my accent has changed a bit."

Rashid looked at me.

"I think we could apply for an original Afghan passport for you in Karachi, and if we pay them a bit more, you can receive it on the same day. The problem would be the visa for Greece."

"You don't think we can get a visa for Greece if we go to the embassy."

"The embassies are in Islamabad. Which is about 900 miles away from Karachi."

"That is manageable," Arif said. "We can fly there from Karachi." Things were happening fast for me, but none of this was my doing. "Rashid," Arif said, turning to Rashid again, "do you think you can get the Afghan passport?"

"Yes, I can take Ben there myself and testify that he is an Afghan, pay some money and get the passport. The problem is that he cannot travel anywhere with an Afghan passport without a visa issued by each separate country he intends to visit."

Sahib turned to Rashid.

"Ben can stay with you. You can take him to the Afghan consulate within the next few days. I will send a driver to take you there as it is a long drive."

Arif considered this before speaking, then turned again to Rashid. "I think we should leave Ben in the small guesthouse next to the garage; do you know where I mean? I met with you there a few years ago."

"Yes, that will be a good place and very cheap. It is full of Afghans and is also run by an Afghan. You can certainly improve your Afghan accent there, Ben."

"Just so it is safe. Remember, I don't have any ID."

"How about this then," Rashid said. "Why can't you go to the UNHCR and apply for an ID as a refugee? You get an ID with your picture on it and if you are asked by the police to show your ID you will have it. I can ask a friend to take you there."

"I have all the time in the world," I replied, realising that none of this was my choice anyway. "It will be worth any amount of time to legalise my status here."

It was decided, and despite my misgivings about my fate being so directly in the hands of others, I began feeling somewhat better.

Arif and Sahib asked Rashid to take me to the guesthouse where I was to stay until my passport and visa were ready. Arif took Rashid outside for a private chat. Sahib and I remained inside. He offered me a friendly warning.

"Do not tell anyone about our plan; otherwise we can encounter unnecessary troubles. People who say they will keep secrets never do." Which sounded quite avuncular until he reminded me of my place once more. "And remember, you must not try to escape from us. If you stick to our plan, you will see your freedom decades sooner than you expected and we can also help you get to wherever you want to head after that."

I looked him in his eyes and offered a deliberate nod.

"Understood," I said.

After Sahib and Arif left Rashid's house, Rashid took me to the guesthouse. It was a twenty-minute walk.

The guesthouse was surprisingly comfortable, with a number of small rooms off a good-sized lobby that had traditional beds covered by rugs, carpet and cushions for the guests, and a huge samovar for making tea in one corner. When we arrived, a man was taking orders from the guests.

Rashid introduced me to the owner who was an Afghan in his forties. He greeted me warmly and related that he travelled to Iran four years before and enjoyed his trip. He was well mannered and managed the guesthouse with only a few helpers. The owner was the contact for whatever a guest needed. Almost all the guests were Afghans. And somehow they seemed to know each other.

I was to share a room with an Afghan man, who was away during the day, but came back to his room in the evenings. The guesthouse owner offered that I could come for breakfast and meals in the lobby.

Rashid was happy with my room and said it was fortunate that there was a bed available for me at all. He, too, felt the need to remind me of my place. "Please don't try to go away from here. I will inform the people around the hotel to watch you and they will bring you back. You are in a desert here and there is no way to get out by yourself." I nodded in agreement, but his voice darkened when he added, "Don't cause yourself or me any trouble. The men who brought you to me are very influential and can be both very kind and very ruthless. Don't put your life at risk by crossing them. I am telling you again, don't trust anyone here. I am all you have. These men here – they have already noticed you and know that you are not an Afghan, even if you are wearing Afghan clothes. They know that you are here to leave this country for somewhere in Europe."

"How can they know that?" I asked.

"What else can be the reason for a young Iranian to come to a place here in the middle of nowhere filled with poor and desperate Afghan refugees?

The only reason is to escape from this country. There are many Iranians who have come here for that purpose. It is unfortunate that you ended up with those two Pakistani people, but there is still hope that they can help you."

I wondered if he meant 'fortunate' rather than 'unfortunate', but let it go. I was curious about his connection to them, so I asked, "It appears that you are Arif's friend, but do you know them well?"

"I do business with Arif, as you have witnessed. My specialty is in passports, travel documents and fake visas. If he needs me, he comes to me. I would say a few times a year."

I nodded, wondering how much more I could ask, but Rashid was all business.

"By the way," he said. "Arif asked me to take passport photos of you and keep them with me. It is late now so we will take the photos tomorrow. You should wash your hair for the photos."

I thanked Rashid for what I had to believe was his honesty and I promised to stay at the guesthouse.

The guesthouse was far from spotless, but acceptable and better than the other places I had seen since the beginning of my journey. There were two toilets and a wash sink in the building, but no shower. Each room had two single wooden beds. A thin soft mattress lay atop an old, concave-shaped, duckboard base. It did not look particularly comfortable, but never mind: the idea of spending a night in an actual bed was wonderful.

Now that I was finally in a space where I could wash and refresh myself, I needed a number of things. I had some money left from my watch, but since I couldn't leave to get them I asked the owner for his suggestion. He dispatched his boys to shop for me and I was soon the proud possessor of a towel, a razor for my thin facial hair and clean underwear. I felt nearly civilized again.

I was lying on my bed in the late afternoon when someone knocked at the door and entered the room without waiting for a response: the other guest who shared the room. We exchanged smiles and handshakes. There was an instant connection between us. It soon felt like we had known each other for years. Jahan was thirty years old and I was glad for his company.

"Are you happy with your bed?" Jahan asked. "Or do you want to have mine?"

I indicated the one I had was fine and thanked him for the kind gesture.

Jahan asked where I was from and how long I had been in Pakistan. He also revealed a bit about himself. He was an Afghan refugee, had a degree in history and had been helping a friend in his shop to earn money. He showed me the ropes at supper in the lobby and our conversation continued through the meal. He was a knowledgeable man and I liked the way he viewed things in his life.

Back in our room, he grew more comfortable, comfortable enough to ask me pointedly, "Why are you staying here, Ben?"

"I just imagine you know why," I said calmly.

We both smiled.

"You are going to Europe or Canada like many others," Jahan responded.

"Bingo! That is correct. I am certainly not here to join Afghan Mujahedin in their fight against the Russian soldiers. I think, perhaps, you were one of them."

"Yes, like many others, but I became exhausted from the war and needed a break. I might join them again, but not now. "

A silence fell between us. I did not like to think of him returning to war; that was another world away.

"Do you know who is going to transfer you abroad?" he asked.

"Not yet, but someone is working on that."

"How long will you be staying here?"

"Not sure, maybe only a few days. It depends on several unpredictable variables."

"Most Iranians, like you, only stay here a matter of hours as there is nothing here for them. You need to go to the big cities like Karachi and Islamabad where there are many smugglers."

"That is part of the plan," I said.

We both slept soundly that night. Jahan must have got up early and left the room because when I woke he was gone. I made myself ready for Rashid, who arrived quite early. We walked to a local photo studio and had six passport photos made. Rashid also brought me a selection of books to read to lessen the boredom he knew would soon set in. I needed to have conversations to improve my accent so I planned to spend time in the lobby.

I asked Rashid to let me call my parents and let them know I was doing well, even though I couldn't give them the actual details of course. To my surprise, he approved of it and took me to a nearby telecom shop.

I talked to Mother.

"I am fine, Mother, and there is no reason for concern. Ask Father to call the lawyer and tell him that Maher is useless, unreliable and good for nothing and that he should avoid him in the future. He should stop sending money to anyone until I ask for it. I'm looking to find someone else to do Maher's job, but it might take a while."

My mother was of course worried but I tried to reassure her at the end of our short call.

"I am fine. I will give you a call again next week."

I was relieved to have spoken to Mother. I had not realised how much I'd been missing her – but I dared not tell her of my travels so far. I focused on the positive steps of getting to Europe, and that seemed to help her mood.

Rashid suggested that we should drive to Karachi late in the evening so that we could be there early the following morning. He thought it would be cooler and there would be less traffic on the motorway. Rashid needed to talk to Arif first – to arrange for a driver, I assumed. He would tell me the plan that afternoon.

I remained at the guesthouse mostly listening to the others speak in order to hone my accent.

Later that day, while I was sitting in the lobby reading, a man with two teenagers entered the guesthouse and sat not too far away. I suspected that the boys were from Iran and the man was the transporter or smuggler – they went by many names. After a short while I stood and crossed to join them.

"You folks coming from Iran?" I asked.

The man said yes, assuming I had also left my country.

"Who brought you from Iran?" he asked as casually as others spoke about the weather.

"Maher. Do you know him?" I responded.

"Are you serious? Where is Maher now?" he chuckled.

"Yes, I am serious. Unfortunately, we had a falling out and he has left me on my own."

"Maher has never been to Karachi himself and he hardly speaks English. He thinks he is a Jack of all trades, but he is master of none. He cannot do anything for you. I am surprised he made it this far. How long did it take you to get here?"

"About three weeks," I answered.

He looked at his boys.

"And you are unhappy it has taken us forty-eight hours," he said, wagging his finger. "This is called professionalism." And he patted his chest with the end of his fist.

"We were arrested and things went out of control, but never mind," I said. "I am here now."

"My job is to take these boys safely to Karachi and hand them over to a man who will do the rest. If you want, you can meet them there. The boys could then ask their smuggler to transfer you, too."

"I am tempted to consider it. Where are you going to stay in Karachi?"

"I am writing the name of the guesthouse here for you as we speak. It is a safe place where I usually take my passengers."

"You are being very kind for no apparent reason. Many thanks, I really appreciate it."

The man excused himself for the toilet. The older teenager, Ramon, started talking.

"He is talking rubbish. It took us forty-eight hours, but we were also arrested by the police here in Pakistan. He paid some money to them and they set us free."

"Be happy that you didn't need three weeks and that you did not go to jail," I said. "Who is your man in Karachi?"

"The main man is one person in Tehran and he allocated the task to two people. One man would take us from Iran to Karachi and the second one from there to Europe. The man in Karachi must be very influential. Try to see us in Karachi when you arrive there."

"I might do that; you never know."

I left them and went to my room. I felt sad for my situation and really envied them their trafficker and his expertise. I remained in my room where I wallowed in self-pity for several hours. Later that evening, Rashid came for me in a pickup truck with a driver, and we were soon heading towards Karachi. Rashid explained that we would not wait at Arif's house but go directly to Karachi.

We arrived in the city early the following morning. Rashid asked a taxi driver how to get to the Afghan consulate. The morning traffic was heavy and it took us a long time to cross the city to our destination.

Before entering the large consulate building, Rashid said that he would do the talking and I should only speak to answer questions directed at me, and I should keep my answers short. We sat in the waiting area and completed several forms related to the passport application. Rashid suggested that I should say I was two years older than I really was, because it would make travelling easier for me. I took him at his word, not really understanding why. When I'd completed all my forms, Rashid entered the consulate clerks' room alone with the papers.

A few minutes later he came back for me. Then we entered together. Taking Rashid at his word, I nodded at the clerk rather than speaking.

"Why do you need a passport now?" the clerk asked.

"I had a refugee ID when I was in Iran that I showed for my identification. I am fed up with living in Iran and would like to go back to Afghanistan."

"What will you do in Afghanistan?"

"Probably do my military service. I don't know for sure."

"Why don't you want to stay in Pakistan?"

"I was already in a foreign country for years. Why should I start all over in another foreign country? I could have stayed in Iran. There was no need to come here."

That explanation seemed to satisfy, as there were no further questions.

Rashid told the man I was his cousin and asked if I could wait in the sitting area again while the two of them talked. The man nodded brusquely, and I walked out and waited for Rashid. I felt uneasy, but I had no choice but to do as I was told.

Minutes later Rashid joined me, wearing a big smile.

"Almas, come with me."

And just like that, I had a passport in hand – my first genuine passport issued by an official authority! So what if it was not my real name? My Afghan name was Almas and my passport was valid for one year.

"I need to phone Arif now," Rashid said, "and let him know how well things went getting the passport. He will probably want you to go to his house first – it is on our way. He might be ready to take you to the Greece embassy soon. In that case he will probably want you to stay with him."

"I'm just part of the cheap help, Rashid. I don't make the decisions."

Rashid offered a quick smile. At the driver's suggestion, we bought food and Pepsi and ate in the car on the way back in order to save time, as we were all anxious to get back. We drove straight through only stopping along the road to relieve ourselves. Along the way, Rashid explained to me that his job was finished and Arif would take over from there and arrange for my Greek visa.

We arrived at Arif's house in the evening. I handed him the passport and he examined it.

"Very good, but unfortunately it will not get you anywhere without a visa in it."

He turned to Rashid.

"Plans have changed. I want you to take Ben to Islamabad. You will drive to Karachi and then fly the rest of the way and obtain the visa. I am sure you will do a good job. You will be well paid. You know that."

"I could do it, but I need to be at home during the next two days. I can take Ben back to the guesthouse again and take him to the Greece embassy in three days. I will make a phone call to the embassy and ask the latest requirements to make sure we will have what we need. He will need to show them some money as Greece doesn't allow vagrants to enter their country," Arif said, "I will give you one of my expensive wristwatches that Ben can wear. You will also need to lend him a pair of clean, unscuffed shoes and some high-class clothes. At the embassy they should think that he is a rich young man and is going to Greece for a few weeks of sightseeing. That will suggest he is prepared to spend a lot of money there. Greeks like foreigners who spend money. I will give you some money for him to carry while at the embassy."

And that was the plan. Which seemed straightforward enough.

By the time the driver took us back to the guesthouse where I had been staying, we were all physically exhausted. I was amazed the driver had been able to stay awake during the drive. I went to bed that morning as soon as they dropped me off. I slept around the clock and had only been up a short while when Jahan returned to the room that evening.

Rashid had left a message for me with the guesthouse owner that he would come for me the following day. He then dropped by the guesthouse late. Plans had changed — of course — and he informed me that we would travel directly to Islamabad the following evening, skipping the flight. The new plan was to drive overnight, arrive in Islamabad the next morning and would go directly to the embassy.

I felt like a chunk of driftwood being thrashed about in a heavy sea, having no control over my destiny whatsoever. But at least this felt like forward progress, and I had to admit I let myself become excited about finally going to the Greek embassy in Islamabad. I could pay my dues to the men and leave the country with their help.

Jahan greeted me and motioned me into our room at the guesthouse, a little too urgently. "Do you know anyone who can guarantee they can fly you from Karachi to Europe illegally?" he asked.

"No, I don't."

That got me a little worried – wasn't I in the hands of experts?

"Well, I don't want to dash your hopes, but I have learned that no illegal passengers have left Karachi over the past several months due to tightened security."

Whether he wanted it or not, my hopes were feeling a bit battered.

"I think most of the passengers who arrive from Iran wait in Pakistan for months and even years."

Now they were plummeting.

"Some of them," he continued, "try to go abroad through UNHCR, but even that can take years."

I felt my stomach knotting.

"I am just informing you about the situation in this country," he said matter-of-factly.

"How do you know that?" I asked.

"Most of these trafficking rings for Iranian and Afghan refugees are run by Afghan smugglers. I know some of them. I have also heard from some of the Afghan passengers who had been duped by the smugglers and lost everything they had. They talk at the shop where I work. I just want you to be alert and watchful."

Getting over my initial shock, I held onto the hope that Jahan didn't know everything there was to know. There had to be a few competent traffickers beyond his range of acquaintances who could transfer people to Europe. I would find them.

"I appreciate your concern and the information," I said calmly. "I am sure I will find a way to get away from this country, because my mind cannot accept any other thing."

Jahan laughed and nodded.

"You are young and you are allowed as many dreams as you want. I like you, Ben. I've enjoyed talking to you and sharing the room with you. And that's why I don't want you to get disappointed and become mad at the world. I really like young people to have big goals in life, but if your dreams are too big, you cannot achieve them – and you will become depressed and disappointed. Some people cannot cope with setbacks and failures. Sometimes they even fall quite far – even using external help to cope with negative events and experiences. I don't want you to go down that route."

"What do you mean by external help?" I asked.

"I mean things like alcohol and drugs. You will see many young people in big cities like Karachi who have become alcoholics and are addicted to heroin, opium and other drugs. It is the sure sign they have given up."

"I assure you I am not one of them."

"I hope you are not one of them, but believe me, at one stage in their lives, they thought the same way about themselves as you think today."

"I understand what you are saying," I said, grateful for his concern, "but I am hoping that I keep hating opium and other drugs; I hated seeing my grandfather smoking opium, as his addiction has affected generations. Similarly my kids and grandkids will probably suffer the consequences of my poor choice today."

"An interesting view and I hope you never touch such things."

Frau Bosch rustles the papers and exhales.

"Is it alright?" Ben asked, wondering why she's stopped, seeing she still has ways to go in the pages he's brought today.

"It's the way you knew at such a young age who you were. Most impressive, really. The way you always circle back to your grandfather's experience with opium. I am moved by that. I have had some personal experience in my own family with alcoholism."

"I seem to have more to say than time allows," says Ben. "I find I am becoming more contemplative the further I get into this project – thinking before I write. In the beginning I concentrated on getting the facts right and keeping it all organised for your benefit. Recently, the things I write seem to call for my assessment – like to meet my own needs. And yes, I do think quite a lot about drug addiction – and how opium ruined so many lives in the place I come from."

"It's fascinating," Frau Bosch admits. "And — do you find the writing cathartic?"

"Yes, very," Ben says without hesitation. When the psychologist does not look up again, he says, simply, "Maybe you should try it."

The psychologist raises her eyebrows. Ben is not sure what that means, but it doesn't really matter. By now, the telling of his story has become his project rather than her assignment.

CHAPTER NINE

MEN IN SUITS

Getting to the embassy proved difficult, of course. Not because of road repair or physical blocks. Not because of paperwork or other such issues. No, getting there came down to my reliance on a set of people who, for whatever reason, had other things that got prioritised over my escape and my life.

Unfortunately, one of Rashid's relatives was ill and he needed to take care of him.

"When do you think you will be free to make the trip?" I asked.

"Probably next week. I am not going away. I will be here; my relative lives right here. I will be taking him for tests and treatment during the days, but I may be able to see you in the evenings."

I sighed.

"I thought," he continued, "Arif could find someone else to take you, but he said he wanted me to do it. I am his only associate who speaks your language."

I may have even rolled my eyes. But what else could I do?

"It seems that waiting is the essential part of my journey," I said, a little downcast. "You know that I am not escaping from here, because I have no place to go."

Rashid looked happy that I was being so agreeable.

"Could I go out with Jahan, the person I share the room with? He is a nice guy and he could show me around."

"Yes, I will trust you for that, but please, don't cause me trouble."

Rashid's response brightened my outlook.

And it made me glad to know he thought I'm an honest man — a man who's good for his word. For some reason, even dealing with shady characters who worked their way round the law as a profession, who lied and cheated and did who knows what other criminal activity, this was important to me.

Living at the guesthouse, I got to know the regular comings and goings of the community. And I met some interesting people who made my time there memorable, and even enjoyable.

One day I met a man whom I'd seen frequently at the guesthouse, entering through the small back door, using the guesthouse toilet and leaving the same way.

This day, I grew curious and went outside to follow him when he left. Next door was a garage with a store that sold tyres and auto parts. I learned that the man I had followed was the owner of the garage and the store. He was a local Pakistani man of around fifty years of age; he was friendly, offering his hand to shake and welcoming me to his garage. We managed a conversation through the little bit of English he knew.

The man, Imran, whistled and a younger man poked his head out the door of the store. Imran asked him to join us and said something to the young man in their local language and the other man — who turned out to be Imran's much younger brother — translated it into English for me.

Imran knew I was not from here — he had seen me at the guesthouse and asked around. I told him that was correct, that I was from Iran and had been there for a short time. I continued that I would soon be going to Karachi. I offered a few carefully chosen episodes from my experiences since leaving home. From there, our conversation moved from topic to topic. I learned that Imran did not have any children. I learned that he'd wanted children. I also learned he could adopt me as his child and I could stay there and study in the city — safely and legally.

I laughed. "I think you are pulling my leg. How can you adopt someone you just met? Besides, I already have parents."

"You can still have your parents, but you don't live with them now. You left your country because you didn't like to be there. Now, you are in my country and you could stay here. I could help you with everything, but you need to promise to stay with my wife and me in our house in this city. What do you want to study?"

I suddenly felt as if I was in a fairy tale — a bargain with a kind but unknown stranger, a wrong turn, a deal that seemed too good to be true...

"I am really flattered by your offer," I said, "but I have other plans in mind. Initially, I wanted to become a fighter pilot, but gave up on that when the war in my country started and I witnessed the terrible destruction caused by such planes. Now, I would like to study medicine."

"You can study medicine here in this city and stay with us," he said, eagerly – and I felt the pressure growing. "I would even pay for the university. Isn't it a good offer?"

"That is an amazing offer," I readily admitted. "But I think you must see a doctor soon as your offer does not sound healthy for your wallet."

We laughed and I came back with a counter offer, which had little chance of fulfilment, but since we were telling fairy tales anyway, I said, "You could have me as your son and pay for my travel cost and study in Europe. What about that idea?"

"I don't like that idea and wouldn't do it," Imran responded.

Over the next few days, he came to the guesthouse routinely and asked me to have tea with him in his garage. Imran was a kind-hearted man and continued trying to persuade me to stay in Pakistan. I was determined to journey to Europe. Eventually, the kind man understood – but I would be sorry to say goodbye to him.

On another day, while sitting in the lobby, I was approached by an Afghan man, accompanied by a thirteen-year-old boy. The man sat close to me and began chatting – typical conversation, asking about my native country and its tourist attractions. I had seen him before in the guesthouse and noticed that many people greeted him whenever he entered. He appeared to be an affluent man – I had seen that much from afar. Now he spoke with me softly, telling me he had several shops and other businesses in Quetta. His name was Karim. I did not ask, but I assumed the boy might have been his son.

Karim invited me to his home for dinner one day. He suggested that I should ask one of the men in the guesthouse to take me there since most of them knew where he lived. I thanked him for his invitation and said I would certainly try to take him up on his offer one day during my stay.

Later that day when Jahan returned to his room from work, I told him about my encounter with Karim. Jahan smiled and said that if I wanted to go there he would take me to his house, but not enter it. He offered no explanation other than to say it was a matter of preference. He would accompany me but he would not visit Karim himself.

Two days later, during the late afternoon, the young boy who had accompanied Karim came to the guesthouse lobby and delivered Karim's invitation for dinner that evening. I accepted, of course; I was curious to learn more about this apparently influential man, and Jahan had certainly piqued my interest further.

On the way I asked the boy whether he was related to Karim.

"No, but I have been with him for three years and he has been kind to me and my family and takes care of me."

"That is very noble of him. He must be a good man. What about schooling?"

"I can read and write a little. My family and I left Afghanistan several years ago and since then I have not gone to school."

"Do you speak the language here– Baluchi and Urdu?"

"Yes, a bit, but I am surrounded with Afghans so we speak Farsi."

"How do you spend your days?"

"I stay close to Karim and go wherever he goes. Sometimes I am a messenger, like now."

"Don't you want to finish school, or are you enjoying life without doing any homework?"

The boy laughed. "I don't like going to school. I want to be a truck driver. I mean a really very, huge, big truck with at least eighteen wheels." His eyes widened as he spoke.

"So, you like driving? Have you driven a car yet?"

"Yes, I enjoy driving and Karim lets me drive his car sometimes – to take him to places that are not too far away."

"I have a younger brother who is almost your age," I said. "One day he took my father's car, opened the gate and drove the car to the street. Luckily, one of our neighbours saw him and took the car away from him before he could take it onto the main road. I hope you don't try to drive on your own. It could be dangerous for you."

"Did you drive a car, too, when you were my age?"

"My father required me to take driving lessons when I was fourteen years old. I took them with two friends. I think we had twenty hours of lessons and then I started driving my father's and uncle's cars. I still don't have a driving license!"

After a twenty-minute walk we arrived at Karim's house. I was ushered into the living room, where Karim and four other men sat. There were carpets on the floor, but no chairs, dining table or sofas. Things were strictly traditional there. The four men seemed to work for Karim, and they had very little to say. Karim carried on with his own style of monologue throughout the evening. I learned that Karim was a married man with two young daughters, but they didn't sit in the living room where we were — in fact, neither wife nor daughters were anywhere to be seen. Quiet servants brought in the food and we were amply fed throughout the evening. The food, an Afghan national dish called Kabuli pulao, was delicious. It was made of rice, chicken pieces, pistachios, carrots and various seasonings.

When I thanked Karim for the evening and made ready to leave, I was asked to stay overnight and go back to the guesthouse the following morning. Karim said I could sleep in the living room where two of the four men would also sleep.

It had grown late. I complied.

In the middle of the night I was awakened by a scream from the next room. It was disconcerting to say the least, but the man in the room with me assured me it was probably a young boy with a nightmare. It had happened in the past, he said. Go back to sleep, he said.

The next morning over tea and bread, the boy entered the living room and stood next to me. He looked frightened and seemed to be in pain; one side of his neck was bluish and had bite marks. I looked at him and asked what had happened. The boy started weeping and said one of the men who slept in the same room with him had hurt him. He didn't like the man to touch him, he said, but he did anyway. I could only assume the man was molesting him. I was horrified.

The other man — the man eating breakfast with me — tried to stop the boy from talking, but I pulled the boy closer and encouraged him to sit beside me. I asked him to talk slower so that I could understand what he was saying. He said his bottom end was in a lot of pain and he could not sit comfortably.

I felt tears welling up. I felt sick to my stomach.

I turned to the man sitting across from me.

"The boy is saying he was raped in this house last night by one of your friends, and you just sit there and don't do anything? Where is Karim?"

"Karim left the house early in the morning."

I tried to comfort the boy and asked him if he had spoken to Karim that morning. The boy nodded and said that he had.

"What did he say?" I asked.

"He said I would be fine soon."

"Didn't he say anything to the man?"

"No, the man and Karim left the house together. They are good friends."

Now I felt even sicker.

The boy continued. "I was told that when I turned thirteen I would enter a new phase in my life here and that my allowance would increase. My birthday was last week."

I suggested that the man there with us take the boy to a doctor.

"He will be fine soon," he said gruffly. "It takes some getting used to. You must not make a mountain out of a molehill."

I could not believe the man's reaction, his nonchalance at such an offense.

"If the boy were my brother, I would put the perpetrator up against a wall and shoot him dead." I was so angry I was shaking.

The boy eventually calmed down, stopped weeping and said that he could still walk me back to the guesthouse. I insisted that the boy have some tea and bread.

I left the house devastated, telling the man in no uncertain terms: "I think this is not a place for me to ever visit again."

I went directly to my room in the guesthouse, flopped onto the bed and screamed my anger into my pillow. All afternoon I could not stop thinking about the poor boy.

When Jahan arrived later that afternoon, he was at first amused by my lying about. "Someone went partying last night, didn't they?"

He had intended it as humorous.

"I wish I never went there," I said, my despair clearly showing.

"What happened?" asked Jahan. "You look very upset?"

I sat up on the edge of the bed with my pillow across my lap.

"The food was good and everything seemed to be fine until this morning when I saw the young boy — you know, the one who is with Karim all the time. He was raped and bitten by one of the men and no one did anything. I cannot believe it. I am furious and tormented by the fact that the boy is still living with the perpetrators."

Jahan's eyes widened, but he did not look surprised. Rather, he looked very concerned, like a secret has been spilled. "Now I can tell you why I don't like Karim and people like him," he said. "I did not want to tell you before – I did not want to paint a bad impression. But I suspected this. They are called *Bache baz*, paedophile, in my country. They take young boys from their parents, who cannot afford to raise them. They promise the parents to take care of them, but they abuse them for their own entertainment. Not only for their own pleasure, but they often allow other men to abuse them as well."

I was trying to take this in – the very idea that this is a cultural habit that society allows.

Jahan continued, speaking softly. "I know it is sickening, but nothing is ever done to stop it. Now you can understand my antipathy towards Karim. Many of the men who come to the guesthouse with a young boy are only showing off their trophy."

I was speechless for some time. Eventually, I spoke. "I didn't know about the practice before. I don't even know if there is a similar practice in my city back home. I know about paedophiles and also boys who had sexual relationships with other boys, but most of them were the same age. I only know it as a matter of mutual consent. That doesn't equate with what I saw this morning. And the most terrible thing is how they seem to get away with it with impunity."

"*Bache bazi* has been a part of my culture for centuries, and it will not be eradicated. There was no punishment for these people when they lived in pre-war Afghanistan. There is certainly no punishment for them here in Pakistan, because no one would talk about it or take any legal action against them. There are too many other pressing issues here, issues that people believe need to be addressed and solved long before that one," Jahan explained.

"It is so unfair."

"Some things that are unfair can be rectified. Some cannot. *Bache bazi* is one that can't," Jahan said. "Focus on other things where you can make a difference."

That experience stayed with me for days. I felt sick and helpless; there was nothing I could do for the boy. I held the image of the abuse in my mind even though I had not witnessed it personally. I wondered if I were overreacting because of how it dredged up the fears and feelings associated with my time in jail. I knew I had not dealt with those: they sat somewhere in a locked box within my subconscious. My inclination was to leave them alone. But now I felt pushed to reassess that stance.

I did not see Karim in the guesthouse after that night, and I heard that he felt deeply insulted by my comment about shooting paedophiles. I wondered, briefly, if my comment would put me in danger, but I could not take it back – nor would I. I remained outraged at the injustices advanced against that innocent boy. I had to doubt if Sahib's quotation from the Quran applied for the boy: *Verily, after every difficulty, there is relief.* I saw no relief in this boy's future.

I wished I hadn't gone to Karim's house, but I had. I should have listened to Jahan, but his reluctance did not do enough to stop me. I think it is a developmental task for all adolescent males — learning to trust in other's wisdom without having to learn every lesson for oneself. What I had witnessed could not just be erased. But perhaps that, too, was not such a bad thing — one of the consequences of the path I'd chosen. Certainly, I'd seen more than I bargained for since leaving home — and I knew how well I had it, compared to this poor boy.

At last the time for the trip arrived. I was annoyed by the delay but at least I had polished my accent. Rashid and I had the same driver as the one who had taken us to Karachi. We drove throughout the evening and night and arrived in Islamabad early in the morning. In the darkness there had been little to see along the way.

We first stopped at a top-end hotel and entered the washroom. I cleaned up and changed into the special clothes Rashid had borrowed for me. Once I had slipped on the expensive wristwatch I looked and felt the part I was meant to play. Rashid had also borrowed a piece of hand luggage for me to carry — an excellent finishing touch.

I examined myself in the mirror and admired my suit. I looked *good* — but I was not the man in the expensive clothes even if I needed to act the part. I was filled with excitement, and then dread. I flashed back to Karim and the young boy — how wealth came so easily, and created such barriers. How Karim held himself so confidently, how his suit shone in the afternoon sun, how he sat in the guesthouse for people to admire him, his wealth, his... his trophy boy. My stomach lurched. I would remember this boy, if for no other reason than to tell his story one day.

I smoothed the front of my suit and turned from the mirror.

When I was ready to leave, Rashid spoke again.

"We will go together to the embassy and you are going to introduce me as your driver and personal assistant. I will sit outside, but you need to find an excuse to mention me to the clerk."

"I will do my best. I hope I don't panic."

"Why should you panic? The passport is original, fully legal, and there is nothing wrong with it. Now, you just need to play your part. You are legal in every way — you must buy into that. It is like playing poker."

"I wish I would have gone to a drama class or at least would have learned to play poker from my maternal grandfather. He was good at it."

"Be relaxed and think positively and you will be fine."

We left the hotel and drove to the embassy. The driver said he would sleep while we took care of our business.

Inside, I was told it would be at least a two-hour wait before it would be my turn. Rashid fell asleep in the chair, but I remained awake, rehearsing answers to the questions I expected. After two hours, I was shown into the office. The clerk was a young lady who appeared exhausted. I hoped that wouldn't affect my interview.

I walked to the desk with an air of confidence. I greeted the clerk with a full smile.

"I am here to apply for a visa to Greece. This is my passport."

"What is your job and why do you want to go to Greece?"

It had been delivered in that bureaucratic monotone I had heard before.

"I am going to start at university soon and would like to have a holiday first."

"Why Greece?" she asked.

"I have always been impressed by the Greek contribution to world civilization and would like to see some of the famous attractions. Some of my relatives live in Germany and they will meet me there so we can see the sights together."

"Where are you going to stay in Greece?"

"In a hotel."

"What is your father's job?"

"He is a businessman in Quetta; he is in the carpet business."

"How can you assure me that you will return to your country and not stay in Greece?"

"I have a good life here with a driver and a lot of support from my relatives. Why should I stay in your country? I don't know anyone there. I don't even speak your language and find it very challenging to learn. My plan is to go to the USA after finishing my university training in Pakistan."

"How much money can you take with you?" she asked.

"I don't know how to answer that. Enough. Plenty. Do you want me to ask my driver? He is sitting outside and can phone my father's personal assistant. He may know or can ask my father."

The clerk waved off the matter.

"No, obviously money is not a problem for you. I am writing in your passport under your visa stamp that you need to show at least 500 US dollars when you arrive in Athens. You need to have that money with you; otherwise your entry to Greece will be refused."

"I have that much with me now if you want to see it."

"That won't be necessary. Please wait outside for a few minutes, while I confer with my supervisor. It is just routine."

I waited outside next to Rashid. After twenty minutes, the clerk called me back into her office and said the visa had been approved for a period of four weeks to begin anytime during the next six months. I thanked her and left the office.

"I am sorry," the psychologist says, "but I need to cut our session short, Ben. I am feeling unwell and need to go home. I will see you next week."

Ben feels helpless. He stands, and says nothing as she leaves.

CHAPTER TEN

IS IGNORANCE BLISS?

Rashid was clearly pleased that I had received the visa. He would now phone Arif so he could begin making the preparations for my journey to Greece.

We went to a local McDonalds-like, fast food restaurant and had a meal. The city impressed me; it looked very clean and quite different from Quetta. After leaving the restaurant Rashid told the driver he wanted to visit the Faisal mosque, the biggest mosque in the country and a landmark in Islamabad. Rashid went on to explain that the Saudi's king had financed the mosque that was designed by a Turkish architect, and it cost over one hundred million US dollars.

I was happy to go and have a look. The mosque was an architectural masterpiece located at the base of the scenic Margalla Hills. It had four minarets, each of them over ninety yards tall, and a magnificent and impressive main prayer hall that could accommodate more than fifty thousand people. It was unbelievably huge and astonishing in every way.

"They have spent a huge amount of money on this mosque. I am not sure I would have put so much money into a building," I said.

Rashid shrugged.

I continued. "With the money spent here, think of how many shelters could be in its place – homes for needy people and individuals who have to sleep on the streets. If I were the King of Saudi, I would have spent the money differently – more on the worshippers and less on the building."

"I don't think it is a bad thing to build an elegant mosque," said Rashid. "In Europe and the USA rich people donate money to churches and keep building bigger and more ostentatious structures. Why shouldn't we build bigger mosques?"

"I think people in Europe are generally better off; many fewer are impoverished like they are here," I said. "I wouldn't mind spending money on mosques if most people had enough to eat and weren't forced to sleep on the streets. And anyway, I wonder why we need to compare everything with Europe or America. Just because they do something doesn't mean they are right. Because they increase the size or splendour of their churches, we don't have to do the same with our mosques. I personally don't think it is a valid point, but as you pointed out the other day, I am still young and my attitude might change."

I managed a smile in his direction.

"I am not disagreeing with you, Ben," he said. "I think you can show off more if you build a massive mosque than two or three hundred apartments for homeless people. I personally don't like wealthy Muslims, who spend vast amounts of money on the Hajj but don't help their poor neighbours who live close to starvation and may even have to sell their children for food. We live in an unfair world."

We eventually left that discussion and the city of Islamabad.

Back in Quetta, I settled back into the guesthouse. Rashid arrived again the next morning and announced, "Arif will be buying the flight ticket to Athens soon. Then you will fly to Greece."

"How soon?" I was excited.

"Arif needs to coordinate the flight dates with his middleman at the airport, because the middleman must be on duty when you depart. I think it may take as much as one or two weeks."

"One or two more weeks! By then the city fathers will make me an honorary citizen of this town!"

"Arif has to make sure that everything is working well and the circumstances are favourable, "Rashid explained.

"I don't understand what you are saying, you know." I was quite irritated by all the waiting. "My passport is original and I have an authentic visa for Greece. Hypothetically, I could fly to Athens even now. If taking two rugs is allowed, as I have been assured time and again, could you tell me what the problem is?"

"Arif is a bit pedantic — compulsively well organised. It is one reason he has been such a successful businessman. He just wants to eliminate any possible flaws in his plan since the rugs are extremely valuable. A one- or two-week wait does not change anything for you, and I will bring you some more books."

I knew he was right: what difference would two weeks make in Neverland? My life was on hold and even if I was not content with Rashid's explanations, there was nothing I could do to change my situation. I scolded myself for being so impatient; I need only look around to see how much better off I was than most others in the guesthouse. I had the luxury of free time, time I spent on my back on my bed, eyes closed, picturing the better life I was seeking somewhere in Europe. I thought of the boy, too – the boy whose life I could not imagine, a boy who would be beholden to a monster the rest of his life. I kept telling myself that my situation was temporary and would pass, and I would not be a resident of the guesthouse for all eternity.

Nonetheless, there were times when I could not comfort myself and I felt extremely weak, vulnerable and anxious. There were even times when I could not stop being tearful. Sometimes when I first woke in the morning, before I opened my eyes, I was uncertain where I was. It was as though I was floating in an oppressive, thick fog that precluded both seeing beyond it and my ability to initiate physical movement. Those moments caused deep panic.

Two of my main concerns were the overwhelming loneliness I felt, and the fact that if something harmful happened to me, nobody could help me and my family might never know about it: I would just disappear from their lives with no trace.

During the day I managed to keep my thoughts under control. I could turn off flashbacks and suppress negative feelings and emotions. I kept my mind occupied. At night it was a different matter. The darkness seemed to unleash the torment from my subconscious. Between legitimate insomnia and my fear of falling asleep, nighttime became terrifying. Awake, I relived the events I had experienced, and they grew more dramatic, more troubling, while not sleeping in the black of night. Asleep, I was plagued by the most unnerving sorts of nightmares, in which the darker moments of my life took on mammoth and irrational proportions. In some ways, the nightmares were better because they typically arrived masked, coming in unfamiliar forms that could not dredge up the actual, disturbing images from life's real experiences.

And as the waiting stretched from days into weeks, the nights grew longer. Many times each night I awakened with heart palpitations, hair soaked and matted against my face, bed sheet drenched in sweat, and waves of anxiety that not even wakefulness could immediately quell. Often, my sleep-time images gained such full control of me that even slapping myself awake and sitting up on the edge of my bed would not send them packing.

Darkness was my enemy.

"Ben, you were fighting with someone in your sleep last night," Jahan said one morning. "It takes a lot to awaken me, but I heard you. Your face looked pained and you tossed and turned on your bed. You were very agitated and restless. I wondered if I should awaken you. I am sorry for you."

"And I am sorry that I disturbed your sleep," I responded.

"Back when I was fighting in the war, I had nightmares as well. They seldom come anymore," Jahan said.

"I am hoping that I will leave them behind when I finally fly out of here, when I settle in my final destination."

"I guess I didn't understand the depth of the trauma you have been through. Again, I am sorry for you, my young friend." He was silent for a moment. "I read somewhere that American soldiers reported similar symptoms when they returned from the Vietnam War. It is called posttraumatic stress disorder or something similar to that. Everything is given a name these days, you know."

"I may have heard about that, but I don't know whether I have a similar condition. Anyway, I think labelling myself with a psychological diagnosis at this age is counterproductive."

"I suppose so. I have heard talking about such things often helps. I am a good listener," Jahan said.

"Really? There is one dream that recurs almost nightly. Life would certainly be easier without it. Sure you want to hear?"

"Certainly."

He sat across from me on his bed.

"It takes place at the spot where I crossed the border into Pakistan. It is pitch dark and then suddenly a huge spotlight illuminates the place where I am squatting. A number of border guards rush at me with guns fixed with bayonets touching my chest. They pull me to my feet and talk among themselves. One relates a new directive that all men trying to cross illegally into Pakistan are to be shot. They stand me up against the wire fence and tie my hands to it, out from my sides. The six guards take their positions ten yards away. I hear the platoon leader begin the countdown. '*Ready. Aim. Fire.*' I can see six flashes and six bullets leave the barrels of the six rifles. It becomes ultra-slow-motion. The bullets sail closer and closer. They are within just inches of my chest when I wake up, terrified and unable to breathe. Back home I read that we dream to heal, forget unpleasant experiences, solve our problems, and fulfil our wishes. I feel that my dreams tend to consolidate my horrible memories and make my troubled life unbearable. No sign of healing in my case. Sometimes I think I should drink a lot of coffee or take something at night to remain awake."

"My goodness, friend. That is worse than anything I ever experienced. I don't know what to say. I have no words that will be of any consolation. I'm not sure we can survive without sleep for more than ten to fourteen days. Therefore, I don't think you would be better off avoiding sleep."

He grew silent. There was nothing else to say. Jahan cleared his throat and changed the topic.

"When are you leaving here? Didn't you contact a smuggler the other day when you were away?" Jahan asked.

"Sort of, but I need to go to Karachi first and they might be able to do something for me over there. I cannot tell you how much, as I was advised not to say anything. You know what happens if the transfer fails? The trafficker will blame the passenger for the failure because he talked to someone even if the person did not reveal anything to anyone."

"I completely understand. If you are not to say anything, please don't."

"I will send you a picture postcard when I arrive at my destination one day," I said with a smile.

"And I just imagine you will."

"I have been thinking about that black box, Ben."

"Which —?"

"The one that holds all your feelings. I became very emotional while reading your pages before. I have recovered now, you see. Your story is moving at so many levels. You have shown a great deal of strength — especially at such an early age. I wonder just how large that locked black box must be. I think you're finding a way to express those feelings — in some way, even if you are not talking about all these events in your life."

"I function well — my grades and social life, my health."

"Yes but one day you'll have to open the box more. You know that, right?"

Ben offers no response.

"How are you sleeping? I haven't enquired for a while."

"Actually, you have never asked. Some nights good. Some not so good. It seems to be correlated with what I've been writing before going to bed," Ben answers. "One does not sleep well in jail. Recounting those days is always hard. Though I did get rather used to the routine of it all."

Frau Bosch realises he is right: she has never asked him about his sleep.

"Do you still have nightmares, Ben?"

"Not much as before but they still occasionally plague me. I would like to learn how to change the story of my nocturnal dreams as I read recently that some people can control their dreams and use it for their advancement. I presume it requires a lot of knowledge and practice. There was a famous Dutch painter who claimed that he dreamed his painting and then he painted his dreams. Imagine I could learn my college subjects in my dreams."

"Nothing is impossible, Ben".

Frau Bosch starts reading the new pages.

Days dragged into a week and then three more. Finally, Rashid received word he was to take me to Arif's place to make ready for the journey to Greece.

"The time has come now that you show us what you can do, Ben," Arif said, sitting in his living room. "We need to buy you a suit, a couple of shirts and prepare you for the trip. We will buy everything in Karachi prior to your flight. I will be coming with you to the airport. I have an apartment in Karachi and we can stay there. Your flight is not until tomorrow evening so we have time to shop for you."

"Where are the rugs? How big are they? Are they heavy? When do I get to see them?" Now that the time was here, I had a lot of questions.

"The rugs are with my friend in Karachi and we will get them tomorrow before the flight. There are two rugs, and you will have two pieces of luggage. Each will carry one rug. Flyers are allowed one piece of luggage so you may need to pay for the excess baggage at the airport. You need to take one or two sets of underwear, a toothbrush, a comb, a razor and so on. We can get you a small wash bag, too."

"The clerk in the visa office said I need to have 500 US dollars with me as you see on my visa."

"I will give you 1,000 US dollars in case you need to pay customs fees for the rugs. They need the receipt of purchase so that they can calculate those charges. The rugs are very expensive, but they won't know it. The price of the rugs on the receipt is very low and will seem reasonable. They have no way of determining their actual price," Arif explained.

"What if there is a problem and they want more money for additional customs fees, which I can't pay?"

"They would confiscate the rugs temporarily, give you a receipt, and you would need to go back later, pay and release the rugs. If it happens, my friend over there will take care of everything. He will pick you up from the airport and he will take you back when the time comes. That is really nothing to be concerned about. It is just a matter of paying the fee. Things like that happen all the time."

His explanation made me feel better.

"We have thought about every possible problem. You should be relaxed and don't think about problems."

Late that evening his driver took Arif and me to Karachi and we went to the apartment he kept there. It was on the fifth floor of a residential building opposite a housing complex for military personnel. It was a modern apartment with three rooms, a shower and toilet – reinforcing my idea that Arif was a very wealthy man.

I lay on the sofa, the driver on the floor. Arif slept in his bed.

We woke up around noon. I took a proper shower with warm water, soap and shampoo for the first time in months. I didn't want to get out.

Arif's driver, who was also his assistant, took me shopping in a retail area, about thirty minutes from the apartment. I was fitted out in a new suit, two shirts, new socks and other essential things. I also had my old scruffy shoes repaired and polished by a skilled shoeshine boy; it took him about twenty-five minutes. The shoes looked great afterwards.

Later that afternoon Arif returned with an officer who worked at the airport. He drew a map of the airport for me and explained where I should wait for him. He asked me not to approach him if I saw him at the airport but wait for him to talk to me first. He emphasised that he would come to me and greet me when the time was suitable. He would take me to the check-in desk and later to the border control officer who would check my passport and apply a departure stamp. He reminded me that my documents were authentic so I had no reason to be concerned or frightened.

I had never been on an international flight so was unfamiliar with the processes that were involved. I was sure I would learn them with ease. I asked the officer to run through the normal procedures at each point in the flights. He was patient and quite competent, and I appreciated that. The officer explained that my ticket to Athens would include a stopover in Istanbul but I would not need to carry my carry-on luggage from one plane to the next, and that transfer would happen automatically. I felt relieved and quite comfortable after the thorough debriefing.

Arif brought two matching pieces of luggage into the living room and showed me the folded rugs inside each one. He asked me to lift the cases and see if I could carry them without any difficulty. They posed no problem; I estimated about thirty-five pounds each. I put my shirts and underwear in one and the wash bag in the other. Arif also provided me with a man-bag for the passport and the money – 1,000 US dollars, in hundreds and fifties.

Several hours later the driver took Arif and me to the airport. Heavy traffic created delays, and I grew tense, but there were still several hours before my departure. The driver dropped us off in front of the international terminal and Arif helped me put the pieces of luggage on a trolley. He shook my hand and wished me good luck. He advised me to remain cool, to not be nervous.

I wondered why I would need 'good luck' if everything was like they said it was. But there was no time for such deliberations.

The airport was crowded with passengers and there were long lines at many of the check-in counters. I scanned the departure board and found the counter that was allocated to my flight even though I knew I needed to wait elsewhere for the officer. I went to that spot and waited.

The officer eventually arrived and greeted me; he showed me exactly where to stand in line.

"You stay in this line. It moves slowly. When you reach the counter and it is your turn I will walk up beside you and help you with all the details."

It took fifteen minutes. When I arrived at the counter, the airline clerk asked me to show my ticket and passport. I had them ready and handed them to him. By then the officer moved in casually beside me. He spoke to the clerk, first in Urdu and then in English explaining that I was his friend's son and going on holiday to see my relatives. He added that I was a bit nervous, since it was my first international flight. I did my best to look the part – it took little acting.

The clerk smiled at me. "There is no reason to be worried, young man. It is like a domestic flight, but it takes a bit longer. The seats are better, and the food is tastier. I am giving you a window seat from here to Istanbul, but today I cannot choose your seat from Istanbul to Athens."

The man did not ask about the content of my luggage but did request additional money for the excess baggage fee. In a hushed tone he explained that he was only charging me half the required fee because of my relationship with the officer. I offered a smile and a simple thank you.

When I was about to hand the money for the fee to the clerk, the officer whispered to me to put an extra fifty-dollar note on top of the money. I did as he suggested and I handed it all to the clerk. He received the money and gave me a receipt for the payment – less the fifty-dollar 'gratuity'. He handed me the boarding card and pointed me toward the allocated border control gate.

The officer made sure I got in the correct line and left. He showed up next to me once again when I arrived at the passport control counter. The officer conversed briefly in Urdu with the clerk in charge there. He smiled at me and put the departure stamp on my passport. He showed me the way to the transit area from where I would move to the gate.

I was glad everything had gone smoothly and felt relieved once I arrived in the transit section. I walked through the duty-free shops, but did not have money of my own to buy anything.

Soon, I boarded the plane to Istanbul.

A reserved Pakistani couple sat next to me, making for a quiet flight. I fell asleep soon after take-off. Several hours later I was awakened by a bout of terrific turbulence. I didn't sleep after that and began worrying over potential problems I could face at the airport in Athens. The flight to Istanbul took seven hours.

After a three-hour wait for my connecting flight, I was given an aisle seat. The plane's condition was less than impressive even though both flights were run by the same airline. The contrast with my previous flight was obvious from the moment I boarded: the threadbare condition of its seats revealed they had been used hard for many years. I was glad it was a short flight – only two hours. The plane landed at the Eleftherios Airport in Athens in the early afternoon.

The border control officer asked me what I was going to do in Greece and wanted to see the 500 US dollars indicated on my visa. I answered his questions and showed him the remaining money in my bag. He flipped through the banknotes to make sure it was enough. He affixed the arrival stamp on my passport and handed it back to me.

I followed the other passengers to the baggage claim area to collect my precious luggage. My first case arrived almost immediately, but I had to wait nearly ten minutes for the second one. I placed my luggage on a trolley and pushed it toward the exit.

At customs, an officer put his hand on my trolley and asked me to stop. He wanted to see my passport. While he looked at it, he asked me why I had come to Greece. I did my best to appear calm and repeated my practiced answer – that I had come to Greece for sightseeing and pleasure, that I would meet some of my relatives who were coming in from Germany.

"You are not planning to stay in this country?" the officer asked.

I tried to act surprised at the question.

"Stay here? Why should I stay here?"

"Some people come here to seek asylum," the officer responded.

I repeated the routine I had used successfully before.

"I don't understand the Greek language and think it would be very difficult for me to live in this country. No, I am not staying here. I will go back."

"Can I see your ticket?"

I offered him my ticket. He frowned.

"Why are you going to leave us in just two days?"

"I just want to see my cousins from Germany and they cannot stay here long, so I am going back when they leave in two days. My university starts soon. They have been here often and assured me we can have a great time in two days."

"What do you have in your luggage?"

"Clothes and souvenirs for my cousins as they just married. It is a tradition in our country to give gifts to newlywed couples so my father asked me to bring two gifts for them."

"Please open the luggage," the officer said.

I opened one case and he took the rug out and unfolded it, laying it back over the luggage case. He asked me if I had a receipt for them. I nodded, pretending to have trouble finding it, and seconds later I offered it to him. It showed the price in US dollars.

"Sorry the receipt is so wrinkled," I offered, helpfully. "I didn't know you would need to examine it. I am glad that I have brought it with me."

"Where is the other rug? The receipt is for two rugs," the officer asked.

"I have a similar rug in the other piece of luggage. I split them up to even out the weight."

"Why did you bring two rugs?"

"I am going to see two of my cousins and each is to receive one rug from my family. They have both been married within the past year."

"Open the other case so I can see the other rug, too."

I opened the luggage and the officer lifted the edge of the rug.

"You need to clear customs for the rugs. This means you need to pay customs' fees."

"But these are gifts and my cousins have to take them to Germany in a few days. Will they have to clear customs too?"

"You didn't have a connecting flight to Germany. Greece is your final destination and therefore you need to clear customs here. You need to pay customs when you enter the country. What you are going to do with the rugs afterwards is none of our business," the officer explained.

"How much do I need to pay?"

"Not very much. I will need to find out for you."

While the officer was talking to me, a female Greek passenger started shouting and cursing loudly at one of the customs officers nearby. They were only a few yards away from us. The situation escalated. When it reached a physical state of disagreement, the officer who was detaining me said, "You can go through. Skip customs and enjoy your stay here. I need to go over there and help my colleague."

I thanked the officer for his generosity and I hurried away from the customs area. I went on to the arrival hall where I waded through a noisy crowd, each person trying to find their passenger. I had been told to wait near the exit.

"Are you Ben?" said a man who came strolling up. "I am Antonios and I am here to pick you up. Arif is my business partner in Pakistan."

"How did you find me so easily?" I asked.

"Arif described you to me as a charming young man who would be carrying two expensive pieces of luggage and waiting for me right here. He also faxed me a copy of your passport with your picture. I hope you have had no problems along the way?"

"The customs officer here seemed awfully picky about my rugs, but he was called away and let me go with a caution!"

"You must have a very good song and dance routine, because you are required to pay customs for two rugs. I have been told you are a young man of many talents."

His comment made me wonder if he or Arif had arranged that altercation waiting in the wings in case I needed a diversion. I had been told Arif was compulsively thorough. I managed a smile through a long sigh. "I think I was fortunate."

"Can I have your man-bag, Ben? I am assuming your money and passport are in the bag."

I handed him my bag as he asked me to.

"Ben, you will receive the bag when you are flying back home in two days. You don't need your passport and money here because you are with me all the time. I have reassured Arif that you will catch your plane back to Pakistan, and I don't want to break my promise. Now look at the two men sitting in the black Peugeot on the other side of the road and wave at them."

I waved at the men and they waived back to us.

"These men work with me and they won't let you out of their sight until you are on your plane. Please remember that, Ben."

"I will."

"Now we need to celebrate your arrival. I have a small apartment about thirty minutes' drive from here, and you are to stay there. I will drop you there and leave you alone for a few hours so that you can recover from your flight. I am staying at my friend's house on the other side of the street and will come back to you later; we will then go out for a meal. You can see some of our attractions if you like."

"Sure. That sounds very nice," I responded.

On our drive, Antonios talked about his country's poor state of economy, its crippling debt and high unemployment rate. He described the inflation rate in Greece at around twenty per cent whereas at the same time it was around one per cent in Germany and around three to four per cent in the USA. Considering his explanation and my own research before my flight to Greece, I knew that Greece was an unattractive final destination for many asylum seekers in the eighties, but one could probably use it as a springboard to the other European countries.

We soon arrived at the apartment, which was in a remote area far outside the city. Inside, I removed my personal items from the luggage and Antonios took both cases with the rugs. Before going to bed I weighed up the possibility of going to Germany from Greece. I was still in possession of a gold coin in my shoe so I probably had enough funds to give it a go even though Arif and Antonios warned me against breaking the trust and made it quite clear that I could not escape from them and their people. I was in a strange place – a kind of no-man's land: in a free country and enjoying the benefits of a passport and visa, yet unable to leave or even move about on my own. Like it or not, despite how far I'd come, I was still a prisoner. I was not free. Not yet.

I grabbed a small knife from the kitchen cabinet drawer and pried open the heel of my old shoe. I was ready to examine the gold coin I'd placed there before I had departed Iran. I wriggled the knife, careful not to cut the shoe. I finally pried the sole loose and created enough of a gap to reach inside. My fingers felt around, and found –

Nothing.

The compartment where I'd placed the coin was empty.

How was this possible? A panic welled up in my chest. Someone had taken the gold coin. But who? Where? I had kept my shoes on all the time in jail, always aware of the physical danger. Same goes for my long car rides with Maher and his cronies. I never took my shoes off, for fear of them being stolen. *Think, Benjamin.* The guesthouse? Unlikely – my roommate was a good soul, an honest man. Then I thought of my visit at Karim's. I had taken them off at his house. Yes, that is where it happened. There were only a few suspects: the boy and the men. I had a sinking feeling in my gut that one of those horrible men had taken it. But I hoped the boy had found it and was able to use it to finance his escape.

I lay down on the bed but my shock prevented me from falling asleep. Later that evening Antonios knocked at the door and hesitated briefly before entering the apartment. Unlike me he seemed elated. I tried to conceal my disappointment and anger about the loss of my coin.

"The stuff is great! The best I have seen recently. I cannot believe they could produce something so incredible in that corner of the world."

"I think our Persian rugs are good, too, and could be even more valuable," I said flatly but trying to share in Antonios' excitement.

"Who is talking about the rugs? I am talking about the good stuff woven into the rugs."

"I don't understand what you mean. What was inside the rugs?" I said.

"Are you an imbecile! Didn't you know that there was heroin inside them? Surely you knew what you were transporting."

I had no words. *Heroin?* It wasn't that I hadn't suspected something was not right about the whole transaction — but heroin?!

The double whammy hit me hard — first, the loss of my coin, now this. My knees buckled and I slid down the wall and sat on the floor. I couldn't believe that I had been a party to such a thing.

"I'm sorry, Ben. Arif said you didn't know, but I couldn't believe it — a young man of the world like you."

I knew the name: mule. People who are used to smuggle drugs, sometimes even unknowingly. I couldn't believe that I let myself be duped into being a mule. I could have rotted in prison if I had been caught. Or worse. I suspected Sahib was not the benevolent man I thought he was.

Antonios saw that I was close to hyperventilating. He brought me a glass of water and told me to drink it and breathe more slowly.

"You can see I am terribly upset, Antonios — I am beyond upset. I am angry, outraged. I feel disappointed. Dirty." I practically spat out the last word.

"I am sorry, but this is the truth that everyone knew, apart from you. If Arif had informed you about it, you would not have come. This is the beauty in these deals: the person, or as you said, the mule, should not be aware of it. Otherwise no one would risk it."

"What if I had been arrested at any of those three airports on my way here?"

"You could not have been arrested in Karachi, as our man at the airport monitored you; nor in Istanbul as there was no further check over there. I doubt you could be caught in Athens, as they would hardly have thought of this means of transport. They could have asked for more customs fees, but they would not have detected the heroin woven into the rugs."

As if all that would make me feel better, after the fact.

"You are a star, since as far as I know, and you are the first one who has managed to transport our valuable stuff this way. Don't sit there and sulk, my young man — this needs to be celebrated!"

I moved from the floor to a chair and looked at Antonios, who sat there blithely lighting one cigarette after the other.

"You are playing with the life of an innocent person, and you clearly don't care. All my hopes for an education and a lifetime of helping the sick were just a hair's breadth from having been ruined. And you want to celebrate!"

My anger was rising even more at the thought of celebrating.

"I think it was cruel, criminal, thoughtless and unscrupulous – I could go on! If I had been arrested, I would have named all the people who were involved."

Antonios laughed.

"You are truly naive. Do you really think they would have initiated an investigation in Pakistan if you were arrested at the airport here? Where do you think you live? We are in Greece, not America. You would have ended up nameless, buried in a Greek prison. Greece is a European country, but the corruption here equals the level of the third world countries. Our Prime Minister, Mr Papandreou, is inept and unable to improve the country's economy. We brag about our thousand-year-old civilization, but we have many areas in this modern country that need improvement." He exhaled dramatically, cigarette smoke filling the air between us. Then he burst out laughing. "I will admit that people like me don't help our current situation."

"I can't really be interested in your country's issues, since it does not help me understand what happened to me."

"But, look! Nothing has happened to you. You are alright! And if I hadn't told you about the damn drugs, you would not have even known about them."

"I'm sorry, but I don't think I am in a condition to go out with you now. I need some time to digest all of this."

"What about the food? You don't want to eat anything?"

"I have lost my appetite. I would like to be alone if you don't mind."

"I can bring you some food tomorrow morning and will also take you out afterwards. I am not staying here tonight but will come back tomorrow morning. But Ben! Don't wallow in self-pity! Remember, your mission was carefully planned so nothing would happen to you. That should be worth something."

And with that, Antonios left.

I sat on the bed, and all I could think about was how I had been betrayed and mortified by a drug lord. Vengeful thoughts crossed my mind and I let them linger; I even spent time developing them with some degree of sordid pleasure.

Nightmares came often and with brutal power. I got up and made tea. While I sipped at it I stood looking out the front window, gazing at the neighbouring buildings. My self-respect had taken a huge blow. I knew I was blameless in the scheme, but still. The fact was, there were signs I should have seen. There were questions I should have asked. Perhaps I let them go for my own selfish reasons: complete this one assignment and earn my freedom. The more I thought the angrier and more frustrated I became.

I knew that hatred, if left to simmer, can destroy a person. I had to focus on the positive things in my life. I had always worked hard at being a good and helpful person. My plan was to dedicate myself to continuing to be that person. I needed to learn useful lessons from this experience and move on. One of those lessons was that I needed to get my exploiters, Arif and Sahib, out of my life — *way* out of my life.

I suddenly doubted if that was going to be as easy as they had let on.

After an hour of head adjustment, I did feel better and was able to sleep for several more hours. I had been awake for some time when Antonios arrived around ten o'clock.

"Are you feeling better about things this morning?" he asked.

"It is still difficult for me to believe what I did, but I realise I cannot go back in time and reverse things — make it all *unhappen* — so I must move on and learn to deal with the emotional consequences of what you people have so thoughtlessly forced on me."

He cringed a bit, but only a bit — I was coming to understand that men like him nurtured a guilt-free inner life.

"You seem to be wiser now than yesterday," he said, illustrating my point all too well. "Did you have an epiphany last night? We say everything is possible in Greece!"

"Call it what you want, but I think I am doing harm to myself by dwelling on so many negative emotions from things that were not of my doing."

"This is your last day here, Ben," Antonios said, as if I were just a visiting tourist, nothing more. "I am going to take you out and show you some of our tourist attractions to reward you for your good work."

I exhaled deeply and agreed. I would accompany him, but I refused to think of it as a reward for my so-called good work.

We drove in his car toward the city. He stopped at a small café where we had a very fine breakfast. He seemed to be well known there. I figured a man of his girth was probably well known in any number of eating establishments. I took that as a good sign.

After breakfast we visited the amazing Central or Constitution Square. We ambled along the streets for nearly half an hour. I saw the Greek Parliament Building, and he offered a brief history of the buildings and the central square. We then drove toward the Acropolis, which was located on a hill. I could see it from some distance away. It reminded me of the Persepolis in my country that was founded centuries before.

Time passed quickly though I felt too depressed to enjoy the sights; I could not stand hearing Antonios prattle on about architecture, history and culture. Much of it seemed odd coming from him. We ended our excursion at a nice local restaurant.

Antonios drank a lot of soda – a dozen or more in the time we had been together. Even more noticeable was how he chain smoked – I counted two dozen cigarettes. I gave him maybe ten more years to swallow and puff.

On the way back home, we talked about the hypothetical possibility of leaving Greece illegally to Germany or Canada.

"It is extremely difficult to find a reliable human trafficker in this country, Ben. You could be deported back to Greece from Germany if they find out that you stopped in Greece first. The law states that a migrant should apply for asylum in the first European country he reaches and wait for the outcome. I personally think you can get to Germany easier from Pakistan. Please don't put me in a difficult situation, Ben. Don't try to escape, as my men will catch you. And you can get hurt."

"You don't need to worry now. I am flying back to Pakistan and I won't try to escape."

His explanation made clear that I should not stay in Greece even if I could and should return to Pakistan.

Back at the apartment we sat and talked. I asked him how he knew if the heroine I had brought him was of a good quality.

"I do not use heroin myself but know how to distinguish a quality product from others. I also have people who are experts."

I pressed for information, believing he would stop answering when he thought I was stepping over some boundary.

"How long have you been in this business?"

"More or less about five years."

"Have you had any problems with police or have you been to prison?"

He laughed loudly and held his expansive tummy.

"Many times in my life. I have different lines of business. Not just heroine. We are also interested in counterfeit clothing, money, paintings and other such things. I have friends in Italy and they are good at counterfeiting money and paintings. Friends from the Middle East are best for drugs."

"Have you met Arif face to face?

"No, but I know his associate in Pakistan and they work together. I think the fewer people you know first-hand the better for you."

"The safer you mean, really?"

He nodded.

"Why didn't you learn something else – something legal? A trade, I mean?" I could see him doing a lot of different things, beyond heroin smuggling.

"I was not born a drug dealer! When I was younger, I ended up in prison for set-up car accidents. While in prison, I learned many illegal strategies to earn money quicker and faster. With such activities, of course, come more risks. I would say that rather than being a place for my rehabilitation, prison was my school for crime."

"You are saying that prison made you more of a criminal than you had been before?"

"Yes, of course. You learn new tricks of the trade from the other prisoners, and you make contacts. I have never known a person who came out of prison a better man than he went in. It is a universal law."

"Do you want to carry on this way for the rest of your life?"

"A person like me doesn't live long. I am fat, and a heavy smoker. I have lots of medical conditions, including diabetes and high blood pressure. Then there are also enemies. My life expectancy is therefore not great. I don't think I can change my line of work during the time I have left!"

At least he and I agreed on one thing. But it wasn't my nature to let something like that drop. Besides, I quite liked him; even felt sorry for him.

"You could stop smoking, eat healthier and do something about your weight. It is not too late yet – and you should not give up on yourself at your age. You seem to be a nice person who just got off the track. It is never too late to change your life."

I sounded like an old maid librarian lecturing a teen for having spoken out loud in her sacred halls.

"It is easy to say and hard to do," Antonios responded.

And then he changed the topic. "I have business I need to tend to still tonight. I will leave you here, now. Bear in mind that my men are watching you."

"As I said before, no worries. I need a small bag to put all my belongings in to take back with me on the plane," I said.

"You will find what you need in the cabinet, there. Take what you want."

I went to bed early, preparing for the long flight. I must have been more exhausted than I realised. I did not awaken until the next morning until I heard Antonios knock at the door and enter.

I had time for a quick shower and got ready for my return flight. One of the bags in the cabinet was the perfect size for my belongings.

At the airport, Antonios returned my man-bag with my passport and money. He somehow managed to accompany me to the departure terminal. He shook my hand with what seemed to be genuine affection – respect even.

What was it with me and my peculiar relationships with horrible people?

"I hope you achieve what you wish in your life, my young Persian friend. Don't forget that you are from the land of brave Persian kings who ruled my country back before Alexander the Great," Antonios smiled his parting words.

"Thanks for your hospitality, Antonios. I really do wish you the best in life as well, and may it be longer than you expect."

We shared a last smile and I left him to board my plane. I felt him standing there, watching me leaving his country.

CHAPTER ELEVEN

GET OUT OF JAIL
FREE CARD

A 'get out of jail free' card: is that what this had been? Had my task been accomplished enough to set me free from the criminals I'd come to associate with. All this weighed on me as I flew to Istanbul and then Karachi. I thought about nothing other than how to separate from the evil individuals around me before it became too late. I thought about the idea of evil and the idea of it becoming too late. Were these people – people like Rashid – already on an irredeemable path? Was I?

If they had been truthful with me, maybe I would be allowed to walk away from them. I had just made them a huge sum of money. Part of me had never really bought the 'get out of jail free' card they had flashed before me – but now it seemed within my reach. Maybe.

It was late in the evening when my plane touched down at the airport in Karachi. The first thing I did was call my parents from the airport. My father picked up the phone. I shook at the sound of his voice. He asked me if I knew when I could leave Pakistan for Europe.

"I am looking for someone who can send me abroad," I said. "But I need to make sure that the person is not a liar like the other guy, so it is taking some doing." I paused. I knew my father would worry, so I added, "I am doing well, though – everything here is satisfactory."

Those calls were always too short. I never felt good after putting the phone down because I always had to lie about some things. My heart was in the right place – I did not want to worry them – but I had lied. And now my well-meaning heart was heavy with sadness.

I sat down next to the phone booth at the airport and considered my options. I had space between me and Arif and Sahib, with some money. Could I strike out on my own at this point? Could I break free of them, or was I somehow yoked to them still? I needed time and space. No part returning to Arif and Sahib seemed like a good idea.

When I exited the airport, I saw that Arif and his driver were both there waiting for me. The driver waved to get my attention. I walked toward them, but stopped several yards away. They both offered me a hand for a shake. I didn't accept either one. I went on the offensive. I used a loud voice – a voice that surprised us all.

"You lied to me and you betrayed me. You didn't tell me that you had drugs in your rugs. You didn't say I might rot in prison for you. You gave me no reason to think you were a drug dealer. You played with my *life*. You tricked me. Tell me, how many people have ended up in prison because of your callous actions? People like you belong behind bars."

A small crowd had gathered.

"Please, please, lower your voice," Arif said. "You cannot say those things at the airport where many people can hear you."

"I believe I just did and I am nowhere near finished."

"Here you are, fine and safe," Arif said. "I can't understand what you are upset about."

"And that, Arif, shows your most dangerous character flaw. You have no moral compass."

"You are acting like you are possessed by a Greek evil demon, son."

"Never, ever, call me *son*. The very sight of you makes me sick."

Again, the man put his finger to his lips to quiet me. It didn't work.

"I am outraged and really disappointed in you," I continued. "Why are you here? What more could you possibly want from me? My soul, perhaps?"

"We belong together. We have a good thing going. Don't damage our friendship."

"Friendship! You used me for your goals, for *your* advantage – certainly not for mine. If I had been sent to prison you would have written me off and gone shopping for your next chump. I have to wonder how many young lives you have already ruined. *Friends?!* We can never be friends. You are an evil parasite, feeding off good people and the rest of society."

"I am warning you to watch what you say and come with us without resisting." Arif was starting to look agitated. "I can make you disappear with a snap of my fingers."

"I think you just threatened my life in front of all these witnesses." I was feeling confident now. "You are dumber than I thought."

The crowd began to disperse. I hadn't counted on that.

Arif, for his part, changed his tack. "I understand your anger and I am sorry for it. I will never ask you for any illegal business anymore. I promise."

"I have no intention of coming with you now. I want to go my own way. You just made a huge amount of money because of my courage, and I will tell you it required a great deal of skill — more than you will ever realise."

Arif remained calm, but firm. And only a few stragglers remained from the concerned crowd. "You cannot walk out on me whenever you wish. Come with us and don't aggravate the situation by unnecessary arguments."

"No," I said flatly. "I will scream for security."

"You cannot escape from me. I will have the airport surrounded. Give me the money I gave you," Arif said.

"I don't have any money. I spent some in Athens and lost part of it."

"Antonios said he paid for everything for you in Athens."

"And you believe him? You should hear the way he talks about you."

"If we were not out here now, I would strangle you with my bare hands." Arif now made a fist with his hand.

"And you want me to come with you. To get strangled and beaten. You're an idiot as well as an amoral prick."

Before Arif and his driver walked away from me, he said, "We will see each other again very soon. No punk kid has ever talked to me that way and lived to tell the tale."

The driver went to a shop and used the phone. That couldn't be good for me. I understood Arif really could carry out every threat he had made.

I went back inside the arrival hall and sat on a bench. It was only then that I realised I was trembling. I could not believe what I had just done. All that anger had somehow found its way to the surface. Other than believing I would soon be dead, I felt better than I had in a month — months even. I was in a state of mental and emotional turmoil. I needed to simmer down before making my way out of the airport.

I asked one of the shop clerks about alternative exits to those out front. He said he knew of none. I wasn't sure if I should believe him. I sat back on the bench; Arif and his driver were watching me from a distance.

By then it was the early hours of the morning and there were not many people at the airport. I could move around inside the airport as much as I liked; neither Arif nor his driver moved to follow me. But each time I returned to the doors to check, they were there. They knew that I had to walk past them if I wanted to leave. They remained next to the exit, as if they had all the time in the world. I moved back inside out of their view and sat on a bench for an hour.

Next time I went back to the exit doors, Arif was gone but the driver was there still – with two men I had never seen. Henchmen. The phone call, probably. They were looking around and pointing. I slunk back inside the airport and moved as far away as I could, sitting on the floor in a corner next to several squatting Chinese people.

My anxiety and panic took over. I buried my head in my hands and raised my knees as support. My mind wandered to the possibility of being caught and the inevitable aftermath. I became tearful. I felt desperate. I stayed that way, frozen, for an hour.

But enough. Sitting frozen in a corner of an airport in a city I didn't want to be in was not going get me anywhere. I needed to start working on a solution.

It was early morning and the shops in the arrival hall were beginning to come to life. I asked the Chinese men sitting near me to watch my bag and I walked toward the exit. Arif's men were still there standing on the pavement. He was persistent – I had to give him that.

I returned to where I had been sitting and retrieved my bag. I thanked the old men and entered the washroom. At the sink I splashed cold water on my face. When I looked up, I saw the reflection of a young Arab man in the mirror. He looked striking in his long garment and headdress. We were alone. I turned and greeted the man. He smiled and asked me in Arabic if I was an Arab. I understood his question but responded in English: "No." He asked where I was from and I told him. He beamed and said that he had spent time in Iran before the war and he liked it very much.

I relaxed and asked him where I could buy a headdress like the one he was wearing. The man said he bought it in Saudi Arabia – his country; he didn't know where to buy one in Pakistan.

"I am looking for something exactly like that. Any chance I could buy yours?" I said, feeling somewhat shy.

He smiled.

"I have another one here in my luggage. I will be happy to give it to you, my brother. I cannot take money for it. I have many of them and now I am flying home so have no need for the extra."

"Thank you so much."

He opened his luggage on the counter and removed a red and white headdress and a band ring.

"For you, my new friend," he said.

I accepted it, reiterating my thanks. In his luggage the man also had a number of long Arab garments that caught my eye.

"You may regard my behaviour as too forward," I said, "but would you sell me one of your long garments? I would feel better while I am flying back home."

"I am a bit confused now," he answered, and I could see his brown furrow. "Why would you, an Iranian, want to wear them at all? By the way, they are called *dishdasha*."

"My best friend is an Iranian Arab from South Iran and he will be there to collect me from the airport. I would like to surprise him by wearing the traditional Arabic garment and headdress," I responded. I wondered briefly if I was getting a little too good at lying.

"The headdress is free – my gift to you – but you would need to pay for the garment."

I nodded. And I was about to pull out my money when he added, "Do you need anything else here before I close my luggage? I must say that I travel a lot, but I have never before experienced anything like this – becoming a clothing merchant in a washroom."

We exchanged another smile. I tried to make light of it by chuckling and nodding.

"Will fifty US dollars cover the cost of the *dishdasha*?" I tried to sound casual and confident.

"That will be fine," he said and handed over his white garment.

I went right into the toilet stall, changed clothes and put the headdress on. When I exited the stall, the Arab was gone.

I assessed my look in the mirror. I looked acceptable, but I still looked like me from the shoulders up. Anybody looking at my face would recognise me. I could not just walk out looking like that. I needed even more of a disguise. Lucky for me, the shops offered inspiration: trainers and inexpensive sunglasses – big sunglasses. The last step was ditching my bag; I removed the remaining money and discarded the bag in a waste bin.

Now, I was totally unencumbered; what I possessed was all I had.

I walked toward the exit wearing the long garment and sunglasses.

I was sure that I could not be distinguished from other Arabs wearing traditional clothes. But I wondered about my gait pattern: should I move in long strides, projecting confidence, or move slowly, taking in everything like a tourist?

My pace was somewhere in between. At the outset I felt confident. But the closer I got to the big glass wall with the exit doors, the more anxiety I felt. My mouth went dry and I found my breathing had become laboured. I started trembling. My nervous state was mostly hidden under my garments, but even so, my heart began beating wildly and I became almost lightheaded. None of that had been a part of my plan. *Plan?* What *plan?* I felt foolish in my new trainers and shades. This was no *plan.* With each stride I realised there was really very little plan to my plan.

I stopped and pretended to read a plaque on the wall; I needed to calm down. *Breathe, Benjamin, breathe.*

A small group of travellers approached, moving toward the exit. I worked myself in among them. They set a relatively slow pace.

Arif's men were just ahead, standing with arms crossed, one of them also wearing sunglasses and looking very mean. I covered the side of my face that would pass closest to them with the hanging part of my headdress and walked on with the group. As much as I wanted to, I didn't allow my eyes to wander in their direction. I passed not five yards in front of them. Outside, the members of the group went their separate ways. Since I had not been accosted, I let myself believe I just might have pulled it off.

At the kerb I stood with my back to the goons and hailed a taxi. Once inside I asked if the driver knew of a guesthouse run by an Iranian. He nodded and we pulled away. I sat back, thinking there was less chance of being seen in that position.

"Whew!" I released the sigh of my life.

A block into the trip, the driver qualified his nod and said, "More honestly, I know some affordable guesthouses in a nice area not far away from a shopping centre. They are frequented by Iranians."

I nodded. I had no other options.

We drove on for the better part of an hour. I figured he was taking me by the long, and more lucrative, route, and I did not mind: that might even work in my favour. I began to relax a bit.

The building was located on a street of two- and three-star hotels.

"The one I would recommend," the taxi driver said as he nodded and pulled to the kerb.

Again, I nodded — I didn't want my conversation to be memorable in case he was later questioned. I paid the fare, added an unremarkable tip, and entered the guesthouse. The daily rate was reasonable and I booked a mid-range room for one week. I was asked to show my ID. I used my Afghan passport, and it was accepted without any question. In the room I locked the door, opened a window, and fell exhausted onto the bed. I slept deeply and well, awaking sometime later, surprisingly refreshed.

The following day I walked to the nearby shopping centre and bought three shirts, underwear, a pair of jeans, a razor, hairbrush, shampoo and soap.

The room had an electric kettle to boil water. I bought tea and sugar, and also bread, biscuits, and cheese — so I wouldn't need to go outside to find meals. I figured I should not go out in the open any more than necessary.

Ben tries not to fidget. Frau Bosch doesn't look up. He wonders where she is in the pages he's provided this week — not very far in, he can see. He clears his throat but she does not budge. Not a move of her head, or a twitch of her hand. A small strand of hair flutters in the breeze and brushes her cheek, but she doesn't reach a hand up to swipe it away. She seems fully engrossed. He wonders if she'll say something soon — something about these sessions is becoming important to him. Her remarks, her observations. Their brief dialogue. Few words are ever actually exchanged, so he isn't sure why he feels this way.

He fidgets.

Karachi was a terribly crowded city, people filling the streets regardless of the time of the day. There was a large population of beggars sitting on the streets. Many of them grabbed at pedestrians' legs and arms as they passed by, asking for money. I had seen beggars before, but it was disturbing to see young children in rags working on the streets for coins. Heart-breaking.

A large part of the population chewed Paan, or betel leaf, mixed with tobacco — which meant the streets, pavements, and the sides of the buildings were stained red from all the necessary spitting. Paan is addictive, inducing a mild state of euphoria and other effects of a psycho-stimulant. Users start young. Even some young teenagers' teeth showed the tell-tale red stain. Any time of day, I saw people chewing and spitting.

There was a small café close by. I could access it through the alley behind my building. It was reportedly a place visited by smugglers who would transfer passengers like me to Europe and Canada. After several days I felt it was time to strike out on my own and try my luck with finding my own smuggler. Luck — now there's a word. Had I already used up my allotment? Was I pressing my luck to try this on my own?

Only one way to find out.

I decided to target Afghans and Iranians. I knew that Iranians living in Pakistan were often looking for someone to transfer them abroad and that Afghans had a corner on the smuggling market. No contact surfaced immediately. I became chummy with one of the night receptionists at the guesthouse. He was a few years older than I. One evening, after I had become comfortable with him, I indicated that I was looking for a smuggler who could get me a visa for Europe. He said that he could ask around for me.

The next evening, while I was making small talk with him, a young man approached me and joined the conversation. He asked me where I was from and what I was doing in Karachi. The man's name was Bashir and he was a former teacher turned property developer. He was putting up a new hotel just down the street. Bashir invited me to come see his project. I agreed, thinking it would be interesting to see the construction.

The next morning Bashir took me to the site. It would have a hundred rooms over six storeys and was designed like many high-end hotels. The project was financed by Bashir's father, who was a wealthy businessman. Bashir was the project manager and would later be the hotel manager.

After the tour, Bashir took me to a café.

"I heard you have been here in Pakistan for months and are looking for someone to send you abroad," he said. "But tell me: Why didn't you stay in your country? I think you have a beautiful country with a wonderful history. If I were you, I would have stayed there. Why do you want to go to Europe?"

"It's true, what you say about the beauty of my country," I said. "But there is not the kind of freedom there that I could have in a European country. The current situation in my country is disturbing and destabilised. There is an on-going war, and there are many militant opposition groups that want to overthrow the ruling party. Those factors prevent many people from living a peaceful life." I saw him nod slightly – as if he could perhaps relate. I continued. "I'd like to choose the way I want. I don't want to be told what to wear or what to say or that I must have a beard and how long it must be. I desire freedom for myself and respect other individuals' right to their freedom. I don't want to be unemployed or banned from studying in a university because I am not actively practising my religion or because I oppose some of the government's policies."

"If you are a Muslim, why don't you practise your religion?" Bashir asked.

"I was *born* Muslim – I was not given the option of choosing."

"What would you be if you were asked to choose?"

It wasn't that I hadn't thought about that before, but I had never really come to a conclusion.

"I am not sure," I replied honestly. "I've probably not put as much thought and effort into it as I should have. It just irritates me to be expected to accept what my parents and grandparents did without being offered a choice. And, if I don't follow in their footsteps, I will be punished by the establishment. It is something I can neither comprehend nor accept."

"If you could choose, would you want to be a Jew or a Christian or –"

"Why do I have to have a religion at all?" I responded – this was something I had thought about, even if I'd not completely arrived at all the answers. "Why can't I live in this world without religion? Do you really think that religion is the key to success? To happiness? To prosperity in this life?"

"I think the world's religions have helped people enrich their cultures and provide answers to some of the difficult questions in life that otherwise can't yet be answered. I think faith gives meaning to an individual's life. Having a being or entity with extraordinary power on one's side can comfort people emotionally and psychologically. It also has a positive impact on health and well-being. I think the benefits of being affiliated with a religion outweigh the down sides."

I listened, but took issue with some of his points.

"I don't think that religions provide the best answers to the big questions; to me, they seem to promote ignorance. Have you forgotten how many thousands — maybe millions — of people have lost their lives throughout history because of religion? Look at my country. It was occupied by Arabs for centuries and Iranians had no option but to convert to Islam if they wanted to live. A choice between converting and dying was really no choice at all. And then there were the Christian Crusades in the Middle Ages and the Spanish Inquisition a few centuries ago. All those monstrosities happened in the name of religion. One could say more atrocities have been committed under the name of religion than anything else."

Bashir offered a gentle rebuttal.

"I could name you some people in our century who killed millions and not in the name of religion. Think about Hitler from Germany, Stalin from the Soviet Union and Mao from China. Go and read what they did to mankind. Those men didn't belong to any religion. What I mean to say is evil people have always been around. Some wrap themselves in religion and use it as their excuse to commit their atrocities; some pretend no religious motivation and the others achieve their personal ends in the name of nationalism. I cannot say that religion *per se* is an evil thing. The way it is interpreted changes, based on the location, time, needs and the individual's knowledge."

"You might be right," I said. "But my basic question is why we cannot *choose* our religion ourselves. We cannot deny that different people have different tastes and needs, even if they live in the same geographical area. They should be allowed to practise a religion that meets their needs. They should be agnostic or atheist if that better satisfies them. I don't see any problem in that as long as they respect one another and reasonable government laws. I think the government in a country has to be secular — religion-neutral — so all people of all religious beliefs living in that country will be equal in the eyes of law. There should not be a religious group that is either privileged or disadvantaged by state law. Unfortunately, the current practice in many non-European countries is just the opposite. The leaders in some countries protect one religious majority and create unfavourable circumstances for minorities. When that happens, regrettably, people with different religions who had, for decades, a symbiotic and peaceful relationship are turned against each other."

"I agree with much of what you are saying, Ben. Inaugurating a single, sanctioned religion establishes privilege and forces division, which virtually requires religious influence on all aspects of society and even culture. Like you suggest, the only thing that really changed was the ruling party or the government that installed a state sanctioned religion. It certainly can be the reason for altercations between the faiths. In such environments, politicians become free to use religion as a most effective tool to manipulate the population. But I don't see *religion itself* as the problem. It is the people who do evil things under the name of religion. One needs to see those two things as separate."

It seemed we found common ground. I was glad the discussion took on the tone of mutual affirmation rather than confrontation. I loved — no, craved — that kind of give and take — where dialogues remained at an intellectual level without degenerating to the irrational emotional level.

"I wish all people would think the way you do, but my experience shows me otherwise. During the past months I have met men — too many — who use religion to justify their despicable actions.

Since I have been in this country, I have often been asked about my religion, as if that needs to be settled upfront — as if it defines me. Then they seem dumbfounded when they hear I don't practise it. My insistence for intellectual control seems fully inconceivable to them. I certainly don't think I am a lesser human being because of it. I do understand I am nearly alone in that contention, however."

Bashir seemed to be listening with interest so I went on.

"One's values and moral centre do not have to grow out of religion. In fact, by mindlessly accepting those from a religion, one abdicates all personal responsibility. If I do as my religion tells me to do, I am a good person — but that's too easy. It's a get-out-of-jail free card, is it not? You can do no wrong, as long as you do whatever you are doing with God in the supporting role."

I thought back to so many of the men I'd tangled with in recent months. Unlike some of the so-called religious men I'd been forced to deal with, I hardly drank alcohol since I didn't like its taste and, more importantly, I didn't want to lose control. I didn't inflict hurt, and I didn't steal. Unlike some of these individuals, I didn't keep youngsters as slaves; I didn't abuse children sexually; I didn't distribute drugs. The men I'd come to associate did all that — and all in the name of their so-called faith. These amoral, unlawful and unethical men. These men, who presented a verse from the Quran or a Hadith as support for their actions — even if their actions defy logic, the wisdom of the ages or common decency. And if anyone could convince them, even slightly, that their actions were possibly wrong, or even inappropriate, there was always *towbah* — repentance. They would be forgiven.

"I personally cannot understand," I said, "that you can do any despicable thing you want and then be forgiven easily by God, just because you are a Muslim. That irritates me immensely. I find it impossible to comprehend."

"All religions have built-in ways so mortals can control their gods," Bashir responded. "I understand your frustrations, and I wish there were ways to educate mankind about the true religion so they don't use their unenlightened, layman's interpretation of the holy books."

I balked at the idea of 'true religion'. "But it is the interpretation that is the problem. Don't you think that following a few basic values suffices to be a good human being? Values that serve positive social function, regardless of religion? If one could create a universal or hybrid religion, a religion that teaches those basic human values shared by all religions, don't you think we would be better off?"

"What I think," he offered, "is that there are more than enough religions around. You don't really want to add one more to it! We need to encourage people to use correctly what they have. Religion is as old as mankind's need to create it and it cannot be removed from society. It doesn't matter where you go, you will find out that religion plays an integral role in many people's lives. I went to the USA a few years ago and could not believe that so many Americans are religious and attend church regularly. It doesn't fit their image on the world stage. I went to Germany last year to visit my cousin in Munich. I've learned that the church or religious organisation owns many hospitals, personal care homes, apartment buildings and companies. I think the church is one of the biggest employers in Germany. Members have to pay annual church tax that cannot be avoided as long as the person belongs to that church. The thing that amazed me most was that church bells sound early in the morning on Sundays – no one living nearby could sleep in. My point is that religion is just a tool and it cuts both ways. Imagine a knife; you can peel an apple with it to give to a hungry person or you can use it as a weapon and kill an innocent person. No sound person would consider a knife as an innately evil tool."

"I can see that we could talk about this topic for hours and still not reach agreement."

"Hours?" he said, chuckling. "People have not succeeded in answering some of these questions after *millennia* of discussion."

It was time to shift topics.

"You mentioned Germany," I said. "I need to find someone who can provide me with a visa to Germany or Canada. I have money to pay. Do you know someone competent – and trustworthy?"

"Do you mean an authentic visa?"

"Yes, if possible. I'd rather not settle for a fake, but understand I may have to."

"I will see what I can do, but I suspect it is not easy to obtain an authentic visa from a consulate here. It will be more difficult for you because you are not a Pakistani. I'm afraid you will be told you must apply in your own country."

Could I trust Bashir with my secret? Did our religious debate create enough common ground to share my illegally obtained ID? "I have an Afghan passport," I said. "An original, issued for me by the consulate here in Karachi. Which means for this purpose my nationality is Afghan."

He nodded – a positive sign. "That might work since most foreign embassies in Afghanistan have been closed down because of the war. In that case you should be able to apply for a visa in Pakistan. Why don't you go yourself with your passport and ask for a visa?"

"I fear they will reject my application and put a stamp of refusal in my passport. Then things would be very bad, you see."

"Don't give up on your hope, my young friend."

I thanked Bashir for the fine time and returned to the guesthouse. I extended my reservation, week by week. Over the next few weeks I continued researching how to obtain a legal visa from one of the west European embassies. I came up empty, and Bashir did not contact me.

My frustration increased. I became more depressed with each passing day. I could not sleep at night, I lost my appetite. I stopped shaving my facial hair and did not leave my room for days at a time. I occasionally phoned my parents to tell them I was doing fine.

Lying seemed to be getting far too easy.

On one occasion when my money had nearly run out, I called my maternal uncle in Germany and asked him whether he could send me an invitation to visit him in Germany. I was hoping if he sent it to the German embassy in Pakistan, I might be issued a time-limited visa like the one to Greece. He didn't think it would work, but did send me 1,500 US dollars.

One afternoon, Bashir came to the guesthouse with a man named Farooq: tall, fiftyish, with a big belly and a face pocked with acne scars. He did not make a positive impression on me, but I have learned not to judge a book by its cover.

Farooq, it turned out, was a secret police officer. Someone, that is, who might be able to help me with a visa. Bashir said he could vouch for the man, but that he had to be left out of things regardless of what I decided or what happened. He said I should listen carefully to Farooq's proposals and make up my own mind

I agreed, of course. Bashir subsequently left us alone. The notion that I was talking with a member of the secret police was unnerving. After dealing with so many untrustworthy individuals, this was, in a way, taking it a step further. At least those characters were admittedly unsavoury. Here was a man of the law but who dealt as part of his profession, and with no doubt impunity, in lies. What if he were there to trap me?

My options had run dry, however, so I listened. We sat in a corner and spoke in voices just above a whisper.

"Am I correct that you want to go to Germany or Canada and you need a visa?" Farooq asked.

I explained the way I obtained my Afghan passport and about the trip to Athens – minus its illegal, drug-related aspects.

"What did you take to Athens?"

"Just two rugs."

"How much heroin was inside the rugs?"

I hadn't seen that coming.

"Heroin? I took two rugs. Where are you coming from – heroin in rugs?"

Farooq laughed.

"You are good, I will say that, young man. Of course, there was heroin in the rugs; otherwise the story would not add up."

"I am not aware of that so I cannot verify what you are saying, but what I could see in the luggage were rugs."

Farooq raised his eyebrows and continued.

"Never mind. How much did you get for taking the rugs to Greece?"

"I didn't receive any money at all." I decided to continue with my story, sounding the innocent. This man was police, after all. "This may sound unbelievable, but the truth is, I was sold to one of the people involved by my former trafficker and was required to take the rugs to Athens in order to pay my debt to my owner. It was my only alternative to a life of servitude. I was naive and that was my only crime."

"Did they just let you go after you returned to Karachi?"

"Of course not. I had to escape from them and assume I must still consider myself on the run, so to speak. I don't like to talk about it now as it aggravates my soul and makes my blood boil."

"Why didn't you stay in Athens and escape from there? I am sure you were better off there than here."

"Greece seems to have a very good system for detecting such things. They deport illegals with virtually no legal process. I feared I risked being pegged as Iranian and being deported back there. That would put an end to my dreams."

He seemed convinced. "I will check with my friends and will see what I can do for you," he said. "But it will cost you a lot."

"How much is 'a lot'?"

"In the neighbourhood of three to four thousand US dollars."

I gulped.

"Really, why so much? The ticket would cost no more than a few hundred US dollars. Are you saying the middleman requires that much money?"

"Yes. You seem to understand the system."

"I should understand it. I've been a part of it for too long already. Can you tell me the general plan? I don't have the money with me and will need to have it transferred to me. I need to be able to make a very good case to my father or uncle. I have already spent a great deal of my father's money. And I'm still sitting here with no prospects for entering Europe."

"Give me a few days and I will come back and update you," Farooq said.

"Thanks. Okay. You know where I will be."

Part of me felt my spirits lift. Part of me had become cynical, and that part of me remained pessimistic about ever leaving Pakistan. And where would I get more money if my father said no? Perhaps I should try for a job. Sure, me get a job, with no saleable skills in a land with a hundred labourers for every available position.

The psychologist places the pages on her desk and leans back in her chair.

"It is always difficult to know how to respond to your story. It is clear that this criminal world was not your world – that the criminal acts you performed were not of your choosing. I am moved by how much you endured just to survive."

She pauses. Ben shifts on the leather chair. A wasp is caught in the corner of the window and crashes repeatedly against the pane.

"What I am learning is overwhelming and disturbing beyond most anything that has ever come to my attention. You have managed to come back from the edge of death time and time again. As horrific as that is – was – I hope you understand what a tremendous feat this is. That you are even here to tell the tale. Well. Ben... My motherly inclination is to feel sorry for you, and part of me does. But look at you: debating religion on philosophical grounds, lying – well, trying – to the secret police. You seem to have grown strong from the experiences. I'm not sure any of these things can be taught. You learned a life's worth of lessons that most people never do, in ways that no other experiences could provide."

"My grandpa once told me that the first time I got my hand burned by reaching into a fire to retrieve a stick I said, through my sobbing: 'No more fire ouchies.' And there never have been. I have said it before: 'What was was. What is yet to come is yet to come.' I don't dwell on past difficulties."

"Yes, but there's a reason you've been asked to recount all of this for me."

"Of course. I understand that, too. I'm just saying, I learn from those difficulties and I work hard to resist being frightened by what the future may hold."

"Ah, yes. And that answers a question I have been wondering – How do you manage to keep writing about these horrific episodes in your life?"

Ben manages a weak smile and a shrug. "My little black box seems to have an infinite capacity to expand as necessary."

The psychologist returns smile for smile. She understands nobody could just pack that much agony away – one either dealt with it in the light of day or lived out his life in the dark shroud of madness.

CHAPTER TWELVE

DOWN THE RABBIT HOLE

Ben and Frau Bosch arrive at the office door at the same moment. She turns the knob, pushes the door open, and motions for Ben to follow her inside.

Ben speaks first, removing his pages from his folder.

"I haven't thanked you for the opportunity you are giving me, so, thank you."

"Opportunity? We have not really even begun your therapy."

"Yes, but for me, this is an opportunity I'd not really imagined. To organise and evaluate my past by writing about it. To understand it. The therapy *has* begun. I know that now. I fully approve of the method you have wisely selected for me," Ben responded.

"As I recall, it was you who selected the method."

Ben smiled, suddenly realising she was right.

She made ready at her desk. He'd come to know the characteristic signs: her cup of coffee arranged just to the left of his papers, her pushing her heels to the side, so she sat – comfortably, he presumed – with her feet flat on the ground.

He really didn't know her, but he trusted her and approved of her and, perhaps, even liked her.

Days dragged on and Farooq did not contact me. My existence had become one long, continuous, tedious, boring, life-consuming wait. It was frustrating and often discouraging. Every day I expected Farooq to knock at my door with news about the plan. Ten days passed; twelve, thirteen.

On the fourteenth day he returned. We talked in my room.

"I am sorry I could not come earlier," he said. "It took this long for me to do a thorough market research on getting the European visa – plus other means of illegal departure from Karachi. I have learned a lot."

"What is the upshot? Have you learned anything useful for me?" I was eager to know exactly what would happen next.

"I have been unable to get you a genuine visa for Germany or Canada. It is your age: too many youngsters your age are seeking the very same thing you are. They are afraid you will arrive in their country, disappear, and stay illegally. What I can do is ask for a fake visa for Germany in your name."

"I don't understand what you mean by a *fake* visa. Do you mean it is a genuine visa stolen from the embassy and my name is written on it, or the visa itself is a fake, like counterfeit money?"

"The visa sticker is a fake – like you said, like counterfeit money. It is not issued by the German government, but is manufactured by a forger here in Pakistan. We will write your name and date of birth on the visa and stick it to your passport."

"How much would it cost? Surely the fake visa cannot be expensive to make." My mind was already racing ahead two or three steps. "And what about the check-in counter at the airport in Karachi? Would they not be able to detect a counterfeit visa to Germany?"

"That is the sticking point. We need to buy the airport too," Farooq said.

"What does it mean – *buy* the airport?"

"We would need to bribe the check-in counter and also the officer who carries out the border control – the one who checks your passport and puts the departure stamp on it."

"How can that be done? It sounds impossible to bribe so many people at the airport. Some people are not bribable, I suspect, and approaching one of them would certainly compound the problem."

"Here in my country you can buy almost everyone; it is only a question of price."

"Is there no other way to leave the country?"

"Yes, you could be employed on a freighter and travel by sea."

"How does that work?" Perhaps the sea would be an easier route. I'd had enough of dodging people in airports.

"You could be employed as a deck boy on a freighter. For that you can get a special visa through the shipping company. In that case, you go where the freighter goes. You eventually jump ship when you get where you want to be. The other way is that you are employed as a *workaway*, someone who works on a freighter for his passage and does not earn any salary. You travel by freighter, and it will take much longer than by plane. I personally would not recommend it. Living conditions for the crew are typically crowded and substandard. Also, a young man your age could be abused on a freighter of the type that would take you with no experience."

I felt his eyes on me. He seemed to look right through me.

"You are not the kind of person for either of those jobs," he said with finality. "I don't recommend that you consider either one."

"Where does that leave me? What would you suggest, now?" I felt a bit desperate. My options did not seem to have broadened after his period of research.

"I could use my airport connection to find one person at the check-in desk and one officer at the border check who would do the job for payment. It may take a while, but I will eventually find the correct people for the jobs. I will need 500 US dollars to cover my costs."

I delivered one of my sighs. I'm not sure what message they conveyed to others. To me they represented my helplessness in the presence of what might be an attempt to con me.

"I hope I will see you again after today," I said, looking him directly in his eyes.

"I will not trick you," Farooq said with a smile.

I had heard that before.

"When do you think you will be back?" I asked.

"I cannot tell you, but hopefully soon. I do have my regular life and job to attend to, you understand."

It was good to hear that. I had not thought about him in that way. Still, I had to wonder about his *regular* job.

"Is there any way for me to contact you?"

"No. Contact between us is always risky — even here, now. I will contact you when arrangements have been made and the time has come."

"It is frustrating not to know when I will hear. It really leaves me in limbo. I once read about a psychological experiment with rats in which nothing in their lives was predictable. They still had food and water and time to sleep and exercise, but it was different every day. They soon found a corner and died. If I don't answer the door when you come back, search the corners."

Farooq looked at me as if I were insane. At least that's how it felt. I was relieved when he said, "Here is what I can do. I will meet with you in one week and update you – if I have not already contacted you. Will that help?"

"Immensely!"

Six days passed. I heard nothing from Farooq.

On the seventh day, he materialised as promised in the guesthouse. He needed more time, but he seemed to believe the following week would produce the desired results. I felt somewhat better. Having sensed my boredom, he had brought me several books to help occupy my time – a kind gesture, to be sure.

Out of My Life and Thought by Albert Schweitzer: my reading material for the next few days. It was published before the Second World War. Farooq had put some thought into selecting this book for me. I appreciated that.

A few days later Farooq arrived with a German visa sticker.

"This sticker is your German visa. We will need to place it onto your passport and write your name and passport number on it. I still need to find one German embassy stamp to place next to your visa." He seemed as if he did this every week. Until he added, "What do you think about the visa?"

"It is a counterfeit visa and it looks fake," I said. I could not admit to being very impressed. "Even a child could tell it isn't real. I certainly expected better. Do you really think something this sloppy can take me through the airport in Karachi?"

"The visa is not important," he said, waving his hand dismissively. "The people at the airport are the essential part of this enterprise."

"If what you are saying is true, why do I need a visa at all?" *And why did he bother asking me what I thought of it?* "I could just enter the airport with my passport and go to the guy you bribed at the check-in counter and on to the border control officer who will also be expecting me."

"Hypothetically you are correct, but others may unintentionally glance at it so you need to have what will look enough like it for just a second to not raise suspicion. We cannot risk sending you there without it."

I supposed it made sense.

"What about the flight ticket? When are you going to buy the ticket?" I asked.

"I am going to buy it soon. You should be in the air within two or so weeks."

I studied the visa sticker again.

"I am sorry, Farooq, but I can't accept that visa. It is terrible. When I pay for a counterfeit I expect that implies a certain *quality* – and this certainly does not have that quality."

That time *he* sighed. I could tell he knew I was right.

"Alright. I will ask around some more, but you must understand there are not many people trading with fake visas for Germany."

"I suppose I must believe you, but this is Pakistan. I have learned that anything is available on most any street corner here."

"Like I said, I will give it one more try."

"Thank you. See what you can find, please. I suppose in a pinch I'll have to try this one. What's the sentence for using a fake visa?"

Farooq smiled. "Probably nothing. Court officials are easier to bribe than airport clerks. And speaking of that: I will need money to buy the ticket and also to bribe the people at the airport. You need to ask your parents or relatives for some money soon."

"I'm sure you will negotiate for the lowest 'bribes' possible."

It sounded ridiculous.

"I will do my best. You just make sure the money is available by the end of next week."

The following day I telephoned my uncle in Germany again and had a long conversation with him. He was a textile engineer and explained that he did not know much about smuggling humans to other countries. He hoped I would investigate all the available options and use my common sense. My uncle kindly agreed to transfer 2,000 US dollars to me through a Pakistani friend and, sounding very much like all my uncles, asked me not to waste the money.

I was able to hand a total of 3,000 US dollars to Farooq for the visa, flight tickets and other expenses.

"I am giving you a lot of money now," I said as I counted it out. "I hope you don't mess up because I cannot get any more money from my relatives."

"Insha'Allah, you will be in Germany next week. You need to be ready each afternoon next week at five o'clock. One afternoon I will pick you up."

"I don't understand. The flight must have a date if you buy a ticket, right? So you should be able to tell me the date in advance."

"The flight ticket has a date, as you say, but the date is also flexible so we can bring it forward if we want. We need to find a golden opportunity for your transfer at the airport."

"How will you know when the condition is most favourable for my flight?"

"My middlemen at the airport will keep me updated." He made to leave. "Remember, you need to be ready next Monday evening at five o'clock."

"I will certainly be ready."

Later I spoke to Bashir about Farooq's plan. He had nothing of any importance to tell me. Either I trusted Farooq or I dropped him; it seemed that simple to Bashir. Easy for him to say. His entire future was not dependent on the unknown skills of a near stranger. But I understood his reluctance to offer opinions. It was not his line of work.

"I have to tell you my honest feeling about Farooq," I said. "Something inside me tells me that his plan won't work. This sort of operation demands precision, and he doesn't seem to be a very 'precise' type. I've had that sort of feeling before."

"Was it confirmed, this feeling before?" Bashir asked.

"Yes. I didn't have a good feeling about the man who brought me to Pakistan – and he turned out to be an incompetent, greedy liar for starters. And he ended up selling me into slavery."

"Somewhere I heard an expression that seems to fit your situation, now. *Hope for the best and prepare for the worst.* If you expect failure and disappointment in your mind, you will experience them."

I had heard that one before – and I wasn't at all convinced by Bashir's philosophy lesson. My thoughts couldn't control any outcome – that was certain. The outcome here was in the hands of other people. But I didn't contest his point; I kept my pessimism to myself.

"You can count on me if you need any support," Bashir said – which was a welcome boost of positivity. "Whatever you say remains confidential. I won't share this with Farooq."

"I really appreciate that."

Without Farooq, I had nothing – so I let my doubts slide and made steps toward departure. I operated all week in what could vaguely be called a sense of cautious optimism. Come Monday, I prepared for my flight just like Farooq had asked me to do.

And then I waited all day. The longer I waited the more impatient I became.

He eventually arrived at eleven o'clock.

"The airport was very tight tonight," he said with urgency. "We could not risk sending you. We need to postpone things to another night."

I was crestfallen. "Why didn't you call the guesthouse and inform me about cancelling the trip?"

"I would never use the hotel phone for this kind of confidential communication. Come now. Use your head." He sounded irritable and spoke as if he was talking to an imbecile.

"Okay. So what is the plan now?"

"We are going to try it again this coming Friday and we hope that the conditions are more in our favour."

"And if not?"

"We have to wait for another day. Understand all of this precaution is for your protection and the success of your transfer," he said irritably. "I thought you were a smart boy. Stop asking me unintelligent questions."

I should have been pleased he was being so cautious. His role was to make it safe. Mine was to wait. I understood that. But something nagged. I had the unsettling feeling that Farooq's behaviour had changed since receiving the money. Why was he so brusque? Did he not understand my obvious concerns?

Snap out of it, Ben. I tamped down my feelings. I breathed. I needed to stop weighing up every word I heard. I needed to stop second-guessing the man who was trying to help me.

I picked up *Out of My Life and Thought* and started over from the beginning again. I fell asleep while trying to memorise *'Impart as much as you can of your spiritual being to those who are on the road with you, and accept as something precious what comes back to you from them.'*

"Get your luggage. Today's the day."

It was Friday, and Farooq was in a hurry.

"Do not check out of the guesthouse. I will take care of that once your journey has been safely completed. We will leave through the back door so your luggage case doesn't make anyone suspicious. You will be landing in Frankfurt, Germany."

"I would like to see the ticket before we leave," I asked.

"It is with my middleman at the airport."

I felt akin to that chunk of driftwood.

Farooq left through the back of the guesthouse, and I bobbed along behind.

We took a taxi to the airport. As usual the road there was crowded. The trip seemed to take forever. We arrived at about 7 pm for my 10 pm flight. Farooq asked me to stay in the departure hall and wait for him to return. He would consult his inside people one more time.

I waited.

I waited two hours.

Finally, Farooq approached from across the hall. "My middleman thinks we should forget the flight tonight because there are many inspectors and security policemen here doing random checks on passengers. They may have been alerted to some bigger problem," Farooq explained.

"Why didn't he tell you before?!" I nearly shouted. "He must have known earlier!"

"He initially thought the obstacles could be surmounted, but changed his opinion over the past two hours."

"Can I have a look at the ticket now?"

"He still has the ticket – and your passport. It appears you don't believe me that you have a ticket for tonight. You have no trust in me, Ben?"

"If I could see the ticket, I would be calmer and less frustrated. You have to know nothing you've done so far has filled me with confidence."

He looked tired, but repeated simply, "You can believe me that you have a ticket for the ten o'clock flight, but it is just not safe for you to go through the process."

"What is the next date your middleman has set?" I asked.

"He has no way of knowing until the time draws near. Sometime next week, I am sure."

"So, I'm going back to the guesthouse now?"

"Yes, and be ready and wait for me on Monday afternoon."

I took a taxi by myself. During the ride I did my best to convince myself to see the glass half full. In terms of the big picture, I had never been so close to a flight to my destination in all these past months. I was close. That buoyed up my spirits a bit.

Two days later Bashir visited me at the guesthouse.

"I came to check to make sure you were still here. I hoped you might have been able to leave for Europe."

"I was very close last Friday, but I had to leave the airport and return here due to tight security checks."

"God did not want you to leave here before gaining more experience, I think," Bashir said with a smile.

"If you have a direct line to God, please ask him when I will leave this country."

"He would say whenever the time is right you will fly away from here."

"Perhaps there is a big check mark on God's calendar with my initials on it for one day next week," I said.

We both smiled.

Monday, I waited up until midnight. No sign of Farooq. I told myself not to be disappointed and went to bed. He didn't appear on Tuesday either, but on Wednesday evening he came to explain his inattentiveness – a sick relative and a business matter.

He did say we'd try again.

"My connection at the airport thinks we will be able to finalise the flight to Frankfurt next Monday since all members of his group will be present at the airport so he can have all bases covered."

"This appears to be very good news, *again*," I said. "I am looking forward to it you know."

"I know. I am really sorry about the long delay."

On the following Monday evening Farooq arrived at the guesthouse and took me to the airport. I had been living out of my luggage, but had done a hand washing that morning so I was ready. Like before, we arrived at the airport about 7 pm and the flight was scheduled for 10 pm.

He asked me again to wait for him in a corner. He returned in less than thirty minutes. He removed my passport and a ticket from his pocket and handed them to me. My hands were shaking as I took them.

We walked as we talked – things were happening fast now. "My middleman had to leave the airport unexpectedly," Farooq said quickly. "But you shouldn't be worried as things look satisfactory tonight. You should go to that check-in counter on the right-hand side –" he indicated with a quick nod of his head, "– and get your boarding card first. The clerk is ours. Once you have completed that, come back to me and I will tell you which border control officer should look at your passport."

It took fifteen minutes to reach the counter. When I approached, the man asked me for my passport and ticket. I handed them across the counter to him.

"Do you have any other luggage to check or is it just this one?"

"Just this small luggage and my handbag."

"You are travelling very light."

"Yes, my older brother lives in Frankfurt and whenever we get together he always buys me clothes. I guess you could say he tries to make up for the way he ignored me when I was young."

My little story produced the slightest smile from the clerk.

"Have you been to Germany before?"

"No, this is my first time. It's why I'm so excited, in case you noticed."

Calm down, Benjamin. Don't over-explain yourself!

The agent held the passport up against the ceiling light and looked at the page where the German visa was attached.

He's being awfully thorough – more thorough than Farooq said they'd be.

My palms began to sweat. This man wasn't acting like he had been bribed, not at all. Had I gone to the wrong counter?

The agent turned through the passport pages and looked at each of them against the light. He asked me if I obtained my visa myself from the German consulate or if someone else had got it for me.

I did not know how to answer the question so I tried to buy time.

"You are confusing me, Sir. The fact is that I have the visa and it seems to be irrelevant if I got it myself or through a travel agency."

"Your visa does not look similar to the other German visas I have seen here tonight. I think your visa may be a counterfeit and, therefore, I would like to know if you went to the consulate physically and received the visa. I need to know if you can verify the authenticity of the German visa."

"Oh." Gulp. "I see." Breathe. "Yes, I received the visa from the consulate myself. I think the date is on the visa, isn't it? Why would the consulate provide me with anything but a genuine visa? I really do not understand how that could be."

"Please wait here one minute," the ticket agent said.

My inclination was to start running and not stop until I was back in my room in my parents' house, but I stood trying to appear unruffled and patient.

A few minutes later the airline agent returned with a soldier who was holding my passport and ticket in his hand. The soldier asked me to follow him, and he escorted me to a room on the other side of the airport. I looked around for Farooq — Was he watching? Could he see what was happening? He was nowhere to be seen. My heart was pounding. I had the feeling that things were falling apart fast.

The soldier led me to a small, empty room and asked me to sit on a chair. He phoned someone, speaking in Urdu.

Two more officers joined the party, an older one and a younger one. The younger man took my passport from the guard and examined it carefully. Then, he looked at my ticket. He passed them on to the older officer. Without saying a word, the older man stepped toward me and slapped me across the face so hard I came close to falling off the chair. He then cursed at me in Urdu. I hardly understood.

"Tell me where you got the fake visa, you parasite," the old man demanded while swearing at me.

I worked to maintain my balance on the chair.

"You could have asked me without slapping me on the face."

A bad way to begin — I could see that as soon as I'd said the words. But, so long as I had already begun in that vein I continued, "You must feel like a big man, hitting someone half your size while he sits in a chair fully defenceless."

I braced myself for a second slap. Instead, I received a hard fist to my upper arm.

I tried to stand. He put his hand on my shoulder and forced me back onto the chair. Why did I insist on doing such foolish things?

My arm hurt like hell, but I didn't let on. The man pinched my chin in his hand. It felt like I was in a vice.

"If you don't tell us who gave you this visa, we will beat you to death. So, now, once again: who gave you the visa, you Afghan dirt?"

"I met an Afghan man in Karachi about two weeks ago. He offered me what he said was an authentic German visa for 500 US dollars and I took it. He told me the visa was original and he received it from his friend in the German consulate. I don't know who this man is, but if you go to the Holiday Inn lobby you will probably see him. That is like his office, you could say. He didn't give me a name. That is the truth, and I don't know what else to say." I was probably talking too much. Liars always do. "He was a tall man with a scar on his right cheek. He was balding – a very high forehead. He usually wore a suit with a tie."

The officer spat on me. I wanted to throw up.

"You Afghans are like parasites; you have ruined our country with your drugs and fake this and fake that."

The tall officer was about to punch my arm again when he was stopped by the younger officer. So he started interrogating.

"It is in your interest to cooperate with us and give correct answers to our questions. Now, once again: are you sure you don't know the visa man?"

"I know him by sight and I can show him to you if I see him, but, of course, I don't know his real name. An acquaintance once called him Hassan, but I doubt if that was his real name."

A serious situation had just become desperate.

The older officer approached me unexpectedly and kicked my left calf with his right shoe and instructed the soldier to take me to the local jail.

I played my 'poor little orphan boy' card.

"Surely you can forgive a parasite like me for such a silly decision. I am not very bright and I was just trying to get to another country – out of your hair, so to speak. Can't you overlook it this one time? I will leave Karachi this very night if you want."

The officer looked angry and said he didn't have any mercy for an animal like me. Said we all needed to be eradicated. He instructed the young soldier to put handcuffs on my wrists. The officers left the room and another soldier entered a few minutes later.

To say I was terrified is an understatement. *I was going to jail in Pakistan.*

Two soldiers accompanied me to a small police car in their parking lot. We drove for ten minutes. We arrived at the police station and the soldiers pushed and shoved me toward an officer sitting at a small desk. He had more stripes on his shoulder than the others. He was eating a sandwich.

The soldiers talked in Urdu and handed him my passport and ticket. Then they left.

The officer looked at me for some time. He looked at my passport, but only briefly. He continued eating, but spoke in a reasonable tone.

"Where are you from?"

"Afghanistan."

"Where did you want to go?"

"Germany."

"Why?"

"I have relatives in Germany and wanted to go there and live with them. No offence, but Pakistan has not been very kind to me."

He raised one eyebrow.

"Why didn't you get a genuine visa?"

"I thought I had. I thought it was an authentic visa."

"You get a proper visa from the embassy and not from a man on the street. Maybe you should remember it for your next trip. This visa in your passport is really a terrible forgery. It was not a good job. Let me show you a real good work of art."

The officer opened his drawer and removed a passport, apparently with a fake visa. It was from one of the countries in eastern Asia. It was a stamp on a page of the passport. He pointed to it.

"Now, this is a good fake visa. Very difficult to distinguish it from a genuine visa."

I didn't understand what was going on. Why was he showing me better fakes?

"But that man was arrested, too?" I asked.

"Not for this visa, but for something else – and we then found out his visa was forged. Do you know anyone who can put up bail for you?"

"No, I'm alone in the world and don't have anyone. What happens now, Sir?"

"Without any relatives or friends here, things can get a bit difficult. You will be going to jail in the adjacent building, and you will stay there until you go to court. A judge will sentence you for your crime, and you will eventually end up in prison. Didn't you know that before going to the airport last night?"

I was shaking, but I tried to remain calm and repeated my story. "Like I said, I thought it was real, second-hand maybe, but real. I didn't know I would be arrested and beaten. How long is the prison sentence for this offence?"

"Beaten? You were beaten?"

"Yes, by an officer before coming to you. He slapped me around, kicked me and hit me in my shoulder."

"A few slaps or kicks would not kill anyone. You've heard that what does not kill you makes you stronger, right?"

"With all due respect, I don't think it is appropriate for law enforcement to beat up an individual in the twentieth century," I said.

"You must have annoyed and insulted the officer by your action and he may have overreacted. You should not forget that you had a fake visa and committed an offence. That officer was not dealing with an innocent person."

"I don't deny my crime, but the officer should not have taken it personally. He kept referring to me as an Afghan parasite. I cannot understand how an educated and rational person could become so aggressive, abusive and physical towards an individual he didn't even know. I imagine he treats all Afghans that same way. There is nothing right or just about that. I didn't harm anyone and didn't bring any suffering to any human being here. That came at the hands of the officer. I just wanted to leave this country since I don't belong here for obvious reasons."

Surprisingly, the officer had let me get all that out. I was feeling emboldened, slightly.

But then he said, "Don't play the innocent man, now. You are lucky that you were just slapped."

"I suppose so, since he threatened to kill me right there and then – for being Afghan, I surmised, not for the visa crime. It seems fully unjust to judge a man by his country of birth or religion or skin colour."

"We are human, and we judge people through our human eyes." He had an answer for everything, this one. That's why they gave him the office for eating sandwiches. "Those things you list are important. I am not inclined to continue this discussion. You should be more concerned about your current predicament than lecturing me on social issues, young man."

"I believe those issues are far more important than the situation of one poor Afghan boy. Excuse me for that. I have often been called strong-minded and I tend to speak my thoughts." I figured I could not make my situation any worse so I decided to talk about practical matters, too. "Could you tell me what my punishment will be?"

"I am not a judge, but I think it is about six to nine months and you will probably get fined, too."

"Do I have to hire a lawyer?"

"Lawyers will be provided for you once you are in custody."

The officer asked me to follow him to the jail in the police station – the one in the adjacent building. He said I would be transferred to a more substantial jail in a few hours. He handed me over to the guard who was in charge there. He took my small suitcase and hand baggage. I was offered no receipt. I was ushered into a tiny cell where my handcuffs were removed. The cell was tiny – about nine square yards. There were already six other men, all lying on the concrete floor. Some of them were asleep and didn't rouse at my entry. I sat in a corner and leaned back against the wall. It felt dreadfully familiar.

Despite my exhaustion, I did not feel like sleeping. I looked at the dirty walls and floor and at the other dishevelled prisoners. It was Dalbandin all over again. The old feelings surfaced: I'd been abandoned and left for the dogs again. Farooq – where was Farooq? I wondered if he would raise a finger to get me released.

One of the men who had been looking me over since I arrived spoke to me in Urdu. I let it go by. Then he tried English.

"Why are you here? What did you do?"

"Nothing important."

I didn't want to talk to anyone and looked away. The man persisted in a more demanding voice.

"I want to know what you did."

I stood up, walked to him and leaned in toward him, as if to speak confidentially.

"I strangled my roommate with my bare hands tonight because he messed with my girlfriend."

The man scooted away. I sat down, closed my eyes and pretended to be sleeping. There were no more questions. Over the months since Dalbandin, I had decided that if I were ever imprisoned again, I would not present

241

myself as weak and frightened, but I would take it to anybody who looked cross-eyed at me. So far, it seemed to be working.

Around noon a prison van took all of us to the bigger jail. My small suitcase and handbag were returned to me, but once we arrived at the new place I had to hand over them along with my other personal belongings – my belt and about 500 US dollars that I had left. I was taken to a tract consisting of four cells. There were no doors on them and the inmates could move freely from one to another. There were eight of us, and we were asked to select a home cell. They all looked alike to me. The others rushed to establish squatter's rights. I could have cared less so entered the one at the far end. It held the fewest men. There were no beds, covers or chairs. The floor was bare. The toilets were awful. There was no soap or provision for washing.

I shared a cell with seven others, two of them foreigners, one from China and the other from India. The Indian man was the only one of them who spoke fluent English. The Chinese prisoner knew some basic English words, but it was a challenge to converse with him. I sat next to the Indian who was gaunt and about fifty years old. The other inmates in the cell spoke Urdu. The prisoners roamed from cell to cell reacquainting themselves with old friends.

The living condition in the jail was deplorable, and the food was awful. We were served three meals a day, always stew and always provided in a large pot. We were provided a bowl and spoon, which were returned each time. They often came to us unwashed from the previous meal.

I figured I would die from a terrible disease before I would finish my sentence.

Several lawyers arrived just after noon. I was told to talk to one. The lawyer was a young man – thirty, perhaps. He asked me questions about my arrest and my counterfeit visa. He said the case would be brought to the court and I would have to appear in person.

"What will be the sentence for me, according to your experience?"

"You will stay in prison for two to six weeks and pay a fine before your release. It is not that horrible."

"Two to six weeks in this hell hole sounds like two to six years."

"We cannot change that. If you have friends and relatives they could bribe the guards and smuggle you some food and cigarettes from outside."

"And the other guys in here will just sit back and let me keep the good stuff for myself? I don't think so. Anyway, I don't have anyone. It is not only the food that is horrible – there is nothing to sleep on here: no mattress, no blanket and no sheet."

"This is a short-term jail so you will not be offered the luxury items you mentioned," the lawyer said with a smile. Yes, he actually smiled.

"Is there any way to be released from here earlier?"

"If you know very influential politicians here, they could accelerate the whole process, but not without high-profile connections."

"I guess that leaves me out – or, in, actually."

We shared a short chuckle.

"There is a fee for my work and I will ask you for that later. I usually ask for some money in advance, but you can pay me when you are going to pay the fine. I have been told you have money on deposit – the five hundred dollars you brought with you."

"That's correct. Can I have your contact details, please?" I asked.

He handed me his business card and left. He didn't offer to shake. In his place neither would I. The men in prison were filthy beyond imagination.

I heard nothing more for several days. On the third morning a guard called me and said Farooq had been in contact and wanted the name and phone number of my lawyer. I was surprised – no, *astounded* – at that news.

A week passed as it does in jail. Sleep. Dream. Wake. Eat. Defecate. Sleep. Repeat.

On Monday of the following week several other prisoners and I were taken to court by the police van. I met my lawyer in the courtyard. He said that he would talk on my behalf in the courtroom. He said if I were sensible, I would not say anything.

We were handcuffed and followed the prison guards into the courtroom. We stood there and waited for the judge. He entered almost immediately: a grumpy looking old man with a short beard. He dispensed with formalities and indicated for the clerk to begin. Either he was efficient or just wanted to get things over in a hurry.

The court speaker said something in Urdu and then read the name of each prisoner, who in turn was asked to step forward while the charges were read.

The judge did his part: he listened. The offender did his part: he stepped back into line.

That was the court trial. It took less than two minutes for each prisoner.

Certainly not what I thought it would be, based on what my lawyer had said. My presence seemed fully irrelevant. We were taken to the police van and then back to our jail.

The lawyer came back to the jail that same afternoon.

"The verdict is six months in prison and a fine. You can buy the prison sentence, but you need to remain here for at least two weeks. It will cost around 1,000 US dollars including my fee for you to be set free."

My heart sank when he mentioned the cost. I'm sure he sensed my reaction from the way my body slumped and my head dropped.

"I already talked to Farooq and he is going to pay the whole amount. I think we did a good job for you."

Another rapid depression followed by an unexpected bright moment.

"I have to admit I don't understand the Pakistani judicial system," I said. "But I really appreciate your work for me. It all happened without any real trial – no give and take between the defence and the prosecution."

The lawyer smiled.

"The outcome is what is important. Not the procedure itself. The lawyers talked with the judge later and worked out the appropriate verdict for each offender."

"I really have to stay here one more week? This is a terrible place."

"We might be able to get you released sooner, but we will need to pay a bit of money here. Shall I look into that?"

"By all means – since Farooq is paying."

The lawyer left and I returned to my cell. The Indian inmate, Kunal, asked me when I would be freed.

"Next week, if all goes well. I am so eager to get out of here."

"Only a few more days is nothing. I would say enjoy the rest of your time here."

"I don't have any choice other than being here. *Enjoying* it is another matter entirely. I wish it were next week, already."

"It is not that bad here, believe me," Kunal said – and I did. I believed he knew much darker places. I could tell by the way he added, "There are places in this world which are much worse. You should regard yourself fortunate to be in this jail."

"I have seen another jail in this country, too, but it was no better than this one. Where were you which was worse than here?" I asked him.

"I have been in a few prisons in my life, but the one in Thailand, Bang Kwang Central Prison, was the worst for me. Many foreign prisoners in Thailand are kept there and if one survives that prison, he would survive any other prison in this world. I would say, in comparison, this is paradise."

"I don't want to ever see another prison anywhere. How long was your prison sentence in Thailand?"

"Twelve years, but it felt like twenty. I was granted amnesty so I could be released after six. After my release I stopped going to Thailand. I think any prisoner released from there does the same."

"May I ask what the charges were?"

"I was arrested with one kilogram of heroin in my luggage at the airport on my way to Taiwan. I would say that was unfortunate."

"How did you manage to stay there for six years without going mad?"

"I am a mess and my presence here is proof of that. I meditate on a daily basis. That helps some. After my release I had nightmares for years, but I don't have them these days."

"What is your job or what did you do for a living?" I asked him.

"I didn't have any formal education or an interesting occupation. I was a rickshaw driver during my early twenties, but did not earn enough money. I met a man who promised me prosperity and a golden future so I gave up my job and joined him in his business. He was not an honest businessman. We were a kind of small Natwarlal."

"What is Natwarlal?"

"You don't know of him?"

"Is it a person?"

Kunal smiled.

"There are movies about Natwarlal. How come you don't know him?"

"I am sorry, forgive my ignorance. Tell me who he is?"

"Natwarlal was a well-known fraudster from India. He is infamous for having sold the Taj Mahal and the Indian Parliament House to tourists – multiple times. He also sold other public buildings to foreign buyers. He forged signatures and was involved in cheque fraud. He was imprisoned many times, but usually managed to escape. In some ways he became a folk hero."

"So, you are saying you and your partner did the same things?"

"Almost the same things, but we did not sell the Taj Mahal or public buildings; we sold our clients buildings – buildings, you see, that we didn't own or, even better, that did not exist. We also forged signatures and cheques."

"Were you also involved in drugs? I am asking because of the Thailand thing."

"Not initially, but later I used it as a means to earn money faster and quicker than before."

"Do you have family and children?" I asked.

"No one at all. I never stay in one place very long so I cannot have a family and kids. I think the family would curtail my freedom."

"You said you have been in prison many times. It sounds to me like you actually did not have much freedom in your life."

"You are correct and therefore I have to value the limited freedom I have and don't curb it by family responsibilities."

"What is your charge now?"

"Not drugs, but I don't want to disclose it."

"Never mind, then. I didn't mean to pry."

Kunal was the only person I ever talked with while there in that cell. I can't say we became friends and I really didn't miss him when he went to court and did not return.

"I have come to expect violence and disappointment in your odyssey, Ben. And this week's instalment is lacking in neither."

Frau Bosch seems agitated by the section she has just read.

"Those times were awful. It's interesting that when I wrote about them I had to stop and work to remember the *feelings*. I could describe the situations with no problem – the people, the conversations. But all of that has somehow become detached from the feelings."

"Once written," Frau Bosch asks, "what seemed the most real?"

"The situation or the feelings, you mean?" Ben responds.

She nods.

"A fascinating question. I must think about it and get back to you. I feel like that part of my life is trying to slip away from me. Those feelings... they are virtually... *gone*. I am doubly grateful for this opportunity to capture it on paper."

"And I am grateful to you, Ben."

It's an odd thing for his psychologist to say, Ben thinks, but it has a definitive note for the time being.

She goes back to the pages.

I was released from jail the following week and went back to the guesthouse that still had a room available for me. As I expected, Farooq showed up at my door that same afternoon.

I met him with a well-rehearsed verbal barrage.

"That was a very lousy performance from you. I don't think you bribed anyone at the airport; you just sent me there to try my luck."

"I am sorry it didn't work out, things got out of hand on that evening. I am truly sorry you had to go to jail, but I was monitoring you from outside. I was the one who talked to the lawyer and made sure he would release you as soon as possible. I paid for everything."

"I have my passport and ticket," I continued as if ignoring everything he had said. "How much can you get for the ticket now? I want all my money back."

"You don't have any money left. I paid for the lawyer and your fine and that was 1,000 US dollars. I also paid for the ticket: 600 US dollars."

I did some quick figuring in my head.

"If you deduct that from the 3,000 US dollars, I gave you, you still have 1,400 US dollars left. I need to pay for my room and I need the money."

"The rest went for the expenses."

"*Expenses?!* What kind of expenses? There was no one at the airport to *help* me. I didn't get any help -- I only found people who beat me and threw me in that appalling jail. I think you didn't hire or bribe anyone. I think you lied about your connections. I think this whole thing was a *con*." I was feeling beyond exasperated. I threw up my hands. "I don't know why I always find such incompetent and greedy people to *help* me."

"Watch your language and don't insult me."

Farooq's face had darkened, but I didn't care.

"Like I said, you still owe me 1,400 US dollars. I didn't pay you 3000 US dollars to end up in prison."

"Honest to God, I paid for the visa and the middleman at the airport. I don't have any money left."

I didn't believe him for a moment, but that was not for him to know. I could play the lying game too.

"I phoned my uncle in Germany and he said he would send me 5,000 US dollars at the end of next week. I need money to pay for the hotel and would like to have at least 500 US dollars from you now. Once my money has arrived, I will pay your money back. You will need to find a better way to use that money and get me to Germany."

"I am sure I can do a better job with more money."

"Please bring me the 500 US dollars tomorrow, then."

"I will borrow some money for you and have it here tomorrow."

Men like Farooq are predictable. I had already come to know too many. He'd easily come up with 500 US dollars in order to receive 5,000 US dollars in one week's time. Greed begets greed.

I was finding it easier to lie to men like Farooq. I wasn't sure what that said about my own moral sense. I worried some days. Most days, I let it go.

Farooq brought me 500 US dollars the following afternoon. That made a total of 1000 US dollars with the 500 US dollars that was returned to me upon my release from jail. Farooq wanted my passport, but I refused to give it to him.

"I am going to the Afghan consulate tomorrow. I want to exchange my passport. I don't think I can go anywhere with it anymore. Not since they removed the fake German visa sticker. It's damaged now – I need to get a new one."

"How do you want to do it?"

"My idea is to pour tea on it – to damage it. I could then take it to the consulate to replace it. Do you have a better idea?"

"No, that sounds reasonable."

The next morning I checked out of the guesthouse and left. I didn't think he was capable of sending me abroad. It had been another expensive lesson, and I was disappointed in myself for my poor judgment: I had hoped

Farooq would provide a stepping stone to my freedom, but he turned out to create more of a stumbling block. I did not want to have anything more to do with Farooq. Maybe I should pay attention to my intuition in the future.

I walked to a main road about one mile away from where I had been staying. I asked a rickshaw man if he knew a guesthouse on the other side of the city. That would put me nearly an hour away from my old place. The rickshaw took me to a small guesthouse similar to the previous one but less expensive; it was very far out of the way. There would be a hundred guesthouses between where I had been and the new one. Farooq would have to search quite a lot if he decided to try and find me.

I paid rent for a week, then went looking for the area where Iranians lived. I got the names and addresses of three Iranian restaurants. From there, I could get directions to Iranian guesthouses. I soon had the locations of several that sounded promising.

I asked a restaurant owner if he knew of a smuggler who could transfer me abroad. This was Iranian to Iranian so I knew the request would remain confidential.

The man laughed. "In this country everyone will tell you they can send you abroad. They will take your money and leave you in their dust. Watch your money, boy, and don't trust anyone."

A sober assessment – disappointing, but brutally honest.

After seven days I moved to an Iranian guesthouse. I rented it for a week. I had decided not to stay in any one place longer than that. It was comfortable there, with a shared kitchen where people met and talked as they ate. Mostly Iranian boys my age. It was busy all the time – a place for exchanging information. The main news was usually related to passenger transfer. There were constant updates about who had escaped from Pakistan and who had failed.

I learned that most of the other young men had been living in Pakistan more than a year, and one man had been waiting two and a half years. Almost all of them had a similar story to tell: they had paid money to a smuggler in Iran in order to be sent to Europe or Canada, but they ended up in Pakistan. Smuggling us out of the country, Pakistan, was nearly impossible. They received money from their families. Many were depressed and had turned to drugs to make their suffering bearable.

Basically, every new resident told the same story. I shared very little of mine. To them I was still a newcomer. Nobody had any information that gave me hope.

I asked about university opportunities. No one had really looked into it. "Did you really come here to study or go to Europe?" one man asked me. "If I wanted to stay in Asia I would have stayed in Iran, where the living standards are substantially superior to here. I came here to fly *away*, not to take roots."

"But you don't know when you can leave here," I said. "It seems that it may take many years — and these are the best years of your life. It does not make sense to go abroad at thirty or forty without any formal education. Starting over there with no profession would be too challenging," I said.

"So, then, what is your solution for this problem?"

"I don't have any yet, but it appears that we must become creative and find new ways to leave this country. These traffickers aren't smarter than average people. Certainly, the men I have met were not particularly talented. And you — you just stay in your room all day long waiting to be saved by somebody who doesn't even know you exist. You eat and chat and listen to music and then go to bed. You repeat the same routine the next day. Eventually, you will celebrate your fifth and then the tenth anniversary in Pakistan. It will be because you didn't take steps to solve the problem yourselves."

They all laughed at me. Then one said, "We thought like you when we arrived here, too. Such optimism. Just wait and see — you will still be here this time next year."

Maybe they were right. It had taken me months to get to Karachi while others managed it within days. Perhaps I was being completely unrealistic, maybe deluded. Even so, I did not like being told this was my fate — that I had no choice.

"I think you might need significantly longer, probably decades, to leave this country," said the same man.

We would see.

Without hope I had nothing, and I knew if I had stayed around these hopeless people, I soon would be one of them. So I tried to avoid them. Over the following days, I gathered the names and addresses of all the guesthouses they knew about. My new plan was to visit them and search for the two boys I had met earlier. The older boy was Ramon, named after a warrior from Ferdowsi's Shahnameh. I had forgotten the younger one's name. I'd have to look for Ramon. That would have to be enough.

To my surprise, I found them only a few days later, still together, and not that far away. I was really delighted to see them, though Ramon's news echoed what I had heard from the others.

"Our smuggler thinks it is impossible to go abroad from the Karachi airport with a fake passport. He does not want to risk it. He is looking for a new way to transfer us. He is looking into sending us to India because he thinks he can send us abroad easier from there."

"How do you get to India if you don't have a passport?" I asked.

"We don't know yet."

"Can I speak to your smuggler?"

"He lives in India, but one of his friends is taking care of us. We have been told that he will come here next week to assess the situation in person."

"Will you let me know when he arrives? I would like to ask him to transfer me, too. I have talked to others, and all of them said what you say: that it is impossible to go through the Karachi airport directly to Europe. I think we could try Islamabad or Lahore. I personally can no longer use the Karachi airport. I was arrested there a few weeks ago. I have to use another one."

"Are you saying that you tried and failed?" Ramon asked me.

"Yes, but it was an ill-devised plan and cost me a lot of money — and time in prison. I knew it was a bad idea, but my desire made me careless. I think I have an idea how to go to India, provided someone can transfer us to Europe from there."

"You need to wait for our man from India. I've heard a lot of things about him. He is a very smart Afghan man who has been living in India for decades. They say he knows what he does. We believe he has sent many people to Europe and Canada from New Delhi."

"That sounds promising."

Tarek was obese and short of stature. He was a chain smoker and suffered from respiratory disease, which was hardly surprising. He always carried an inhaler in his pocket and used it immediately after he put out each cigarette. He claimed to be fifty, but he looked older than sixty. He also claimed he had lived in many countries in Asia, but during the past ten years his main home had been India.

"Can you help me go to Germany or Canada from India?" I asked.

251

"Of course I can. It is much easier from India. It will cost you some money, but it would only take me a few days to transfer you to Europe from New Delhi."

I had to wonder why he hadn't already done that for Ramon and the other boy if it were really all that easy.

"I think Ramon will vouch for me. I am not sure if I need someone to testify to my good character — I don't recall ever meeting anyone who said that he had successfully scammed a trafficker, good character or not."

Tarek laughed.

"You are right, son. I get my money and no one messes with me. If you want me to take over your case, you have to pay my fee. Do you have money?"

"I will have to telephone my relatives and get the fund. I don't think money is an issue."

"It will cost you 4,000 US dollars for the whole trip."

"This is a lot of money. I could understand if I was starting from Iran, but I am out of Iran and therefore the amount seems to be high from here."

"Okay, you pay 3,500 US dollars. That is my final concession. Are you happy now?"

"It is still high, but I assume final means final," I said.

Tarek offered his hand for a shake. The deal was set. I just had to come up with the money. Ramon seemed happy to have me join them, and suggested that I should move into their guesthouse.

I asked Tarek about his plan and how he would transfer Ramon and the younger boy, Safa, to India since neither of them had a passport. Tarek opened his Samsonite handbag and showed us nearly two dozen fake passports from different countries in Europe.

"With a person's picture I can make him a passport in no time. I have done it often — even some I have used for myself."

"What about the visa and date of entry to Pakistan and the other necessary details?"

"I can do all those things for you — your passport will look genuine in every way. It will appear to be the passport of someone who came to Pakistan as a tourist and is ready to return home. They are scrutinized less than the others."

252

"I can't leave through the airport in Karachi. I was arrested there a short while ago. Security is thorough."

Tarek paused, then nodded and said, "We could fly to Lahore and from Lahore to India. The airport security in Lahore is relaxed. We could get through it easily."

He certainly sounded confident.

"I have an Afghan passport and I could use my passport for the trip to India, but I would have to get a visa from the Indian consulate in Karachi. I don't know how difficult that is," I explained.

"How did you get an Afghan passport?" Tarek asked.

"An Afghan man took me there and we claimed I was an Afghan who lived in Iran for a time, but didn't want to go back there."

"Alright, then, I have the solution – ingenious, if I do say so myself. I know someone who works in the Afghan consulate. I will take photos of the three of you to him and tell him the same story you used before, Ben. You will all have Afghan passports in no time. With the passport we will be able to fly to India legally. I will need to bribe the man at the consulate, but it is doable."

"I already have an Afghan passport, so don't think you can obtain another passport for me?"

"Forget your old passport. The consulate doesn't know you. I will take your picture there and get you a new passport with a new name. Do not worry about it."

The three of us were to provide him two passport photos each by the following day. He left the guesthouse for the upscale hotel where he stayed.

Tarek collected the photos on the following day and headed to the Afghan embassy on his own. He came back to the guesthouse later that day and bragged that he would receive the passports delivered at his hotel that same evening. I was impressed. I even felt hopeful.

The psychologist pauses.

"It must have seemed like the journey was endless, Ben. I am impressed that you could still muster hope after all you had been through. For all your bad experiences, you seemed to trust quickly with little evidence to actually support it."

"My grandfather had a saying: *'Life is more tolerable if you trust people until they prove to you that you can't.'* I guess that is my default in human relationships," Ben responds. Then he considers further. "It may have led me astray at times — I can see that as I look back over things."

"Are you saying that long-held belief has been badly tarnished?"

"I would like to think not. It would be a personal defeat to allow the likes of the scum I had to deal with change me in that way. Now, I am just more careful when I assess people's trustworthiness, I suppose."

"The story leaves the reader with a sense of despair. I suppose more importantly it leaves the reader with a sense of your resiliency and determination."

"I wonder if the two go hand in hand."

CHAPTER THIRTEEN

AN AFGHAN AND A SPANIARD

And now I was Hafez, the famous Persian poet from the fourteenth century. It said it right there, on my new Afghan passport.

And there, right next to me, was my brother. Safa.

This was Tarek's brilliant plan, anyway. When he returned the next day with our passports, he waved two in the air.

"Where is the third passport?" I asked.

Tarek handed one to Ramon and then held the other up for me to look at. The second one – mine – had two photos in it.

"How can there be two people in one passport? A parent and a child, yes – but this?"

"If you pay, you can get anything you want," he said calmly. "I could even get your neighbour on your passport if it served my purpose."

"But –"

"Safa is now your younger brother. They wrote the explanation there on the last page so it should not be a problem. It can only work in your favour – big brother taking care of his orphaned younger brother." Tarek indicated crocodile tears running down his cheeks with his fingers and continued. "It won't be any issue here. Maybe in Europe but not in Pakistan or India."

Tarek said he needed to obtain a tourist visa for India for us to fly to India. He would need to bribe someone for that, of course.

"You seem to believe that money can buy you anything," I said.

"Of course. By the time you are my age, that will become apparent to you as well. It works everywhere. Everybody has a price, and you just need to find it and decide if the favour is worth that amount to you."

255

I hoped that was not true.

Ramon was a pessimist. He seldom let himself believe the possibility of good. He didn't retreat; he just didn't allow himself to feel hope. He was the only son in a family with three sisters. His family had lived in the United States for a long time. He missed his parents, especially his father. He worried about his father's health. Unlike me, Ramon did not want to enter a university, but hoped to complete a technical course. He wanted to be able to get a job and begin earning a living as soon as possible. Becoming independent at the earliest possible time was important to him. Perhaps it was to prove his worth to his father; I really couldn't tell.

Ramon and I got on very well.

Safa was fifteen years old. He would occasionally steal a cigarette from Tarek's pack and smoke it. I figured it was his way to be more like the older boys. He appeared unhappy — about his situation, I assumed. There may have been other reasons as well. I wondered why a boy so young was travelling without his family. He said his parents were waiting for him in New Delhi. From there they planned to go to Sweden because they had relatives there. Most of his story seemed plausible.

Tarek needed one more week to obtain the visas. Apparently, he had a contact in the Indian consulate. The appropriate bribe would get him everything he needed. They would be transit visas, but that would be sufficient. Once in India we would no longer need the passports.

I admired Tarek's confidence, but doubted whether money could buy him anything in life.

Two days later, the four of us took a taxi to the Karachi airport. On the way I felt the old anxiety growing inside me, and I wondered if I could ever overcome the fears associated with this airport. Tarek comforted me by reminding me that we would be using the domestic terminal for the flight to Lahore, not the international one where I had my difficulties. I had not considered that already; I felt mildly better.

We arrived at the terminal in the early afternoon and checked in with no difficulty. Security appeared to be non-existent for domestic flights. Ramon and I sat next to each other in one row, Tarek and Safa in the row in front of us. The flight took almost two hours and we landed in the early evening. The flight from Lahore to New Delhi was on the following morning so we stayed overnight in a small hotel at the airport. The hotel room was small, but it had four beds. Tarek snored and wheezed through the night. I didn't sleep.

Next morning was our flight to New Delhi. We had no problem at the check-in counter, but the border control officer asked me why I shared a passport with my brother. I explained that it had been the consulate's decision not to issue my brother a separate passport. I said that apparently they did not think it was appropriate to issue my fifteen-year-old brother a separate one. I closed by saying we had no choice in the matter. The officer looked at me and then at Safa. It appeared that he swore under his breath in Urdu but went ahead and applied the necessary departure stamp.

Once well past the border control counter Ramon gave me a high five. It felt like I was already in Europe. We were overjoyed. Even the usually sullen Safa.

On the plane, Ramon and I sat next to each other again. Ramon hit my shoulder and repeated, "We have made it, Ben. Can you believe it? The others back at the guesthouse wouldn't believe it."

"Do you know what happens to us when we arrive in New Delhi?" I asked.

"I think you will continue to be Tarek's passenger and he will arrange to send you to Europe. Safa and I are not really his passengers. He was commissioned to take us to India and hand over to our smuggler who is awaiting us in New Delhi."

"Where are you going to stay in New Delhi?" I asked.

"I imagine that Tarek will immediately hook Safa up with his parents, and I will join my smuggler."

"You mean you are going to live with your smuggler's family in New Delhi?" I found that arrangement unorthodox.

"The plan is for me to be their cook as long as I am in New Delhi. I could also do ironing, babysitting and gardening. It isn't supposed to take very long," Ramon said jokingly.

"I can't believe how long all this has taken me," I said.

"Be happy, Ben. We are better now than yesterday. Imagine you could still have been in Pakistan."

"Yes, you're right. I think we should go to the UNHCR in New Delhi and register as asylum seekers. In case we cannot escape from India immediately, we could use their support. Besides, we need to have an ID to show police if we are asked for it."

"You shouldn't think about the possible complications. You need to believe that it is really easier to go abroad from India than Pakistan."

That seemed odd coming from my friend the pessimist.

"Getting an ID from UNHCR does not compromise our plan, but may provide us with more security. I don't want to make the same mistake again and just rely on the smugglers. Somebody – Einstein, I think – said, '*Stupidity is doing the same thing over and over and expecting different results.*'"

Ramon nodded and said, "If we need to do it – I mean going to UNHCR – we should do it without telling Tarek and the others."

The flight took about seventy-five minutes and the plane landed in New Delhi on time. We were all excited. Soon we would gather our things and leave the airport. That would be the point where we knew we had really made it.

There were forms to fill in, of course. We exited the plane and found a place to the side to complete the landing form for India – important, Tarek explained, before going to the border control. Ramon filled in his form, and Safa's, too. Tarek asked me to also complete his form, because he had misplaced his glasses.

After completing mine, I started on Tarek's. I asked to see his passport because I needed to transfer some information from it. I knew Tarek's nationality was Afghan, but I was surprised to see his passport was Iranian.

It soon became clear to me that it was an original passport, but not really his. In an Iranian passport the name and date of birth are typed in both Farsi and English. Iran used its own national calendar, which differs from the Christian calendar. Tarek's date of birth according to Iranian calendar did not match with the Christian calendar's date. According to the Iranian date of birth Tarek was twenty-six years old and based on the Christian date he was fifty years old. Only a person who could read Farsi would notice the discrepancy in his passport.

I filled in his landing form according to the English section of his passport so he was more believably fifty years old. I didn't mention the calendar discrepancy to him. I handed him the form, and he signed it.

At border control, the officer on duty reminded me that my brother and I needed to leave the country within one week. And then we walked on through.

Another high fiving high in the air – this one even more exuberant.

By the looks of it, Tarek lived well. We travelled to his apartment, which turned out to be a penthouse in an affluent area of New Delhi. We stayed two days.

Tarek was not married, but he had a maid he called Bolbol; it is the Persian word for nightingale. Bolbol was in her mid-twenties and had a room in the same apartment. It was soon apparent that she was not merely his maid. Their relationship resembled marriage, in fact: shouting and frustrations. And he occasionally beat her. I had to wonder why she would stay in such an abusive relationship; the reasons were strictly financial, of course. Tarek paid her better than she could earn anywhere else. He had found her weakness, and he took all the benefits he could.

The smuggler who was in charge of Ramon's transfer to Europe was a man named Peeruz, born and raised in Afghanistan. He had studied literature in a university in Tehran and was married. His wife was Iranian and had studied the Russian language and literature in the Tehran University. She was a kind woman but seemed to be depressed and unhappy. They brought their two sons, aged eight and three.

Peeruz and Ramon greeted each other warmly. Ramon introduced me as a friend he met on his way to Karachi.

Peeruz was in his mid-thirties, bald with a moustache. He looked like Lenin and was, in fact, a Lenin admirer; he spent a good deal of time talking about Marx and Engels and their socialist views.

Peeruz wanted to transfer his family to Canada. He had relatives there and planned to join them. He apparently knew Tarek from his home country, Afghanistan, and called him Kaka, which means uncle. Both Peeruz and Tarek drank a lot of whisky. Peeruz entertained Ramon and me with stories about Tarek and praised him for his bravery and business talent. He described Tarek as a kind of Afghan Robin Hood. He said many Afghans would associate his name with good deeds.

By the end of the evening, however, Ramon and I understood that in addition to his many laudable achievements, Tarek had trafficked both drugs and humans, and at one point, money laundering had been his speciality.

At some point during all the storytelling, my suspicion around Tarek was confirmed; he was illiterate. Which was why he needed me to complete his form at the airport. Ramon and I were both astounded that a man so gifted in speaking a number of languages could not read or write. His English was better than everyone else's in the room and he spoke Farsi with an Iranian accent better than Peeruz, who studied Farsi literature in Iran.

Tarek built his reputation on lies – big ones. The central deception was that he posed as an Afghan embassy ambassador before the start of the war between the Soviet Union and Afghanistan. The belief among those who knew him was that he had graduated from one of the most prestigious universities in Asia. I had to admire his ability to portray such a grand self-image, even if it occasionally seemed to be pretty pathological; despite his obvious character flaws, I wished I could exchange my battered and bruised self-image with his.

By the end of the evening, Peeruz had asked Tarek to hand over my transfer to him so he could send Ramon and me to Europe at the same time. Tarek agreed, but I was not happy about it. Tarek tried to put my mind at ease, muttering something about how he and Peeruz were from the same extended family, so it did not matter who received the money for it.

I was not sure I liked that arrangement. I wanted to leave India as soon as possible. I was not sure how competent Peeruz was.

But what choice did we have? I was so close to being free – I could taste it. So when Peeruz rented a small room for Ramon and me, I had to see it as a step in the right direction. Call it optimism. Besides, it was a place with two single beds and a small kitchenette so we could cook, on the top floor in a big house owned by an Indian family. Here we were in the new town of New Delhi, a place that resembled a European city – and a place that was clean. Most people who lived in the new town were wealthy, with a driver, a cook and often a gardener. Labour was inexpensive in India and a doctor or banker could easily afford to pay for lots of help.

The owner of the house across the street was a banker who had four people working in his house. His driver, who sat in front of the main gate most of the time, was a number of years older than we were. He visited us in our room several times. He explained that he lived with his employer's family, the owner of the house. His food and accommodation were free and he earned just enough money to pay for his cigarettes and a few drinks. He found it difficult to save any money on his very small salary.

That was the bitter truth in New Delhi. As we stayed on, I came to see the economic inequalities – they were obvious in every nook and cranny of the city. Most of those unfortunate people remained with their employers, despite mistreatment and abuse, since it was difficult to find new work. We witnessed our landlord and his wife shouting at their gardener frequently. They even threw objects at him and slapped him in the face. The man never said a thing and would apologise, accepting full blame for whatever the issue, even when it obviously had not been his fault.

"Could you live the way the help has to live here?" Ramon asked me one evening while we were eating.

"I don't think I am the kind of person who can be subjugated by another individual. I think most of these people are not free in their minds.

They cannot even dream of being free and having a life on their own. I read something when I was in Karachi that said you are what you think about most of the time. That means you are the product of your own mind. If you think you are free and you believe it, you will be free. These folks believe the opposite."

"You would not blame their circumstances and their parents for their condition?" Ramon asked.

"No, I would not. Look at your family and siblings. You say most of them have a PhD degree and earn a lot of money, but you are happy with much less – very little, in fact. You all had the same parents, but you decided to pursue a different life than your three sisters. I don't blame the environment at all. I am sure that not all people from poor neighbourhoods remain poor. I have put a good deal of effort into finding the secret to success for myself over the past two years – especially the past few months. I read a lot of interesting conclusions from various wise men; most of them concluded that we alone are the masters of our destiny. They all say that wealth and poverty originate in our mind. In order to be prosperous and have wealth in life we have to develop a kind of 'prosperity consciousness' and work toward it. I think most of these people we see working as labourers cannot even imagine being rich in their dreams. What I mean is, they do not believe that they deserve to be wealthy; otherwise they would not be in their situation. They have a kind of thermostat in their brain telling them that they cannot earn more than ten dollars a month or that they can never become financially independent."

"I don't think I agree with your view," Ramon said.

"Suit yourself, but that is what the experts say and if I look back in my own short life I think the experts' view is correct. I always wanted to leave my country and whenever I mentioned it, my friends laughed at me, but I made it happen. I remember the argument I had with the young men in the guesthouse. They bet that I would remain in Pakistan for years like they had? It was like they needed to prove to me that I would fail in order to make their lot seem more reasonable. Where are we now? We are not in Pakistan anymore, but they are still there. Believe or not, we are the creators of things that happen to us and no one else is responsible for it."

"Maybe, but we are not in Europe either," Ramon said.

He spoke the truth. Even so, I maintained my position.

"Your negativity verges on hopelessness; it's almost a medical condition. You must focus on what we have achieved up to now as a success and be grateful that we are here and not in jail in Karachi or Dalbandin. I think your view would be significantly different if you had had to endure jail for a few weeks."

"I am not ungrateful to God or whoever is in charge," Ramon said. "But I didn't expect to have to go through so much suffering in order to get to Europe."

"Let me tell you how I see these things. We didn't do our military service in Iran, which is touted as an institution that makes men out of boys — assuming one survives to grow up. Now listen to this, I personally regard this trip to Europe as a process that can also make men out of us and transform us into competent grown-ups, a character-building journey. This trip has already given us many experiences that will be beneficial in our future lives."

"You must be out of your mind, Ben. How can you use the interactions and stresses with the scumbags who brought you to jail in Pakistan as helpful benchmarks? How can that experience be useful in your future life? You must be out of your mind. The only things I have received from my trip have been nightmares and depression. I don't see how that can be regarded as valuable in any culture."

"I have all those things, too. I wanted to believe if I didn't talk about them, I could just forget them, but the fact is, they don't forget me, and they visit me almost every night. I have set goals in my mind, so I don't dare surrender to those negative thoughts and feelings. They can't prevent me from achieving my objectives. I just tell those thoughts I don't have any time to deal with them at the moment and they should come back to me when I am less busy. You see, I try to cut those thoughts off whenever they come to me. I think it is a learning process. There was a time when I surrendered to them, but I think differently these days and I know I feel better about myself and life and my future."

"You are just living in a dream world, Ben. It is called being a Pollyanna. I think I am too sober to live that way."

"Try it my way for a while. What do you have to lose? I'll help. Stop thinking about your misery and suffering. It just makes you more depressed and clouds your rational judgment. Like the fellows back in the guesthouse. No need to feel sorry for yourself — oh cruel life! That's how those others live — never believing life can get better. They come to believe their sad lot in life is all because of uncontrollable outside forces. You may get some empathy, but empathy won't change your situation. If anything, empathy often just proves to you how bad off you are because others see it, too."

"I don't know what I need to do now," Ramon said.

"Do nothing and just enjoy life as much as you can. We are fine at the moment. We have better prospects than we did just two days ago – you said that yourself. You enjoy cooking. So you should do the cooking and I will do the thinking – like a traditional married couple!"

He threw a pillow at me.

"You are mean, but I don't mind cooking for us. I relax when I cook."

"I am glad that I am living with you, then. I don't enjoy cooking that much and I relax when I'm thinking."

Peeruz and his family lived in an apartment that was a thirty-minute walk from our room. He asked us to go to his place and meet other people who were also waiting for their transfer to Europe and Canada.

One evening we walked to his apartment. It was located in a nice neighbourhood in New Delhi. We met three Iranian families that had all been waiting for transfers for months. That didn't boost my confidence.

Among them was Hamid, a twenty-six-year-old single man from Tehran, who was a dental technician and came to India with a genuine tourist visa waiting for Tarek to send him to Sweden. I realised that he was the original owner of the passport, which Tarek had altered – unknown to him, as far as I could tell – in order to travel to Pakistan.

Hamid was related to Safa. He was there with Safa's parents, Safa and his younger brother.

There was also a middle-aged couple with two children who had also been waiting in New Delhi for several months. The husband was quiet and looked very unhappy. He kept pressing Peeruz about when they would be able to fly away from India.

There was a young woman with her three-year-old son, and they were waiting to go to Canada. She was related to Ramon's mother and knew Ramon well. The young woman's older son and husband, who was a successful engineer, lived in Montreal, Canada and were waiting for her to join them. She said she had not known that it would take so long, otherwise she would have tried the legal way through the Canadian embassy, which usually took one year. By comparison, that no longer seemed so long.

At the heart of Peeruz' plan was his own desire to go to Canada with his own family. He had contacted Tarek to arrange the illegal transfer – which would cost a good deal of money. Peeruz thought he could bring several families to India that were looking for ways to go abroad illegally. His commissions for his part in the transfer would pay for his family's transfer – which meant that he really had no clue about the business of human trafficking. He believed what he had been told by Tarek. Many of the people who were at Peeruz's place had already realised that he was a victim of his own stupidity and credulousness. They also knew that Tarek was really the man who had to transfer them abroad. Most of them had already handed over the money for their transfer to Peeruz, who then gave it to Tarek. The families did not have any money left to negotiate with another trafficker – and I had the impression that Peeruz could not retrieve any of the money back from Tarek for the families.

That evening the atmosphere in Peeruz's apartment was extremely tense and some of the women started crying about their miserable quality of life in India. Peeruz was generally a quiet man and did not really try to defend his actions. He only said that the situation to move out of New Delhi was unfavourable at that time and they needed to wait and see what time would bring.

His explanation was not convincing. Some of his passengers left the apartment, clearly despondent. Neither Ramon nor I said a word. I talked with Peeruz's wife, Sara, who also understandably suffered under the pressures of their situation.

Peeruz, for his part, drank well into the evening.

Sara explained to me about her life in Iran and the challenges they faced before coming to India. She defended her husband: he was a decent man and not into human trafficking. He wanted to help some of these families with the connections he had in India, and the money had not been the motivating force.

After most of the guests had left, Sara and Peeruz prepared a traditional Afghan meal. Despite the discomfort of the evening, the meal was delicious. Ramon and I could not help but enjoy it.

On our way home, Ramon said, "Do you realise what Peeruz has done to these unfortunate families? He has sucked them dry."

"Yes, and I think he was conned by Tarek. I think he believed those empty promises. I think he is a victim, too. His wife portrayed him as a Good Samaritan, but I think he is not totally innocent in it all."

"I agree; he isn't. He took all these people's money and they are left without anything. They had to sell their houses and land and whatever they had owned and all for false hopes."

"What you say is correct, but these families have to take some of the responsibility, too. Why would they hand over all their money in advance and not follow the usual arrangement – half at the beginning and the other half later on?"

"Did you transfer any money to Peeruz?" Ramon asked.

"Yes, I asked my father to send him 2,500 US dollars a few days after our arrival. I gave him 500 US dollars from my pocket and the rest was sent to his relative's account in Tehran. I know it's a gamble, but I hope we can leave here soon."

"I wish you had not given him any money."

"You know if they don't see any money they will not do anything, so I had to send him the money."

"Knowing what we know now, do you think Peeruz can do anything for us?" Ramon asked.

"He relies on Tarek. I suppose it depends on how much help he gets from him. Of course I have my doubts. You need a lot more than a suitcase full of false passports to get somebody out of the country. I met a man near Quetta who also had various counterfeit passports, but he could not send anyone to Europe just by the fact he had them. The smuggler needs to know officers at the border control and airline agents. Many of these families have no idea about what really goes into exiting this country."

"You didn't know it either."

"I took the responsibility for my own life, but if I were responsible for a whole family or other people, I would have done things differently. Besides, I am still a teenager and these people are old enough to be my parents. My father was against my illegal trip but respected my wish. He probably knew he couldn't stop me so he didn't try to fight me about it."

"Personally," said Ramon, "I cannot trust Peeruz at all, and I am very suspicious about Tarek."

"I am still optimistic about our trip and think we are now one huge step ahead of where we were when we stayed in Pakistan."

"But just look at our situation, Ben. Geographically we are now farther away from Europe than we've ever been."

"Okay, start crying now because you think it is the end of the world, that our future is bleak, and that we will end up miserable and defeated here in India. If that option makes more sense to you, choose it. I can't believe that you have lost all hope."

"You are being silly now, Ben. We should not talk about it for a few days and see what happens."

We did not hear from Peeruz during the next few days so we decided to go to the UNHCR in New Delhi and register as asylum seekers so we could obtain our identity cards.

There was a long line for registration; we waited hours. While we were waiting in the queue, we saw a number of Iranian people surround a man. They were shouting and cursing at him. The Iranian men called the other man terrible names: thief, scumbag, parasite, drug lord and so on. Probably one of the human traffickers who had taken their money and abandoned them. No one came to his rescue when he was pushed onto the pavement.

"Do you see what I see, Ben?" Ramon said pointing. "The man escaping the angry crowd? That is Tarek!"

"Yes. I see. You are right. It is Tarek with one of his associates or accomplices. I think we should turn away so that he cannot see us. It would put us in a compromised situation if he recognised us and exposed our connection to the others."

We turned and maintained our slow progress in the line.

Ramon was the first to say what we were both thinking.

"So, it appears our Tarek has brought misery to a lot of people. None of those here today were at Peeruz's place. Which means Tarek has had more victims than we can imagine. Who knows, maybe Peeruz is his accomplice in all these cases. Maybe Peeruz was the man who looked for passengers for Tarek in Iran. I told you these guys are scumbags and parasites, so low they crawl on the bellies of worms."

"You must know the animal kingdom very well," I said, "as I have difficulty finding species low enough to include them."

Obtaining the IDs was a positive step for both of us. We were relieved to be at least legal, even without up-to-date visas.

But there was no progress over the next few weeks. None of Peeruz's families had left the country. The pressure on him from his passengers increased. People turned from impatient to angry to enraged. He subsequently increased the pressure on Tarek. One day a nasty fight broke out between them.

The story we heard went this way. One evening Peeruz went to Tarek's place and asked him to give him the money back – the money which was given to him to send the passengers abroad. Tarek apparently said he did not have any money left because he had spent it in Pakistan to pick up Ramon and Safa. Apparently, that is when Peeruz lost his temper and attacked Tarek with a fruit knife from the coffee table. Despite Tarek's maid's intervention,

Peeruz must have beaten Tarek so badly that he needed to be taken to a local hospital. He was hospitalised for several days and was finally discharged without any long-standing complications. He then began legal action against Peeruz. Police went to Peeruz's place to arrest him. He had been forewarned and disappeared for several weeks.

And now none of his passengers knew where he had hidden.

We went to Peeruz's house and were informed by his wife that he was safe but needed to stay in hiding until things were settled. She went on that one of their friends had employed a lawyer to represent Peeruz and the lawyer would soon have things sorted out. Sara continued that Tarek had also taken legal action against *me*, claiming that I was involved, with Peeruz, in his beating. Peeruz's lawyer had shared this with Sara. He'd said that I was to stay in my room and not leave the house until things were back to normal.

Ramon and Hamid later confirmed the fight between Tarek and Peeruz and that Tarek had initiated a suit against me, too. I could not understand why Tarek took legal action against me. I had not seen Tarek since the night of the arrival celebration in his penthouse. Tarek had allocated my transfer to Peeruz, so I did not have any reason to even be associated with Tarek anymore.

Ramon was of the opinion that Tarek wanted a commission from Peeruz for giving me to him as a passenger; when Peeruz refused it Tarek added me to the suit in order to try to get the money from me.

Hamid speculated that Tarek was probably ashamed and embarrassed to tell his friends and associates that he had been so badly beaten by one man and, therefore, he claimed that he was assaulted by the two of us. In that scenario, it seemed like I was just handy.

"This is crazy, as I have never done anything to Tarek. Does he know where we live?" I asked.

"No, because Peeruz did not tell him," Hamid responded.

I immediately became concerned for our safety.

"Tarek has a number of henchmen around him who clean up his messes. They would do anything for money. They can easily find us here and either take care of us by themselves or inform the police about our location."

"You should not be afraid of police here. You are being sued, not arrested. Tarek's men, however, are a totally different story," Hamid explained.

I didn't leave our room for two weeks. Ramon did our shopping and occasionally walked to Peeruz's house to see if he had come out of hiding. It had taken his lawyer that much time to settle the dispute in court so Peeruz could return to his family. The court awarded no payment to Tarek.

Thinking the immediate threat was over, I left the room one morning and went to a nearby shopping area to get food. It felt so good to be outside again. I enjoyed the fresh air and sunshine. Enjoying those distractions made me less cautious than I should have been. Two of Tarek's men, who were probably only in the area by chance, saw me. They followed without me noticing them.

On my way back home, they approached me from behind while I was walking along a narrow street in a quiet neighbourhood. They asked me for 1,000 US dollars. They said it was the money I owed Tarek for transferring me from Pakistan to India.

I tried an explanation – mostly to buy time.

"Tarek transferred my case to Peeruz on the day of our arrival in New Delhi, so my father sent the money to him. I just spent what money I had on bread and rice."

The two 'debt collectors' would not let me go.

"I must say I am surprised that your boss is so poor he has to try to extort money from a penniless, displaced teenager."

Appealing to their humanity didn't help. One of them put his hands around my throat and said, "We could easily eliminate you here and nobody would care. Tarek wants some money, now."

"I understand what you are saying," I said congenially – as congenially as one can be with another man's hands around one's throat – "but do you think I would walk around here with a thousand US dollars in my pocket? We'll have to go to my place and I will give you some money, but I only have a few hundred dollars."

That seemed to appease them; something was better than nothing. They escorted me to my place and walked very closely behind me. I was hoping to escape along the way, but I looked left and right – to no avail. There was simply no place to duck away from them. So I continued walking toward the street where my house was located – slowly. *Think, Benjamin.* I needed a plan – and fast. We were approaching my street, but I was not about to give up my exact location.

The driver from the house across the street – the young man who occasionally came up to our room to talk and have tea with us – was standing next to his gate. When he saw me approaching he waved. I decided to walk directly toward him, stopping a few yards away from the gate. I hitched my head as if to indicate the men behind me.

"Raj," I said trying to sound nonchalant. "Will you open the gate to *my* place here for me? My arms are full so I can't manage it." Raj caught on quickly. He could tell something was not right. He opened his gate and let me in. I stepped through – a few paces ahead of the goons with me – and we closed and latched the gate immediately.

"These men have been following me and have demanded money from me," I explained hurriedly. "Quick! Call the police!"

The thugs became furious and tried to get through the gate by pushing on it and shaking it. Raj removed a twenty-four-inch machete from behind the gate post and approached them. They took several steps back.

It was time to send a message to Tarek.

"Go back to your pathetic boss and tell him he needs to sort out his problem with Peeruz, not me. I'm *broke*, got it? Just like the others he has cheated."

The men were upset and began spewing what all thugs spew in that sort of situation: They would catch me one day. Then I would wish I had never been born. Et cetera.

They then walked away. I thanked Raj for his help and promised to make it up to him by buying him his favourite cigarettes next time I went shopping.

"Your 'little friend' there really impressed me," I said, nodding to his machete.

Raj smiled and responded.

"It has impressed many men trying to break and enter here."

Once the intruders were out of sight, I crossed the street and opened the gate to our house. I found myself trembling with fright. Upstairs, I sat on my bed and looked at myself in the mirror on the wall. I wanted to cry, I wanted to scream, I wanted to throw things. But I felt too weak to do any of that. I flopped back and tried to regain my composure. I looked up at the ceiling and felt despair wash over me. I missed my family. I missed being a kid. I was tired of trying to figure out everything for myself. Who was there to protect me? How did I get so embroiled with drug lords and human traffickers? I wanted to be a little boy again, surrounded by my loving family. In my safe house. In my familiar city. I remembered the feeling of sitting on my mother's lap. *Safe.*

A distant concept.

I knew there was no one to blame but myself. It was I who had burned all my bridges — I left my country, I left my family and support team. And now I had even left the relative comfort — or at least familiarity — of Pakistan for the unfamiliar and unbelievably crowded country of India. I had separated myself from former friends and safe havens and subjected myself to outright liars and enemies. All around me were false friends who turned on me, unscrupulous men who took my money with no compunction — even one who thought he had the right to own me.

I had only myself to blame. The problems I had caused were problems only I could solve. This was all on me.

Maybe tea would help.

It had been a useful chat with myself. Gradually the 'me' I loved, respected and revered returned. After all, I had just handled my latest problem with creativity and poise. I had dispatched two burly thugs back to their lair. Sure, Raj's 'little friend' had probably helped some. Sure, I wasn't all that brave. But I'd kept my wits about me. And that had to count for something.

When Ramon returned, I told him how Raj had probably saved my life.

"I think we should stop going out alone anymore," I said. "The thugs made it clear that Tarek is out to take revenge on Peeruz and if he cannot get to Peeruz directly he is going to try to do harm to his passengers. That means you and me. I think we are safer if we go out together. And probably with Hamid when he's available.

"I'm sorry I wasn't there for you today, Ben."

"I think it was all a coincidence. They seemed as surprised to see me as I was to see them. They really weren't expecting me."

And so we implemented our buddy system. We didn't see any more of the thugs. We did not hear anything from Peeruz, either. We only left the room when absolutely necessary and then included Hamid when we could. We used the back stairs leading to the back door and the alley.

Evenings, I scratched in my notebooks.

"What are you writing all the time?" Ramon asked one evening. "Not letters because you never send them. Diary, maybe?"

"I am writing about what I have gone through during my journey here. I think it is a good way to cope with boredom and frustration. I am sure when I am older, I will read it. I hope to learn things about myself. Maybe I will see things differently then."

Ramon was interested. "Do you write about me too?"

"Yes, you are the hero in my writing, Ramon."

He didn't believe me. He seemed to know I was pulling his leg.

"I could not write about such things. It would just make me upset. I want to forget these people once I have reached my destination and never think about this time again."

"Who knows? I might feel that way later as well, but for the time being, I think writing helps me to calm down and keep my frustration at bay. When I write down the feelings I have experienced, it is like I am sharing things with another individual. Somehow, that is soothing."

"You could share your issues with me."

"That is kind of you, and I do, some of them. But there are many things I cannot share with you."

"Give me an example of something you can't share with me."

He found his joke hilarious.

"You are getting on my nerves now," I said directly, but not, I hoped, unkindly. "I cannot share what I think about you and I cannot share my feelings with you or anybody. It makes me uncomfortable."

"Come now. What do you think about me?"

"At this moment? A silly juvenile boy who can be a nuisance!"

He frowned. "As a punishment for that, I won't cook anything tomorrow."

"I think you would suffer more than I would. You enjoy cooking more than anything else. Maybe you should write a cookbook."

"Interesting. A cookbook for asylum seekers. I could call it, *Eating on a Nickel a Day while Running for Your Life*. On the cover could be a kid running while stirring something in a frying pan he is holding out in front of him."

"That's actually quite clever. It is a good idea and worth thinking about. You might even find someone who will publish it for you."

He looked out the window.

"You know, Ben, I think I could live in India for the rest of my life. It is a beautiful country and if one has just a bit of money, he can have a good life."

"It is a good place if you don't feel suffocated by all the people – and have money, as you say. But as a foreigner you cannot earn any money here.

271

The unemployment rate is very high and people like us would not likely be able to get a reasonable sort of work. Maybe we could assist some households like Raj, opening and closing the gate and doing a bit of gardening, but you cannot make a living out of it. Haven't you been listening to Raj complain, Ramon? I would say you should not change your plan now. Our destination should be Europe and nothing should alter the plan. We must not settle for *here* just because it seems difficult to get *there*."

"It was just a thought. I have thoughts sometimes, too, you know."

I managed a smile in his direction.

"I think you must cut out those kinds of thoughts and don't waste any time on them. Try to work on your willpower, buddy."

The two of us enjoyed each other's company most of the time, but, I suppose, like any people who have to live in close contact all the time, we got on each other's nerves sometimes. We also had disagreements. Sometimes we wouldn't speak for several hours at a time. Once it lasted a whole day. Those things always ran their course and things worked out. Usually, it was Ramon who took the initiative to restore our relationship. He seemed to need people – and their approval – more than I. I had really never thought about that before – how much I need or don't need other people – until then.

I had to give Ramon credit for getting out more than I did. He went to the old town to exchange money – the private exchange offices there offered a significantly better rate than the banks in India. Ramon saw a bit of town on his outings. I had not taken time to do much sightseeing.

One afternoon Ramon came home looking terrible: broken glasses; torn shirt and trousers; scratches on his face, arms and torso. Hamid was with him. They both looked frightened.

Hamid explained, speaking quickly as soon as they entered our room.

"We were in the old town, you know – going to one of the small currency exchange shops. On the path between shops, Tarek and his men saw us and followed us into the exchange – they were sitting in an open café. They closed the door behind us and Tarek started cursing at Ramon. Said he and you owe him money, said he's not received any from Peeruz. His men asked Ramon for money – Ramon said he didn't have any and they... they *beat* him! They tore his clothes and broke his glasses."

I examined Ramon's bruises on his arms. Hamid continued, wild with fright. "Tarek was such a changed man from the one we saw at the arrival party at his house. He was angry – intimidating. He swore at Ramon, and at you and Peeruz. The shop owner and I intervened. We begged them for mercy and forgiveness. I was scared, Ben. Really *scared*. For whatever reason, they stopped and left."

I didn't know how to respond. I was sorry for them – of course. But I was also perplexed.

"I am really sorry about what happened to you, but why were you even in that area? You knew that Tarek's accomplices hang out there. You should have known better. This was your own fault."

Ramon became angry.

"What happened to me is *your* fault!" he came back. "If you were not here I would not have had the problem. What I got today was really meant for you."

"No, I told you about Tarek's men and that we needed to be cautious. I warned you. Don't blame me for your carelessness and stupidity. Stop being a juvenile and take responsibility for the really dumb thing you did today."

Hamid intervened.

"Arguing who is to blame will not change anything. We are all upset, emotional. We're under massive psychological pressure. I don't think if you two throw punches it will improve our current situation. I think we all should go to Peeruz as soon as possible and ask him what progress he is making toward getting us out of here. He is the one who has to be blamed for his incompetence and shortcomings. We must find a way to light a fire under him – make him do what he promised."

Ramon and I remained silent, not looking at each other. It had been a dumb thing between us and we both understood that. Still, we gave each other the silent treatment for the remaining hours of that day and went to bed without our usual 'good night, see you in the morning'.

The following morning Ramon woke up first as usual. It was as if he were standing there just waiting to see my eyes open. He began with no introduction.

"If you are going to write about my fight with Tarek and his men in your notebook, you need to get the details right. I punched Tarek in his face so hard that his inhaler jumped from his pocket like a missile. It hit his first accomplice in his eye, then bounced back and hit Tarek's head; it bounced back once again and hit the second man's forehead so all three men fell to the floor from just one punch from me."

"I will take your word for that and will certainly record it just as you described it. I will also explain that you injured yourself and broke your glasses because you tripped over their bodies, which were lying deathly still on the floor. I think you have seen too many Bollywood movies."

He sat on the edge of his bed, a bit deflated.

"The problem was that I could not defend myself against all three people. I knew I needed to be cautious because people like that usually carry a knife. Besides, it all happened so unexpectedly and I was so shocked by seeing them that I froze. Hamid will attest to it."

"I think we have both been lucky that we did not sustain serious injuries from those criminals. Please don't go to that area again. Better yet, don't go out at all. I don't want you getting hurt again."

He nodded. We didn't need to say anything more. The problem between us had dissolved.

The next morning, we made our way to Peeruz's house through alleys and back yards. He seemed pleased to see us and asked us to sit in his living room.

I began.

"We heard you trounced Tarek in a fight a few weeks ago – sent him to a hospital. You need to know that he and his men have tried to hurt us on two separate occasions. Once, they followed me and threatened me. Then, just yesterday, he broke Ramon's glasses. They seem to be trying to get to you by going through us. We have also learned that the police are not looking for you anymore so you are able to move around freely. So, our two questions are: why haven't you contacted us, and have you found a smuggler to get us to Europe?"

I thought I had succinctly covered all the bases.

"To be honest with you, I have not found any competent person who can do the job. Tarek was my hope, but I have already found out that he lost his important connections. As you know, I have given him a lot of money that he says he cannot pay back, so I need to find another solution for you and the other passengers."

Ramon exploded. "I am really fed up with you, Peeruz. You took our money and now you can't produce the results you promised – the results we already paid for. How long do you think we can stand this waiting? I have given up all hope in you – and that means I have given up all hope of ever getting a transfer out of here. I'm going to rot away in the slums of the old city."

"I am sorry that you feel that way, but this kind of job does not have a deadline. We need to wait as long as is necessary. Don't forget that my own family is also waiting to go to Canada. I have you guys on me all the time, *plus* I have my own family nagging about the delay. I think I cannot take it anymore."

Ramon grew silent and Peeruz left the living room to tend to his sons, who were fighting in the yard. I told Ramon that he should try to control his emotions because that sort of discussion would be counterproductive.

He surely wasn't much, but Peeruz was all we had.

But Ramon remained agitated. "He has got my money and also yours. He has to do *something* for us!"

I had to calm Ramon down before Peeruz returned.

"Tell me, Ramon: what can you do if Peeruz kicks us to the kerb? What power do we have if he says he cannot pay us back, and he does not want to see us anymore? The answer is *nothing*. He can do the same thing with us as Tarek did to him. You cannot sue him here and you cannot take any legal actions against him in Iran, because none of us can go back home anymore. We can't be so confrontational – it will just add to our problems."

"I cannot accept that, Ben. He promised my father to send me to Europe, and he took a lot of money from him," Ramon responded.

Peeruz entered the living room again and Ramon continued.

"You promised a lot of things to my father and now you don't care what happens to me. It is unfair. Call it cheating, fraud and or whatever, but it is not what a decent person would do. Nobody has forced you to do this job; you chose to do it of your own free will and now that you have the money you don't give a damn what happens to us."

"Now, you are just being rude to me, Ramon. I don't like people talking to me that way. Who do you think you are? You come to my house and insult me. Say one more negative word about me and I will break your jaw. I am warning you."

They had both crossed the line.

Sara had shown up by then and tried to cool things off. But she ended up just defending her husband. Which did not help.

Emotions were out of control. I suggested we leave and try to talk again another day.

"I agree," Peeruz said. "You could come here tomorrow. I should have some news for you because I am going to see a trafficker this afternoon."

Ramon stomped out of the house without saying goodbye. I shook Peeruz's hand, apologised for Ramon's behaviour and followed my friend.

On the way back home, Ramon continued cursing Tarek and Peeruz, sometimes under his breath and sometimes out loud.

On the following day Ramon and I went back to Peeruz's house. Ramon had calmed down by then.

"I saw a man yesterday who knows his business," Peeruz announced. He thinks we should not try to leave this country through the New Delhi airport because Tarek has all my passengers' photos and he can give us all up to the authorities. I personally agree with him."

"What are the other options, then?" I asked.

"It looks like Bombay is the best option."

"Do you know if it is easier to be transferred from Bombay?"

"I believe for us it will be. In Bombay we won't have Tarek's men following us. We can move more freely. We don't have to be frightened when we leave our houses."

"You could be right about that. What do you think, Ramon?"

"I don't know," he said, still surly. "Maybe there are more competent smugglers in Bombay than here. We sure haven't found any here. I think we should try it."

Peeruz asked Ramon and me to go to Bombay first and promised to join us after a few days. It would be less conspicuous, he explained, if only a few of us made the trip at a time. Besides, Tarek might have eyes on Peeruz. He also promised that he would transfer the two of us before anyone else because of all we had been through and the money we had thrown away during the process.

It sounded good, but both of us had been at 'sounded good' many times before.

Peeruz asked his connections in Bombay to book an affordable hotel room for us where we could stay as long as we needed to be there. Peeruz's long-term plan was to ask all his passengers to move to Bombay – without Tarek's knowledge, of course.

We would leave by train the following day. Peeruz provided the tickets. We went home and packed what we had, which was actually very little. Ramon transformed what food we had into meals for the train. It was to be a long trip.

We made our way to the station by a circuitous route, hoping to lose anybody who might be following us. We saw no one, but we didn't dare take any chances. Train seats were first come first served so we were there waiting when the train arrived. It was slow, overcrowded — as they always were in India — and made many stops along the way. We needed to change trains three times. In the end the trip took us twenty-six hours. Even though we were able to have actual seats the whole way, by the time we arrived in Bombay every square inch of our bodies ached. I wondered if my head would ever again be able to swivel on my neck.

The hotel where we were to stay was small, but looked clean and was good value. Our room was quite small and sparsely furnished. There were two single beds and a small dresser. The hotel did not offer meals, but guests could buy tea, coffee and other beverages in the kitchen on the main floor behind the main desk. The room did not have a window; we had to keep the light on whenever we were in — otherwise it was pitch dark. We walked a lot, but kept very close to the hotel. The only stories either of us had heard about Bombay were horror stories. We usually bought food from small, neighbouring grocery shops and took it back to our room to eat. The quality of the food was poor but edible. Typically, we had bread, cheese and sausage. Sometimes we bought takeaway grilled chicken because it was the only prepared Indian dish that was not way too spicy for us. We heard the spices killed bacteria. They also killed our taste buds.

Little by little over the next several weeks Peeruz and his family, plus Hamid and some of the other passengers, joined us there in our hotel. Hamid slept in the room with Ramon and me. We took turns, rotating, one sleeping on the floor and two in the beds.

Most of the hotel guests were Iranians waiting to leave India illegally for Canada and Europe. It gradually became warmer in Bombay and subsequently in the hotel rooms, which were not equipped with a fan or air conditioning. Ours became oven-like. In the evenings, the three of us often went for a walk along the promenade adjacent to the Taj Mahal Palace, one of the famous hotels — a ten-minute walk from our hotel. At times we sat in the air-conditioned Taj Mahal Palace's lobby, but were usually asked to leave after a short time because we didn't purchase drinks.

The city was teeming with the homeless. Thousands slept on pavements, in front of shops, between shops, under the stairwells and under bridges. Late at night in many areas of the city, the pavements were littered with sleeping individuals. Pedestrians were forced to walk in the roads and streets, dodging the cars and motorcycles. Bombay drivers were among the worst in the world — I had heard that before; now I could confirm it.

I noticed that spirits were much higher among the passengers here in Bombay, related, no doubt, to the generally held belief that it would be easier to leave from here.

Peeruz found a number of smugglers who claimed to be capable of sending passengers to their destinations. Most of them were originally from Afghanistan and had moved to India after the start of the Soviet-Afghan war. It was challenging to distinguish between competent and incompetent smugglers – they all were smooth talkers. Every one of them claimed to have sent many people to Europe and Canada and even the USA. None of them could prove it. All of them required their fee up front.

Peeruz occasionally talked to me about his progress in finding capable smugglers. Unlike Hamid and Ramon, I really did not possess any antipathy toward Peeruz. I became the one he trusted and confided in. On occasion we even enjoyed talking together about current events and politics. Peeruz occasionally asked me to accompany him to a hotel lobby for a drink and a chat.

A month to the day after Ramon and I arrived in Bombay, Peeruz confirmed that he had things set for me to go Europe – most likely Germany.

"How do you mean to do it?" I asked.

"I have agreed to work with one of the human traffickers who I think has better credentials than the others I have met. I found people who vouch for his success. He promised to charge me less than average since there are nearly twenty of us for him to send abroad. I asked him to send you first, then the other single individuals followed by the families. At the end, my family and I will leave."

"What travel document will I use?"

"You will laugh, but you are going to have an original Spanish passport with your photo on it. The problem is that the owner of the passport is twenty-six years old, so we need to make you appear older for your trip. Let your whiskers grow."

"What about the visa?"

"You don't need a visa for Germany because your flight is to your home city, Madrid, and you will have a stopover in Frankfurt Germany. Once you arrive in Germany, you will ask for asylum and the rest is up to you."

"When can I fly?"

"Maybe in two or three weeks, when we have made sure that there are no flaws in the plan. My contact has used similar approaches before and says they have always worked."

"I am looking forward to it. Now I need to learn how to speak Spanish like a Spaniard, I suppose?"

"It would be helpful if you learn the basic vocabulary and common phrases over the next few weeks. Practise short answers to the usual questions. You have been there before. The airport officials will probably not be speaking Spanish, however, so it probably won't even be necessary. You could learn to speak English with a Spanish accent."

"I will buy a book this very afternoon and start a quick course. A voice coach could be very helpful."

I was somewhat hesitant to break the news to Ramon. We expected to make the trip together. So it was a great relief to see how genuinely happy he was for me. I could tell the news improved his spirits. Just knowing that Peeruz had finally started the ball rolling changed everything.

My Spanish name was to be Juan Diego Cortez – it couldn't get more Spanish than that! – and I had been born in Madrid. The photo was changed perfectly and no expert could doubt its authenticity. I even looked Spanish in the photo. The flight was to depart at 3:15 in the early hours of the morning, via Pan Am Airlines. I was advised to pack a small suitcase and one very small hand luggage for books and things that I might want to carry with me.

It was difficult to believe I might actually make it that time. The plan appeared to be a good one – it had always been that visa that tripped things up.

I waited with my packed bags, practicing my rolled rs.

The psychologist looks up from the pages.

"I think your life – the one I am reading about at least – can be summed up as suspense floating on a sea of fear."

"Very nice," Ben says. "Perhaps you will be the writer between us."

They exchange a smile.

"I see now that you started this process a long while back, didn't you? Capturing the story on paper, I mean."

"Oh yes – quite right. I wrote down many details even when I was with Ramon in our small room. I was determined to remember it all."

"And do you think it helped – having those notes from that time?"

"Most certainly. But you know…" Ben hesitates. "I must still work very hard to summon forth the feelings – they are quite buried. I think they needed to be. Buried, I mean."

Frau Bosch smiles.

"Until now."

CHAPTER FOURTEEN

ON BEING CONFIDENT AND ENTREPRENEURIAL TENDENCIES

Confidence. I was feeling a great deal of it. This time things had to work. I had a passport that was authentic, a visa which was flawless and an excellent name. I could say either thank you or something more dismissive if need be with flair. I was ready.

I said my farewells to Ramon and Hamid, and Peeruz took me to the airport.

At that moment, I felt genuinely sorry for the man: he seemed beaten, despite our imminent success, and his first step toward freeing his own family. I hoped my successful transfer would bolster him. I shook his hand and wished him luck — and I meant it.

Everything at check-in seemed in order. The airline agent asked for my ticket and passport. He looked at the passport and at me and smiled. I had none of my earlier fears weighing my chest.

And then. Just as the airline attendant was about to issue the boarding card, an older airline agent appeared behind him. He took my passport and examined it. He held the passport against the light in different angles and asked me when I arrived in India. I repeated the entry date, which was on the passport. According to it I had been in India for about six weeks.

The officer leaned toward me.

"Why does the entry date have a watermark? See? It is slightly discoloured. You can see it if you hold it against the light."

He held it up so I could see it.

I smiled.

"I remember what might account for it. A droplet of tea fell on this part of the passport while I was showing it to my Indian friend in a café. I immediately tried to dry it by blotting it with my handkerchief – I wasn't thinking. Could that have caused damage to the page?"

The agent, who was in fact an airport inspector, smiled.

"Yes. That makes sense."

He handed it back to the first agent with a nod, but stayed and watched. Seconds later, when the airline agent was about to hand it back to me with the boarding card, the airport inspector looked at me a second time.

"I only have one more question before you take the boarding card. Could you tell me the name of the airline you travelled to India on that day?"

I had done my homework. I knew that the owner of the passport had the exit stamp from Rome before coming to Bombay.

"I came to Bombay from Rome via Alitalia airline, Sir."

The inspector took the passport and boarding card and asked me to wait for him next to the counter.

My heartbeat began to rise. I could see Peeruz watching from a distance. I signalled that the inspector went to check something. Inside my head I kept repeating, 'God, Mohammed, Moses, Jesus or whoever is on call tonight, please let there have been a flight from Rome to Bombay on that day because I cannot take any more of this.'

After fifteen minutes the inspector returned.

"There was a flight from Rome to Bombay with Alitalia the day after your entry date, but not on that day. Something is incorrect in your passport. It seems you've altered your entry date. I suspect you've done so in order to stay here longer."

He paused to measure my reaction, but I remained still. I was gathering my thoughts, trying to keep my body from shaking.

The inspector continued. "If a tourist wants to stay here more than three months, he needs to go to the bureau of immigration and extend his tourist visa against payment. Some tourists don't want to pay the fee for the visa extension, you see, so they try to change the date on their own or with the help of forgers."

Another long pause. My throat went dry.

"I think that is what you have done."

There it was. I'd been found out again. A liar, a cheat. Not a boy who just wanted to get to freedom, but a criminal. *Well, Benjamin, what will you do now? Obviously, there was no divine intervention tonight. Think. Think. What story can you tell? What tale can you spin? What small deception can you offer to keep you out of jail this time? Go on, think. Find the lie. Make it a good one.*

I told the truth.

"Yes, Sir, you are correct. One of my acquaintances did it for me, but I am happy to pay the penalty for it now so I can take my flight."

I mean, I told the truth – sort of.

"I am afraid you cannot fly away tonight. In fact, you are under arrest now. Please follow me to my office. You can bring your belongings with you."

"Sir, I am really sorry for my wrongdoing and stupidity," I begged. "Please let me take the flight now. My relatives are expecting me today. Sir, I am more than happy to pay the fine for my forgery."

I felt a huge lump in my throat with a trembling voice. I asked the inspector to forgive me; I appealed to his sense of humanity while trying to control my emotions. But he did not show any mercy and seemed determined to see his version of justice through. It seemed that I would take another trip through another court system.

He asked a policeman to come and sit with me until the airport detective or interrogator arrived. We sat on a small hard bench in a small room.

When the interrogator arrived, there were no introductions or formalities. He merely opened his small notebook and began.

"Will you tell me why you changed the date of arrival to India in your passport?"

"I know it sounds stupid," I began, "but I wanted to extend my stay in India without paying a fee for extending the visa."

"Are you really twenty-six years old? You look younger."

"Yes, I am twenty-six years old. Sir, can I take my flight now? There is only a tiny bit of time left for me to still catch it."

"No, you cannot fly today. The court will have to make a decision on your situation."

"If I cannot fly now and have to go to the court, what is the point in asking me these questions again and again? I can answer the questions in court."

The detective smiled and left the room. He said he would be back soon. The policeman stood in front of the glass door looking out at the people in the hall.

Time dragged. It came to be 3:00, then 3:20. My plane had no doubt left. I grew more upset and frustrated. The fact was, I had noticed the watermark and discolouration in the entry date and asked Peeruz about it. He'd said nobody would care about the date of arrival, just about the photo in the passport and the visa. If only I had spoken up then, I could have been on the plane by now.

I became concerned about my escape story – the one I'd written in my notebook, which was in my carry-on bag. My real identity was in that notebook. I could not risk that being discovered– I would have to let it go. When the policeman looked away, I slipped my notebook into the rubbish bin. I had already written over 200 pages.

The interrogator returned.

"We don't know what to do with you here; therefore, you will be taken to the police station. They will tell you what you need to do. Either they confiscate your passport and you'll need to appear in court, or they will fine you and you will be released. It is quite early in the morning and there are no supervisory personnel here who can advise us on this."

Perhaps it was time for the truth. The real truth.

"I am sorry to cause trouble for you, Sir," I said, "but my passport is not genuine – and I am not a Spanish citizen."

The interrogator held the passport up against the light and turned the pages again and again.

"Of course, it is a fake passport, you son of a bitch. You tricked us, you bastard."

I was taken aback by his gruffness, but really, what else could I expect. The handcuffs would come soon. Then the cell.

The interrogator left the room and came back with the inspector who had initially suspected me. Both of them sat across from me. The inspector spoke.

"Where are you from?"

"Afghanistan," I responded.

The inspector became angry and started cursing in Hindi, his native language. He lifted his arm to hit me, but the interrogator told him to calm down. He continued with swear words and pounded the desk.

That second interrogation consumed another thirty minutes. I told them that I had a passport, which was issued in Pakistan, and that I had travelled legally to India, but wanted to go to Germany to live with my relatives.

I was handcuffed and two airport policemen transported me to a police station nearby. The policemen waited with me until eight o'clock for the day shift officer because the officer in charge of new arrivals was busy with cases that needed to be dealt with before mine.

The day shift officer began with my case. The questions were the same as before and the officer recorded the answers on a form. In the end he said I needed to go to the holding cell there in the building and wait for the transfer to the local jail.

The cell was tiny – two by four yards. My handcuffs were removed before I entered. There were already seven men sitting and standing there. We were apparently all new arrivals. The area was filthy and had no chairs. It was crowded and uncomfortable. I selected a spot by a relatively clean section of the wall and leaned against it. The air was pungent with body odour.

After several hours I began feeling ill. A tall, middle-aged, Caucasian man joined us. I had seen him handcuffed and guarded by two policemen at the airport. He stood next to me for a while and then sat down.

I closed my eyes and leaned my head against the wall, still feeling nauseated. The Caucasian man asked me if I was well. I explained that my stomach was upset from the stale air and odour.

"You only have to cope with this place for a few more hours. Then we will be taken elsewhere. This cell is temporary," he explained.

That was the last thing I remembered. I slid further down the wall as the room went black.

When I opened my eyes, I was sitting handcuffed in the police van between the Caucasian man and another prisoner. We were taken to the local jail to wait for our court appearance. At the new place, we had to undergo a body search and were required to hand over our shoes, belts and other personal belongings before entering the cell tract.

The tract where we were sent consisted of five cells, which were each about sixteen square yards. Some cells had more prisoners than others. My cell contained six prisoners – all of us were Non-Indians.

Andrew was a fifty-year-old man from Manchester in the United Kingdom, Pierre forty-four years old from Lyon in France, Abtin, an

Afghan from Kabul and seemed to be thirty years old, and Gen was forty or so – a Chinaman.

David was the sixth person in my cell; he was in his mid-forties, came from Detroit, USA and had been arrested at the same time as I. Like me, he had spent some time in the police station jail. I learned that David and another prisoner were the ones who carried me to the police van at the time of transfer to the main jail. He explained if I had been transferred to medical, my stay would have likely been extended; they were sure I wouldn't want that. I didn't have any clue what he was saying but thanked him for his intervention.

The prison cells were enclosed by walls on three sides and were open on the front so the prisoners could use the toilets at one end of the hallway. At the other end was an iron exit door. The tract was separated from the outside world by a four-foot-high brick wall with barbed wire that extended up another six feet. My cell was located on the first floor; there were also prisoners in cells on the ground floor.

The walls and the floor of the cells were made of concrete – filthy concrete. We were not provided with beds, mattress, pillows or a sheet or cover. Our choice for sleeping was to sit or lie on the naked floor.

The language was different, but so much about this prison – the management style, its design, the meals – was similar to the prison in Karachi. The food was inedible and the toilets were worse than the toilets in Karachi's prison. There was no tap water inside the prison tract. There were three metal barrels containing water in front of the two toilets in the hall. The water was undoubtedly contaminated and looked disgusting. It was meant for drinking and washing hands and body parts. I did not think anyone would dare drink it. But I had been wrong about so many things already – and clearly most of the prisoners were not concerned about sanitation and health.

Most of the local prisoners spat mucus or phlegm at the outside prison wall and at the barbed wire above the wall. The area was covered by thick slime, making the view stomach-churning. The meals were the same every day, consisting of a warm drink and a piece of bread in the morning and a kind of gravy with bread for lunch and supper. Several of us ate the bread and nothing else.

Pierre would swear in French every time a meal was served. I quickly grew accustomed to his outbursts, loudly expressing his displeasure, saying the food was not even fit for rats.

Andrew muttered something under his breath all the time, frequently using bad language. I couldn't determine if he cursed out of anger or excitement.

David – the American – did not talk much and tried to eat his meals without complaint. The Afghan and Chinese inmates did not talk much and ingested whatever they received.

I was the youngest prisoner in my cell. In fact almost some of the inmates in my cell could have been my father. Andrew was curious about how I ended up in that prison. He cautioned me over and over that I would not have a promising future if I started my prison career as a teenager.

David encouraged me to ignore Andrew's remarks. He said life was not always as predictable as some people thought. But even he asked me the same question.

"Why *are* you here, boy?"

"I tried to leave this country with a fake passport and was caught at the airport."

"That is not what I thought. I thought maybe you got caught with drugs like our Afghan and Chinese mates here," Andrew said, nodding toward the others.

"No. What about you?" I asked.

"No drugs for me either. I had smuggled some gold from Thailand and did not declare it."

"Why gold?"

"Because I earn bloody good money with it and it is something I am good at – usually."

Andrew turned to David.

"What is your story, mate?"

"Nothing, I am innocent and I have been mistaken for someone else."

"I am sure you were! I hope you have not killed anyone, my friend."

David flashed a smile. "Not yet."

Andrew had passed through Iran by car on his way to other parts of Asia many years before when the Shah governed Iran. He said he enjoyed his trip through Isfahan, but found Tehran unpleasantly overpopulated. He tried to entertain the other prisoners and often cracked jokes that many of the inmates did not understand; he laughed loudly, and often had to announce at the end that his story was meant to be a joke.

Prisoners were required to hire lawyers to represent them in the Indian court. The lawyers usually arrived at prison around noon. On my second day there, I also hired a lawyer. I advised him to contact Peeruz through the hotel reception desk and inform him that he was representing me. I explained to the lawyer that Peeruz knew me by a different name than the one by which I was registered in prison.

The lawyer explained to me that I would probably be fined for my offence and would be sentenced to four months that could be bought. He made me feel better about things. The indication that my case would be settled within weeks and that my prison time would be minimal and temporary was a great relief.

Several of us were taken from jail to the court building by the police bus. The lawyer met me there. He said that he would talk to the judge in the court and, like my previous lawyer, told me to keep quiet even though I had to be present.

Police accompanied a group of seven of us into the courtroom. We were handcuffed in front. We sat on a bench and waited for the judge. The lawyers stood in one corner. The room had one large door on each side. The doors were open all the time so people could enter and leave.

The judge entered the courtroom and took his seat. He was a short middle-aged man who sat down and perused the papers placed in front of him. He asked the court speaker to begin. They all spoke in Hindi. I could not understand a word.

After a few minutes a policeman motioned for us to stand. It was the same general procedure I had experienced in Karachi; the offender stepped forward when the speaker announced his name. I did not step forward when my Afghan name, Hafez, was announced, as I had completely forgotten my Afghan name. It was called a second time and the lawyer signalled me to move forward.

The judge looked at me and nodded, indicating I should step back.

We were escorted out of the courtroom and taken back to the van where we waited for a few hours in the blistering heat. One other prisoner and I were transferred from the van into a smaller police car. The lawyer approached me and related that the judge's verdict had gone just the way he expected; a prison sentence of six months that could be replaced by a fine: roughly 800 US dollars, which would cover both the fine and the lawyer's fee. I asked him to contact Peeruz for the money.

I was returned to my cell. David asked how things went and what my sentence was. David, Andrew and several of the other men appeared genuinely happy for me. They took it as a good omen and believed they would also be released very soon.

Andrew asked me why I did not buy a bottle of whisky for the others in the cell to celebrate my release. A joke.

I smiled. "Whisky and champagne will be delivered later in the afternoon by a bevy of dancing girls."

Smiles, nods and finger whistles.

"Will you retry going abroad after your release?" Andrew asked.

"Sure, I will certainly try," I said. "Again and again if necessary until I leave this country. I didn't come here to take roots, just to pass through."

"I admire your determination. They say that where there is a will, there is a way."

I had heard it, too, of course. It was trite, but I hoped it was true.

Two days later the lawyer informed me that I would be released later in the day. At the counter where I was to collect my possessions, I was told my shoes had been lost. I knew what 'lost' meant. I thought one of the guards must have needed a pair of shoes. They were not inexpensive.

I walked out of the jail barefoot.

I took a rickshaw and returned to the hotel. Not knowing for sure what was going on back there I knocked on the door of the room where I had been staying. Hamid opened it, clearly both relieved and happy to see me – barefoot or not.

Ramon explained that they had not been able to visit me in jail because they did not have any acceptable ID. I understood that. In fact, I had not expected visitors. I was not upset at them for that.

I was upset at Peeruz, however. I could not understand why he did not follow my case in jail.

"But of course I did, Ben," he said. "We were all very distressed about the turn of events. I got a lawyer – ask Hamid and Ramon! But he could not find your name."

"Really! Did you think I would tell them my real Iranian name? I was afraid if I let them discover my true nationality and name, they would send me back to Iran. I used my Afghan name."

Poor Peeruz. I saw the lightbulb moment of realisation. Sometimes I worried he was just not quick enough for the job. "I am really sorry that it didn't work for you," Peeruz said.

"Me, too. The passport was really good," I said. I thought he should know that. "But the date of arrival messed up the whole thing. The passport was confiscated, but I got the ticket back. I don't know how much we could get refunded for it."

"We need to ask the travel agency about that."

I was ready to get down to business again.

"Have you found any new ways of transfer? Any new smuggler with a better passport?"

"You just left the prison, Ben. Wait a few hours before you talk about leaving the country; aren't you afraid of ending up in jail again?"

"I've been there so often I'm becoming an old hand at it. Do you have any other plans? Now we know how much it costs to be released from prison – so it's not like it is a life sentence."

"It is not a life sentence, but it is a lot of money that is sacrificed each time our plan fails. Added all up – the jail fine, the price for the fake passport and the ticket – and we have invested about 2,000 US dollars. That does not include the emotional suffering for everybody."

"Yes, I understand." I knew the others had also worried over me during my absence. They were genuinely interested in my welfare. By now we'd all come to mean something to each other. "Where did you buy the Spanish passport for me and how much did you pay for it?"

"From the smuggler. I paid 600 US dollars for it."

"That is a lot of money."

"It was an original passport, so it was expensive."

"Over the weekend," Frau Bosch begins, "I was talking with a colleague – confidentially, of course – about your journey. He was most interested. I could not tell him the end, of course, since I don't know it yet myself. He said he wondered how I slept from session to session not knowing."

"Been there myself," Ben said offering a modest smile. "Alright."

Ben notices how she doesn't sit back in her chair the way she has on previous occasions, but places the sheets on her desk and leans over them, sitting forward on her seat. There is a new intensity about her.

He wonders if it's proper for the patient to be analysing the therapist.

She glances at her watch, continues.

"Maybe we can buy passports ourselves," I said. Peeruz had left the room. Ramon, Hamid and I continued the conversation.

"What do you mean?" Ramon asked.

"In the evening when we walk along the promenade next to the Taj Mahal Hotel, we see a lot of European tourists who smoke dope. That costs a lot of money. I have seen them trying to sell their possessions to people who pass by. Some of them who are more severely addicted might be willing to sell their passports. They can always get replacements for them at their embassies. I hate to say it, but they must know their lives are not going anywhere – not in their present state. I bet if we play our cards right, we can get passports for not more than 150 US dollars. What do you say? Are you game?"

Hamid was not game.

"I thought you came here to leave this country, not to start trading in passports and become a smuggler. I heard that people in prison don't rehabilitate, that they just become more criminalised. I think you are now a living example, Ben! No sooner are you out of prison and you have new corrupt ideas!"

"That new corrupt idea is all my own. I didn't learn it in prison. I am sorry that you feel irritated at me for the idea, but could you tell me how you will leave this country without a valid passport?"

"You know what will happen to you if the police catch you engaging in the buying of passports from tourists?"

"I think your guess is as good as mine. I know better than any of us. I was the one who was just released from the jail, remember!" I was annoyed at Hamid, after all I'd risked. "What I have learned," I said, "is that fear and indecision do not help our situation – they do not move us toward our goal. We need to take our destiny into our own hands. What makes you think that Peeruz knows any more about this than you and I? He does not have a clue. He has to depend on some ill-mannered traffickers and forgers for directions. Peeruz is older than us – and that is the *only* difference between him and us. This business is uncharted territory for him. I think we can find a way for ourselves. I, for one, am no longer willing to wait around for him to learn the trade by making mistakes with my life."

"But, we don't have any money," Ramon said as if perhaps he might be warming up to the idea.

"I understand that, but perhaps money is not the solution. We have to find a suitably sophisticated method, first, and then we can probably find an investor for our illegal start-up."

Hamid remained silent. Ramon had questions.

"What do you want to do now?"

"I think we should go out and try to buy some passports. Test the waters, perfect our methods. Maybe we can sell them and earn some money. The idea crossed my mind while I was sitting in the police van yesterday. "

"Sell them to whom?" Hamid was sceptical.

"To the people who sold them to us or Peeruz."

"Most tourists here seem to speak English," Hamid said. "I cannot speak English so I do not see how I can help."

"My English is also limited to a few words," Ramon added.

From Hamid the language barrier had been offered as a good reason to exempt himself from the plan. From Ramon it seemed like an unwanted handicap.

"Language does not need to be a problem. I can do the talking, but I would not dare venture out alone on my own. You both know that."

"Hamid, sleep over it?" Ramon said.

I was glad for Ramon's intervention. Hamid remained silent.

"I will come with you," Ramon said.

"I think I will just wait for Peeruz to get me a visa," Hamid said. "Unlike you two, I have an original passport."

I had been wondering when to tell Hamid what I knew about his passport. Now seemed the right moment.

"I don't want to upset you, Hamid, but you should know what Ramon and I know," I began, apologetically. I was not sure why I felt so apologetic – it was the rat Tarek who'd done the damage. "Tarek modified your passport so he could use it and go to Pakistan to collect Ramon and Safa. He changed your photo and date of birth."

I saw Hamid's bushy eyebrows shoot up.

"Put simply," I said. "Your passport is a mess and entirely useless to you now. I don't think Tarek has given it back to Peeruz – and even if he had, you cannot use it anymore."

"I'm sorry, Hamid, but what Ben said is the truth," Ramon added. "You must forget your Iranian passport. It is doubtful they will issue a replacement for you in India."

Hamid stood and paced, all the while swearing at Tarek and Peeruz, suggesting inventive ways for drawing and quartering them both. Ramon and I just sat back and let it run its course. Much of it was humorous, but we didn't let on.

I needed to sleep. I had not slept well in jail.

On the following morning I was awakened when someone started knocking on the other side of the wall. It went on for several minutes. I thought that a child might be in the next room playing some game against the wall with a ball. Moments later Hamid returned from the washroom.

"I thought you would be sleeping all day," he said. "I thought you were exhausted."

"I am, but I think a child has been knocking on the other side of the wall. It woke me up."

"It is not a child; it is a girl who is with a one-armed man speaking Arabic."

"That doesn't explain why she knocks on the wall."

"I saw her in the hallway the other day and smiled at her. Since then, whenever she is alone, she knocks on the wall and I knock back.

"Is that all? Probably she fell in love with your green eyes, Hamid. I imagine they can be very tempting."

"I suppose it is juvenile, but what else can I do?"

"Ask her to go out with you."

"Are you nuts? She is with the Arab man. She may be his wife or fiancé. I can't go out with her. Soon you will hear, through that same wall, the man making love with her. He is really loud and rough!"

I could barely visualise love making. I had *no* reference point for *rough* love making.

"I don't think I want to hear them making love. Obviously, she is interested in you. Maybe she needs more than one lover. Maybe she is a nymphomaniac or less happy with the current lover. We can find out what the story is. Have you talked to the man?"

"With which language? The man sits in the reception area and watches Indian movies on television in the afternoons. God, I hate this guy. Maybe you could find out what the deal is for me."

"What do you want me to ask him? 'Excuse me, Sir. Do you mind if my friend dates your wife?'"

"I don't know why I wasted my time being worried about you when you went to prison. You don't respect your friends' feelings at all."

I could see that my attempt at humour had fallen flat.

"I am sorry, Hamid, but what you are asking sounds mad. You can hear them getting intimate and yet you are still interested in the girl. I don't understand you, but I will see what I can do for you. I have never worked as a *procurer* before, but as people here say, *'Everything is possible in India'*. It should not be difficult for me to find this one-armed man."

"Just think of it as you being a friend who is going to help out a friend in need. There is no pimping to it. I won't pay you, you know!"

"A friend in great need of a woman, it would seem. I will do my best to satisfy your needs – no, that did not come out right. Anyway, I just wish you would have found a woman who was single. Or at least alone."

I was not sure why I took on this challenge. As if I did not have enough to worry over already! But I seemed to be the one in our little group who could envision how to get things done. Even it meant luring a young woman away from her rough-sex one-armed man.

That afternoon I casually wandered into the hotel's reception area and eyeballed the one-armed man. Sure enough, just like Hamid said: there he was with his movie. I took a seat next to him and offered a casual greeting. He nodded and asked me where I was from.

"Iran. What about you?"

"Saudi Arabia."

"Are you here for sightseeing? A tourist?" I asked.

"Yes, for four weeks. I haven't seen you here before," he said intending it to be a question.

"Unexpectedly, I had to go on a short business trip so I was away for a while, but my associates were here, in the room next to yours, I believe. Are you enjoying your stay?" I asked.

"Yes, it is okay."

"Are you alone or with friends?"

"I am alone. You?"

"Like I said, I'm here with some associates."

"Associates?"

"Yes, we are doing business with Europe and waiting for our partners there to seal a deal. A bit nerve-racking at this point."

"You seem so young for deals and partners."

"That's what all the girls say, too, I'm afraid — too young."

He smiled and nodded, then continued the conversation.

"I have not been to Europe yet, but I come here once a year and stay in this hotel."

"May I ask what line of work you are in?"

"I am a driver working for the police in Madinah."

"Are you married?"

"No, but maybe soon."

He removed a bottle of Johnnie Walker from his handbag and asked whether I would like to drink a glass of whisky with him.

"Thank you, but no. I must admit I have never tried it. I'm just too young, remember, you suggested it yourself. I think it would be very strong for me. Maybe in a few years!"

He laughed.

"It will put hair on your chest. I like whisky very much. I drink it whenever I come to India. Alcohol is illegal in my country — I could not buy it freely."

"Alcohol is strictly forbidden in Iran, too, and those who are caught consuming it can be punished with a public lashing according to the Islamic laws. Some Iranians make a home brew, but the ingredients in the wrong proportions can lead to blindness and even death. I figure they must be desperate to chance it."

"Do the police have breathalysers in your country?"

"Not to my knowledge — of what use would they be in a country where there is no alcohol?"

He winked at me and laughed again.

295

Presently, I excused myself, thanking him for the conversation.

Later that afternoon I asked the receptionist whether he knew who the girl was with the Arab man.

"Such rich men come here regularly and hire girls through some agencies," he told me. "Some of them keep the girls in their rooms for a few weeks. They do whatever they want with those poor women. Unfortunately, there is no law that can stop it. It is a business here."

"I thought the girl with him was his fiancée."

The receptionist smiled.

"Fiancé for a week, perhaps. No, these girls prostitute themselves to feed their family members. You know, in many poor families that profession is passed on from one generation to the next. One could call it a family tradition. Women and female children are the only source of income for many families. Many prostitutes like to be with men like the Arab man because he'll keep one girl for several weeks. That way the girls don't have to find new clients so often."

"I feel sorry for the girls who have to rent their bodies for money, but there is nothing I can do to stop it."

"The girls would be displeased with you if you stopped it. For many, their bodies are all they have to keep them and their families alive."

It was hard to believe. I wasn't so naive that I didn't know about prostitution, but it had never touched my life before. I was disgusted.

"You should go to the red-light district in the city," the receptionist suggested, mistaking my questions for genuine personal interest. It has been there since the nineteenth century. The British military established and maintained many of the brothels for their soldiers. There are prostitutes who were born in the very whorehouses where they now work. Many of the young teenagers and even preteens have been bought from their families and sent there to learn the profession. Once a girl ends up in one of them there is no way out for her. Many die of terrible diseases."

"It sounds distressing and deplorable. I don't know if I want to hear more about it. I think it makes me feel embarrassed and ashamed for humanity when I learn of such sufferings and injustice – and it seems to be everywhere I have travelled recently. We moan about our petty problems. When compared to things like that, they amount to nothing. We forget to appreciate our freedom."

"India is a very diverse country and has both limitless poverty and wealth!"

Was this an excuse? A justification? What I heard him say was: that was the way it was and that was how it was going to be – *the end.*

Back in the room, I broke the news to Hamid about the status of the girl of his dreams. He stomped around. He swore, got angry and threatened the man with despicable actions. I think there was more drawing and quartering.

After that ran its course – and it always did – he said he would invite the girl to our room when the Arab man was at the reception areas the next day. I tried to point out some weaknesses in his plan.

"What do you want to do with the girl? You can't speak her language and she cannot speak yours. Would you just sit and look at each other all the time?"

"I don't know, but I really like her; she is very sweet."

I knew none of what I said made any difference to him.

"Are you in love now? Once the Arab man goes back to his country are you going to propose?"

"You must be a lunatic. I'm more convinced than ever that jail has ruined your character completely."

"I am sorry that I touched a nerve, Hamid. If you'll stop taking my jokes so seriously, I think I can help you with your love affair. The Arab asked me to drink whisky with him yesterday, but I rejected his offer. He sits in the hotel lobby most afternoons."

Hamid interrupted. "Yes. Between his lovemaking sessions, he goes to the lobby to rest and regenerate. I hate him and could punch him."

"It seems you know his timetable and must know when he goes to the lobby! Listen up; don't start a fight with him over a girl you don't even know. Besides, you are half his size even if you think size doesn't matter. Maybe I can go out with him so you can bring her to the room and she can look into your beautiful eyes and touch your moustache or whatever boys and girls in love do."

"You are not taking my feelings seriously."

"Okay. I'm sorry. Do you want me to ask the Arab away from the hotel for a walk around the area so you can be alone with his girl?"

"Yes! Very much! That would be great. You are a genuine friend and I won't forget it."

"Hamid, I take your praises about as seriously as I do your swearwords."

The following day I made the effort to find the Arab man – Aleem was his name – while he was in the lobby. I took a seat next to him and offered small talk. Eventually, I asked Aleem if he would like to go for a walk to the Taj Mahal Palace Hotel for an hour or so after it got cooler. We agreed to meet in the lobby around seven o'clock.

Hamid was happy. So happy he said he needed to shave for the second time that day; he wanted to look very good for the girl.

Aleem and I left the hotel and walked along the promenade to the Gateway of India that spread out in front of the Taj Mahal Palace. We walked into the lobby and sat there for nearly an hour. Aleem ordered a shot of whisky for himself and a beer for me.

We talked about a variety of topics, but our conversation narrowed quickly around the restrictions in Islam and what a Muslim should and should not do. Aleem shared his ideas quite openly. His views represented an odd menu – a sampling picked according to his wishes from the teachings. He was fine with drinking alcohol, which is forbidden in Islam, and seemed to be all for prostitution, but he strongly opposed eating pork and non-halal foods. I pointed out that alcohol does more harm to the body than non-halal meat, but Aleem was not about to be persuaded.

We returned to our hotel two hours later. I went to my room – knocking before entering. I didn't want to interrupt any intimate eye-gazing.

Hamid was sitting on the bed with a huge smile on his face. He thanked me for taking the Arab out."

"Did the girl come to you here?"

"I knocked at her door when there wasn't anyone in the hallway and asked her to come to our room."

"When are you planning to get married?"

"You are being silly again. She is a very beautiful girl, just nineteen years old."

"Hey, in Iran the morality police would demand a marriage."

Hamid ignored me.

"Did you kiss her or anything?" I asked, somewhat surprised that I actually found myself interested.

"Yes, we kissed each other and the rest is for adults and I am not telling you anything more."

"Good! I don't think I approve of what you did."

"What do you want me to say? It was wonderful and very relaxing. I think I need something like that after months of being Peeruz's captive."

"I suppose I should be glad it worked the way you wanted it to. Didn't Ramon disturb you here?"

"No. He was very cooperative and went to watch a movie in the hotel lobby."

"I hope you don't fall in love. You must not forget why you came to this country in the first place!"

"No, I won't. I am going to buy her a present tomorrow."

"A ring?"

I burst into laughter. He ignored me again.

"Maybe a nice necklace that I can afford."

"It is nice of you and I think she will probably remember you for the rest of her life."

Ramon returned and he and I walked to the Gateway of India where many tourists were walking or leaning against the short wall on the side of the promenade. One of the tourists stopped next to me and asked for a cigarette lighter. I said I didn't smoke and didn't have one. The young man asked me if I knew anyone selling hashish.

"No, we don't know anyone. Where are you from?" I asked him.

"Denmark. My name is Sigurd. Have you been to Denmark?"

"No. How long have you been here?"

"Two months."

"Are you working here?" I asked.

"No, I'm here to enjoy life and not for work. I have to go back soon as I'm about out of money."

"Would you like to sell your passport so you can have some money and stay here longer? You can get an ID from your consulate here and go back home without any issues."

"What do you want to do with my passport?"

"We have a friend who has lost his and needs one to travel to Europe. He's in a real bad spot."

"Why can't he go to his embassy and get a new one?"

"He has some sort of problem about it and can't get a replacement easily. Anyway, think about it and if you like we can meet up here tomorrow evening at the same time. I will pay you 150 US dollars. You should go to your consulate and get a new passport or something that takes you back home before we complete the deal."

"I'll think about it. 150 US, right?"

"Correct."

"Why did you ask him to sell his passport?" Ramon asked.

"I don't know. I guess I just wanted to see how people react when you ask them that question. Blond hair and blue eyes – he certainly wasn't an undercover cop."

"Are you crazy?" He pointed at his own head of dark hair. "Blond hair! Blue eyes! Neither of us could use his passport."

"Not for us. For a trial run. I have been thinking we should buy some passports and sell them in order to make some money here. Then we can afford to leave this country."

"Who would buy them?"

"Human traffickers like the man who sold Peeruz the Spanish passport I tried to use. He received 600 US dollars for it. I think they are always in need of new passports."

The next afternoon we showed up at the same spot. The Danish man was waiting for us. He said he had called his consulate and discovered that he could get a temporary ID for returning home. He said he would like to sell his passport for 200 US dollars. I negotiated with him and in the end we agreed on 160 US dollars.

"You will need to accompany us to our hotel. I never bring money into this district."

Ramon remained with Sigurd in the lobby while I went to our room and asked Hamid to lend me the money to buy the passport. Within minutes we had a new, fully authentic, Danish passport. How simple it had been. Before we parted I asked him where we could meet Europeans.

He named two cafes that were not far from our hotel.

I talked to Peeruz about the idea of purchasing and reselling passports and he seemed very surprised that I had taken the initiative. He added that he could certainly sell the passport I had acquired to any number of smugglers who were desperate to purchase original passports with authentic visas.

A few days later I went to one of the cafés European tourists frequented. There were many people coming and going. I took a seat and pretended to be waiting for someone. I wanted to know what kind of things went on there. I soon realised that, for one thing, there were a number of people selling hashish and other drugs. Nobody seemed to be monitoring them.

The following day I went back. There was a young man wearing hippie clothing sitting alone at a table. I approached him and asked him if his name was George. The man, who was going on thirty, looked puzzled and said he wasn't – that I had been mistaken.

"Sorry. I was told by a mutual friend to come here and meet George who would be wearing something like what you are wearing. He is a journalist and wanted to hear my story. I thought you might be the man, that's all."

He smiled and repeated that he didn't know George. I asked where he came from.

"The Netherlands. My name is Klaas."

He offered his hand and motioned for me to take a chair at his table. After a few minutes when things seemed comfortable between us I got down to the point of my visit.

"This will probably sound a bit weird, and you are not obliged to continue the conversation, but I have a European friend who is looking for a European passport to fly back home. He would like to buy an original passport. Do you know anyone who might be interested in selling one? The person wouldn't be stranded here. He can get a replacement from his consulate for a small amount of money."

"No, I don't know anyone, but just because I'm nosy, how much would your friend pay for the passport?"

"I think he said 150 US dollars, maybe it was 125 US dollars."

"I could do it myself. I am experiencing a cash flow shortage at the moment, but I couldn't risk it for less than 200 US dollars."

"I'm not sure if he will go that high, but I will ask him for you. Be sure that you really want to do it. If yes, we can meet here tomorrow and I will tell you what he said about the amount. If we can strike a deal, I will give you the money in return for your passport. If I were you, first, I would call the consulate and see what they need for issuing a temporary ID."

"I will do that immediately and I will see you tomorrow."

I told myself I was doing him a big favour – money for something he really didn't need. I cautioned him to take steps necessary to protect himself and required that he take time to think about it. With those things in place I felt okay about myself.

I met him the next day. I asked to examine the passport. I had learned a lot about what to look for over the past months. I agreed to his price and the exchange was made — with care, under the table.

I left the café and walked a quiet street back toward the hotel. Two young, rough looking Indian men approached me from the back. They grabbed me and started beating on me. They didn't say anything. I was soon on the ground. They kicked me in the legs and back. I lay there helpless in terrible pain. The larger of them eventually spoke.

"You will not come to the café anymore. It is our territory."

Territory for what I wondered. Then it hit me.

"I am not into selling drugs. My line is something else entirely."

They each kicked me one more time.

"You will not come back or we will kill you."

They left no doubts about the sincerity of their message.

I gradually regained my composure and walked — limped, really — back to the hotel.

Ramon promised to accompany me the next time. I felt rather stupid. I had violated the first rule I had set for us about venturing out alone.

I gave the passport to Peeruz to sell to the smugglers and asked him to put the amount he received for it against my future expenses with him.

A few days later there was a knock at my hotel door. The Danish man was standing there.

"Why are you here, Sigurd?"

"I need twenty dollars for my food over the next two days while I wait for my flight."

"What makes you think I will give you money? We completed our deal. I can see I made a mistake letting you know where I am staying."

"You seemed like a kind and honest man and I am desperate. Once I am in my country, I will send you the money back — to your room at this hotel."

"Sure you will, probably with interest. Here, take this twenty-dollar bill and please go away. People may think I am dealing drugs. I can't have that. Please don't come back as it is embarrassing for me and dangerous for both of us."

He thanked me and left.

Hamid, willing to risk his health for the girl of a one-armed Arab, could not abide this risk. "You should not have brought him here."

"He was my first client, and I realised that it was a mistake. I didn't do it with the second. Today I have learned several good lessons – and as soon as my ribs heal, I will probably be more able to appreciate them."

Ramon and I began a late evening routine, walking along the promenade close to our hotel. It was cooler and many tourists left their hotels to take walks at that time of day. When we saw a potential client – a European man who looked to be in need of money – we would approach him and offer to buy his passport. We always asked them to think about our proposal for twenty-four hours. I wanted the deal to really help them as well as us. We occasionally used dark corners in one of the nearby hotel lobbies for exchanging the passport for the money.

Ramon became fascinated by our work. His head ran way ahead and way too fast. He thought we should start our own business transferring passengers abroad because changing photos and other details on a real passport was obviously less of a hassle than obtaining a genuine document.

We knew that there was a huge demand for such a service. Hotel after hotel was filled with Iranians and Afghans who were desperate to find a way out of India.

I reminded him that we had not come to India to get involved in human trafficking – not from that side of the arrangement, at least. Our future in that business would be bleak and would be a waste of our real talents.

One afternoon later in the week the hotel receptionist came to our room and asked me to come and meet a friend. He did not say who the friend was. I could hardly believe who was standing there. It was David, the American inmate from the Bombay prison.

"How did you ever find me here?"

"I remembered the name of the hotel and I just thought I would drop in and see if you were still here."

"I am, but then I guess that is obvious at this point. When were you released?"

"Yesterday. I am staying in a small hotel not far from here. Do you want to join me for a drink? We can walk a bit on the streets."

We walked and eventually found ourselves sitting in the lobby of the Taj Mahal Palace. David ordered a whisky and I asked for a beer. I seldom took more than a sip or two, but the fact I had something always seemed to make the other person feel better.

David asked if I had found a competent smuggler yet.

I told him no and explained that I was purchasing passports from Europeans and reselling them to earn money for my passage. I had been depending on my relatives and thought it was time I took that responsibility for myself.

David smiled and seemed interested.

"How enterprising. Maybe you could buy one or two passports for me. I need one for myself."

"There are many people here who ran out of money and they are happy to get some extra cash, and selling a passport is an easy way. Do you have someone to exchange the picture on the passport for you or should I find someone to do it?"

"Actually, I am very good at doing that myself and I also know some friends in New Delhi who do a good job."

I suddenly felt the need to know more about him.

"I don't know why you were arrested at the airport. Is it a private thing or can you tell me the reason?"

"Put it this way, I was arrested because the police thought I was a spy because I had a fake passport like you. I am not a spy. I could not tell them what I really do because that is not a legal business. I think I should not tell you either because the less you know the better for you. I am not a killer, rapist or dangerous person."

"That is comforting, but I never took you for an abusive person. Where do you live when you are not in India?"

"Most of the time in Singapore. I have friends and a girlfriend there."

"When do you go back to the USA?"

"I have no plans to do that for the time being. I have not been back home for almost ten years. By the way, I visited Tehran a few times before the Islamic Revolution. I also lived in that area for six months and worked as a mechanical engineer. I had a Persian girlfriend while I was there. She was strikingly beautiful, but a bit mercurial. I think she was probably interested in me because she wanted to go to America as most of her relatives lived there. The last time when I was in Iran was 1977. I don't think many Americans visit Iran since the revolution. I suppose we are your enemy now."

"That is only what Iranian and American politicians claim. It is not most people's view. I find it difficult to hate someone because of his nationality or because his government is not on good terms with mine. That goes against common sense."

"I am a Jew, but I am not a practising Jew. Maybe you can start hating me now!"

"As long as you don't compromise my freedom, I won't hate you, David."

We exchanged smiles and left the lobby, each heading to his hotel. David promised to see me again in a few days. He said he would talk to some of his friends about the prospects for getting me to Europe.

"What a rollercoaster!" the psychologist says, almost amused. "I'm exhausted just reading about it. I keep saying it, Ben, and I'll say it again: your life story is incredible. You have lessons you could teach all of us."

"I must get my own house in order first before I attempt to present lessons. It is astounding how much better things are in my life since I began all this," Ben responds.

"All this? Meaning . . .?"

"You, me, here, writing. Fewer nightmares have led to more fruitful sleep, which in turn has led to a more productive life. My teachers say they notice the change."

"That pleases me, you know."

"Yes, I know."

"You understand this has been a most unusual approach for me."

"Yes. Tailor-made to my needs. I appreciate that." Ben offers a quick smile.

"I sense we are coming to the end of your story. I am eager to read more."

"I'll do my best, assuming I don't get arrested and thrown in jail again."

CHAPTER FIFTEEN

IN LOVE AND LEAVING

Ben hands his last set of pages to the psychologist.

"You will be amazed to hear that I never did get out of India."

She looks puzzled.

Ben lingers in the moment.

"Kidding. Absurdities. I'm coming to enjoy them. It's my way of accepting all of them that have followed me around the past year."

Frau Bosch smiles and starts reading the pages.

"Would you like a cold drink?"

Who, me? Was she talking to me?

"Excuse me, would you like something cold to drink?"

I managed to stutter a weak *yes*.

I was standing in a travel agency with Peeruz, sweating in the heat of the building. I happily accepted the offer – and I noticed she had not extended it to any of the other young men there. I probably would have accepted the cold drink even had it been ten below zero. She was that stunning.

She left and came back with a bottle of soda. She didn't speak, but smiled again and went back to her desk.

Peeruz had asked me to accompany him to the travel agency, as he wanted to cancel his return ticket to New Delhi. It was crowded so we were asked to wait in the waiting area for the appropriate customer adviser. While we were waiting, I had noticed a beautiful young woman working at the desk behind the counter. By chance, the two of us made eye contact. Or maybe it was not by chance. She glanced away, but then came back. She had a wonderful smile. When Peeruz moved on up to the counter to speak with the representative, I moved to the side. That's when the young woman approached me and asked if I would like a cold drink.

I had never had a girlfriend — that was very complicated in my country. My relationships with girls had been either strictly platonic or hormone driven fantasies.

I let myself believe that this young woman had some interest in me. I plucked up my courage and moved to her desk, asking for a piece of paper and pencil. She seemed happy to provide them. I moved back to the counter and wrote down my name, the name of the hotel and the hotel's phone number. I returned to her, slipped the sheet into a magazine on her desk and handed her the pencil. I thanked her for the drink, turned and left. By that time Peeruz had finished his business and we walked outside together.

Peeruz turned to me and asked if I had seen the attractive girl who was sitting behind the desk.

"I saw her. She brought me a fizzy drink, in fact."

"You old fox. Make a date?"

"I am inexperienced in such things, but I left her a note about how to contact me. I guess it will be up to her now."

"She could be a model, you know," he said. "A natural beauty."

I nodded, confirming his contention.

"You need to be more forward in such a situation. Show the woman you are in command. Women love that in a man."

"There was no opening back in Iran for me to practise such things, you understand. Boys and girls are not really allowed to mingle."

"You need to make up for it now. Here you see boys and girls together everywhere. Take advantage of the freedom."

"It's a wonder there has become a new generation in Iran, in light of that prohibition."

We smiled. I had talked about such things with boys my age, sharing our ignorance, but never with an adult. It was not comfortable. He continued.

"I think your generation will have deep psychological problems because you have been kept from getting to understand women first-hand. They are put together differently."

"I have noticed, and I like the difference very much."

I had missed his point and he clarified it for me.

"I mean: psychologically different. They have different takes on life than men. It is good to let some of that rub off on us, I think."

I knew that just from watching my relatives interact. I assumed that sooner or later I'd gain my own first-hand experience with girls. But I was not sure when or how it would happen. Peeruz was right – I was lacking certain knowledge of how to even approach them. He blamed the new governmental regime that had come into power after he had been a young man. And it may have been their fault, yes, but I could never change that. I still had to make do with my own knowledge and experience – or lack thereof.

But this wasn't just about girls.

"If I recall correctly, your generation was the one that was not happy with the way the former officials were running our country," I said. "You brought about the government change, allowing the clerics to take over. Some people think your generation had a lot of freedom before the revolution and did not know how to use it wisely. If it hadn't been for the way you messed things up, we wouldn't be here in India now, waiting our lives away as asylum seekers, looking for smugglers to transfer us abroad."

"Much of what you say is true, of course. Sorry, but we didn't know things would take a turn for the worse. Still, at least you do have an opportunity while you are here to bring yourself up to date on the female gender."

"I think I am a late bloomer!"

"And you will stay one if you don't provide yourself with your own base of personal experiences."

I knew he was right. After all, in some circles I was *Juan Diego Cortez: twenty-six!* It was high time I learned a thing or two.

We were soon back at our hotel. Hamid asked me to occupy the Arab man for an hour again so he could have some quiet time with the Indian girl. I had been against it before, but after my chat with Peeruz, my resolve was weakening. Hamid wanted to give her the gift he had bought her. He didn't say what it was. I thought it was odd, this compulsion boys had to buy girls gifts at the beginning of a relationship. Perhaps with more experience I would understand.

That afternoon while I was sitting with the Arab man to keep him distracted and occupied, the receptionist called me to the phone. It was from a woman, he said repeatedly raising his eyebrows. He humorously tried to make it into a big deal. I tried my best to ignore him.

It was the girl from the travel agency. I recognised her voice. My heart began beating faster. My mouth went desert dry. It produced a series of strange sensations. She introduced herself as Sandy and said that, even though she thought she was a few years older than I was, she would like to meet me. She suggested the following day. We agreed to meet at my hotel in the reception area the following afternoon.

I hung up. I could not believe my luck. She had done almost all of the talking, I realised. I had the feeling that she knew I was shy and inexperienced in dealing with girls.

I was immediately excited at the prospect of seeing her. It seemed like a dream – a dream that was actually going to come true. I didn't tell anyone about it because I wanted to wait and see if she would really show up. I knew back in high school girls would sometimes promise things to boys and then not carry through on them. They seemed to think it was funny. The boys never did.

But Sandy was as good as her word. She arrived at the hotel just before six o'clock the following evening. Peeruz was sitting with his two children in the lobby watching television. He was clearly taken by surprise. He motioned me to him.

"Why didn't you tell me?" Peeruz asked.

"I didn't tell you because I wasn't sure if she would come."

"Take her to a nice café; I would say you take her to the café in the Taj Mahal Palace. I will pay for the drinks and don't worry about the cost. I think you deserve a treat after your jail time! Leave a nice impression on her. Mesmerise her!"

"Thanks for the tips, Peeruz. I will do my best." I had no idea what he meant by *mesmerising her*, but I would certainly try.

In the Taj Mahal Palace, we were seated in the café. I ordered a coffee. She preferred cappuccino.

Sandy was an upfront sort of person. She said she was a Jew and belonged to Bene Israel ethnicity. She went on to say that her family had moved to Bombay generations before. I figured that explained why she did not have the dark Indian complexion, but looked more like Iranians and Turks. She was twenty-one years old and already had a degree in chemistry. She could not find employment in that field, so she took the job at the travel agency. Sandy had been single for almost a year after separating from her boyfriend who cheated on her with her best friend. I couldn't figure out how any man would cheat on a well-mannered and attractive girl like Sandy.

Rather than telling Sandy I didn't have a passport and was looking for a way to leave India via a smuggler, I told her that I was waiting for a visa for Germany and would leave India when the visa was ready.

Our conversation went on for hours. Neither of us was aware of the time.

She looked at her watch and noted that it was very late and she needed to return home.

"The time went by so fast," I said. "My physics teacher told us that Einstein was once asked to explain the theory of relativity to a layperson and he said: *'When you are courting an attractive girl, an hour seems like a second. When you are sitting on a red-hot cinder, a second seems like an hour. That's relativity.'* After tonight, I understand that."

Sandy laughed and looked at her watch again.

"It has been a very nice evening. Ben. Thanks for explaining the relativity theory in a simple way!"

We left the hotel and kissed each other on the cheeks before she got in her taxi. Sandy promised to meet me again in two days.

I had kissed many female relatives on the cheek before, but it felt *nothing* like that!

The two-day wait seemed like an eternity to me. I couldn't explain the feelings I felt for her because I had never felt that way for any girl before. I began to understand about Hamid and the Indian girl.

I returned to my hotel room and told Hamid how my first date – ever – had gone. He asked me if I was in love.

"I don't know the signs of being in love so I have nothing to compare my feelings with. I do know that I really like her very much and want to see her again and spend as much time as possible with her. Would you regard that as love as an older and more experienced friend?"

"Probably, yes. Many don't believe love can happen so fast. I think they are wrong."

"If it is love, you need to make some space for the lover and his beloved one soon."

"What do you mean by that?" Hamid asked.

"I have asked her to come here in two days, so you and Ramon need to leave the room for a few hours. Now you can return my favour."

"We will be happy to stay away so you can have privacy so long as she goes home at the end of the evening because Ramon and I don't want to sleep on the street."

"I will make sure she goes back home after a few hours."

Frau Bosch looks up, smiles. "Our narrative has taken a turn."

"I had to write this hurriedly. I hope it is satisfactory."

"More than. I find it interesting that you had time for the finer things in life, even as you were honing your skills as a smuggler."

Ben is not sure where the psychologist has got to in the notes.

"*Coffee,*" she says. "You never forget that first kiss."

Ben blushes. There is a lighter air about them now. Frau Bosch seems to be enjoying herself.

And so is he.

David came to the hotel the next afternoon and took me to a café in another local hotel.

"I have talked to a friend in Nepal. He said he could get you out of Nepal easily, but you need to go there first."

"How?"

"You can go to a border city and from there smugglers will have no problem getting you into Nepal. I think it is similar to the way you left Iran and came to Pakistan, but far less dangerous. That border is not really patrolled. Once you are there you need to go to Kathmandu."

"It sounds very scary. Nepal is so far away from Bombay. It means going farther away from Europe again. I am sorry, but it sounds to me like another failure in the making."

"Do you know Henry Ford?" David asked.

"No, wasn't he one of your presidents?" I responded.

"No, he was the founder of the Ford Motor Company; he manufactured cars."

"Like the Ford Mustang?"

"Yes, that's the company."

"Did he go to Nepal, too?" I asked.

"No. He was one of the most successful men in history. I was going to tell you something he said. *Failure is only the opportunity to begin again more intelligently.*"

"Would you please ask Mr Ford how many times I need to fail before good things start to happen?"

David smiled.

"He passed away a long time ago. If Nepal is not of any interest to you, I will check for other options and let you know. You seem to be happy today. Has something important happened to you?"

"Yes. Two things actually. I received money in an envelope from a Scandinavian man – money I loaned some time ago. I had never expected to see it again. But, that is not the best of the news."

"I'm listening."

"I met a girl and already had a date. In fact, she is a Jew like you. I didn't know there were Jews in India.

"Yes, much to the chagrin of many people, you will find us everywhere, no matter where you go. You know if you have a child with the girl you dated the child will be a Jew and not a Muslim."

"Really? I can't say I really know anything about interfaith marriage, but I think in Islam, if the father is Muslim, the children will be considered Muslim. It seems a Muslim-Jewish marriage would cause a lot of issues. I personally don't care much about my children's religion. In fact, I prefer that they choose one for themselves when they are old enough. Besides, I thought you were not practising your religion!"

"That's right. I feel that morality is important and it is not necessarily connected with any religion as it existed prior to any religion."

"I heard something similar before. We should change the theme before I forget the other important news."

"What is it?"

"I have bought a few passports recently. I gave them to Peeruz, the man who takes care of us. There was nothing for a man your age since most people who look destitute here are younger."

"No worries about the age, I can have the dates changed easily," David said with a smile.

"If the age is irrelevant, it is easy to find you passports. I will ask around tomorrow."

David had things to do so we parted. I returned to my hotel, collected Ramon and went back to the promenade to look for tourists who would sell their documents.

"I need to purchase a passport for my friend from prison. He says the age on it doesn't matter," I explained to Ramon.

"So, now you are getting passport orders first and then looking for specific sellers. I would call it a custom, made-to-order service!"

"Name it what you want, but at the moment we don't have any other way to earn money."

Over the next three days we bought two more passports. I was getting very good at picking my subjects. Interestingly, none of the people I picked said no. When we didn't make a deal it was because the passport owners asked for too much money. One man from France asked for 1,000 US dollars and one from Austria asked for 500 US dollars. We stayed under 250 US dollars unless we had a specific order from a wealthy client. We were looking for an American or Canadian passport, but found they were difficult to come by.

Sandy started coming to my place three or four evenings a week. She would leave before midnight. We usually stayed in the room throughout the evening. She often brought food so we didn't need to go out. It was my first love affair, and only Sandy's second. I found the relationship very comfortable – and comforting. Sandy was not only beautiful, but also thoughtful and compatible with me in every way. I thought the affair helped me grow emotionally stronger and increased my self-confidence.

On one occasion I mentioned my morale-boosting affair to David. He laughed and said, "It is always interesting at the beginning, but things change over time. We say that women are like a hurricane: at first warm, wet and wild, and in the end they take your house and your car and leave you with nothing. That is just a piece of advice – caution, perhaps – for you to tuck away for later in life."

"That is funny, but I think at the moment I don't have to be afraid of such things." I chuckled at David's view. A man of clearly more experience than I. "By the way," I said, changing topics. "I have bought two passports for you to look at. I forgot to bring them today, but on the way back you can see them at my hotel

David looked at the passports and said he would take both of them. He had a valid passport but it was held up from when he was in jail. I had paid 340 US dollars for the two, which was all I asked from him. He insisted that I make at least a modest profit and gave me 450 US dollars.

I was starting to feel like things were moving in the right direction. I asked Sandy to bring one of the flight timetable booklets from her travel agency so I could study the flight routes to Europe.

Over the next few days I studied them to learn about the various routes to Germany. I spent so much time with them that Hamid and Ramon teased me, asking if I had given up girls for flight schedules. They thought it was hilarious. I kept quiet but, knowing what I had learned by then, I knew I would never give up girls.

One evening when David and I met for a drink at a hotel bar, I took out the flight schedule and asked several questions about the options. There was a flight that had caught my attention; it took off from Bombay and carried both domestic and international passengers. It landed in New Delhi where the domestic passengers were dropped off and then took the international passengers on to Frankfurt. I wanted to know if the international passengers had to leave the plane in New Delhi and take another plane, or if they remained on the same plane.

David smiled and nodded and thought about it for just a moment.

"They do remain on the same plane. It is an ingenious plan if you mean what I think you mean."

I went on to explain so there could be no misunderstanding.

"If it is the same plane, I wouldn't even need a passport to go to Germany. I can purchase a domestic flight from here to New Delhi. For the same flight number, using your fully legal passport and visa, you could purchase an international flight from here to Frankfurt with a stopover in New Delhi. Once the plane landed in New Delhi, you would leave the plane and I would remain on the plane occupying your seat. Maybe, I should occupy your seat in Bombay before the plane takes off. In that way I don't need any passport at all. We just buy the two tickets for the same flight, one domestic ticket with my name and one international ticket with your name.

The problem would be the departure stamp on your passport, but you say that can be easily removed."

"Like I said, young man: ingenious. I don't see how anybody could be caught using that plan. It has to succeed. We are looking at a hundred per cent success rate."

"I need to ask Sandy tomorrow to do a search for me to make certain that the international passengers remain on the same plane."

The excitement and anticipation overwhelmed me. I didn't sleep well that night. I did not tell Ramon and Hamid about the plan, because I wanted to make sure it would work. Sandy confirmed that it was the same plane that would fly on to Frankfurt. Only the domestic passengers would leave the plane and then additional international passengers would board and occupy their assigned seats.

This was it. There was no stopping me, once I put the plan in motion.

But it was more difficult than I figured, informing Sandy that I would soon be leaving India for Germany. I felt a bit awkward. My throat was tight.

"I think I will miss you a lot," she said, "but I don't want you to stay here. I know your future will be much brighter in Europe."

I felt sad, deep inside. I would miss her immensely. Her amazing spirit, her beautiful smile. Those eyes. And the softest skin I had ever imagined.

I met with David the next day. I was floating on cloud nine. That didn't last long.

"There is a flaw in the plan. I cannot participate because my passport has not been released yet."

"That makes the situation more difficult, doesn't it?" I asked.

"All may not be lost. I have a friend who could do it for me, but you will need to pay him, maybe 500 US dollars. His name is James and I already talked to him. He wanted to think about it first."

"How long do you think you have to wait to retrieve your passport?"

"I don't know yet. I haven't received any information about its status."

"I need two people," I said.

"What do you mean by that?"

"One of my roommates, Ramon, needs to go, too, and I think we should go together. I don't want to leave him behind. He has supported me all the way from Karachi to here. If I fly first, he would remain here. Either I fly with him or he flies first and I fly after him."

"I hope he appreciates your friendship," David responded.

"I'm sure he would do the same for me."

"Two on one flight might call attention to the switch. Maybe James can take him away and I will find someone else for you."

"I don't know how to thank you for that. You are a great friend and the only good thing that ever came to me from having been in jail."

"We do what we can to help each other."

I explained the plan to Ramon. He was initially reluctant, but came around when I laid it out step by step. We needed to talk to Peeruz because he would have to fund our transfers. With the large number of passports we had procured for him, I didn't hesitate asking.

I explained my plan to him. He could not believe that there was such a simple and fool-proof way to leave India. He knew of no smugglers who had ever thought of that. I told him that, after Ramon and I were safely in Europe, he could use it to send his passengers, but had him promise he would not share the plan with any other smugglers. He agreed.

Peeruz was pleased to pay for the tickets and send Ramon as the first passenger.

David brought his friend, James, to meet Peeruz, Ramon and me. James agreed to take 500 US dollars to depart with Ramon from Bombay and leave the plane in New Delhi according to my plan.

James and Peeruz set a date to go to the airline agency and buy the tickets.

On June 25th, Ramon was ready to make the trip. Peeruz took James and Ramon to the airport and they boarded the plane. As planned, they swapped seats in Bombay. James left the plane in New Delhi and my friend, Ramon, continued his flight to Frankfurt. Ramon called me at the hotel reception desk on the following morning and said that he arrived safely in Frankfurt and there was not so much as the hint of a problem at any point along the way. He had applied for asylum.

Those of us still in India were overjoyed. Clearly the plan was idiot-proof. It was a huge relief to know no one needed to be afraid of being arrested at the airport for whatever reason.

That evening, Peeruz, Hamid and I celebrated with drinks at the Taj Mahal Palace. Hamid's emotions flowed after a shot of whisky.

"Ben," he said, gripping my shoulder. "You are the youngest one among us but your discovery ended the misery of at least twenty people who have been trapped in India for almost a year. I will never forget you."

I was the next in line to leave. David still did not have his passport so he introduced me to his friend, John, who agreed to do what James had done. He also wanted 500 US dollars for his service. Peeruz, John and I went to the travel agency and purchased the flight tickets following the same route. The flight was scheduled for June 30th, five days after Ramon's flight.

David and I met at the café one final time. David was clearly happy that I would finally be on my way.

"I've got used to having you around, inmate," he said. "I have grown to really like you."

We smiled. Our friendship had begun in a dark place and got us here.

"Now," David said. "You need to get your hind end out of India and make a wonderful new life in Europe. I know you are going to make something special out of your life. You should believe in yourself. Don't let your external circumstances make you change your goals, adjust your plan of action but not your goals. I think you already know these things but I want you to implement them as often as you can. You should also know that repetition of the same action develops into a habit."

"Thank you. I will do my best to put my knowledge into practice in my life, David."

"Just one more thing, Ben. Don't be upset about leaving your girl behind. You are very young and your life spreads out in front of you; first love is always something special, but *first* love would not be called *first* if there weren't to be a *second*! You will certainly find another girl with whom you will be happy."

"That helps put it in perspective for me. As you said, the first time is something special, and I will never forget her. It will always be one of the finest parts of my life – as will my time with you, good friend."

Sandy and I met for the last time before my departure. We both felt very sad because it was unlikely we would ever see each other again.

I wasn't at all sure what I would say and intentionally did not rehearse anything. I wanted it to come from my heart.

It did.

"I want to thank you for the amazing time we shared together and for your kindness and your patience. You have changed my life over the past weeks and brought me a kind of happiness that I have never had before. And for that I am grateful to you."

She became tearful.

I kissed her cheek and tried to comfort her.

"Over the past eleven to twelve months I had to face a lot of setbacks and go through emotional and physical pain. I've never revealed that to you. I had some terrible, terrible experiences. But you... You —" Now it was my turn to be choked up. "I regard you as the best reward for me chosen by the supreme power for overcoming the obstacles in my way. Believe me, I could not have thought of any reward more fulfilling and complete than you. Maybe it is a sign that my creator knows me better than I do!"

Sandy smiled and embraced me.

"I have been so lucky to get to know a person like you, Ben. You have also changed my life. I feel better prepared to go forward now, having known you. I am sure that you will be successful in your life. Promise me that you will always share your wonderful smile with those you meet and maintain your boundless enthusiasm for the rest of your life."

I blushed. But I forged ahead.

"I have to thank you for — I'm not sure how to say this — the intimate times we shared. It was my introduction to manhood, I guess I could say. And through your gentleness and patience I learned about a brand new, wonder-filled, aspect of love. That is a one-time experience. Nobody else will ever be able to do that for me. In so many ways you have enriched my life."

I had stopped blushing.

We shared a final kiss.

Sandy got in the rickshaw and rode out of my life. It was sad. It was wonderful. It was right.

The time had come for me to get ready to leave for the airport. Peeruz shared a taxi with me. John and I had agreed to meet there. We both carried small carry-on bags — less hassle and less likely to draw attention. Our check-in counters were located in different places. I took my boarding card and went to the departure hall. There was no border control check for me. John had to pass the border control check and received a departure stamp on his passport. We sat next to each other there as we waited to board, but didn't talk. I discreetly flashed my seat number to him: 23. John did the same for me: 16.

Once we boarded the plane, we occupied each other's seats. I found myself sitting next to an old Indian woman who did not speak English. After the plane took off and we were free to move about, we put the next phase of our plan into action. John walked toward the magazine rack at the front of the plane. I followed him a few moments later. We stood there side by side as if not aware of each other. The rack was filled with a wide variety of magazines. John picked up one and flipped through the pages as if to decide whether it held any interest for him. He slipped his boarding card inside it – page ten as we had planned – and put it back on the shelf. I did the same with another magazine. I took John's magazine and John took mine. He returned to his seat first, and I went back to mine a few minutes' later. As I feigned interest in the magazine I managed to remove the boarding card and slip it into my pocket. We were both legal in case there would be a seat check.

The plane landed in New Delhi after 140 minutes. The domestic passengers, including John, began to disembark. He managed a final smile as he passed me.

The stopover was meant to take sixty minutes, but there was an announcement about a technical problem with the plane. The stopover would take longer.

I became nervous knowing that technical problems were sometimes mechanical problems and sometimes a code word for something else. I asked one of the flight attendants what the issue was and if we would have to leave the plane. If we wouldn't, I would begin a nap. She assured me that most times technical problems could be fixed while they waited on the tarmac.

The wait dragged on as I feigned sleep. I became more and more concerned. Men in airport garb entered and exited the plane. Federal agents? This was how they disguised themselves – I had seen such things on TV. Anything was possible, and after all my failed attempts it was hard to believe there would not be a setback here, too.

I worked to calm my runaway imagination. When the announcement was made to fasten our seatbelts, that we were preparing to take off, I uttered an *"Oh, good"* out loud. I got several looks, followed by friendly smiles.

I would not let myself believe it had happened until I felt us lifting off. The last leg of my journey had really begun. It was a night flight and lasted eight-and-a-half hours. I may have dozed, but I was far too excited to have a good sleep. We landed at the international airport in Frankfurt just after the sun appeared in the east.

I was still slightly nervous when passengers started disembarking. I left the plane as the last passenger. Once out onto the passenger boarding bridge I was asked by two German police officers to show my passport.

I responded that I had dropped it in the toilet on the plane and it flushed away. Playing the helpless card I asked for the policemen's recommendation about what I should do. They responded in a kind manner and said that the only way for me to stay in Germany was to apply for asylum; otherwise I would be deported to India on a return flight. Once I had been accepted I could then take steps to get a new travel document. I thanked them and asked where I needed to go. They motioned for me to follow them, and I accompanied them across the airport.

I had known all along, of course, that an asylum application was the only way for me to enter Germany. We soon entered a separate section of the airport where many asylum seekers were waiting to have a short hearing and become registered. I looked around. So many faces, so many paths to here. I wondered how many of them had an arduous journey like mine. I knew that I would never know. We all had something in common – we were all here, after all. And yet we each had our own set of stories to tell.

I needed to complete several forms and had to explain the reasons for my asylum application. Finally, the police took my fingerprints and I was then allowed to walk inside to the transit terminal where I was to wait until further notice. That might take days.

No matter – I had become a world-class waiter.

It had been a long, long trip. I was still in police custody but I'd made it here – Europe. Germany.

And there was Ramon, my companion in misery and in happiness.

Waving at me.

On free ground.

Ramon was the first person I saw when I left the police station inside the terminal. We embraced and cried tears of joy for minutes. It was our way of restoring emotional equilibrium. He said he was being sent to an asylum seekers' camp near a city called Karlsruhe. We sat together quietly for a long time. Hours. It didn't matter how long we sat there – we had all the time in the world.

I called up my uncle and informed him that I was in Frankfurt. He had already consulted with his lawyer who advised me to wait until I arrived at my asylum seeker camp and then contact him.

It took a week. For a week my home was the Frankfurt airport. What a strange new home this was. We had to remain in one area of the airport and were not allowed to leave until we were officially allocated to an asylum seekers' camp. Among us were many women and children from different parts of the world. Young men walked around in the airport terminal during the day and slept on the seats in the waiting area after midnight when the terminal closed for the normal passengers. Some looked to be my age; some were older. Some of the asylum seekers became unhappy and dissatisfied after a few days of waiting and demanded to leave the airport as soon as possible. Me? I was on cloud nine and could not believe that I had finally made it to Germany. No amount of days in a crowded airport terminal could detract from the freedom I felt here. I was not about to be sad over my misfortune at having to wait a little longer. No complaints from me. I kept in mind Saadi's saying: *'I cried because I had no shoes until I met a man who had no feet.'*

Shoes or no shoes: I had arrived.

I left the airport one week later and was sent first to a small hotel that had been converted into an asylum seekers' stopover in a town called Schwalbach. After a two-week-stay there, I was transferred to a city named Braunschweig, which was close to Hamburg. My stay in Braunschweig lasted for two more weeks. After that, I was moved to an asylum seeker accommodation in Oldenburg.

I was not to leave Oldenburg without official permission from the city authorities while my asylum application was running. There were rules.

But the rules that governed life were fluid. I'd learned this the hard way. I'd come too far to be cramped up and waiting any more.

I began studying at the college in Cologne the very next year.

The psychologist smiles.

"I knew of course that you would make it here because here you are, but still, your words helped me relive every step of your journey – every setback and every success."

Ben smiles back.

"I realised early on that this was not a story about 'Would you make it', but one about, 'How in the world would you ever make it?' In some ways I feel like I have made the journey with you. I know I'm exhausted!"

"I'm glad you could come along, too. I'm happy I could share it all with you. I was as honest and open about every aspect as I could be – more so than I often wanted to be."

"Yes, I know. But that's why you are doing this. To open yourself up, to explore the journey, step by step."

"Had it not been for you I think my inclination would have been to gloss over parts of it and play the hero where I wasn't."

"That in itself tells me a lot about you, Ben. You are self-critical, as you are critical of the world. You retain a view that allows reasonable perspective. You refrain from rationalising away your mistakes, find sound lessons in defeat as well as success and give credit where credit is due."

Ben fidgets. "So, this is it? The last session? I am going to miss you. I have come to look forward to this time together."

"We will pass here and there on campus. Be sure to stop me and keep me informed about your life."

"I will do that."

Frau Bosch pulls a file from a drawer. "Here. For you, Ben."

He studies the paper: confirmation that he has completed his counselling.

"Thank you. You have been very kind, Frau Bosch."

"Yours has been an extraordinary journey, Ben. May it continue and may you flourish. Without any further jail time, of course."

"Of course."

CHAPTER SIXTEEN

THE END IS NOT THE END

And what about the rest of Ben's story? There are hard parts, but nothing so hard as everything that has come before. There are happy parts. There are new friends, new advisors, new studies. There are girls, too. But the journey is ongoing. The psychologist's evaluation is accepted by his head teacher. He is allowed to take his final exams, even without a passport. Advisors and teachers are supportive. He is congratulated on his courage, inventiveness and willpower.

He studies. He gets the highest scores possible. There is no other way.

He applies for medical school, using his undergraduate ID to help his application along.

He is congratulated on his high marks. He is declared a solid citizen of the university undergraduate populace. He has discovered *his* community.

And, alongside those other outwardly declared successes, he has been declared saner and more stable than most of the rest of us.

When the letter arrives from medical school, Ben does not open it at first. He lets it sit on the counter all afternoon. Only toward evening, as the sun sets across the greening campus in the cool spring evening, does he pick it up.

Ben has not anticipated how nervous he would be. He hesitates just a moment before opening the envelope.

Ben's entry into medical school represents a significant turning point in his life. All that has come before has strengthened his resolve to build a meaningful life. He has seen the darker side of human existence and the grand potential of the human spirit. Now he would move forward. He would carry his past with him, always. From torture to beatings to the first gentle kiss. Those were his story, yes. But those were no longer his only story.

We begin in the middle. We end there, too.

THE END

Printed in Great Britain
by Amazon

18313862R00192